Fair Play

Book 7 of the Branwell Chronicles

Judith Hale Everett

Evershire Publishing

Published by Evershire Publishing, Mapleton, Utah
ISBN 978-1-958720-08-0
Library of Congress Control Number: 2025908374

To Kat

Whose positivity and determination are an inspiration.

To my readers:

Make sure to read the Author's Note in the back for historical information on concepts and events described in the story.

Fair Play

Prologue

August, 1818

THE JOURNEY FROM Jamaica to England had been a comfortable one for Eliza Willoughby, so far as such long journeys could be. The William Miles, though primarily a cargo ship, was provided with excellent accommodation for its relatively few passengers. But nearly two months of confinement to two levels of a ship had been wearing, even to one of Eliza's sunny temperament. When the West Indiaman entered the mouth of the River Avon, therefore, she joined her fellow passengers on the deck in a cheer.

As the ship maneuvered its way into the Floating Basin at Bristol, Eliza turned from the rail and hastened belowdecks to her quarters, where her maid was finishing the packing.

"Make haste, Muncey!" she cried, taking up one of the garments laid out upon the bed and folding it swiftly and neatly to lay it in the portmanteau. "I think I shall die if we do not instantly escape the ship when she docks."

Muncey grunted, replying in a grim tone, "No hurry. You will die of cold in dis place, anyway. All de way across de ocean, I felt de cold in my bones."

"It's not so bad," said Eliza, folding another garment. "I scarcely feel a chill, and I've been on deck since we sighted the Bristol Channel."

Muncey only tutted, casting a deprecatory look at her young mistress. "You will feel it soon enough. When all dis excitement dies away, you will wish you were back in Jamaica. I told you not to come."

The click of the clasp on the portmanteau sounded in the following silence. Eliza did not look at her maid as she said, "I already miss Jamaica, Muncey, but you know there is nothing left there for me."

After a slight hesitation, Muncey reached to take her mistress's hand, giving it a fierce squeeze. Eliza squeezed back, closing her eyes for a moment before giving her maid a sidelong look and conjuring a grin.

"You nearly undid me there, but I am resolved that nothing today shall dim my joy. I am having a grand adventure, and whether you like it or not, you are having it with me. Now, we had better go up and greet our new home!"

With a resolute set to her shoulders, Eliza took up the portmanteau and hastened out the door, while Muncey, grimly setting her lips, followed more sedately with her own bag. Eliza hurried up the steep stairs to the deck, skirting a group of seamen intent on furling the sails as they drew alongside the dock. The captain gave the order to drop anchor and within minutes, several seamen had swarmed over the side, while others wound out ropes to toss to the dock.

Eliza leaned out over the side to watch as four sturdy seamen made ready to run out the gangplank, but she immediately drew back in shock and disgust. The air of a port was often pungent, but the stench that assailed her nostrils from the murky waters below made her eyes water. Blinking, she pressed her handkerchief to her nose and glanced at Muncey, who had joined her by the rail.

The lady's maid stood stoically. "Maybe I was mistaken, Miss Eliza, and you will die of de smell before you die of de cold!"

Eliza grimaced beneath her handkerchief. It was not the welcome she had dreamed of these many weeks, indeed. The rank stench of rotting fish mingled with human refuse rising up from the water below seemed impossibly strong.

"Well," she said in a voice muffled by the handkerchief, "it cannot smell so foul everywhere. Come, Muncey, let us disembark and await Mr. Findlay on the dock. The sooner we are away from the water, the sooner we will feel more at home."

Lifting her chin and squaring her shoulders, Eliza took short, shallow breaths as she stepped onto the gangplank and made her way down onto the stone dock. No sooner had she touched stable ground than her legs wobbled uneasily beneath her, and she stumbled sideways into a carter as he pushed his load. With a little cry, she stepped backward, colliding with a fishmonger.

"Oh, pardon me, sir," she said, lowering her handkerchief. She instantly regretted the lapse. Replacing the handkerchief and backing unsteadily away, she bumped into a stack of trunks and cried out when a hand grasped her elbow.

"Best get out of de way, Miss Eliza," said Muncey, steering her across the dock to a corner beside the window of a small shop. She settled Eliza on a whiskey keg and went off to find a porter to take their trunks.

The energetic woman's legs seemed unaffected as she dodged seamen, crewmen, dogs, and passengers on her way toward a young man waiting with a cart for hire. Eliza smiled as Muncey sized up both the young man and his cart before pointing an imperious finger at their trunks that had been piled haphazardly beside the dock, entirely at ease.

What happened next, Eliza could not tell, for the cacophony of the docks engulfed her. Ringing bells, pounding feet, creaking ships, calling gulls, shouting seamen, and banging hammers drowned out everything else, and the constant flow of traffic up and down the dock made it impossible to see much at all. Eliza quickly gave up the attempt to follow Muncey's doings and glanced about her new surroundings.

The harbor at Bristol was a fairly recent addition, having been completed less than a decade earlier. The captain had kindly informed his handful of passengers that the tidal nature of the River Avon had made it necessary to create a harbor so that ships would no longer be in danger of running aground at low tide. The river had been diverted and locks installed at either end of what would come to be known as the Floating Basin, providing the stable water level required to support the high level of ships' traffic to Bristol.

Eliza noted that improvements to the docks and surrounding buildings seemed continuous, and added both to the general chaos of the place and its utility. While nothing was particularly charming about the architecture, nor the humanity swarming about the docks, Eliza was determined to admire her new home and could approve its industry if she could not detect much beauty.

So intent was she on her inspection that she did not notice a gentleman approaching her until he addressed her directly.

"Miss Muncey?"

She glanced up quickly to find a man of middle height and age, with a worried brow and a dusty frock coat, gazing intently at her through round spectacles as he, too, pressed a handkerchief to his nose. "No, sir, I am Miss Willoughby. That is Miss Muncey, my maid, over there."

He glanced at where she indicated but quickly returned his gaze to her. "Forgive me, ma'am, but I did not expect—" He stopped, his brow furrowing. Then he tipped his hat and cleared his throat. "I am Mr. Findlay, of Windle, Windle, and Findlay, London. Welcome to England, Miss Willoughby."

"Oh, thank you, Mr. Findlay!" She sprang up, holding out her hand. "It is delightful to meet you at last."

He took her proffered hand and bowed punctiliously over it. "I see Muncey has secured a porter. May I take your portmanteau?"

"Yes, thank you. I must own I am glad not to be the only one offended by the general smell," Eliza said with a mischievous look. "It quite took me by surprise, for I doubt even Kingston is ever so noisesome as this."

Mr. Findlay's smile was pained. "It is the stagnant nature of the Basin, ma'am. The problem has yet to be solved, though I know not what has been attempted. But you may rest assured that the smell does not extend farther than the city, and the problem certainly does not afflict other English ports."

On this patriotic defense, he assisted her across the busy dock to where Muncey stood with the loaded cart, and Eliza made the introductions. Then, with the facility of a man secure in his own capability, Mr. Findlay took matters into his own hands, signaling to the porter and leading the whole party off the dock to where a traveling carriage waited. He handed the ladies inside before stepping back to make arrangements with the porter for the transfer of the trunks to the carriage, then climbed in beside them.

Looking on his companions in a fatherly, if somewhat condescending way, he said, "You are still determined to live at Penhurst Lodge with your brother rather than stay here in Bristol with your former governess?"

Muncey made a strangled noise and Eliza quickly answered, "Yes, sir. Miss Tibble is expecting us only for the night."

"Very good," he said, though his mouth pinched in disapprobation. "I have a room at the White Hart, which is not far from her home."

The carriage jolted to a start, and after some minutes, Mr. Findlay cleared his throat. "I shall be obliged to collect you rather early in the morning, I'm afraid. It is over a hundred miles to London, and we must be on our way betimes."

"London?" inquired Eliza. "But were we not to travel directly to Lincolnshire?"

Mr. Findlay dropped his gaze to adjust his gloves. "Mr. Willoughby has not answered my letters. I do not believe it proper to deliver you to Penhurst Lodge without first ensuring his—well, that he is in residence. I have resolved upon taking you to London until we might discover his whereabouts."

Muncey tutted. "An ill wind," she muttered, shaking her head.

"Nonsense," murmured Eliza with a quick, repressive look, before returning her bright gaze to Mr. Findlay. "That is all the better, for I am curious to see London. As much as I should like to be settled in my new home, I will not mind a sojourn in the Metropolis of which I have heard so much."

He glanced over the light muslin of her gown. "You will wish to have new gowns made, I daresay, that are more in keeping with the climate of our fair kingdom. Mrs. Riddle—the lady I have engaged as your companion while you are in Town—will find a respectable dressmaker to see to your needs."

"You are very kind, sir. Though, a linen draper's would be adequate. Between us, Muncey and I may contrive."

"You are an heiress of no little fortune, Miss Willoughby," said Mr. Findlay, eying her significantly over the rims of his spectacles. "You need not 'contrive.'"

Eliza's smile dimmed slightly. It was only through the deaths of those she loved, and the loss of all she held dear, that she was so wealthy, after all.

"No, certainly not," she said. "I am most fortunate in that respect."

Mr. Findlay seemed satisfied and sat back in his seat, looking out at the passing streets. Eliza did not mind the ensuing silence, glad as she was to put the sorrowful thoughts elicited by the conversation behind her. She was also rather tired from the journey, and grateful once they arrived at the tidy little row house Miss Tibble kept with her sister. Mr. Findlay escorted them to the door before bidding them good day.

"I shall call for you at eight," he said, bowing.

Eliza gave him her hand. "Thank you, Mr. Findlay! You have already been indispensable in your service. 'Til tomorrow."

He nodded and turned away, and Miss Tibble, who had met them at the door, guided her former charge and the maid into the tiny parlor on the first floor. They all sat on the faded but serviceable sofa and chairs and the greying governess clasped her hands before her bosom in rapture.

"Oh, my dear Eliza, what joy it is to see you! And Miss Muncey! It seems only yesterday I consigned my dear charge into your care. But you have done admirably, for she is looking so well! Look at the roses in your cheeks, my dear Eliza, and I do believe you have grown, though it has been only two years. What a lady you have become! You quite take my breath away. How oft have I envisioned this day, when we would be reunited—and I never dreamed of it until I received your letter upon your poor father's death. Oh, my dear, what a tragedy! The palpitations I suffered upon learning of it! It must have been a blow to you, having already lost your dear mama, and so young, too."

Eliza, smiling bravely under this effusion, replied, "It was a blow, Miss Tibble. Neither my father nor myself were quite the same after my mother's death."

"Certainly not," agreed Miss Tibble, her rapture only somewhat impaired by remembered grief. "Poor man. While I was with your family those many years, I can scarce recall a day when he did not speak of her, and lament that he could not consult her in something, whether regarding your upbringing, or the running of the house or the plantation. But you were his greatest consolation, Eliza. So dearly did he delight in your likeness to your mother. Though I did not have the privilege to know her, I never doubted that your father loved her so, like Romeo his Juliet, or like Antony and his Cleopatra. How disheartening that his story was quite as tragic, now it is over."

Eliza bit her lips, blinking away the sudden moisture in her eyes. Having been to all intents and purposes reared by Miss Tibble, she had anticipated her loquacity and known it would likely bring up painful topics. But she had misjudged the strength of her emotions in response. The governess's fond remembrances conjured vivid images of her beloved parents, and the deep grief Eliza had felt at their deaths threatened once more to bubble up and overwhelm her. But she swallowed them down, for she had determined to be brave and to forge ahead on her new path, as was her father's wish.

Taking a deep breath, she said, "They are sorely missed, and ever will be. But I have my dear Muncey, and am with you again, my dear Miss Tibble, and shall soon meet my other family."

"Oh, yes, Eliza! It is a blessing of Providence, to be sure, for I thought you lost to me, but now I may see you, and with far greater frequency than I ever could have imagined. We shall be nearly as close as—well, Lincolnshire is less than two hundred miles away, rather than halfway round the world! And we cannot guess where you will settle in the end, for you will likely marry, and who is to say that your husband's abode might not be in this very county!"

Muncey darted a horrified glance at her employer, who bit her lips against a laugh. Muncey had come to Willow Great House scarcely a month before Miss Tibble had left the family's service, and had declared the governess's volubility to be more than she could stand. But Eliza, somewhat immune from many years' experience, only said graciously, "That would be delightful, my dear. And as my whole purpose for coming to England is to secure a husband and a home of my own, we must hope that all the circumstances attached to my new situation will be salutary."

Miss Tibble nodded emphatically. "To be sure, my love, for you will have your half-brother to assist you. What an astonishing discovery his existence was, I declare! I scarcely could believe it when I read your letter. But it is all for the better, for he will do all in his power to oblige you, I am persuaded. He is your father's son, for all they were never on good terms. But I heartily agree that one cannot fault your brother for somewhat resenting your father's choosing to reside in Jamaica, his being so young when Mr. Willoughby went away. In such a case, one might expect some...disapprobation, or even dislike." The governess looked uncertainly at her former charge. "But surely he will not bear a grudge against *you*, my dear Eliza! That would be ungentlemanly, and he is a gentleman, by all accounts. At least, his estate is quite handsome, from what I have gathered—for all it is in the Fens—and he counts some illustrious personages as his friends."

Eliza laughed. "My dear Miss Tibble! Have you been listening to gossip? How shocking! Must I repeat back to you the lesson you were obliged to drill into my head more than once?"

"Oh dear, no," replied the governess quickly, color tinging her faded cheeks. "It was not gossip, my dear. One knows well enough that one may never find the truth through gossip! I had recourse to the Lincolnshire guidebooks, where I discovered a complete description of Penhurst Lodge and its environs. And it was only a chance comment I let fall at an evening party, to which Mrs. Franklinson was so kind as to invite me, that brought forth the information that Mr. Willoughby was seen to be much in company with Lord Wraglain's eldest son and with Lord Hayes's heir during the Season."

"Very well," said Eliza with mock solemnity, "I shall be content with that. And if, as his fine estate and high-born friends attest, my brother proves to be a gentleman, then he will not be disinclined to put me in the way of some of those high-born friends, and thus secure a husband to take me off his hands."

Miss Tibble exclaimed against the notion that her dear Eliza could be in any way an encumbrance before her countenance assumed a dreamy aspect. "How romantic to be young, with all the world at one's feet. I declare, you will be beset with suitors, so pretty and lively as you are. Certainly there will be many willing to overlook—" She stopped, suddenly blushing scarlet. Putting a hand to her cheek, she sprang to her feet. "Where have my wits gone begging? Here I have been gabbling on, while you are sure to be fatigued beyond measure with your travels. Was the crossing horridly tedious? Mine was ever so tiresome, and I am forever hearing the same from others coming from the West Indies. A storm may have been more welcome than the everlasting blue sky and glinting sea. I declare, my eyes were sore from the sight of it! And I was sick to death of the pitch and roll of the deck—oh, how grateful I was that my seasickness did not extend beyond the first two days. Were you sick, my dear? Of course you were not. You have been on boats in Montego Bay. But a sailing ship is something different altogether, I believe, for—"

She continued her monologue all the way up the stairs, with Eliza nodding or murmuring affirmations appropriately, and Muncey pursing her lips and raising her eyes heavenward.

Chapter 1

MR. FRANCIS MANTELL tossed back the last of his port and stood, replacing the glass at his place on the large formal dining table. Grimsley, the aged butler awaiting his master's pleasure, hastened forward as quickly as his tottering steps could take him to retrieve the glass. With a sideways glance, his master briefly surveyed him before nodding and retiring from the room.

Grimsley was too old, thought Francis as he walked up the staircase in the spacious hall. What a pity. He had grown used to the old retainer as his butler, and Mrs. Grimsley as his housekeeper, but he was uncomfortable watching them struggle with their duties. Good old Grimsley was not quite washed up yet, but it was only a matter of time. Francis sighed, reaching the landing and turning into the family wing of the manor. He did not like retiring loyal servants, and less did he like finding new. It was a lucky thing that Jane would come presently to take his mind off such burdens.

He had dismissed his valet and sat on the bed pondering his problems for nearly a quarter of an hour before the door opened and the housemaid appeared, something like a pout on her otherwise charming face. Jane's figure was petite and light and her face heart-shaped, with a cupid's bow mouth in cherry red, and celestial blue eyes framed by golden curls. It was the wanton invitation in those blue eyes that had first caught his fancy, and when his father had died and left him as master of the estate, Francis had not hesitated to take Jane up on her frequently insinuated offer.

That had been over two years ago, and Francis had come to expect Jane to be available at his whim. Indeed, she had used to be excessively obliging, but of late her demeanor had become somewhat flighty. He could not put his finger on it, but the pout twisting her pretty mouth now attested to some indefinable dissatisfaction.

She was clothed as usual in a modest dressing gown to conceal her true purpose from any other servants who might be abroad at that hour—though Francis did not doubt they all knew very well the relationship between the maid and the master. Once she was in his bedroom, Jane generally did not hesitate to abandon the dressing gown, revealing the lacy negligée beneath, but tonight she only released the ties as she regarded him sulkily from across the room.

Francis admired the rounded lines peeking enticingly from the gap in her gown. "You are lovely as always, my darling. Come here, so that I may admire you more closely."

"Perhaps I've no use for your admiration tonight, sir," she said, one perfect eyebrow arching.

Francis cocked his head at this impertinence, but said, "Admiration is not worth much at all, to be sure. Come and have something far more to your liking."

Tilting up her chin, she merely stood, her gaze meandering up and down his form in a somewhat appraising manner. With a tingle of annoyance at this unaccustomed detachment, Francis put out a hand to her. "Well, my sweet?"

She did not come to him, only hunching a slim shoulder, which he knew to be milky white and soft as a dove's wing beneath that dratted gown.

Francis sighed, his mouth pursing in impatience. "What is the matter?"

"I don't know." Her mouth trembled as she cast him a remonstrative glance.

So it was to be more games, thought Francis, looking away so that she did not see the roll of his eyes. Their interactions were meant to be his reprieve from care—a release from trouble and vexation—but of late she had been making such a fuss.

She must have sensed his irritation, for she moved to the dressing table, somewhat agitatedly rearranging the accoutrements there. "Mayhap I'm not in the mood tonight."

"Then why did you come?" inquired Francis bluntly, suspecting she had reached the inevitable point where fascination became greed—a point to which London mistresses came far more quickly.

She turned to face him, her chin high and her bosom heaving under the dressing gown. "I dare not risk my position, sir."

Francis paused, his lips turning down in distaste. "I do not force you to come to me at night, Jane."

She scowled and dropped her gaze, a deep blush reddening her damask cheeks. "There are sundry ways to force a person, sir."

"What can you possibly mean by that?" snapped Francis, his distaste increasing.

But she merely shrugged her pretty shoulders and refused to meet his eye.

Francis was seriously annoyed. He prided himself on the fact that he never took an unwilling lover, just as he never seduced innocents. It had been for his father, famed rake and scourge of husbands everywhere, to exert pressure on unwilling women. If a woman had caught the Colonel's eye, he had approached her, and if she did not welcome his advances, he had found a way to catch her in his toils.

Though Colonel Mantell had gladly exerted himself to instill his values—or lack thereof—into his eldest son, Francis had learned to despise his father's methods. He could see no finesse, no charm, no satisfaction in a forced liaison. To hold a woman in his sway was far more exciting when she desired to be there, and when the relationship palled, there was nothing to oblige either of them to continue.

It seemed his long-held understanding with Jane had not been an understanding at all, if she now felt herself forced to remain. It had not always been so, he was persuaded, for she had entered into their relationship with all the excitement of a school girl—though she was past one-and-twenty years of age. She was also no innocent, he knew, for it was well known that she had enjoyed the attentions of the footman who had since gone off to serve in a London house. But something had changed in recent months, and Francis had allowed himself to ignore it, curse his complacence. Now he must make himself uncomfortable, and all for a goose of a village maid.

With an effort, he schooled his features into a patient smile. "My dear Jane, you are my maid. I pay you to turn out the bedrooms and make up the beds, to dust the picture frames and beat the rugs. If you do not come to me at night, but you perform your usual duties to Mrs. Grimsley's satisfaction, there is nothing to fear. Your position is secure."

Her blue eyes flicked up to his. "Do you mean that, sir?"

"I wouldn't say it if I did not."

"Do you promise, sir?" she asked, gazing keenly at him.

With a pained, slow blink, Francis said, "On my honor as a gentleman."

She blushed, glancing about as though not knowing where to look. "And you'll not tell my dad?"

"Your father? What has he to say to anything, pray? You're of age, aren't you?"

"Yes, but—" She hesitated, licking her lips. "He's set a mite bit of store in my being—involved with you, sir. I suppose he's taken to expect something to come of it. I never did, to be sure, but I'd liefer he didn't know it was my fault nothing happened."

Grimacing in comprehension, Francis regarded her. It seemed it wasn't himself who had forced her after all. "I don't think I have ever spoken to your father in my life, my dear Jane. This circumstance is certainly nothing to cause me to wish to do so now."

"Your word as a gentleman?"

"Of course."

She eyed him uncertainly, but after some moments said quietly, "Then I'd rather not come anymore, if you'll excuse me, sir."

"Certainly, Jane."

Swallowing visibly, she peeped up at him once more, then curtseyed, her dressing gown gaping just enough to afford Francis a delectable glimpse of her decolletage before she straightened and hurried from the room.

As the door closed behind her, Francis heaved a sigh, leaning his head back against the carved headboard of his fourposter. If it wasn't one thing, it was another. Not only did he have an aging butler and his housekeeper wife to retire and replace, but also a former lover whom he must continue to employ as a maid. Perhaps it was time he was off again to Leicestershire, for he certainly was not to find relief in Southam.

The following morning, he was up betimes, taking his favorite ride along the River Stowe and past the Holy Well. The route passed near the town—which this morning was providential, as his bay gelding threw a shoe only half a mile from the blacksmith's shop. The circumstance, coupled with the frustrations of the night before, put Francis in a brown study, and he scarcely noticed his path as he led his mount along the road to town.

He would not miss his liaisons with Jane—he never missed his lovers once they had parted from him, whether amicably or no. If he had learned anything from his father, it was that romantic relationships were fickle, and it was best if one never became emotionally involved. The Colonel's own marriage had been a misery to both husband and wife—even as a young boy, Francis had sensed the disenchantment which quickly grew to dislike and even to hate.

Francis's mother was no less culpable than her husband for the discord at Gracely Hall. The Colonel might have had his *affaires*, but a teenage Francis had felt the justice of a man seeking enjoyment elsewhere, when his home was filled with the harping complaints and shrill demands of his wife. There were rumors that Mrs. Mantell had been a sweet and lively young lady in her youth, but he had seen nothing of it. He could not profess to love either of his parents, for neither had they professed to love him, just as they never had professed to love each other.

He had thus grown to despise marriage and hold women generally in disdain, only caring whether a pretty face could entertain him for a time. His charm and fine fortune held him in good stead in Polite company, but matchmaking mamas hoped in vain—his flirtations never came to anything. His deeper ardor was reserved for those ladies who did not require commitment in exchange for a taste of their pleasures—merry widows, fancy pieces, and the occasional country maid whose inviting glance caught his eye.

Jane's saucy invitations had promised much—and indeed, had satisfied much. But Francis let her go without a twinge of regret. He would simply find another pretty face to replace her. As he considered this, however, he could discover no desire to do so. He was getting bored, he imagined, with the sameness and flatness of his relationships. But what else was he to do? He was not about to reform and settle down. That, he would never do.

So distracted were his thoughts upon entering the high street that he nearly ran amok of the butcher's son, whose vision was obscured by the hindquarters of some beast he was carrying over his shoulder. Francis, regaining awareness of his surroundings only just in time, drew up short and begged an insincere pardon, and was somewhat astonished at the glare of utter animosity he received from the burly young man.

They stood regarding one another—a mildly surprised gentleman in expensive riding dress leading a fine bay gelding, and a surly young man of solid stock with a smear of blood on his cheek and blotches covering his smock from the burden of new-killed meat. After several moments, Master Hatchett gave way before Mr. Mantell's bland gaze and, with a grunt, continued down the street.

Never given to much curiosity, Francis merely shook his head and went on to the blacksmith's shop, handing over his gelding. As there was to be about a half-hour's wait, he elected to partake of a heavy wet at the Horse and Jockey to while away the time. The proprietor, Mr. Potts—greeting his illustrious patron with all the obsequious familiarity of a man who both knows his place and yet has known his guest since he was in short coats—scrupled not to strike up a conversation on the probability of rain in the coming week.

"Aye, it's bound to be wet," pronounced this worthy, "what with all the heat we had last summer. Heat makes the earth sweat, my grandad used to say. All that moisture rises into the heavens until they're full and pours back down as rain."

Francis, unimpressed by this folk wisdom, gave a smile and a nod, glancing about for a barmaid who had taken his fancy on his last visit.

"Rain'll be good for the shooting, I reckon, sir," went on Mr. Potts. "Nothing a bird likes more than to settle with its covey on a wet day. Just ripe for the killing. And wet damps the sound, as well, so's they can't hear a body coming." Potts went on, unheeded for the most part by his guest, until the door opened and he greeted the new customer.

"Hallo, Jacob. In for a rest? I saw your dad's got you hauling mutton all over town."

Francis turned to see the butcher's son, still in his blood-stained smock, glaring in his direction. He raised his brows in indifferent inquiry and the young man clenched his fists, the muscles in his forearms rippling. Mr. Potts, glancing between the two in some anxiety, stepped quickly out from behind the bar, somewhat forcefully resuming his jovial air as he wiped his sweaty hands on his apron.

"What'll it be, Jacob? Ale as usual? There's a table, just there, by the window. Why don't you set yourself down and I'll have your ale to you in a wink."

Young Jacob Hatchett never took his eyes off Francis's handsome and disdainful countenance, shrugging off the helpful proprietor's hand as he attempted to guide him away to the table. Potts stood uncertainly between them, chuckling and nervously wiping his hands, until Jacob said he'd take his ale at the counter, striding forward and sitting beside Francis.

Mr. Potts, eyes wide with horror, hurried behind the bar and drew the ale, his gaze flitting nervously between the two men before him. When the mug was full, he thrust it at Jacob, sloshing a bit onto the counter in his haste.

"Here you are, my boy! On the tab, as usual. Drink up!" He chuckled, mopping at the spill with his towel and closely watching the young man taking leisurely sips from his mug while he gazed straight ahead as though he were alone in the room.

Francis, after a sidelong glance at his silent companion, returned to contemplating the depths of his own mug. He was quite comfortable despite the waves of hatred emanating from the other man, feeling only a mild curiosity as to the cause. At last—after what must have seemed an eternity to Mr. Potts—Hatchett pushed away his mug and stood, nodding curtly to the relieved proprietor and striding from the pub.

Potts's shoulders sagged as he took up the mug and began wiping it with his towel. "That was as near-run a thing as ever I've seen." He blew out a sigh and replaced the mug on the shelf behind the bar. Turning again to Mr. Mantell, he bent to lean an elbow on the counter and said in a confidential tone, "Right smart of you to keep your tongue, sir. That Jacob's got a punishing right—took a prize at a fair not long ago—knocked their fighter clean out of the ring, he did! So they tell me. Best to keep quiet and not give him call to exhibit."

He winked, straightening and wiping down the bar. "All blow over in time, I say."

Having listened in growing irritation, Francis gave a slow blink. "Are you suggesting I am afraid of Jacob Hatchett?"

Mr. Potts looked up from where he had spat on the bar, his towel poised to polish it in. "Why, no, sir—no one never thought that. Only we'd never none of us blame you, sir! Why, young Jacob's twice your size—that is to say, he's not only a big'un, but he's got science, that one. Meaning no offense, sir, to be sure! Only thought you was wise to him—begging your pardon! But now you know, you'll pardon my taking the liberty to suggest—best act as though nothing's going on."

"As nothing *is* going on, Potts, you may keep your suggestion," replied Francis, leveling his most supercilious look on the unfortunate proprietor. "You had better leave off the flattery and speak plainly. Do you mean to suggest that I could not take master Jacob in a fight?"

"What—" Mr. Potts blinked, straightening quickly and clutching the towel between his restless fingers. "No, sir! That is, you may well strip to advantage, sir, but no one—that is, it might look bad, to be sure—considering how things stand. Couldn't make that sort of a rumpus, or the goose would be well and cooked! Very wise to refrain, and a mark of your extraordinary condescension, I must say."

Francis stood, his penetrating gaze pinning his host. "I still have not the pleasure of understanding what you are insinuating, and am becoming annoyed. Whatever young Master Jacob has against me, he would be wise to think twice before raising those ham-hands of his in my vicinity."

"That's the ticket, sir!" cried Mr. Potts, tapping his finger beside his nose. "Bluster's better'n bruises. Ain't nothing going on, to be sure." He bent forward over the bar, lowering his voice. "But can't blame poor Jacob for feeling a mite ill-used, your honor having blighted his hopes, so to speak."

Narrowing his eyes, Francis spoke slowly. "How the devil am I supposed to have blighted the hopes of the likes of the butcher's son, pray?"

"Oh, well, I suppose she is a mite above his touch, having worked for your family so many years. Though we don't take it to mean she's ties to the family—oh no, sir! We none of us pays any heed to her dad, when he gets bosky and starts carrying on about her grand expectations. We knows just how it is, depend upon it, and don't none of us blame your honor for taking her up. It'd be different were she unwilling, but you know—" He tapped the side of his nose again. "It's clear to every Bob Cull hereabouts she's always been a game pullet."

He winked, straightening to polish the bar again with a knowing look, and Francis, gazing now in blank astonishment, began to comprehend the matter. Jane's odd manner the past several weeks, topped by her sudden refusal to continue their liaisons last night, became almost clear as crystal. With a distinct feeling of annoyance, he closed his eyes, massaging the suddenly tight spot between his eyes.

What sort of muddle had she thrown him into? With an exhale, he deliberately resumed his seat.

Chapter 2

REGARDING MR. POTTS with strained long-suffering, Francis inquired, "You are speaking of my maid, Jane?"

Mr. Potts looked surprised, and put a finger to his lips. "No need to bandy her name about in public, sir. There's some who'll take offense. *We* both know who the young lady is. All's right and tight as long as mum's the word."

Francis placed his open hand firmly but quietly on the bar, giving his head a little shake as he bent toward the tavern keeper. "Allow me to ensure I understand you, sir: young Master Jacob hates me because I am—" He lowered his voice, "on an intimate footing with a certain young lady in my employ?"

The proprietor blinked, his smugness slipping. "Well, yes, sir. Didn't you know?"

"I feel sure I made it clear, at the outset of our very enlightening dialog, that I did not, Potts."

"No sir—that is to say, I would never have presumed, sir—" Mr. Potts bent to look into his guest's face. "You really had no notion of the way the wind was blowing, sir?"

With an effort, Francis contained his irritation. "Need I repeat myself, Potts?"

"No sir! Oh, no, sir. It's just that—I never reckoned you couldn't know that young Jacob has been head over ears in love with our young lady these three years and more. Calf-love, his dad thought it was, but nothing's changed, even when you took her up—that is, even when she went to work at the Hall."

Francis closed his eyes and sighed. "Had I any idea it would have pitchforked me into a village drama, I'd not have done it, I assure you, Potts."

Mr. Potts whistled. "Now here's a fine kettle of fish. If I'd the slightest notion you weren't fly to what's been going on, I'd have warned you, depend upon it, sir. Abel Potts'd never run a rig on you, sir!"

"No, do not apologize." Francis waved away his protestations. "I find it immensely tiresome. But you may explain, if you please, why master Jacob did not make his sentiments known."

"I should have thought—" He was silenced by another look from his guest and he revised his speech. "Well, sir, everyone knows he's had a fancy for—well, the young lady—ever since she put her hair up. At first, you may guess, he kept his tongue out of shyness, worried as she wouldn't give him a thought, being the prettiest girl in the village, you know. But there wasn't never much hope to begin with, what with his situation and all, and when she started up with you, sir, he seemed to give over."

"On the contrary, he seems to have nursed an excessively fierce grudge against me."

Potts scratched the tip of his nose. "There is that, but none can blame the poor fellow. Likely seems to him you've got far more than you deserve—though no one disputes your right to all you've got, us all being born to our place, to be sure. But you can't blame him all the same."

"Oh, I shouldn't blame him even if you did believe me outside my rights, Potts," said Francis dryly. "What fascinates me is that he should think so ill of my—shall we say, position with her, when he has never even made a push to fix her interest."

At that Potts coughed and looked away.

Francis sighed. "No, no, do not hedge—simply tell me what is going forward. You interest me excessively."

"Well, he didn't precisely try to fix her interest, you understand," said the proprietor, looking exceedingly uncomfortable, "being as she is spoken for, you might say—but he did recently take to carrying her things when she came into the village, and walking her home of a Sunday. Wasn't no more than neighborly, and good manners, to be sure, and he weren't encroaching—that is, she weren't more than passably pleased 'til it'd been going on a month or so. But though some might say she's been haunting the butcher's, I'd not say there's any call to worry yourself, sir."

"I'm obliged to you for not saying it," said Francis, pushing away his mug. "But do not spare me any longer, Potts. I may not show to as much advantage as the butcher's son, but I can take a blow or two without flinching. Just how involved are the young lady and Master Jacob?"

"I wouldn't know, sir," Potts answered, looking shocked. Then, glancing quickly side to side, he bent forward and added in a low tone, "However, I suspicion she's either leading poor Jacob a merry dance or can't make up her mind, for he's only got more and more rusty, 'specially when your honor's mentioned. When you come in today, cool as you please, and in he walks right after, I thinks, the reckoning's come at last. But you're as lucky as the day you was born, sir, for young Jacob kept his wits about him and never even tried to—"

Francis cut him off with a look. Then, ruminatively tapping a finger on the counter, said, "So it is the young lady's indecision that has kept him from declaring himself in form?"

"I wouldn't say that, sir—at least, I can't imagine she would hear of it. Not with you in the picture, sir. Nor would her father." He shrugged, saying expansively, "And it's all very understandable."

"Indeed, it is not at all understandable, and I could wish someone had knocked them both on the head long ago." With a huff, Francis stood, reaching into his waistcoat pocket. "Well, Potts, your converse has been exceedingly enlightening, and I cannot express my obligation enough. Here is for your trouble, and I beg you will use some of it to pay up the butcher's account."

He tossed a guinea on the bar and took his leave of the blinking Mr. Potts, emerging into the late summer sunshine and making his way down the high street to the blacksmith's shop. After retrieving his gelding, he mounted and made toward home, once again ruminative.

What a bumblebroth! He well knew Jane was the prettiest girl in the village—he would not have taken up with her if she had not been—and it did not surprise him that another man could have admired her enough to form a *tendre* for her. It was a situation in which his late father would have thrived—nothing delighted Colonel Mantell more than to cuckold another man.

For that precise reason, Francis found the circumstance distasteful in the extreme. He liked his *affaires* uncomplicated, with no jealous lovers waiting in the wings to muddy the waters. That he could go so long without discovering Jacob's *amore* for Jane was rather mortifying. He had long assumed, by looks and rumors overheard, that the more part of the village pretty much knew what was going on at the Hall. He had also assumed, as Mr. Potts had so frequently attested, that no one thought much of it—for sweet Jane was, indeed, willing, and her father as well. It was something for a village maid to snare the interest of a gentleman.

Francis could wish, however, that his consequence had not stood him in such good stead in this case. How much time had he wasted with Jane, while her attentions had been divided? He had begun to sense her dissatisfaction a month or six weeks ago, but until last night, she had not openly addressed it. But it seemed she had not truly addressed it at all.

To discover in the manner he had done that Jane had fallen in love with another man was mortifying to Francis. He was not a vindictive man, but nor did he enjoy being made to look foolish. For all he knew, Jane could be entertaining both of them at the same time—something his pride would not allow.

He must let her go. It was to break his promise, but she would not repine—at least, not long. It seemed she returned the butcher's son's sentiments—was that not what had brought on her dissatisfaction? Knowing she was loved by Jacob, she chafed at being bound, however temporarily, to a man who had never professed to love her, and never would.

But even as he acknowledged this as being the case, he could not comprehend it. What was so attractive about love that it could sway one's reason? How could a woman even consider a future of love in a cottage when she commanded the easy attentions—non-committal though they were—of a handsome and wealthy man? He supposed young Jacob to be well-looking, in his burly way. But how could Jane be tempted to give up her pampered existence in Francis's house for that of a housewife obliged daily to clean a blood-stained apron?

It was inconceivable, but it seemed to be the case. And it was too fatiguing to consider the matter any longer. Francis determined to release her, and she could run into the arms of her burly butcher's son with his good wishes.

But as he dismounted at his stables, he was distinctly uncomfortable regarding his promise to Jane last night. She would not have desired to retain her position if she could be secure with her butcher's son. He must be missing something.

Consigning his horse over to the head groom, he inquired abruptly, "Hatten, why have you not married?"

The groom, who had been with the Mantells since Francis was very small, looked surprised but replied, "Never had the chance, sir."

Francis frowned in thought. "But if you had a lady in your eye, and she seemed to return your affection, would there be anything else to keep you from declaring yourself?"

"Well, sir," Hatten said, looking off at the fields in the distance, "it's been a long time since I gave up marriage. But if I were young, and had the chance, I imagine my only concern would be for money."

"Money?"

"Yes, sir." He shifted his weight and returned his gaze to his master. "Begging your pardon, sir, but for men in my situation, marriage ain't something to consider lightly. For instance, I couldn't well bring a bride to live above the stables, could I? So I'd have to find the means to get lodgings for the both of us. And then there'd be two mouths to feed, and likely within a year or so, more. And even if she had work, it would stop when the babes came."

Francis's brow furrowed as he contemplated the plight of the common man for perhaps only the second time in his life. "I see."

"Yes, sir." Hatten looked as though he did not believe his master saw at all, but merely began to lead the gelding away to its stall.

Francis blinked and shook his head, in the manner of a man trying to rid himself of a disturbing idea. "Hatten."

The groom turned. "Yes, sir?"

"How can it be worth it?"

"Beg your pardon, sir?"

"Marriage." Francis waved a hand. "Love. If it is so much trouble and expense, why bother?"

Hatten gave a wry grin. "I wouldn't know, sir. That's something you'll have to discover for yourself, I reckon."

A grimace transformed Francis's handsome countenance and Hatten huffed a laugh, turning away once more with the horse. Shaking his head again, Francis made his way up to the house.

He sat long after dinner over his port, irritated that the matter of Jane and Jacob continued to niggle at his brain. What did it matter to him how they managed after he turned her off? For he could not very well allow her to remain as a maid in his house under the circumstances. And he might not have given the lower classes more than a passing thought, but he did know the butcher was one of the wealthier men in the village. Surely he could assist his son in achieving the dream of going into wedded shackles with his lady-love. Living over the butcher's shop could not be so distasteful if it was what she wished.

He went to bed, snuffing the candle and drawing the bed curtains to lie down upon his pillow. But somehow, Jane's wish to retain her position troubled him so greatly that he found it impossible to sleep. After tossing to and fro for over an hour, he at last sat up, gazing with narrowed eyes into the darkness and grimly pondering the avenues available to him. It was another hour before he arrived at a resolution that relieved his mind of care, and he was able to sleep.

The next morning, Francis awoke at his usual hour and dressed for riding. His first destination, however, was not the stables, but the housekeeper's room. Mrs. Grimsley, the butler's wife of two-score and more years, did not approve of how her master had turned out, but knowing as she did both his mother's and his father's characters, she could not bring herself to fault him for it. She knew exactly what services Jane had been providing to the master beyond turning the bedsheets and beating the rugs, but she had, out of loyalty and a softness for him, never said a word.

She was stunned, therefore, to receive from his lips the command he gave that morning, together with the information that Jane was about to change her circumstances for the better. If he had stayed to hear her opinion on the subject, she could not have given it, for there warred within her breast the desire to give him a piece of her mind and the hope that he might be shrugging off the influence of his odious father at last.

But Francis did not stay, striding from her gaping presence to the stables, where his mount was ready. He rode out to the village, arriving just when the women and servants were about their shopping. Tying his horse outside the butcher's shop, he entered, glad to see the proprietor and not his son at the counter.

"Good morning, Hatchett."

Francis did not think he imagined the disapprobation beneath the smile on the man's face as he replied, "Good morning, sir. What can I get for you?"

Gazing about the shop with spurious interest, Francis said, "I've come about your son, Jacob."

The smile froze. "And what of my son, may I ask, sir?"

"I hear he is considering matrimony."

Mr. Hatchett's mouth tightened in apprehension. "P'raps. Never can tell with boys his age. Always falling in and out of love, but if he's got marriage in his mind, it's the first I've heard of it, sir."

Francis sighed, looking away. "I highly doubt that, Hatchett." He took another leisurely step toward the counter, returning his wry gaze to the butcher's face. "A daunting prospect, marriage, or so I've been informed. Not a step to be taken lightly."

"To be sure, sir," said the butcher, lifting his chin. "But it's a darn sight better'n frittering away the best years of a maid's life before casting her aside, sir—no matter how willing she is."

Francis's brows raised a trifle, and the butcher's fierce gaze wavered under his satirical regard. But the man stood his ground, and Francis at last gave a small huff. Perhaps not everyone was as expansive in their acceptance of the rights of a gentleman as Mr. Potts. It was something that Francis could almost respect.

Breaking their mutual gaze, he came forward the final few steps to the counter, crossing his arms over his chest. "If your son wished to marry a certain young lady who is at present in my employ, for example, you would give your blessing?"

The butcher did not reply at once, and Francis watched as a multitude of emotions flitted over his face. Fascinating, he thought, that hope and fear and pride and hatred could live so easily together in one mind. At last, the man said, through gritted teeth, "Ain't her fault she was tempted beyond what she could bear."

"Then you would give your blessing to the match?"

"Don't matter, sir, as there ain't no hope of her leaving 'your employ,' as you say."

Francis shrugged. "Oh, I could arrange that—indeed, I already have. But I wish to be assured that she will have someone else to protect her—someone with whom she would be happy to stay."

"Someone who loved her, you mean, sir?" ground out the butcher.

"You could say that."

Mr. Hatchett's mouth worked for a moment, his narrowed eyes searching Mr. Mantell's face. At last, when he had commanded himself enough to speak, he said, "You can be sure she'll be a fair sight happier with my Jacob than she has been with you, sir. She won't have baubles and furbelows like she has with you—it'll be hard enough for Jacob to scrape together a few pounds for a proper wedding, much less provide a roof over her head. But nor will she have empty promises and heartbreak looming, he'll see to that! You can leave her to his protection, for no matter what you might think, my Jacob loves her, sir!" Then, looking away, he added in a low mutter, "Little though she deserves it."

Francis regarded him, torn between fascination and distaste. What strange creatures, these common folk, with their intense emotion and complex loyalties. He considered inquiring into it, but mentally shook himself, reminded that he had little time and less interest in such tawdry subjects, and had better close the dialog and get on with his ride.

Reaching into his pocket, he withdrew a purse and placed it on the counter. "That is for your young Jacob. I would be obliged if you would see that he gets it, and even more obliged if you will tell him to waste no more time in making the young lady in question his wife. And pray do not weary me with your misplaced pride, Hatchett. There is nothing attached to this purse but my good will, and the overwhelming desire to be done with the matter."

Mr. Hatchett, who had been eying the purse with mingled incredulity and affront, looked at Mr. Mantell as though uncertain how to act.

"Take it, man," said Francis, adjusting his riding coat and dusting his sleeves. "I have forgotten it already, as I have the young lady."

And with that, he turned and walked from the shop, mounting his horse and turning it back toward Gracely Hall.

Chapter 3

HIS DIALOG WITH Mrs. Grimsley having established Jane's removal during the course of the morning, Francis was spared a scene which he would have found tiresome in the extreme. He was never one for feminine tears, and though he could not guess whether they would have been from grief or gratitude, he was certain Jane would have indulged freely—and likely spoiled his neck cloth, if not his coat. As it was, he easily escaped Gracely Hall for the remainder of the day by calling on Charles Wraglain, his lifelong neighbor and friend, who resided with his adopted parents at The Knoll.

Charles Wraglain was the son of Lord Wraglain's erratic sister Margaret, who had been on the brink of making a respectable match when she ran away with a captain on leave from the army. Captain Finchley was handsome, charming, and described as a great gun by his cronies, which to the discerning was warning enough. Unfortunately, Meg had never been possessed of much discernment, and her elopement was not viewed by anyone but herself as the coup she believed it to be.

Four children and thrice as many changes of quarters later, Meg had been thoroughly disabused of her fanciful notions regarding her marriage, and she at last turned to her family for assistance. Her father, by that time, had gratefully left the world and his daughter's shame behind, but her brother's succession to his honors only sharpened his anxiety regarding her situation. As the new Lord Wraglain, he exerted himself on behalf of Meg and her family, but as Captain Finchley seemed little disposed to exert himself likewise, nothing was accomplished by way of amelioration.

At last, Lord and Lady Wraglain extended the last olive branch available to them: an offer to adopt their eldest nephew, Charles. This offer was gratefully accepted by Meg, and Finchley viewed the circumstance with equanimity. For while he continued to receive a stipend and the use of a cottage and farm on a family estate in Somersetshire, there was little about which he could complain. Thus, Charles was reared in the family of a lord while understanding that he was not truly theirs, for his origins kept him firmly out of reach of the usual privileges of an elder son.

Francis thought little of all this. Though he rated highly his own social standing, he was not so squeamish as to split hairs over where his friend came from, for they had been practically inseparable since childhood. As few knew all the details of Charles's situation, there was little chance of their acquaintance causing a scene. Besides, though Charles tended toward the prudish, he was an agreeable companion, cheerful and sharp as a tack, and game for nearly any lark his friends could think up.

Arrived at The Knoll, Francis consigned his curricle to a groom and went into the house, being ushered into the library by the staid butler, Petrie. Here he was not left kicking his heels long, for after only a few minutes Charles came in, all eagerness to know what his friend was about.

"I heard the devil of a rumor at the Horse and Jockey, Mantell!" he said, dispensing with the usual pleasantries. "They say you gave a purse to young Hatchett if he would take Jane off your hands! But I know it can't be true. You said she's as game a pullet as ever there was—you're never keen to be rid of her so soon. It can't have been more than a year she's been under your protection."

Francis took a sip of the Madeira Charles had offered him while delivering himself of this speech. "Two years. However, she never was under my protection, precisely, as you ought to know, Charles. It was merely an understanding between us."

"And more to the point, she cost you far less than any of your London high flyers ever did! I ask again, what are you about?"

Wrinkling his nose, Francis took another ruminative sip. "She wished to end the arrangement, and to be frank, I had begun to find it rather tedious myself."

"These little *affaires* never last," agreed Charles, dropping into a wing chair and sipping at his own drink. "But I still do not see what the purse to Jacob Hatchett had to do with it."

"I had no other choice but to facilitate the marriage, or be obliged to keep her on as my maid. Otherwise, it would seem as though I grudged the end of the arrangement. And I really could not be expected to bear that ignominy, you know."

Charles chuckled, raising his glass in salute. "Then it's all for the best. I suppose it's not really the thing, to have an *affaire* with one's maid."

"Come, Charles," said Francis with a look of distaste. "You aren't going to come over the moralist now, are you? I swear I'll cut your acquaintance quicker than I dropped Jane."

"Never fear, my friend—I learned long ago it is vain to try." But then the smile faded and Charles considered the depths of his glass for a moment. "Though, it's true that taking up with village maidens was your father's game."

Francis's look of distaste transformed into a sneer, and he pinned Charles with an icy blue gaze. Charles did not flinch, however, merely returning the look with one of blandness. After a full minute, Francis turned away, tossing back the remaining contents of his glass.

"Then it's as you say—all the better." He looked back to his friend, his tone heavy with irony. "Heaven forbid I become my father, after all the steps I have taken to distance myself from his legacy."

Charles's countenance softened almost to pity, but he quickly recovered, giving a chuckle as he rose to refill his glass and offer his guest more wine. Raising his glass, he said, "To untrammeled bachelordom!"

"Hear, hear," replied Francis, taking the wine in one gulp.

"I suppose that's what brings you here today, then? Avoiding the inevitable scene?"

"Indeed, and the ruination of my neckcloth. Poor Benton would have the vapors, and I cannot have that."

Charles shook his head in mock solemnity. "It would be to risk his absconding to fairer climes, and I'd be obliged to take him in out of pure charity."

"To your peril," replied Francis, rising and going to the mirror over the mantelpiece to adjust said neck cloth. "The day you steal my valet is the day you name your friends."

"Now, if you were your sister, I should take sufficient warning," Charles said with a smirk. "Clara's twice the shot you are."

Francis glanced at him, a martial light in his eye. "I will have you know, it was I who taught her to shoot!"

"To hold that pretty pistol she cozened you into buying for her, perhaps, but it was Simpford taught her to shoot, sir."

"Then your loyalties are misplaced!" retorted Francis, but he could not hold Charles's gaze. Dashing some more Madeira in his glass, he muttered, "Simpford indeed. He bested me only the one time, you know."

"For friendship's sake, I'll forget the other," Charles laughed, slapping his friend's shoulder. "Now, how shall we amuse ourselves? I assume you've a mind to avoid Gracely as long as possible. It just so happens I've had a letter from the bailiff at Briarwood and it seems there's nothing for it but to see what's to do. Want to come along?"

"To Northamptonshire? The old biddy getting up to her tricks again?"

Charles shrugged. "This time my great aunt believes there are ghosts roaming the attics. More likely there are loose shingles and any number of other repairs needing to be made. As I am to inherit, it behooves me to go investigate and see to repairs, and put her mind at rest."

"It would be better if *she* could be laid to rest," said Francis, with a moue of distaste. "Never did like an old woman. Regular cats, all of them."

"Young and old alike," said Charles, grinning at his friend. "Will you come? We should be three weeks at least, perhaps five, and I'll go mad with boredom."

"With your great aunt to dog your steps? I think not."

Charles brushed this worry away. "The old lady sleeps the better part of the day now. We'll hardly see her—be off about the park. There will be plenty of shooting, you know."

Francis rubbed a hand over his mouth. "It's better than bearing the stares and sly looks of all and sundry in the village. Heaven knows I've nothing better to do. Pritchard has everything well in hand, and barring Grimsley's sudden incapacitation, Gracely ought to do for a month or so."

"Famous! I was dreading the solitude," said Charles, clapping his hands together. "As for now, have you brought your curricle?"

Francis said that he had and Charles grinned, inquiring, "Driving your chestnuts?"

"None other. I thought the situation called for speed."

"I'll get my coat."

Francis thus avoided Jane at her departure, but returning in late September, he could not avoid his mother and sister at theirs. They were off to Bath with Mr. Noyce, his recently-acquired step-father, who really was too good a gentleman to be saddled with such tiresome women. Clara was hot-at-hand—when she was not conniving to get her way in unladylike activities, she was continually flirting, imagining herself to be up to all the tricks. Francis lived in daily expectation of her downfall, which he hoped would be as spectacular as it was fitting. Their mother, on the other hand, was simply bitter, selfish, and nervous—thanks in part to her own temperament, but more to thirty years of marriage to Colonel Mantell.

Neither woman was comfortable company, which made Mr. Noyce's offer of marriage to Mrs. Mantell, coupled with the necessity of offering a home to Clara, so unfathomable to Francis. But what was even more so was that even after several months, his step-father's patience was unending. Francis could only put it down to inexperience. Mr. Noyce was fresh and in love, while Francis, having lived with his mother and sister all his life, might well have strangled the both of them had not Mr. Noyce so felicitously intervened.

Now that incomprehensible gentleman was not only going away to Bath, but carrying his womenfolk with him, which both bemused Francis and suited him very well. He would have—indeed, he had many times in the past—taken the opportunity to escape his female relations, but as Mr. Noyce inexplicably desired them with him, Francis could enjoy a reprieve.

In gratitude of this event, therefore, he acceded to the request that he come to dinner, and comported himself in so gentlemanly a manner that he hardly irritated his mother, and kept his sarcasm to twitting Clara only twice on the conquests—or lack thereof—she was likely to make in a town inhabited almost entirely by invalids.

When the ladies left the gentlemen to their port, Francis breathed a sigh of relief, causing Mr. Noyce to chuckle.

"They are talkative things, are they not?" the older man said, filling Francis's glass.

"And you are to bear with them for how many weeks at Bath?"

Mr. Noyce grinned, 'Til Christmas, or 'til my cursed legs feel the cure. But you need not pity me, my boy. I've been a lonely man for so long that having two beautiful ladies in my house, who spoil and pamper me, is no burden, no matter how they rattle on."

"But that is not all they do, sir, most especially Clara. You will find yourself playing nursemaid to her, for the girl is set on becoming ruined—she flirts with every man she meets! Even poor Simpford has fallen under her spell."

"You do not mean to imply that Lawrie Simpford would ruin your sister," said Mr. Noyce, raising an eyebrow.

Francis snorted. "He wouldn't dare, though he's been mooning about after her for two years at least." He took a swallow of his port, replacing his glass with a click on the table. "It's nauseating, and an affront to masculinity. I wish he would offer for her and be done with it."

Mr. Noyce looked ruminatively at the liquid in his glass. "He has done."

"Done what?"

Mr. Noyce met his gaze. "Lawrie offered for Clara, and she refused. It would seem that he *is* 'done with it'—at least, so she has informed him."

Francis shook his head. "I thought he hadn't the rumgumption to take the leap. And she refused? What a shame—I had hoped for an entertaining episode. Well, she is kinder than I could have anticipated. It is more in her line to gobble a man up than to so tamely let him go."

"It would seem so to the casual observer, I own," said Mr. Noyce with a wry smile.

"As most casual observers are besotted gentlemen, sir, I must disagree. But to one who knows her more intimately than one could ever wish to know any member of my family—excepting you, of course, sir, and perhaps my brother Geoffrey—it is plain as a pikestaff what she is capable of, to be sure."

"Clara is impulsive, selfish, and a flirt, but that does not preclude her being kind. She is unfailingly kind to me, you know."

"You are not a driveling mooncalf."

Mr. Noyce chuckled, but shook his head. "I must maintain that you do not know your sister. Just as you do not know your mother. You Mantells have hidden depths, I am persuaded."

Francis, with a look of disdain, said, "I suppose I am meant to find in that a compliment."

"You need not, if you do not wish it," said Mr. Noyce, pouring more wine for his guest. "But you will not convince me otherwise. There is too much evidence to support me. Take what you have done for Jane, for example."

Francis's keen gaze flicked to Mr. Noyce's face. "So that has come to your ears, has it?"

"It was bound to—such a romantic story could never be hushed up in our sleepy little town."

"Romantic, bah! I merely acted as any sensible man would when faced with a disagreeable situation. Even if my name is worth nothing, I have my position to uphold."

Mr. Noyce considered him for a moment. "The purse to young Hatchett was rather well-done."

Francis shrugged, taking another sip of his port. "It was insurance. I could not have Jane continue in my house, when her husband is a reputed devil with his fives."

"It certainly does not sound romantic when you put it that way."

"Be assured, sir, there is not a romantic bone in my body—just as there is not in Clara or my mother. I am sorry to disillusion you, but so it is. We are incapable of the tender emotions, and wish only to satisfy ourselves."

Mr. Noyce sat forward with a knowing smile, saying, "You have my blessing to think as you will, but I take leave to think as I will. However, I will own that you may well be wiser than the generality of men to close your heart to susceptibility—I am the first to admit that the tender emotions are not at all comfortable. It seems that no sooner does one submit to them than one finds oneself obliged to endure all sorts of responsibility. It certainly is easier to pretend one is insensible than to embrace discomfiture."

"Your persistence in disbelieving me will not change the truth, sir," said Francis dryly. "You would do better not to believe me a better man than I am."

"Never fear, I do not," said Mr. Noyce, and when Francis merely nodded, he added, "It seems you are afflicted with universal insensibility, my boy, for you do not seem to know yourself any better than you do your sister or mother."

Francis did not reply, for though he could not comprehend Mr. Noyce's optimism, he found it impossible to employ harsher means to bring him to a sense of reality. He disagreed with his step-father, but he also respected him. So, rather than defend his own heartlessness to one who would never relinquish a belief in the innate goodness of man, he turned the subject to the treatments available to invalids such as Mr. Noyce in Bath and they whiled away the remainder of their time together in camaraderie.

They soon rejoined the ladies, and Francis watched in bemusement as Mrs. Noyce instantly began fussing about Mr. Noyce, pressing him to sit in his favorite chair and searching for a stool to put under his feet. This could only be a pretense, for Francis had never seen his mother so solicitous—not for her children and particularly not for her former husband. It seemed entirely out of character for her to care so, but he was obliged to own that Mr. Noyce was particularly capable of engaging a lady's affections. And Mr. Noyce seemed truly to esteem his wife, as was evidenced by the gentle admiration radiating from his countenance as she fluttered about him.

Francis turned his back on the display with a mixture of abhorrence and wonder, going to sit beside Clara on the sofa. His mother's actions were entirely unnatural, but perhaps Mr. Noyce was right—perhaps Mrs. Noyce was capable of tender emotion, and had only required the right encouragement. But that did not make it one whit more palatable to Francis, nor did it prove Mr. Noyce's point that all the Mantells were possessed of these "hidden depths." What good was tender emotion when it would eventually fail? It only complicated matters and made the inevitable disappointment all the more unpleasant.

The remainder of the evening passed as quietly as possible, considering Clara declined to agree with Francis in discussing the oddity of Mrs. Noyce's absorption in her spouse's comfort. Instead, she quizzed him about throwing off poor Jane, and he was forced to compass again what he had done for the maid and the butcher's son. But when he trusted that she would understand his true motives, even she failed to do so, perversely attributing his actions to a kinder instinct, just as Mr. Noyce had done. It seemed their step-father's influence ran deep with the Mantell women. But Clara only twitted him for a few disbelieving minutes, and the subject at last dropped.

Francis took his leave, therefore, with no little relief, looking forward to the blessed quiet of his Leicestershire hunting box, whence he meant to remove for the hunting within a sennight. There, he could be certain of clearheaded companions—Charles Wraglain was to accompany him, and then they were to join their old schoolfellow Nathan Willoughby at his estate in Lincolnshire before attending the races at Newmarket. If tender emotions came up at all, they would be properly despised and summarily dismissed, as they should be. Let men like Mr. Noyce make fools of themselves over women—Francis and his cronies certainly would not.

Chapter 4

WHEN FRANCIS SET out for Leicestershire in his curricle at the end of September, he was duly accompanied by Charles Wraglain and Hatten, his groom. A coach followed along behind them, carrying Charles's groom and the baggage at so respectable a rate that the curricle quickly outstripped them. Arriving betimes at the Swan with Two Necks in Rigby, the two gentlemen went into the public room to refresh themselves while the horses were being changed.

Though it was only gone ten o'clock, the establishment was nearly full with patrons, travelers and locals alike, and two serving maids bustled about the tables. Francis and Charles were obliged to wait several minutes before the tapster could take their orders, then they took a small table in a back corner to await the drinks. Soon a serving maid, not in the first blush of youth but very comely, came along carrying two tankards.

She greeted them familiarly as she set the drinks on the table, resting a hand on the back of Francis's chair while she paused to chat. "Back so soon? I declare if you wasn't off to the hunting box only yesterday."

"Ah, but I couldn't stand to be apart from you any longer, Dotty, my dear," said Francis, reaching for her hand, but she pulled it away.

"And here I thought you was running away from that fine estate and all its responsibilities."

"You are too modest, sweet Dorothy," Francis said with an appreciative smile. "You know you have always been the only girl for me."

She sighed gustily, a hint of a smile upon her rosy lips. "If only it were the truth."

"But Dotty, why do you think I keep that poky little hunting box if not for the pleasure of making you sigh now and then?"

Her smile broke free, but when he attempted again to take her hand, she stepped to Charles's side, saying piteously, "Do you hear this silver-tongued fool, Mr. Wraglain? What's a maid to do, when he's so handsome, and says such pretty things?"

"If you want my advice, Miss Dorothy—" began Charles, but Francis interrupted him.

"That is what you don't want, my love! You may be certain Wraglain is so envious of my charms that he would say anything to give you a disgust of me, and then where will I be?"

"On the road to Leicestershire, sir, just like you was before," she said archly, exchanging a knowing look with Charles.

Francis pressed a hand to his chest, affecting an injured look. "You think me so inconstant? How you wound me, and to the very heart! I declare I shall never recover."

"If I believed that, Mr. Mantell," she said, her lips pursing against her treacherous smile, "I'd be dotty indeed. Now, I'd best be on my way. Is that all it'll be for you?"

"I thought I had made it plain what else I'd like," said Francis reaching to encircle her waist.

But she danced out of his reach, placing herself on Charles's other side. "A girl can't trust him to behave like a decent gentleman even for a minute, eh, Mr. Wraglain?"

"Not at all," was the prompt answer.

Francis turned an outraged look upon his friend. '*Et tu, Brute?*'"

Charles merely grinned, taking Dorothy's hand, which was at present resting on his shoulder, and kissing it.

"Ah, now there's a gentleman for you," she said, gazing approvingly down at Charles. "He'll protect me from your conniving ways. Won't you, sir?"

"To my dying breath," said Charles, grinning ungenerously at his friend.

"Turncoat," remarked Francis, but he grinned back, sitting back more comfortably in his chair. "Since there's nothing else on tap at the moment, my darling Dotty, I'll settle for my porter."

She shook her head, a dimple peeping in one cheek. "I suppose you'll never give over this useless game." She turned to bestow a dazzling smile upon Charles and, laying a hand softly on his cheek, said soulfully, "Goodbye, my champion." With a saucy look at Francis, she sauntered away.

Watching the sway of her hips through the crowded room, Francis said pensively, "I ought to call you out for that, Charles."

"Not that I would back away from a challenge, Mantell, but it would do nothing for your case."

Francis slewed about to regard him. "And what of yours?"

"I don't have a case," laughed Charles. "Not with Dorothy, in any event—and it's about time you acknowledged nor do you."

Francis considered a moment, then remarked, "I suppose you're right. She's never taken me up, not in eight years. Fine woman, Dotty—she would have been my first love, you know, if she would have had me."

"Then it's well for her she withstood your charms." Taking a pull of his ale, Charles inquired, "Still, I am persuaded you would have gone with her if she *had* taken you up."

"Certainly. Who wouldn't?"

Charles huffed. "Leaving me to kick my heels here? But I have known for some time you are just such a friend."

"If you were not such a Puritan, you could have found your own amusement."

"I'm no Puritan, sir—*you* are a loose fish."

Francis pursed his lips. "Come now, Charles, it's not as though I've done anything scandalous. I never take 'em unless they're willing. As could you, if you'd put yourself forward."

"Many thanks for the advice, Mantell, but 'taking' women, willing or otherwise, somehow doesn't run with my notions of amusement," said Charles, taking another pull of ale.

Francis eyed him sardonically. "Who's no Puritan?"

"I simply happen to have been reared by an excellent woman, and happen to agree with her strong opinions on the subject."

With sudden comprehension, Francis raised his mug in mock salute. "To Lady Wraglain. May she find joy in wrecking the independent spirit of the men within her reach."

Charles only shook his head, good-naturedly raising his mug as well and allowing the subject to drop. They finished their drinks and left the inn just as the coach bearing their luggage swung into the yard, and after a word with the coachman, Francis and Charles climbed into the waiting curricle and went on their way.

"What did we decide, eh, Mantell?" inquired Charles. "One week or two for the shooting?"

"We didn't, but I have since exercised my prerogative as your host and decided the matter. That is, I've received the intelligence that the hunt will throw off next week, and so we shall enjoy the relative peace of our own company until then."

Charles expressed his agreeableness to the plan. "Then on to Willoughby's? Can't say I'm all eagerness. I wonder who will be there this time."

"Oh, the usual fellows. But I forget you do not like Willoughby."

"I do not care for his set, that's all. Too rackety by half."

"They can be tiresome, to be sure, but there is never a dull moment. Besides, Penhurst is a convenient stopping point on the way to Newmarket. I have a horse running in the second October Meeting, you know."

Charles gave him an expressive look. "As I have as much patience for Newmarket as I do for Willoughby and his set, you'll not take it amiss if I take myself off instead to Somersetshire."

"Ah, yes." Francis grimaced. "Filial duty awaits. I must own that I do not miss the demands of my dear departed father."

"It's my mother who more often desires me to come."

"Yes, well, I do not regret that my mother is too caught up in the delights of her new marriage to think much of me."

Charles was meditative for a moment. "She seems exceedingly happy with Mr. Noyce."

"Exceedingly happy," agreed Francis, in a disdainful tone, "if one can but believe it."

His friend looked quickly at him. "Do you doubt it? Have you not seen them together?"

Francis shrugged. "Not often, for I have made it my business to be absent from Southam for much of the time they've been married."

"Solely to avoid them?"

"Not precisely, no," admitted Francis. "You well know I've had other reasons to wish to avoid Southam. But I do not know what I believe about my mother's sentiments. When I saw the newly married couple at first, my mother was not much altered—only giddy with her own conquest, I supposed. But when I returned from Northamptonshire last month, the change was significant. It was as though she truly wished to please him. If Clara had not told me our mother is always thus, I would not have credited it."

Charles was quiet for a moment before saying, "Mr. Noyce is so kindly a person that one can imagine him capable of great things, including the transformation of a heart of ice to one of flesh and blood."

"One wishes he would have spared himself the trouble. Do you know how distasteful it is to witness the ministrations of a woman in love?" Francis shuddered. "It is enough to put one off marriage forever."

Charles contemplated this. "I have a notion one might get used to such attentions."

"You know not whereof you speak, my friend. They can only wear thin with time."

Chuckling, Charles said pointedly, "Mr. Noyce does not seem at all averse to them."

Francis could only shake his head. "Have it as you will. I have had enough talk of love and marriage. At least I will soon be with gentlemen whose sentiments agree with mine."

"Dear me, yes," sighed Charles. "I do not believe I have ever been surprised at one thing Willoughby has ever done. He is so unoriginal in his complaints and bitterness that one may plot out his next move almost to the end of the game."

Francis laughed. "Comforting, is it not? One always is assured of one's position with old Will."

"I yet reserve the right to abscond at my discretion."

"And leave me to bearlead the lot of them?" cried Francis in mock dismay. "You wouldn't be so heartless."

"You are welcome to join me, if you wish."

"You are too kind, Charles," said Francis with a wry smile, "but your dear mama would, I fear, only think me in the way."

Chuckling, Charles said, "I would not expect to drag you all the way to Somersetshire. I wish only to give you an excuse to remove from Penhurst Lodge at your leisure."

"You dashed well *couldn't* drag me to Somersetshire—not if I have to stay in that drafty old inn again. The sheets were damp, and if there were not bedbugs, I am a lobcock."

"Come now, the dear old Lord Nelson ain't so bad. And even if it were, there's always the cottage."

"Stay with your family? No, Charles. That would be the outside of enough. Have you counted the members of your family? I shall remind you that they outnumber the rooms in the house. I am persuaded I'd have to share your bed and, much as I enjoy your company, dear Charles, my esteem does not extend to that, I assure you!"

Charles laughed heartily. "You are being obtuse. Lyddie is so in awe of your magnificence that she will surely offer to make her bed with Mary and Abigail in the nursery, leaving you with the best room in the cottage."

"How can you suggest such a thing, Charles? I should blush to take your sisters' bed."

"Then you might take William's, for he would think nothing of pigging in with Frederick and Edward."

Francis cast Charles a scathing look. "Your solicitude is overwhelming. Much as I am moved, however, it would be impossible for me to accept, for it would be to oblige myself to Captain Finchley. For all he is your father, Charles, I find him intolerable."

Grinning, Charles said, "But he adores you, Mantell!"

"The word you are searching for is 'bores.' He bores me to death, Charles."

"Oh, but you must admit his tales of heroism in battle to be imaginative. They are grander and more implausible every time I visit."

"They must have been mere grunts when you were a child to have grown out of all recognition of the truth. It's a wonder he expects that I could believe a word of them."

"I think he has even begun to believe them himself."

Noting that Charles's tone had become somewhat pensive, Francis glanced at him. He was not a particularly sensitive man, but he could appreciate the burden of a less-than-perfect father.

"It's the devil of a situation, Charles," he said after a moment. "At least you are far removed from them much of the time."

Charles managed a fleeting smile, but said, "I am never completely removed, however, nor will I be so for much longer. Soon, my great aunt will die, and I will inherit Briarwood, and must take my mother and my father's maintenance upon myself. Lord Wraglain cannot bear it forever. Indeed, it would not be right."

Francis shrugged. "I suppose not. It is a pity, for as your adopted father, he has done the thing admirably all your life."

Charles was silent for a few moments, then said, "Once they are in my care, and close by, it will be all the more difficult for me to show the forbearance I do now. It is easy to laugh at my father when I am not with them, for in between visits I am able to forget with what carelessness he treats my mother and brothers and sisters, and my anger dims. But when I have no such reprieve, I cannot say what I will be guilty of."

"You will certainly not be the first to hate his father," said Francis in a bland tone. "Just as he is not the first man to be careless of his wife."

Charles glanced at him. "No, but it is a shame nonetheless."

"Or it is only the way of things. It is my belief it is the way with most marriages."

"Not so with Lord and Lady Wraglain. They have always been excessively fond of each other, and have scarcely given any of their children a moment's mortification or anger for their care of one another."

"They are certainly the exception, I am persuaded."

"You are merely biased, based on your parents' experience. I could name half a dozen other couples with happy marital relations—your mother and Mr. Noyce for one."

Francis hesitated, musing over this perspective. "I suppose I must own that you have something there, Charles. But Mr. Noyce and Lord Wraglain are exceptional men—much like my brother Geoffrey, whose marriage is also quite different than my father and mother's. There are not many men like them, and therefore, I hold to my opinion that marriage in general is no rosy prospect."

"You simply do not choose to be in company with men like Geoffrey and Mr. Noyce," rejoined Charles. "Therefore, you are no judge. For all you know, your parents' marriage is the exception."

"Perhaps, but no marriage is without its discomforts, and the likelihood of both parties maintaining satisfaction for the duration is very low."

Charles considered this, but said, "Let us agree that much depends on the characters of the persons involved. The union of two caring individuals must produce mutual satisfaction, if not the bliss often dreamed of or written of in romances."

"Very well. But you will not convince me that I must dream of this bliss. Some of us simply are not made for marriage, I am persuaded."

Grinning, Charles said, "Spoil sport. I only pray I shall be present when you discover the perfect woman and you suddenly find that the notion of wedded bliss is not so very distasteful after all."

"I will never."

"It is the way of Providence, my friend. In my experience, it always sends you what you never wish. Indeed, I'd wager that you have not much time left before you are proved wrong."

Francis's glance was speculative. "If you'd wager your grey hunter, I should gladly take the bet."

"If you'll wager your bay, we may shake on it," Charles rejoined.

When Francis seemed seriously to consider this, Charles laughed out loud. Francis soon joined him and, the ridiculous wager quickly forgotten, they whiled the rest of the time to Lutterworth with idle chat.

Chapter 5

Having sent their hunters and dogs ahead, Charles and Francis enjoyed a few days' sport without interruption. The lodge was quite cozy, with a kitchen, breakfast parlor, billiard room, and saloon on the ground floor, and four bedrooms above. The Brubbinses, the middle-aged couple who kept the lodge ready for their master throughout the year, were rather garrulous, but this inconvenience was outweighed by Mrs. Brubbins's way with a partridge pie—that and her broad-minded acceptance of what she and her husband termed "young men's ways."

"There they go, tracking mud onto my clean floors again," Mrs. Brubbins commented fondly to her husband, as Francis and Charles tramped through the hall after a day's shooting. "Not but what it wouldn't go cross-grain with me if they were to be taking off their boots out of doors, but these young men have better things to do than worrit about the floors."

"Just like our Bill, they are," agreed Mr. Brubbins, thumbs in his belt. "Always coming and going, doing this or that. Fine, healthy boys need fresh air and action. Puts me in mind of the summer when Bill was out all night, and come back with that shiner. Looked mighty like he'd come to blows, but 'twere only a stumble into a tree." He chuckled and shook his head. "These young men and their ways."

Mrs. Brubbins wiped a tear from her eye with the corner of her apron. "The house is right cheery with them footprints where none was afore."

With such adoring and indulgent retainers at his service, it was not surprising that Francis took every opportunity to escape into Leicestershire. Even his valet was left behind, for there was no need for so finicking an individual with only hunting and shooting to dress for, and no society to speak of.

The tranquility of this carefree existence was not to last, however. On the afternoon of the fourth day, Francis and Charles were walking up the drive after a successful day's shooting, the grooms acting as general factotums bearing their birds in bags over their shoulders and the dogs gamboling joyfully before, when the sight of a chaise and four in the yard brought them to an abrupt halt. Sending the grooms on ahead, the gentlemen came up to inspect the vehicle, finding Mr. Brubbins struggling at the rear with a large trunk.

Francis, gazing with disfavor upon the showy team of horses, inquired, "Whose set-up is this, Brubbins?"

"It's Mr. Bellerton's chaise, sir," grunted the man as he hauled the trunk off the back. "This'll be the last of the baggage."

"The last—what the devil?" exclaimed Francis, gazing bemusedly after the servant as he and the trunk disappeared into the house.

Charles gazed along with him. "Well, there's an end to our peace, to be sure. As you were about to say, what the devil brings Bellerton here, I wonder?"

Francis turned to Charles, his countenance grim. "Ten to one it's a woman."

"That or his father is after him about money again."

Sighing, Francis clapped Charles on the back and walked on toward the house. "Best find out. Looks as though he means to stay, at any event. Devilish ugly horses, those."

"Bell never was a judge of horse-flesh."

They went into the house to find their guest in the saloon, along with two other gentlemen, around the legs of whom the dogs darted, sniffing curiously.

Seeing no need to call his dogs to order, Francis surveyed his unexpected guests. "I believe it is within my rights to know what possessed you to bring such an ill-favored team onto my property," he observed.

Simon Bellerton, a tall, blond fellow with brown eyes and a somewhat toothy mouth, looked up from where he sat sipping Madeira. "You like my greys? Sell 'em to you. Give you a good price, too."

Francis snorted. "Not on your life—you can't gull me. I never saw such a parcel of bonesetters."

Bellerton cursed him amiably and returned his attention to his drink, while his two companions stood to shake hands with Francis and Charles.

"What brings you here, Willoughby, and Hayes, too? I never imagined you'd so honor my humble abode."

Nathan Willoughby, the older of the two by three years, gave a short laugh, his steel-blue eyes sardonic. "Shoe box, more like. I'd have sold it off the minute it was mine and bought a better. Plenty around here to be had, to be sure."

"Perhaps I keep it because it is too small to house encroaching friends," said Francis dryly.

"Ought to have apprised him," said The Honorable George Hayes, shuffling a bit as his anxious gaze flitted from Francis to their friend.

Willoughby, who had gone over to pour himself a drink, made a careless gesture with his free hand. "Nonsense. Can't be any trouble. Just the three of us, and only for a few days."

'Til the storm blows over," added Bellerton with a meaningful look.

With a heavy sigh, Francis went over to the sideboard and poured himself a brandy. "I suppose I'm stuck with you, so you may as well cut line. What storm is that, Bell?"

Bellerton looked up in surprise. "Not me. It's Will who's in the suds."

Charles, who had resigned himself to the situation, settled on the sofa and prepared to be interested. George, still uncertain that danger had been averted, sat gingerly beside him and watched as Francis turned his bland gaze upon Willoughby.

"Cursed meddling Draffin woman," Will began, seemingly unmoved by this inspection. He caught the look Francis exchanged with Charles and added quickly, "Not the young one, the mother! Insists I've compromised her daughter—dashed lot of lies. Never did more than ogle the chit a time or two."

George put in helpfully, "Said you made assignations—"

"Devil a bit!" retorted Willoughby testily, and Bellerton sniggered. Grimacing, Willoughby tossed off the Madeira and poured himself more. "Cursed scheming Cits trying to worm their way into good society."

A barked laugh from Bellerton did nothing to improve Willoughby's humor. He glared at Bell over his glass. "The Willoughby name's still the best in Swineshead, no matter the state of my finances. Situation's ridiculous—won't tolerate it. Thought it best to remove myself a while."

"So you descended on my hunting box," drawled Francis. "How touching. I never conceived you held me in such esteem. To be the one a friend turns to in his darkest hour—it warms the heart, truly it does."

"Couldn't well go anywhere else," muttered Willoughby into his glass.

"Duns making life unpleasant again?"

Willoughby made an impatient gesture. "When are they not? Flooding last year, and the saboteurs this spring—that windmill cost three hundred pounds to replace! I'd have kissed my fingers to it if I had fins and flippers, but I don't, do I? Can't live in a cursed boat, either." His mouth tightened, intensifying the lines of dissipation in his face. "Never can seem to get my legs under me, thanks to that devilish fenland. It'll be a welcome day when my honored father snuffs it and I can get my hands on the Jamaican plantation."

Francis raised his brows. "Why not arrange an advantageous marriage? Are not the Draffins fairly warm?"

"More like hot-at-hand," muttered Bellerton, but at Willoughby's withering look he sought refuge in his Madeira.

Francis pursued, "By all accounts, Miss Draffin is a cozy armful, and if she's willing to take you—"

"I'd have to be willing to take her, wouldn't I?" sneered Willoughby. "I may be at my last prayers, but even I've not sunk as low as that."

Shrugging, Francis finished his brandy and set down the glass with a weary sigh. "Then we must make the best of the situation. You will, of course, make yourselves at home, and have free run of my small holding here. Though we have done our possible, Wraglain and I have not quite killed all my birds, and the hunt throws off outside Tilton on Wednesday. That ought to be enough to occupy the five of us, however I dislike to admit it. But one thing is certain, gentlemen," he said with a fulminating look. "There are only four bedrooms in this house, and I will not be sharing mine with any of you."

Charles jumped up. "Nor I. First come, first choice, and I was here before any of you."

With that, he bolted from the room, no doubt to bar entry to his chamber. There was a general clamor as the remaining three men called out, jumped to their feet, and made for the door, but George was the unfortunate one who received an elbow to his face and was knocked to the floor, therefore losing the race.

Holding a hand to his nose, he looked pitifully up at Francis. "I'd take a trundle bed."

"There is no trundle bed on the premises," declared Francis, though not unkindly. He did not mention that this was on his direct orders. "Besides, my dear Hayes, you do not possess the requisite, shall we say, physiognomy, to be welcome in my bedroom."

Struggling to his feet, George made one last attempt. "I swear I don't snore."

"There is a garret in the attic," said Francis, setting down his glass and turning to the door. "A servant used to sleep there, I'm told. I have every confidence Mrs. Brubbins will do her best to make you comfortable there."

George could do little more than acquiesce, for his nose began to bleed, and by the time he had located and applied his handkerchief, his host had quitted the room.

George arrived puffy-eyed and disheveled at the breakfast table in the morning, but neither Francis nor Charles—the only other gentlemen present—were at all conciliating.

"Dashed lumpy mattress up in that garret, Mantell," said George. "Didn't sleep a wink."

"Excellent," muttered Francis, not raising his eyes from the paper he was perusing. "Perhaps it will teach my friends not to descend in numbers, unannounced."

Charles greeted the newcomer with a bright smile, pointing him to a chair. "You never struck me as a man of matutinal habits, Hayes. Why didn't you take breakfast in bed? It seems Bell and Will intend to do so."

"No bell pull," George answered mournfully, reaching for the plate of toast.

Mrs. Brubbins bustled in with a fresh pot of coffee and, seeing George, cried out, "Mercy me! Poor man, you look like the cat drug you in. On account o' you slept in the garret, or I'm a blue-spotted ape. Did you fall out of bed? I thought I heard a thump in the middle of the night, and I told Mr. Brubbins, that poor man what had to take the garret has fallen clean out of bed. 'Twould be no surprise, as it's so narrow a body could scarce turn over. Many's the time I thinks, I should've liked that garret room for our Bill, for though he was good as gold, he was a boy after all, and if he'd had that bed, I'd've slept better at night. Ain't never any shenanigans going on in that bed."

George, blinking blearily at her, merely held out his coffee cup to be refilled before she went away again.

Still deep in his newspaper, Francis remarked, "Wraglain ought to trade rooms with you, Hayes."

"Devil a bit!" cried Charles, shooting Francis an outraged look. "It's his own fault he's got the garret. Dash it, you invited me, Mantell!"

Francis smiled, taking a sip of his coffee. "It would be only fair. You are the Puritan among us, after all."

"You, a Puritan, Wraglain?" inquired George, his brow knitting. "Never would have thought it."

Charles's coffee cup clinked as he set it down rather harder than he ought. "I am not a Puritan, Hayes, and do not forget it. Mantell here is only bamming. It's his idea of a bad joke."

"Mark my words, Hayes," said Francis, finally raising his mocking eyes to Charles's face. "If I brought a parcel of fair Paphians here, Wraglain would hide in the stables. What else am I to think than that he is a Puritan?"

"When you bring fair Paphians to this lodge," retorted Charles, "I will gladly change rooms with Hayes."

"Well!" George was clearly moved. "Mighty generous of you, Wraglain, I must say. Always had the highest respect for Puritans, you know." He looked at Francis expectantly, as if he would produce the Paphians at any moment.

Charles crossed his arms over his chest, leaning back in his chair. "He'll never do it, Hayes, old boy, so you may as well give over hoping. This lodge is sacrosanct—the day a female crosses its threshold is the day Francis Mantell dies."

"But Mrs. Brubbins—"

"Doesn't count," said Charles categorically. "To count, the female would have to be younger than Mrs. Brubbins."

"And at least passably pretty," inserted Francis.

George looked for confirmation to Francis, who merely gazed blandly at him before applying himself to some rashers of bacon.

Abashed, George grumbled something that sounded like, "dashed unsporting," and returned to his coffee and toast.

Mrs. Brubbins must have worked some magic on the garret mattress, for in the following days, George did not appear so haggard. It soon became apparent that she had at least, in true motherly fashion, taken to bringing up breakfast to him in the mornings—the cause being, as she observed to Mr. Brubbins that first morning, "He deserves it as much as any of the gentlemen do, and more, for he didn't think to ask. Our Bill would want breakfast in bed, even without asking, and so I mean to take it to him."

So the days passed without much mishap, but without much harmony, either. Charles and Francis frequently repined the fact, loudly and with long, flowing wit, to the high entertainment of their guests. But in truth, they found much in the situation to laugh over, for as Francis had stated, there was never a dull moment in this company.

With the addition of his three friends to the hunt, there was no shortage of hard riding, hedge jumping, puddle splashing, and tosses, with their accompanying shouts, jibes, and curses. Perhaps the most satisfying event was Bellerton flying headfirst into a bramble after having forced his mount at a fence too high for its liking.

"Dashed horse is a Bugaboo," he ground out as he was carried away to a carriage.

"Devil a bit," was Francis's uncompromising reply. "You always were a saphead when it came to fences."

"And when it comes to prads," put in Charles helpfully. "That daisy cutter's no good on the turf, much less put at a fence."

Bellerton did not seem to appreciate this solicitude, as he swore fluently at them and the grooms while they loaded him into the carriage waiting to carry him away to the lodge.

George pulled at his lip as the invalid's carriage drove away. "Lucky the horse did shy. Could've broke his forelegs. Devilish bad riding."

"Trust Bell to ruin all our fun," muttered Willoughby.

Indeed, they had been effectively abandoned by the hunt, and the four remaining gentlemen followed Bellerton's carriage back to the lodge, nursing their disappointment with an excellent vintage of brandy. Once the surgeon had been to see the patient, he reported a wrenched shoulder and twisted ankle but no broken bones. This good news met with a unanimous vote to send up a bit of the brandy to Bellerton's room as a sort of congratulation.

Mrs. Brubbins came back to pass on the injured man's gratitude. "He says you can all go to the devil, he's that put out, but who can blame him, poor man? Just like my Bill, can't stand to lay idle. Too much to be doing to be tied by the heels. But never you worrit about a thing—me and Mr. Brubbins'll nurse him till he's up and doing again. No need to cut up your own pleasure, now."

As none of the gentlemen had intended to curtail their own sport for the sake of Bellerton, this met with their general approbation. Only George suffered by the incident, as Mrs. Brubbins, being called upon night and day to see to the invalid's needs, neglected for some few days to bring breakfast to the garret, and thus obliged its occupant to seek sustenance at the breakfast table.

The effective reduction of their company to four proved propitious, as they all fit round the small dining table, and were less crowded in the billiard room. There was also less argument over who was to sit in the most comfortable chairs in the drawing room, which contributed a sort of camaraderie to their evenings.

"I could almost imagine myself at home," mused George one evening as they sat about the drawing room, sipping at the excellent Madeira.

"I don't," declared Willoughby. "This shoe box is a sight more comfortable than my barrack of a house."

Francis, pouring a bit more wine into his glass, remarked, "I should hope this shoe box is at least as comfortable as Penhurst, Will, as you've invited us all there—or don't you recall?"

"Why do you think I invited you?" retorted Willoughby. "House guests hold the gross realities of life at bay. Once you're gone, it's 'when are we to be paid, sir,' and 'you'd best look after that cottage falling down, sir,' and 'the dike's burst again, sir.' My man of business in London don't leave me alone even for a minute. It's got to where I don't open his letters, for there's bound to be more bad news in them."

"Rotten luck, to inherit property in the Fens," said George comfortably. He stood to inherit a barony in Kent.

"If it were only luck!" snapped Willoughby, going to the sideboard for more wine. "My revered father bought the land on purpose, before I was born—thought it a sound investment! All the drains and dikes were sure to make it viable farmland. Ha! Been holding off the sea ever since. No wonder he ran off to Jamaica. I'd go too, if he wasn't there."

"His plantation there does well, I expect?" inquired Charles.

Willoughby chuckled mirthlessly. "Very well, or he wouldn't have stayed. Though I've no real knowledge—keeps it from me, dear Papa. Acts as though it's none of my business. But it dashed well will be my business—just long enough to get a fine price for it, and then I'll wash my hands of all he built in Jamaica. It'll be a fine revenge on that cheating cutpurse."

"I imagine it does not sit well with him that you will inherit what amounts to the product of his life's work," remarked Francis, tossing off his Madeira.

"Yes, well, unless he wishes to leave it all to that worm of a cousin of mine," replied Willoughby, smirking in satisfaction, "he really has no choice, does he?"

Chapter 6

AFTER THREE DAYS, Bellerton had healed sufficiently to rejoin the group and, to Francis's great relief, was sick to death of the poky little hunting box. Entering fully into his feelings, George expressed a desire for a proper bedchamber—complete with bell pull—and added his importunities that they remove forthwith to Penhurst Lodge. It was only a week to the second October Meeting at Newmarket, and they wished to recruit themselves in better style.

As only a short time had elapsed since Mrs. Draffin's disquieting ultimatum, however, Willoughby declared himself as yet unwilling to take his turn as host at Penhurst. He argued that they could go straight from Leicestershire to Newmarket and stop at Penhurst on the return journey. But Francis and Charles, taking upon themselves the role of advocate for the sufferers, reassured Willoughby that they should shoulder the responsibility of holding any and all Draffins at bay, and he at last acquiesced. The whole party went off to brave the

Fens of Lincolnshire, therefore, in the second week of October, with the expectation that though they might find the estate underwater, there would at least be room in the house for all five of them.

As it transpired, no flooding had occurred during the preceding weeks to halt their progress, nor to wet their feet upon entering the Lodge, but a pile of trunks and bandboxes in the entry hall attested to some sort of interesting development. A brown-skinned woman was directing the disposal of these articles upstairs by the footman, and when the gentlemen came in, she favored them with a measuring gaze before coming over to present herself.

"Who the devil are you?" demanded Willoughby, understandably astonished at the presence of a stranger—and a quantity of strange luggage—in his house.

With a dignified curtsey, the woman replied calmly in a mild West Indian accent, "Miss Muncey, sir. Miss Eliza's maid."

This name meaning nothing to him, Willoughby opened his mouth to demand an explanation when another voice forestalled him.

"Mr. Willoughby? I'm glad you are returned. We have much to discuss."

All the gentlemen turned to see a thin, balding man of middle age coming toward them from the direction of the library.

"Findlay?" Willoughby narrowed his eyes at his man of business. "Why are you here, and who is this impertinent female? What the deuce is she doing with all this baggage in the middle of my house?"

Removing his round spectacles, Mr. Findlay polished them with a handkerchief. "If you had taken the trouble of reading even one of my letters within the past two months, sir, you would be fully conversant with the details of the situation." Replacing the spectacles, he gazed soberly upon his employer. "But as I have deduced from the pile of unopened correspondence on your desk that you have not done so, I should be glad to put you in possession of all the facts at my disposal. You will first wish to see to the comfort of your guests, of course, but I should be pleased to have audience with you at your earliest convenience. I will await you in the library."

With a short bow, he turned on his heel and walked away, leaving Willoughby to gape after him, and the other gentlemen agog with curiosity.

George tapped Francis, who stood next to him, on the shoulder. "Shouldn't have ignored his man of business."

"Stubble it, clunch," hissed Bellerton, gazing with narrowed eyes at their host, who had turned pale.

Looking from the library door to the pile of luggage and back again, Willoughby licked his dry lips and swallowed. "You'll—you'll excuse me. Go—go into the saloon and make yourselves comfortable. I'll send Clayton to look after you." And with that, he strode to the library and disappeared inside.

The four gentlemen standing in the entry hall looked at one another in amazement, then back at the closed library door.

"His revered father has probably come to make a reckoning," speculated Bellerton, waving at the fast-shrinking pile of baggage.

George nodded. "That maid's accent is West Indian."

"As though you would know that," scoffed Bellerton.

George drew himself up. "I lived in Jamaica from the age of twelve to sixteen. Believe I can recognize a West Indian accent, however mild."

"She certainly looks West Indian," remarked Francis, observing the proceedings.

All turned to inspect the lady's maid, who was standing to the left of the stairs, watching as a footman hefted a small trunk onto his shoulder. She was of medium height, with brown skin and dark, tightly curling hair. Her frame was erect and her features elegant, and her carriage as she directed the footman bespoke self-possession. She did not even glance at them, though she must have heard at least some of their speech.

"A no-nonsense sort," observed Francis in an aside to the other gentlemen.

Bellerton scoffed. "I like a spirited woman."

"I'd like to see you try," said Charles with a scornful laugh. "Ten to one, you'd end up with a black eye and a bruised ego, and serve you right."

"I'll take that bet," mused Francis, glancing from the West Indian maid to Bellerton.

But George cut in, "Who is Miss Eliza?"

"Don't know," Bellerton huffed irritably. "Five to one, it's Old Willoughby's mistress."

This elicited a response from Miss Muncey, who turned her head to glare majestically at them all.

"Either you're right," said Francis, amused at this miniature drama, "or you've just offended a very imposing lady. I suggest you consider locking your door tonight, Bell, or you might find yourself missing an appendage in the morning."

"More likely, you'll sicken by degrees," put in George in a low tone. "That's the way with Obeah."

"Oh be what?" Bellerton snapped, his eyes flicking nervously from the maid to George. "What the devil are you spouting about now?"

George bent close to his ear to whisper, "Witchcraft. Common in the West Indies. Used to punish enemies."

He drew back, nodding to Bellerton with a meaningful look. The latter cast a horrified glance at Miss Muncey—who had resumed ignoring them as though they were so many gnats—and drew circumspectly away.

At that moment, Clayton, the butler, came jogging down the stairs, an action in strong contrast to his sober clothing. Indeed, his whole form opposed his position, for he was of middling height and stocky, with a shock of blond hair and a blue-eyed, youthful countenance that spoke nothing of dignity.

None of the gentlemen in the entry hall considered this at all odd. It was well known to them that Matthew Clayton, formerly known as the Mighty Mancunian, had once been a fierce contender in the Manchester ring, and his ascent to the leadership of the upper servants at Penhurst Lodge was due entirely to the fact that Willoughby required a butler capable of tossing insistent debt collectors out on their ear. The former pugilist had even been known to plant a facer on the more aggressive tradesmen who undertook to beard their uncooperative client in his den. Despite this fearsome record, however, Clayton's disposition was amiable, and he could charm nearly anyone he wished.

His eyes alighted on the gentlemen in the entry and he grinned, raising a hand in very un-butler-like greeting. As he neared the bottom of the stair, however, he slowed, his jog becoming a sedate step and his back straightening so his already impressive chest seemed to swell a trifle. Miss Muncey was there, her gaze averted as though she did not perceive the butler, or as though she could care not a button that he was present. Clayton, however, seemed unaffected by this indifference, for he gazed directly at her in open admiration, nodding politely as he passed and grinning upon receiving not so much as a flicker of an eyelid in return.

His jauntiness resumed as he crossed the hall to greet the gentlemen. 'Allo, sirs. And what are you doing 'ere, eh? Lost with nowhere to go?"

"We hoped you would direct us, Clayton," said Francis dryly, "as Willoughby has deserted us for his solicitor."

Clayton glanced at the library. "Eh! So Master's come with you. And well 'e did, for I tell you, there's a bit of a storm brewing, unless I'm dead mistaken."

He gave a significant look at the remaining baggage in the entry, and Bellerton uttered, "Ha! I knew it!"

But the butler did not elucidate further, merely bowing very creditably and saying, "I suppose 'e means for you to take your leisure while 'e and that Findlay are up to their business, so if you'd be so good as to retire to the saloon, gentlemen, I'll get after Mrs. Slade to prepare rooms for you."

Expressing their thanks, the four gentlemen went into the saloon, and Clayton closed the door on them, shutting out the activity in the hall to their view. They were drawn immediately to the sideboard, where decanters of sherry and brandy stood waiting, and they poured themselves generous libations to assist their whirling brains in assimilating the exceedingly strange goings-on.

"Would Old Willoughby really have brought his mistress here?" inquired Charles to no one in particular.

Bellerton leered. "One can hope. Been far too long since there's been a tolerable face in this house. Why not bring an open-minded lady, eh? It's Old Willoughby's house, after all, no matter that he left it all those years ago to Will's care."

"Got every right to bring a mistress," corroborated George, "especially now his wife's dead."

"Better watch what you're about, Bell, for it's just as likely this Miss Eliza is his intended wife," remarked Charles, brow raised in challenge.

Francis gazed ruminatively at the door to the hall, where sounds of activity could still be heard. "It is even possible they are newly married and the maid is so in the habit of calling her mistress 'Miss' that she has misled us."

"Then she'd be a near-miss," put in Bellerton, looking for their response. "You see? Near-miss, as in nearly a 'Miss."

Charles swirled his sherry in the glass. "If she's Mrs. Willoughby, you'll be lucky to have only a near miss for insulting her."

"Entirely possible she's married," said George, ignoring—or perhaps not comprehending—the joke. "My sister's maid called her Miss Hayes for months after the wedding."

Charles looked suddenly gleeful. "Your sister was on the shelf when she married—this Miss Eliza could be a veritable ape-leader. Old Willoughby's no sprig, you know."

"Good lord!" exclaimed Bellerton, his countenance overcome by horror. "It would be just like that old gager to bed a fubsy old spinster. Wish to heaven you're wrong. Much better bring a mistress."

Francis gave a wry smile. "I fear you are destined for disappointment, Bell. But you said yourself, it has been some time since Will had a pretty face about the place."

"No fair Paphians here either," said George, shrugging.

Bellerton snorted, moving to refill his glass. "Perhaps I'll not stay, if Old Willoughby and his fussock of a wife are to cast a damper on us all. There's a game wench in Swineshead, at the Pig and Whistle. Wouldn't go amiss to get some sport about now."

"Your adventures on the hunt not excitement enough for you?" inquired Francis blandly.

But Bellerton merely replied, "Three days trapped in a panny room with only a waggle-tongued old matron to wait on one is enough to give even a saint the taste for something young and obliging. Why don't you pension off those two cacklers and get a pretty young thing to keep up the lodge?"

"You'd only precipitate your unwelcome presence upon me more often," said Francis.

"I'll wager it'd be worthwhile for you, however."

Francis shrugged. "Pretty young country girls are not apt to take employment in a gentleman's hunting lodge. Something to do with protecting their virtue, I believe, and the denizens of Tilton would likely agree. I'd prefer not to deal with high drama at my hunting lodge, at least."

"That's easily mended. Just bring a girl from London," said Bellerton.

Here, George cut in with an air of authority, "Don't signify. Mantell won't allow a young girl to cross the threshold of his lodge."

Bellerton regarded Francis with sneering pity. "Never took you for a Puritan, Mantell."

"Oh, no," said George, with all the air of one with authority. "Mantell ain't the Puritan. That's Wraglain."

Bellerton's wondering gaze swung to Charles, who sighed heavily. "Look what you've done, Mantell. I'll never live it down, not if I take on a hundred mistresses."

"If it drives you to such an exigency," said Francis, sipping at his sherry, "I'll count it a rare triumph."

Charles would then have been obliged to sit through a spirited bout of ribbing and conjecture, but having been enough in company with Bellerton and George to recognize that only the complete exhaustion of the topic would suffice, he upended the subject by remarking, "Old Willoughby must have something dire to communicate, or he would not have come all this way—if he did, indeed, come at all."

"Ain't a thing one undertakes lightly," said George importantly. "Got seasick on the crossing from the West Indies myself. Cast up my accounts for days. Won't do that again anytime soon."

Bell snorted. "Cast up your accounts, or cross the ocean?"

"Either," replied George seriously.

Francis waved his glass to regain their attention. "Perhaps he sent only his mistress—or intended wife—or newly acquired wife—expressly to annoy Will."

Bellerton huffed. "He sent off his first wife quick enough."

"Ought not to have sent her to Will," remarked George.

"This is all just conjecture, my good fellow," said Charles, smiling kindly at George.

"Precisely," said Francis, setting down his glass. "It is just as likely that Old Willoughby himself has returned to Penhurst—along with this Miss Eliza—because his plantation failed and he has no other recourse."

George shook his head. "Will won't like that."

"Dashed bad luck if it is so," agreed Bellerton, tossing down his drink. "Only bright spot is that Old Willoughby will have to take over the estate management, which'll please Will no end. Hates the Fens with a blue passion."

"Won't get him more blunt, however," said George gloomily.

"Not unless Old Willoughby has miraculously discovered in Jamaica how to drain a fen," put in Charles helpfully.

"No fens in Jamaica," said George, but he somewhat more

cheerfully added, "Plenty of swamps, however. Might have learnt a thing or two about them that'd be useful."

"That must be it, then," said Charles, sitting back with his hands behind his head. "Old Willoughby has come back to Penhurst to save his estate from ruin by applying some obscure West Indian wisdom for draining wetlands."

George nodded, looking pleased at this conclusion, but Bellerton snorted and said, "Still don't have a clue who Miss Eliza is."

"We've plenty of clues," said Francis dryly. "What is more to the purpose, is she the sort of female who will add to our stay at Penhurst, or detract from it?"

Their conjectures were cut off by the opening of the door. They all turned to see a young woman enter the room, of about twenty years of age and a stranger to them all. Her fashionable dress of jaconet muslin proclaimed her a lady, though her bearing was almost as jaunty as Clayton's, being a trifle less dignified than Miss Muncey's. Francis concluded she was another West Indian servant, for her coloring was nearly as brown as Miss Muncey's and her hair, though lighter, was still tightly curling. She was taller and slighter, but very pretty, with an oval face, full lips, and a straight nose. But her most arresting feature was her eyes, which were a deep, sparkling blue. He thought with some satisfaction that here was a female who would add admirably to their stay at the Lodge.

Glancing about a bit uncertainly, she said in perfectly unaccented English, "I beg your pardon, but which of you is Nathan Willoughby?"

"I fear none of us is Willoughby," offered Francis with his most charming smile. "He is in the library with Mr. Findlay."

She seemed somewhat daunted, but said, "To be sure. They have much to discuss." After a slight check, she came across the room toward them, smiling brightly with her hands clasped in front of her. "No doubt you will think me quite impudent for doing so in your friend's house, but I took the liberty of coming in Mrs. Slade's place to tell you that your rooms are ready. She does apologize for having kept you waiting so long, but she has been at sixes and sevens this afternoon in getting us all properly settled. She did not, as you may have guessed, know we were to come, though we did make every attempt to apprise the household of it."

They all gazed at her in varying degrees of admiration, curiosity, and interest, but none evinced an iota of comprehension as to her identity.

"Oh, dear," she said, wringing her hands as her cheeks suffused with color. She hurried on in laughing confusion. "I have muddled it already, and I had so counted on making a good first impression. It was my understanding that Nathan would be here in the saloon but, as you have indicated, he is not. Nor would his being here be at all to the purpose, for I have yet to be introduced to *him*, so he could not effect the introductions anyway. But there is nothing for it now, I suppose. I hope you will forgive the informality in making my own introduction, as you will, no doubt, agree the situation demands it. I am Eliza Willoughby, Nathan's half-sister."

Chapter 7

THERE WAS A stunned silence as the gentlemen gazed at the lady, of whose existence their host—to any of their knowledge—had not even been aware. Francis found himself unable to utter a syllable, and it was Charles who at last stepped forward, taking her outstretched hand.

"Charles Wraglain, at your service, Miss Willoughby. Forgive us our stupidity, but we had no notion Will had a sister."

She blinked, her gaze flicking to each of the gentlemen in turn. "I see. Yes, I ought to have guessed—our father never mentioned—that is, their relationship was never cordial, to say the least. And I have never had the honor of corresponding with Nathan."

"To be sure," said Francis, finding his tongue at last. He came forward to offer his welcome.

The others followed suit, until she had shaken all their hands, expressing her pleasure at the acquaintance.

"Pleasure's ours," said George, bowing.

"I greatly doubt that," she said, eyes dancing. "It cannot be very pleasant to arrive at your bachelor friend's home only to find it overrun with strange females."

Bellerton's wide mouth drew into a smile. "On the contrary, ma'am, it's a circumstance one could not but find exceedingly pleasant."

She blinked, as though uncertain what to make of this statement, and Charles called Bellerton to order.

"If you don't take care," he said, elbowing Bell sharply in the ribs, "she'll take a wrong notion of your morals and manners."

But Miss Willoughby put out her hand. "Do not scold him on my account. I do believe I brought that upon myself! It seems there is much for me to learn. I am not used to male company, you understand, my father not being one to invite his friends to the house. But I must learn how to get on, for that is why my father sent me to England, after all."

Francis was rather struck by this unique response. She had neither coquettishly welcomed Bellerton's remark nor been shocked into the vapors by it. Perhaps her father had trained the missishness out of her.

Charles, leading her to the sofa, inquired, "Then that is your luggage in the hall?"

"Oh, not anymore," she said, her eyes sparkling impishly. "That is, it is no longer in the hall. But yes, it is all mine—are you horrified? There is ever so much of it, and I shudder to own that almost the half of it was bought only recently in London. Will it comfort you to know that it is everything I have in the world?"

"Then you anticipate a long stay, Miss Willoughby?" asked Francis with real interest, seating himself across from her on a settee.

"I do," she said, a shadow passing over her features. "It is to be permanent—at least, I hope so, if Nathan will agree to allow me to stay."

The gentlemen's looks askance bespoke their skepticism of this issue, but Miss Willoughby, if she noticed it at all, did not seem deterred in her cheerfulness. Upon learning that George had passed some years in Jamaica, she engaged him in a lively discussion of the beauties of the island, its pleasures, and drawbacks.

"I am not fond of the sand flies," she remarked, after agreeing with George that the beauty of the white-sand beaches was unrivaled.

"To be sure," said George, nodding soberly. "Once knocked into a rotted palm, and disturbed a nest of them. Looked as though I had measles for a week. But fairly easy to avoid. What I'd sooner forget is the spiders. Great, hairy beasts!"

"I find the Orb-Weaver spiders quite lovely, myself," remarked Miss Willoughby. "Though they can be rather disturbingly large, and they find the most awkward places to build their webs. I've walked right into a web that had been built across a path overnight, and more than once. It's quite a shock!"

Francis's brows had gone up at the mention of spiders in polite conversation. This Miss Willoughby was indeed a curious female.

"Orb-weavers ain't poisonous, I believe," mused George. "Still give me the shivers, though."

"But they are simply Anansi, you know," she said, with a teasing note. "How can one be afraid of a mere trickster—and a wise one at that?"

George looked dubious. "Never did comprehend the fascination with Anansi. Devilish—that is, must be mad to think a man-sized spider harmless!"

"It is only a folk-tale," soothed Miss Willoughby. "Made up nonsense to entertain children."

But George was unconvinced. "Didn't work for me, I'm afraid, ma'am. Nothing entertaining about a Black Spider!"

Miss Willoughby agreed, her eyes widening. "They are fearsome-looking, to be sure, with their swollen bellies and red spots. You other gentlemen will be interested to learn that the female of the species has been known to eat her mate! Horrid, to be sure, but only what one might expect of such evil little creatures. One of our grooms was bitten by a Black Spider that had hidden in his boot, and he straightway began to convulse! But the cook quickly applied a poultice of ground nuts, which seemed to stop the poison, and he was soon recovered. He could never again bring himself to put on his boots, however."

"Stuff of nightmares," said George, looking green. "Ought to change the subject—talk of pleasant things."

"Forgive me, sir," she said, her eyes twinkling. "In my excitement to speak of my home, I again forgot my company. But I should like quite as much to speak of the turquoise waters of Montego Bay, or of sugarcane candy."

Visibly relieved, George entered into these subjects with energy. As they continued to reminisce together, Francis languidly watched, both amused and intrigued. George was generally a dull stick, and one was prone to forget that he had traveled to foreign climes, or even that he was capable of conversing agreeably about them. But Miss Willoughby's delight in recalling the wonders of her home almost made Francis wish to see them himself. Instead, he got up and went to the back of the room to refill his glass at the sideboard.

"She'll be a curiosity in the drawing rooms, to be sure," murmured Bellerton, coming up to him.

"A nine days' wonder, perhaps," answered Francis.

Bellerton chuckled. "If my mother ever heard talk of spiders and flies in her drawing room, she'd be more than nine days recovering."

Francis shrugged, continuing his low tone. "When one reflects, one finds her conversation is no different than the usual chit of her age. The subject matter is strange, certainly, but she converses ably enough."

Charles joined them, having heard this last. "With enough wit to delight but not to annoy, and enough variety to please," he said, helping himself to the claret. "Never imagined a sister of Will could be so amiable. Indeed, from what he says of his father, one could easily have expected his female offspring to be a cold and calculating mercenary. I must say, I'm relieved to find her the opposite. I would most definitely have curtailed my stay in this damp locality otherwise. Now, I rather wish I could stay longer to hear more of the fascinating and frightening fauna of Jamaica."

"She certainly seems to be in her element," said Francis, watching Miss Willoughby through hooded eyes. "For one who professes inexperience in male company, she does not seem uncomfortable at all."

"Her father sent her to England to find a husband," Charles pointed out. "Just like any other young lady on her come out, she would have been amply prepared."

"It seems apparent her preparation has been quite dissimilar to most."

Bellerton flicked a sly glance at them. "And what do you think the chances of her success?"

Francis considered, murmuring, "Her obvious African parentage might stand in her disfavor with some, but it's not as though she is alone in that."

"And she may have a healthy fortune." Bellerton continued to observe Miss Willoughby with interest. "If Will isn't bamming us, that Jamaican property is worth a pretty bit."

"One must hope that Old Willoughby loves his little chick more than he loved his son," replied Francis dryly. "He has yet to give any indication to Will that he is a doting, or even responsible, father."

Bellerton grimaced, reaching to refill his glass with brandy. "There is that. The old shaver probably fobbed her off on Will to avoid spending his own blunt. Just what he would do."

"Surely he would not," murmured Charles, his native cheer somewhat disturbed. "Shabby thing to do."

"Even for a man who effectively abandoned his family to live halfway across the world?" was Francis's quiet parting shot before returning to his chair nearer Miss Willoughby and George.

He sipped at his wine, pondering the young lady's situation. If her father had sent her away permanently, Francis guessed that it was due to some hardship, and that could not bode well. The state of Willoughby's finances was terrible, and his status in society precarious. If Miss Willoughby had no fortune of her own, she would do better to resign herself to spinsterhood, and to keeping house for her brother the rest of her life—if Willoughby would allow it. Francis would not be surprised if, in Will's circumstances, he cut her off or consigned her to the poorhouse. It would be a shame, really, for she was quite taking. Not in Francis's style, of course, she being an innocent young lady bent on marriage, but other men would doubtless find her attractive.

As her dialog with George had progressed into more general topics, Francis interposed, inquiring whether she had been long in London. "For you mentioned that you had purchased many of your belongings in Town."

"Yes," she said, turning her startlingly blue eyes upon him. "As Mr. Findlay was unable to reach my brother to apprise him of our arrival, we were obliged—that is, we took the opportunity of staying some weeks in London, to replenish my wardrobe. Jamaica is much warmer than England, you must know."

"And this is not something you were able to prepare before your journey?" he inquired. "Surely there are modistes of decent skill in Jamaica."

Miss Willoughby looked down. "No. That is, there are modistes. But there simply was not enough—enough time."

Francis was sure from her hesitance she was hiding something, and interpreted it to mean that her father had not allowed her enough time, perhaps because he did not wish to pay for a new wardrobe himself.

"Nor do they stock the proper fabrics for winter wear," she went on, raising her eyes to meet his again, clear and calm.

Admirable recovery for one practicing subterfuge, thought Francis. He merely smiled and said, "To be sure. Did you find the London modistes to your liking?"

She assured him she had, adding, "As I did London itself. So excessively dissimilar to anything we have in Jamaica—Kingston itself is a mere village by comparison! I do not know that I expected differently, but it was certainly a new experience going about with Mrs. Riddle, my companion."

Charles, returning to sit beside them, said, "I imagine there is much to which you must accustom yourself. I trust you do not find it altogether distressing."

"England is very different, but I do not find it distressing in the least," she said, turning her smile upon him. "I have lived all my life in one place, Mr. Wraglain, so this is all a grand adventure to me."

Francis set down his glass. "And what by way of adventure could you have enjoyed in London, pray? Unless you deem driving down Picadilly in the middle of the day an adventure. Perhaps riding in a hackney? Though I should hesitate to call it an adventure, precisely, it is always a memorable experience."

"You are quizzing me, Mr. Mantell," she said, a dimple appearing in her cheek as she attempted a severe look. "Certainly, a gentleman such as yourself would not deem those everyday occurrences adventures. But almost everything in London was new and exciting to me. I have never seen so many people together before, and of such variety! And with such strange habits. Do you know, I saw a man on a two-wheeled vehicle in the park. He moved it by pushing at the ground with his feet, almost like running! I have never seen anything like it in Jamaica."

"A hobby horse," said Charles. "It is new here as well, introduced only this summer. It was invented in Germany, I believe."

Miss Willoughby laughed. "Then I was not imagining all the odd looks the poor gentleman got, from more persons than me! He did look quite silly, running along while sitting on that strange contraption that seemed intent upon getting away from under him."

"Tried one myself," put in George. "Devil of a—that is, very hard to handle. Ran into a shrubbery more than once. Never did manage to work the thing out."

"Nor did this gentleman," said Miss Willoughby consolingly.

"Indeed, he was not so lucky as you—he ended by careering into the Serpentine."

"That sort of foolishness, unfortunately, is too often seen in Town," said Francis. "I fear you shall find Lincolnshire a dead bore by comparison."

She laughed, a rich, melodic sound that fell delightfully on the ear. "Oh, I do not anticipate boredom here, sir. How can I, when I am assured the dike is always threatening to burst and to flood us out of hearth and home?"

"Did your father apprise you of the circumstance?" inquired Francis. "It seems an odd thing for him to have done."

"It certainly would be," she replied, seeming amused at the suggestion. "However, I never heard a word of it from my father. Indeed, he scarcely spoke of Penhurst Lodge to me at all. But Mr. Findlay let fall on the drive that he is always being applied to for funds to repair the dike. I do not think even he would have burdened a mere female with such cares, except that he wished to stop so that he might inspect the dike's condition on the way hither."

Charles said, "You found it intact, I suppose."

"More or less—but I am no expert," she answered with a mischievous smile. "Mr. Findlay merely looked grave and returned to the coach. I assumed him to be satisfied, however, for he did not order the coach to turn around, or hire a boat in Swineshead. Indeed, he said nothing more of the business."

"Better not burst while I'm here," said George nervously. "Can't swim!"

Miss Willoughby regarded him with surprise. "Truly? How extraordinary—I thought everyone in the world knew how to swim. I certainly do."

Charles grinned. "Then Hayes may count upon you to fish him out of the fen when it floods."

"Oh, I'd be more likely to capsize the rescue boat, sir," she replied, "Assuming there is to be one. But it would be far more to the purpose to teach Mr. Hayes to swim."

This instantly brought visions of the young lady's form draped in clinging, wet linen to Francis's mind. It seemed a universal occurrence, as all the gentlemen gazed at her in various stages of wonder.

She blushed. "Oh dear, I have muffed it again. I ought not to have made so outrageous a remark, oughtn't I? Well, if our situation was not so dire, I declare I shouldn't even have thought of it. But when every moment one may expect to be drowned, it is my belief that one would wish to be prepared."

Bellerton, who had remained at his station near the decanters, choked, but Charles nodded with smiling gravity. "It was excessively decent of you to offer."

"George seems quite to be looking forward to it," said Francis, directing their gazes to George's bemused countenance. As he became aware of their observation, however, a tide of red crept up his neck and into his face.

"Oh, dear me," said Miss Willoughby again, flicking a helplessly comical look to Francis and Charles. After a moment of mortified silence on George's part, she rose abruptly. "Well, that is enough of that, I believe. I really must be going. It is nearly time to dress for dinner, and I have yet to meet my brother, which must no longer be delayed, I believe, Findlay or no Findlay. You will find your rooms ready for you, and Clayton or Mrs. Slade will be pleased to show you to them. Forgive me for keeping you all so long with my chatter. Goodbye!"

They all stood, bowing as she went out of the room, and when she had gone, Bellerton came forward to lean upon the sofa back.

"Engaging filly, ain't she? And not half bad-looking. Wonder if Will would mind me having a go at her."

"It depends, I fancy," said Charles stiffly, "on what you mean by 'having a go.'"

Francis gazed blandly at Bellerton. "Best discover Will's sentiments for his long-lost sister before talking in so unguarded a manner, don't you think, my boy? He has a wicked right."

Bellerton, whose glass had never gone empty since their arrival in the drawing room, merely chortled, "Chit don't need Will's leave to teach me to swim! Damme if I don't take her up on it."

"Offered to teach *me* to swim, not you," grumbled George.

"Don't be a gudgeon," replied Bellerton with a sneer. "Ain't a need to split hairs—seems to me she'd be willing to teach any and all of us."

Charles regarded him disdainfully. "Seems to me you're too disguised to make judgments on a lady's character."

"If she is a lady," retorted Bellerton, slewing around to face Charles. "Didn't you see her? Got to be nineteen or twenty if she's a day."

George grunted. "Don't make any odds how old she is, Bell. You're drunk as a wheelbarrow."

The bellicose gentleman turned again to him, leering. "And you're a looby. Mrs. Willoughby died fifteen years ago—not so drunk I couldn't work that out in the last half hour. Miss Eliza's a by-blow, or I'm Cock Robinson."

There was a general silence in the room as the men digested this. Francis ought to have suspected it, having known Willoughby since Oxford days, but he had not thought, having been entirely focused on Miss Willoughby's unusual demeanor. Illegitimacy certainly presented a grave problem for her success in English society, far more than her African ancestry. Unless her father had endowed her with a fortune large enough to blind her suitors to this egregious fault, Francis doubted her journey from Jamaica had been worthwhile.

Chapter 8

NATHAN WILLOUGHBY ATTEMPTED to read again the wording of the will, but his hands were shaking too hard, causing the words to skitter on the page. Slamming the paper down on his desk, he exclaimed, "You mean to tell me there is nothing left? That he gave away the whole?"

"Indeed, sir," said Mr. Findlay, in his infuriatingly calm manner. Begging Willoughby's pardon, he took up the will and began to peruse it, summarizing aloud various points. "Eleven years ago, your father freed his slaves, and upon his death bequeathed to each of them a parcel of land belonging to the plantation. The house and all his belongings were either claimed by right or sold at auction, and the monies therefrom placed in trust for your sister Eliza."

"My half-sister," Willoughby ground out, sweeping angrily from behind the desk and pacing about the room. "The daughter of his mistress is to benefit entirely from what ought, by rights, to be my inheritance! What of me? What of his legitimate son and heir? Did he have no thought to the condition in which this would leave me?"

"I believe your father expected Penhurst Lodge was more than adequate recompense, sir." Mr. Findlay placed the will on a stack of papers and straightened them meticulously. After a brief hesitation, he added, "Your father wrote to me of Miss Willoughby's mother after her death, and it was plain, even to the meanest intelligence, that he admired and loved her."

Willoughby whirled on him. "She certainly wormed her way into his affections! I've no doubt she was beautiful, and definitely clever, for she managed not only to become his mistress, but to convince him to marry her after my mother's death and to acknowledge her child as his heir. It beggars belief!"

"Miss Willoughby is your father's child, sir," said Mr. Findlay with absolute calm, "though she was born five years before he married her mother. I have a copy of the birth record listing his name as father. Even were it not so, the Jamaican property, with all its assets and income, was completely unattached to the Penhurst estate, and therefore his to dispose of as he saw fit."

"Oh, and he did so, without thought for the needs of his legitimate heir!" Raking a hand through his already disordered locks, he spat, "But I ought to have known it would be so. Any man who could abandon his wife and son so callously, to settle so far away as to never see or communicate with them again, could not be depended upon to treat them with even a modicum of honor at his death."

"If I may remind you, sir, your parents' separation was at the agreement of both parties, and the deed stated that Penhurst Lodge, Willoughby House, and all income derived therefrom were to be at your mother's and, when you came of age, your disposal. As this has been the case," he lifted an appraising gaze to Willoughby's, "there is no legal justification for your expectation regarding the Jamaican property."

Willoughby only growled in rage, making a backhanded swipe at the nearest object, which happened to be a vase of some antiquity that had resided upon a pedestal in the corner of the library for as long as he could remember. The vase smashed into the wall, shattering into a million pieces which showered onto the rug, twinkling in the light of the fire. Even they seemed to mock his bad luck.

Cursing under his breath, he strode to the chair behind the desk and dropped into it, putting his head into his hand, his fingers covering his eyes. After several tense moments, he commanded himself so far as to inquire in a more measured tone, "What's to be done, then?"

"I beg your pardon?" said Mr. Findlay.

Willoughby rubbed his forehead, his eyes shut tight against a reality he did not wish to acknowledge. "You know the state of my finances. I needed that money—I've been depending on it to bring me about. Dash it, I'm ruined! What's to be done?"

Mr. Findlay cleared his throat, taking up the sheaf of papers on the desk and tapping them into precise order. "If you will permit me, sir, I have frequently advised that there is only one thing to be done. You will pardon my observing that your style of living is, and has been for many years, unsuited to your circumstances. You must retrench."

"Deuce take it, man," Willoughby threw out his hand and gazed up at the solicitor with burning spite. "Is that all you can say? I'm a gentleman, and I've a right to dashed well live like one."

Pursing his lips, the solicitor nodded curtly. "Then there is nothing more to be said."

Willoughby groaned, leaning his elbows on the desk to grip his hair with both hands. "Recollect what I've had to bear these three years! Everything would have been right and tight if that cursed dike hadn't burst and flooded the whole property. And then the windmill was torn down—"

"I beg your pardon, sir, but as your man of business, I advised you to look to the future long before those misfortunes." Mr. Findlay turned to place the papers into his valise. "You live in the Fens, and would have been wiser to prepare for such eventualities as commonly arise in this country than to provide only for your own amusement."

Willoughby ground his teeth, composing in his mind a fitting curse for his prude of a solicitor, but at that moment, the door opened and a woman entered.

Eliza had been waiting outside the door, having heard raised voices when she had at first approached the library. The voices within had quieted, but she was still anxious lest her brother be angry at her for the situation in which he now found himself. He certainly had every right to feel himself injured and ill-used, but she had held out the hope that he would reserve his anger for their father, and not direct it at herself. She really had had nothing to do with the matter, except to be born.

At last deciding to risk entry, she had gone in, but now paused, glancing somewhat uncertainly between the two men. Mr. Findlay looked pained, as he often had during their journey hither, especially when speaking of her brother. And Nathan—Eliza paused to take in his harsh features, easily tracing in them a resemblance to their father. He had the Willoughby chin and aquiline nose, but his eyes were a more steely blue than those Eliza had inherited.

"Who the devil are you?" he barked, jerking her from her reverie.

Darting a glance at Mr. Findlay, she answered, "I am Eliza, your sister."

The shock that overcame his features she had expected, having witnessed it on the faces of all his friends just now in the drawing room. Indeed, she had been somewhat prepared for it in London, where people had stared both openly and askance at her West Indian coloring. But until she had arrived at Penhurst, and seen the astonishment of the servants who had welcomed them, it had never before occurred to her that her African heritage would be unknown even to her brother. How could she have guessed that her father would neglect to mention to any of his English correspondents that his second wife was a freed slave? But she ought to have anticipated some lapse of this kind, for he had treated his family in England as though they did not exist, and could not be expected to communicate with them with any degree of attention.

It had taken his grave illness to bring out her father's confession of his wrongs toward her brother and his mother, and only at the reading of the will had Eliza come to grasp the enormity of her situation. She must go to live with a young man who had been abandoned and forgotten by his father, replaced in his affections by an illegitimate child.

She would rather have remained in Jamaica, for it was all she had ever known and she did love it. But the sentiment toward persons of mixed blood just then was volatile, and being an heiress as well had only made her more of a threat to the hierarchy. In England, her father had insisted, she stood a far better chance at finding security and comfort. Indeed, he had reared her as a proper English lady, with a proper English governess as her preceptress, in order that she would fit perfectly into genteel society.

Unfortunately, this had further alienated her from her Jamaican roots, and she found that once her father had died, she had nothing left to anchor her to the island but her love for it. But this love could not protect her from social injustice, and she was forced to concede the wisdom of her father's last wishes, leaving Jamaica forever to make England her home. Now she could only trust to Nathan's honor and sense of familial duty, and hope that through her persistent and unaffected attentions and care, he could come to accept her, and possibly even to love her as a sister.

She therefore tried to demonstrate her understanding by saying, "I can appreciate your surprise. I did not even know I had a brother until my mother died."

"The devil you did—" Willoughby shook his head, gazing in disbelief at Mr. Findlay. "Good lord, man! Why didn't you tell me?"

"It did not seem relevant, sir," was the clipped reply.

Willoughby seemed to wrestle within himself, his eyes shut tight and his jaw working. At last he looked again at Eliza. "I understand that I am to have the charge of you from now on—you are to be my ward."

"Yes, but only until I am married."

A bitter laugh burst from him, and he regarded her with mockery. "It may as well be for the remainder of your life. Do you have any idea the impossibility—to marry off the illegitimate daughter, no doubt of a slave—"

"My mother was a freed slave, Nathan." She spoke with surety, forestalling the undoubtedly acid words on his tongue. "There is a difference, you know. In Jamaica there is a decided difference. A freed slave may petition to have as many rights as a white person, as my mother did."

"But you are not in Jamaica anymore, my dear Eliza," he said in a tone of disdain. "Daughter of a freed slave or not, in England your antecedents are a decided deterrent, though I could have hoped to get you off my hands even then. But add to that your illegitimacy—how could my father even imagine to get you respectably settled? To saddle me with so hopeless a case, and without allowing me the funds—"

Mr. Findlay cleared his throat. "If I may, sir, Miss Willoughby's fortune is exceedingly large. It will, I believe, ameliorate the fact of her illegitimacy. It often does in such cases as this, you know."

"And it will relieve you of the obligation to put out even a penny of your own money for my expenses," put in Eliza.

Willoughby's lip curled. "Oh, you can be certain of that, my dear sister. As your guardian, I shall be certain to pay all your expenses from your own account."

"Which may be drawn upon only with proper verification of receipts," Mr. Findlay said quickly. "And a yearly accounting to the Court of Chancery is expected."

Willoughby snorted, turning a contemptuous gaze upon him. "Don't mince your meaning, sir. I comprehend you completely."

Believing his fierce disappointment to be the primary cause of his rancor, Eliza said, "I am sorry that my coming to you is a burden, Nathan. If there was anywhere else I could go, I promise you, I should go there in an instant. The last thing I wish is to be a charge on you."

"How very thoughtful," he said, his eyes narrowed. Dropping his gaze to the desk, he ran a hand along its polished surface before raising his eyes again to her face. "I suppose I must take you in. You bear the Willoughby name, and odds are there will be the devil to pay if I do not. But I warn you, I shall not alter my style of living just to accommodate you. Oh, you shall have whatever you desire, to be sure, thanks to our father's generous consideration of his little darling, but you shall not interfere with me in any way. You shall not keep house for me, or attempt to order my days, or take exception to the company I keep—"

Mr. Findlay again cleared his throat. "As I am joined with you in guardianship of Miss Willoughby, sir, I may take exception to the company you keep. If there is any possibility of danger to your sister's person, or more specifically to her virtue, I warn you, I will unquestionably take exception."

"As her virtue is perhaps the only thing next to her name and fortune that makes her even passably respectable," scoffed Nathan, "you may be assured I shall guard it assiduously, sir. How else might I hope to dispose of her in marriage?"

Eliza looked quickly down, containing her hurt at this affront. She could only believe his prejudice must stem simply from shock at so many unexpected revelations, and would resolve in time.

Mr. Findlay's sentiments were expressed in a heavy silence before he said gravely, "It will be my business to correspond regularly with her, and to make unscheduled visits to ascertain her happiness and well-being."

"Certainly," said Willoughby, eying the solicitor with dislike. "She will be well looked after, make no mistake. I only wish to make plain that I do not intend to put myself out for her whims. However she wishes to fritter away her fortune, she may do it, but she does not dictate to me how I shall go on."

"To be sure," said Eliza quickly, giving a significant look to Mr. Findlay. "I would not be happy otherwise."

Willoughby huffed, tapping his fingers on his desk in finality. He glanced at the clock. "It is past time to dress for dinner. I believe I have neglected my guests long enough."

"Oh, they have not been neglected, Nathan," said Eliza. "Clayton saw to their comfort, and I visited with them for nearly a half-hour.

They seemed well-contented, and must since have gone up to the rooms Mrs. Slade has prepared."

He opened his mouth to dispute her handling of the situation, but intercepting a stern look from Mr. Findlay, he merely smirked his gratitude and quitted the room.

Mr. Findlay turned to Eliza. "Now that you have met your brother, Miss Willoughby, is it still your wish to reside at Penhurst Lodge?"

She sighed. "I really do not have anywhere else to go, do I?"

"What of Miss Tibble?"

Eliza shook her head. "She could not house both me and Muncey long-term. She is more than willing to try—" She paused, her lips quirking in a weary smile. "But I believe Muncey would strangle her within a fortnight."

Mr. Findlay looked down, perhaps to conceal his own smile. After a moment, he raised his eyes and said composedly, "We could set you up in a house of your own with a companion, as we discussed in London."

"But whom could you find who would be willing? Mrs. Riddle was rather uneasy in my company, I am persuaded, and without a respectable and well-connected companion, I would effectively be shut off from Society." She smiled faintly. "If my prospects are as bleak as Nathan believes, that would do for me entirely."

Mr. Findlay looked down at his valise, checking the straps for some imagined weakness. "You are a wealthy woman, Miss Willoughby. You need not marry at all. You could live comfortably for the rest of your life, without the need to move in higher circles, or even to see your brother."

"But I should like to marry," she said. "I should like to have children, not just a home of my own. Pray, do not attempt to dissuade me. I must try to do as my father wished, and give my brother the chance to behave honorably. He has given his permission for me to stay."

He sighed, picking up the valise and turning to her. "Perhaps I ought to remain a day or two, just to see you are properly settled."

"Oh, I do not believe it to be necessary, sir, I thank you."

He regarded her through his spectacles, his eyes lingering on her hands, which were clasped before her, the fingers clasped tight in obvious anxiety. "If you will permit me, ma'am, I believe it would be best if I did stay on. As you have witnessed, Mr. Willoughby is a selfish, bitter young man, prone to fits of despondency and anger."

"But he promised to take care of me."

"There are many constructions one who knows him may put on his words, ma'am, few about which I am sanguine."

Eliza looked down, dropping her hands to her sides. "Very well. I own I should be glad to have someone to take my part, and to show me how to go on. But I will not trespass on your kindness for more than a few days."

Mr. Findlay nodded. "The housekeeper has already seen to a room for me. If you will inform her that my stay will be a trifle longer than anticipated, I should appreciate it."

"But sir, I am not to keep house for Nathan—"

"I am not Mr. Willoughby's guest, but yours, Miss Willoughby." He set his hat atop his head and moved to the door. "Whatever he may claim, he cannot deny you the right to properly look after your guests. Should he do so, I believe I shall have something to say to the matter."

He went out and Eliza, bowing under the weight of the entire interview, sank into a chair. It had not gone as she had hoped, certainly, but she strove to convince herself that it had not been so bad. Nathan had agreed to allow her to stay—even to care for her. How that would play out, as Mr. Findlay had warned, remained to be seen. But however Mr. Findlay may mistrust him, Eliza could not allow herself to form an opinion as to her brother's character after only one day. She had promised their father she would give Nathan every opportunity to behave as a brother ought, and she would not give up so easily.

Nathan had surely been at his worst today—who would not be, after the blow he had sustained? Eliza had some idea of Nathan's pecuniary embarrassments, and she could well imagine that her brother had anticipated some relief at their father's death. The intensity of his anger had been equal to that of his disappointment. She could easily forgive his contempt and bitterness toward herself, and only wished that she could give some of her fortune to him. But she knew from the solicitor's information that her trust was tied up so completely for her maintenance and marriage that her brother could have none of it.

Eliza could only engage herself to give Nathan no more trouble than he already had, and to arrange her daily interactions so as to be as pleasant to him as possible. She would use everything within her power—which she was vexed to admit was, indeed, very little—to make him glad she had come into his life, and strive never to give him cause to repent this day's work.

Chapter 9

Eliza WENT UP to her room, finding Muncey there busily unpacking her trunks. The maid glanced up in her usual stoic manner.

"You took so long, I tought you went back to Jamaica," she said as she closed the door to the clothes press.

Eliza chuckled, presenting her back to be unbuttoned. "I should never do so without you, my dear. But you know our returning to Jamaica is impossible, no matter how much we could wish it. I was only detained by my brother's many questions regarding the will."

"Him nuh happy."

"No." Eliza sighed. "He has agreed that I may stay, however. So we must make the best of our new home."

Muncey huffed. "You may make de best of it, Miss Eliza—I will make my own judgment."

"It's less worrisome to have optimism in a new situation," retorted Eliza, shrugging out of her morning dress. "You really ought to try it sometime."

"Maybe I will, when we are not stuck in a cold, grey place wit no life."

Eliza chuckled, laying her muslin over a chair back, but there was something forlorn in her movements that her maid did not miss.

Muncey eyed her askance. "Maybe you should not go to dinner. I will bring you a tray, and tell dem you don't feel well."

"It is tempting," said Eliza, gazing longingly at her bed, "but it will not answer. I must face the monster some time—it may as well be today."

The maid grimaced, turning to retrieve the sapphire blue silk gown she had laid out on the bed. Eliza held her arms up for the maid to slip the evening gown over her shoulders.

"I met my brother's guests," she said, wriggling a bit until the gown settled smoothly over her shift and stays. "I fear they are not quite what Miss Tibble would consider the thing, for all her surmises on high-born gentlemen."

Muncey snorted, doing up her buttons. "Dey have very poor manners for gentlemen. Dey all stared at me like overgrown school-boys. And dey dress as carelessly."

"They were surprised, Muncey," said Eliza, a hint of reproach in her tone. "And they were in all their dirt after traveling—of course they looked somewhat disheveled! They surely expected a restful welcome, not a troupe of strangers overrunning the house."

She was bodily turned around so that the maid could glare her disapprobation of this reasonable explanation as she adjusted the neckline of her gown, tucking in lace for a modicum of modesty. The dress was the height of London fashion—if the very expensive modiste to whom Mrs. Riddle had taken them could be believed. When Eliza had first worn it, she had gasped at the low neckline and blushed to wear it in public, insisting her governess would never have allowed such an exhibition. But Mrs. Riddle had assured her it was quite proper here in England, and that she should be considered a dowd if she wore anything less revealing. They had compromised on the lace.

Muncey had just finished pinning Eliza's hair up in a style Mrs. Riddle's woman had taught her when a knock sounded on the door. Muncey, grumbling, went to open it and there stood Clayton, smiling in his very un-butlerish way.

"I bethought me that you ladies might wish for an escort to the saloon," he said, hands on his coat lapels as he bobbed on his feet. "Seeing as 'ow neither of you knows the way about."

"Miss Eliza has been to de saloon, Mr. Clayton," said Muncey coolly. "You took her dere yourself dis afternoon."

But before Muncey could send him about his business, Eliza jumped up from the dressing table. "You have not been to the servants' hall yet, however, Muncey. It would be so very kind of Clayton to show you the way."

Clayton bowed in his jaunty style. "It would be an honor, Miss Muncey."

Muncey grimaced as was her way, and Clayton, unabashed, turned to Eliza. "And may I say you look a treat, Miss Willoughby?"

"Why, thank you, Clayton," said Eliza, her dimples peeping. "It is all due to Muncey's artistry, you know."

"Did never doubt it for an instant," said the unlikely butler, grinning engagingly. "With a lady of your beauty, ma'am, it must be a delight to 'ave the dressing of you, eh, Miss Muncey?"

At her most disapproving, Muncey bent her head in dignified assent.

"Well, I believe we are ready, Clayton," said Eliza, fastening her pearls around her neck. "Shall we go down?"

Francis and all the other men were gathered in the saloon when Eliza entered, and there was a stir as they each either stood or turned to regard her. More than one gave a gasp of admiration and, to Francis's disgust, Bellerton gave a low whistle. The man was as sophisticated as an alley cat; however, one could not fault the general reaction—Miss Willoughby was certainly striking. In her evening toilette, her hair caught up in a tumble of twists and curls interspersed with white rosettes, and the deep blue of the gown enhancing the unexpected color of her eyes, she would have excited admiration anywhere. The gown's low neckline, though tempered with a bit of lace and the modest rope of pearls about her throat, was also a source of appreciation. Francis thought again that, but for her birth, and if Miss Willoughby proved the heiress she ought to be, he might be tempted.

He was not to discover the precise nature of Miss Willoughby's situation anytime soon, however, or so it had seemed since they had all earlier come back into the saloon. Mr. Findlay had been forwarder than Willoughby in dressing for dinner, and his presence in the saloon on their host's entrance had scotched any possibility of private discussion. All the others, awaiting with bated breath the full story of Miss Willoughby's arrival and the reason for her stay, were obliged to rein in their curiosity, at least until Findlay and the lady had retired for the evening.

But it did not take a shrewd observer to guess that the circumstances did not march with Willoughby's wishes, for he had taken up a brooding position at the mantlepiece, and upon his sister's entrance had merely grunted, returning his gaze immediately to the fire as he kicked a log with his foot. But Bellerton, eyes still gleaming appreciatively, came across the room to take the lady's hand and bow over it.

"Come sit here, Miss Willoughby," he said, offering his arm as he gestured to the settee just large enough for two.

There was an almost imperceptible hesitation before she said gently, "Thank you, Mr. Bellerton." She went gracefully along with him toward the settee, inclining her head to Charles and Francis as she passed, and bestowing a smile upon George, who stood with a slight frown as he watched her on Bell's arm.

Francis noted that Findlay, rather than leap to her assistance, had only nodded deferentially, returning to his perusal of the newspaper. From Willoughby's frequent animadversions upon Findlay's strict morals, Francis had anticipated a more fatherly and protective air from the solicitor toward his charge—for it was evident that he was at Penhurst to smooth her way with her surly brother. His apparent unconcern for the chick among so many foxes was surprising.

It could not be that the older man did not perceive the admiration of the others—if he did not, he was blind. Charles had moved to the edge of his chair, bending toward the lady with his usual polite and cheerful solicitude—what Francis liked to roast him was his "Society face." George had drifted away from the fireplace—and from Willoughby's glowering incivility—and now hovered at the end of the settee, offering his usual sedate commentary on the topic of discussion from time to time. And Bellerton was fairly slavering over Miss Willoughby's decolletage, his glittering eyes never long from the expanse of smooth brown flesh above the dainty lace along the neckline.

Francis simply observed the tableau in mocking amusement. Miss Willoughby, by her unexpected arrival, had caused quite a kick up, and it remained to be seen whether it would enliven their stay, or dampen it. At present, she was the center of attention, but Francis knew from long experience that young ladies of one's class rather quickly became a bore. Miss Willoughby, however, with her slightly improper conversation and impish humor was out of the common way. He conjectured that she would keep them entertained a day or two longer than the average miss—and perhaps longer if she proved to have the wandering Willoughby spirit. He made a mental note to try her in a flirtation as soon as may be.

Their dinner was uneventful, served by Clayton and John, the sole footman in Willoughby's skeleton staff. Conversation was desultory at best, and the daggered looks Will continually shot either his sister or his solicitor served further to stir his friends' anticipation of his explanation of events. As it transpired, however, he was not to satisfy their burning curiosity that night, for after Miss Willoughby retired for the evening, Mr. Findlay requested that Willoughby go with him again to the library, as they had matters to finalize. Will did not look best pleased to be taken from his guests again, but he went grimly away, casting such an evil eye upon Mr. Findlay from the back that Francis surmised, if Will had his pistols, his man of business would more than likely return to London in a casket.

Having been thus encouraged to make an early night of it, all the gentlemen arose the next morning betimes, and Willoughby directly led them all out for a walloping ride over his parkland. Once the boundary of the park had been reached, however, they were obliged to slow and pick their way carefully to avoid running afoul of the series of drains and dikes crisscrossing the land.

When they had got far enough from the Lodge that one could only see its rooftops peeping from over the great oaks that surrounded it, Will led them up a small incline to a spreading sycamore where they dismounted to rest the horses.

The fen spread out before them, the drains and becks, dikes and roads making a cross-hatch pattern. Windmills stood here and there like solemn watchers of the puny attempts of man to wrest control of the land from the sea and, off in the distance, a bell tolled in the steeple of St. Mary's church in Swineshead.

The view could be termed idyllic by those whose livelihood did not depend upon a fickle fate, but Willoughby exclaimed, "Damme if I don't strangle the chit and have done with it."

Four startled gazes turned to him and Charles said, "Good gad, Will. Which chit?"

"If I'm to be a party to murder," muttered George, "best get myself on my way to Newmarket."

Willoughby continued for some moments to glare out at the surrounding landscape, no doubt contemplating with distaste the encroaching fenland. Then he unburdened himself of all he had discovered the night before. It did not take long to recount the salient points of his discussion with Findlay, nor for his auditors to offer their opinions on the matter.

"Dashed like Old Willoughby to pop off without warning," said Bell with a snort. "And to leave you high and dry when he must have known you'd be needing funds."

"There's nothing high and dry about Penhurst, you numbskull," Will ground out. "He knew just what he was about, bolting to Jamaica once he'd realized what a scrape he'd got into here."

"The Jamaican property wasn't family land, then?" inquired Charles.

Will shook his head. "It was another of my honored father's cursed investments. Bought it on the advice of a friend a month or so before he removed there."

"Deuced good investment, too," remarked George, who seemed insensible of the searing glance Willoughby gave him. "Sugarcane is as good or better than privateering to make one rich as a Nabob—'til the slave trade was abolished, that is."

"Obliged to you, Hayes, for pouring salt into the wound," said Will in sneering mockery, "You'd best go back and congratulate my sister on her good fortune before I change my mind and strangle *you!*"

George considered him. "Wouldn't think you'd do it. Even so, oughtn't to speak of a female's fortune—at least not in her presence."

Will rolled his eyes, but Charles put in, "Did your father really cut up stiff over improvements to this place? Penhurst was still his estate."

"Dear old Papa never could recall that trifling detail." Will plucked up a rock from the ground and threw it with a growling sound deep in his throat. "Scoundrel told me the income of the estate was mine to do with as I pleased, and that if I wished for more money, to look to improving the estate."

Francis huffed. "I believe that is the usual excuse; the only trouble is, there does seem to be something to it."

"And pray, how many windmills have you been obliged to rebuild, Mantell?" Will inquired contemptuously. "Or does my memory deceive me that your Southam land stands somewhat higher in elevation?"

"I fear I must concede the point," said Francis, with a mocking nod.

"And now my beloved natural sister has all my money tied up in her dashed trust."

Bell cocked his head like a vulture sighting a fresh kill. "And just how much, precisely, does she have, Will?"

"Enough to make me wish her dead," replied Will, hurling another rock with so much violence as to startle the horses.

George took exception to this, saying, "Can't say such things, Will. Pretty girl, and pretty-behaved, too."

"Come, Willoughby," chided Francis, his lips curling in amusement. "It can't be so bad as that. How rich must the illegitimate, hitherto-unknown heiress of your father be to give your thoughts so violent a turn?"

Will grimaced at them each in turn, shaking his head as though he himself still could not believe it. "Forty thousand pounds." He paused to take in their stupefaction with a mirthless smile. "Yes, gentlemen, my sister is worth every penny of forty thousand pounds. When one takes a moment to calculate, one finds that sum would just about pay all my debts, replace twenty windmills, repair any number of dikes, and set me up in comfort for the remainder of my sorry life. Likely twice over."

Bellerton whistled, a speculative gleam coming into his eyes. "Had a hunch she was a ripe one."

"Don't get any ideas, Bell," Will said sharply. "No man touches her until I've figured a way to get my fair share out of her fortune. The deuce of it is, there's no way around the dashed trust."

"Should be simple enough to pad the accounts," mused Francis. "Pay for ten gowns and keep only three. Get her a broken-down prad and say it was purebred. Buy her paste and present them as the finest quality jewels. Say that woman of hers is paid twice as much."

Will snorted. "That might buy me some time, but in the end it won't fadge. Findlay's watching too closely, and I'll have to account for everything to the dashed Chancery Court as well. But I'll come up with something, though I've only got one year. Cursed chit's nearly twenty."

"Not much time," mused Bell.

They got up and remounted, turning toward the village, where they entered the Pig and Whistle and settled at a table there. Bellerton called for ale, and when the pretty serving maid brought the tankards, he hooked a thumb toward his friend.

"Here, Molly, give poor Will a kiss. He's had a grievous disappointment and wants comforting."

"That so?" She gazed in interest at Will, who was not endeavoring in the slightest to hide that he suffered from something. "Seems you're in a bit of a twist, to be sure, Mr. Willoughby. I'd be glad to oblige if you'll wait until closing time, for you know Barny'd sack me for carousing during work hours, sure as check."

"I'll make it worth his while," Will said, taking the maid's other hand and pulling her onto his lap. She gasped, but his mouth was quickly pressed against hers, and it seemed her employer's prohibitions were forgotten. As the other gentlemen grinned or hooted their approbation, Will kissed the maid thoroughly, leaving her breathless and pink when he at last raised his head. Then, just as suddenly as he had pulled her into his lap, he levered her out of it, saying, "You always were a good sport, Molly, my love."

"I'd call *that* simply good sport," exclaimed Bellerton, pointing at Will as though he were a champion. "I fancy I'm feeling a bit low myself, Molly."

Molly's full lips hitched in a smile. "You'd have to buy the pub, I'm afraid, Mr. Bellerton. Pity, that's all I've time for now." She put her hand out to Will.

Will huffed and pressed a half-crown piece into her palm. "Get on with you, then."

"Come again, sirs," she said, tucking the coin into her cleavage with a broad and general wink. Then she sauntered away, swaying her hips as if to remind them what they could look forward to.

"A fine way to improve one's spirits," said Francis, sipping at his ale. "I'll have to remember sweet Molly next I'm in Swineshead."

"Gamest pullet in the county," said Will. "Prettiest, too."

"There's your sister now," said Bellerton.

George gazed soberly at him. "She's not a game pullet. She's a lady."

Bellerton cast a sideways glance at Willoughby and said, "More's the pity."

Chapter 10

THE WEATHER THE following day mirrored Willoughby's continuing foul mood, grey and wet and unremittingly gloomy. Mr. Findlay had gone to visit the steward and Charles had a letter to write in his room, but the other gentlemen, resigning themselves to a day of boredom, adjourned after breakfast to the billiard room, where Will hoped he would be spared his sister's society. His attitude was so surly, however, that he soon alienated Francis, who could never find patience for anyone's self-pity but his own.

Retiring to the library, Francis thought to ensconce himself with a book in one of the comfortable, wing-back chairs near the fire. He discovered within another inhabitant, however, who was at that moment reaching from her perch on the ladder for a book on a high shelf. The pose caused her muslin day-dress to drape enticingly over her shapely curves, and he thought it the perfect time to try a flirtation.

"May I be of assistance, Miss Willoughby?" he inquired, striding to the base of the ladder and gazing quizzically up at her.

She turned in some surprise to regard him, eyes dancing with her ready humor. "Perhaps you might catch me when I topple from this precarious position, sir."

"It would be my honor," he said, opening his arms with a lazy smile.

The dimples appeared in her cheeks. "I see you are too gentlemanly to scold me for endangering myself, for which I am glad, for I assure you, it would do no good. I know perfectly well I am ridiculous to believe myself capable of reaching so far."

Without hesitation, Francis mounted the steps of the ladder, coming up close behind her. "And for which book are you endangering yourself? I do believe it would be far more prudent to allow me to obtain it for you, for I have a superior reach, you see."

Miss Willoughby was shrinking back against the ladder, her gaze wide and somewhat shocked at his improper nearness. But the harsh sound of someone clearing their throat brought both their gazes around to Miss Muncey, whom Francis now perceived to be seated on the far side of the room, looking daggers at him.

"Ah," he said, leaning an inch or two away from his quarry and bestowing on first her maid and then Miss Willoughby his most engaging smile. "Allow me to assist you down from the ladder, ma'am, and then you may point out the book you wish for me to reach down to you."

So saying, he retreated, holding the ladder steady for her as she followed and taking her hand for the last few rungs.

"Thank you, Mr. Mantell," she murmured, not quite looking at him.

When she was once more on firm ground, she retrieved her hand immediately and skirted him widely. He smirked to himself at her discomfiture, thinking that perhaps she was not so self-assured as she had appeared yesterday, which would be a pity. Nevertheless, he climbed the ladder once more, awaiting her pleasure with an expectant look. Somewhat inarticulately, she pointed to a shelf, and after a few mis-tries, he successfully plucked her choice from among its companions and retreated with it down the ladder.

"Here you are, Miss Willoughby," he said, presenting it to her with a flourish. "I hope it proves as enjoyable as you hoped, and more so than it would have been had you risked your—" He glanced wickedly at Muncey— "lovely person to obtain it."

Then he was permitted to admire how a blush became her tawny skin, and how gracefully her neck curved when she attempted to be civil without looking into his face. But he was even more struck when she peeped at him with mischief in her eyes.

"Provoking man!" she said, fighting to contain a smile. "It is my belief you are an accomplished flirt! If only you had not caught me off-guard, I ought to have guided you to a very different book, just out of that superior reach of yours, for it would have served you right to lose your balance and fall, right on your—" She paused cheekily— "theretofore handsome face."

The sparkle in her eye was nothing less than a challenge, and his interest was instantly re-engaged. When she bobbed a curtsey and would have retired to a seat beside her maid, he would no more allow her to do so than he would withdraw himself.

"The Penhurst collection is a noble one, do not you agree?" he inquired, languidly considering the floor-to-ceiling shelves lining the walls.

She turned back, the book clasped to her chest, glancing first at him in dubious inquiry, then following his gaze around the room. "I do, sir. But my brother must have done much to improve it over the years."

Francis snorted. "Certainly not. Willoughby greatly dislikes this room. He hasn't read more than *The Turf Remembrancer* since he was sent down from Oxford in his second year, or I'm a gaby."

She cocked her head. "Gaby? I suppose that is something like a fool. A useful word to know, I think—especially when one is surrounded by them."

Again, that impish twinkle. Francis decided that Miss Willoughby's coming was undoubtedly an addition to his stay at Penhurst. Too bad she was also, contrary to Bellerton's surmise, a lady. But she was at least willing to spar, which was proving quite enjoyable.

He clasped his hands behind his back. "Yes, my friends are, on the whole, a sad trial to me."

"You are too bad!" she cried, giving him a remonstrative look. "You know very well I meant to roast you." Then she grew pensive and, with a sigh, moved to one of the shelves to touch the spines of the books. "If Nathan had nothing to do with this collection, they must all be my father's." She trailed her hand along the shelf. "He chose them and handled them."

"Which explains Will's dislike, I am persuaded. I wonder that your father did not take them with him to Jamaica."

"Perhaps he thought more of Nathan than either of them supposed. It is quite a legacy, to be sure."

"And entirely lost on Willoughby." Francis watched her as she wandered along the shelves, gazing up and down at the rows upon rows of books in their tooled leather bindings. "Did your father have no library, then, in Jamaica?"

"Oh, he had one. Not so large as this, but splendid in its way. I wish my mother could have seen this collection." She turned with a melancholy smile. "I believe she would have loved it."

"Could your mother read, then?"

A muffled noise emanated from Muncey's corner of the room, and Miss Willoughby flicked a glance to her, biting her lips. Returning her clear gaze to Francis, she said, "It was she who taught me to read, Mr. Mantell. She died of the fever when I was but ten years old, but I remember her melodious voice. I could listen to her reading for hours—as could my father. He loved her so."

This was said with such longing that even Francis was moved. Though he had never been so foolish as to fall in love, he could appreciate the pull of a beautiful woman on one's emotions. That Miss Willoughby's mother had been a beauty, he did not doubt. Will was a well-looking fellow, and apparently took after his father, but one could easily tell that, other than the striking blue eyes, the father's features had contributed little to Miss Willoughby's prettiness.

"How did your mother and father meet, if I may ask, Miss Willoughby?"

She stilled, crossing her arms over her chest, and Muncey jumped up, tumbling a shawl off her lap onto the floor. "It's alright, Muncey," said Miss Willoughby quickly, but her hands belied her agitation as they gripped her arms. "It—it does not pain me to speak of them."

"I insist you do not, ma'am," said Francis gallantly, "if it pains you at all."

She regarded him, her smile warming, but not, he fancied, for him. "It used to, very much. Indeed, it still does, a little. But now that I am well and truly separated from my home in Jamaica, I find myself wishing to remember everything, whether painful or no."

It piqued him that thoughts of her far away homeland gave her more pleasure at this moment than his company. She was right—he was an accomplished flirt, and if she were of the usual sort of young ladies, she would have succumbed to his charms long since. But she was proving to be a most uncommon female, and Francis considered the challenge of winning her admiration worthy of at least a half hour or two of his time.

"But you are cold," he said, observing her crossed arms. He strode toward Muncey, who stood her ground as though daring him to accost her, but he merely bent and retrieved the shawl at her feet. Returning to Miss Willoughby's side, he cast the maid his infuriating smile while placing the shawl tenderly about her mistress's shoulders. "There, now come sit by the fire, and tell me what you please of Jamaica."

"But I have detained you long enough, sir," Miss Willoughby protested. She held up her book, the twinkle back in her eye. "You have done your duty by me, and may go about your business."

Francis spread his hands. "That is the problem: I have no business. I am a gentleman, after all."

Muncey uttered something like a snort, settling back on her window seat.

Miss Willoughby stifled a grin. "Indeed, sir, I fear I had forgotten you were a gentleman."

"And after I have been at such pains—" Francis bent an injured look upon her. "I believe you owe me the opportunity of reclaiming my character."

Miss Willoughby looked skeptical but allowed herself to be led to a cozy wing chair.

Francis settled into its mate and put his chin in one hand, gazing expectantly at her. "Tell me what you miss most about Jamaica."

"Dear me." Miss Willoughby looked about, as though searching her mind for a memory with which to start. "I have already talked about the beaches—"

"And the spiders," put in Francis helpfully. "I wholeheartedly agree there is no need to revisit them. What of your home?"

Miss Willoughby embarked on a colorful description of Willow Great House near Montego Bay, on the northern shore of the island. She described the house as quite similar in design to Penhurst Lodge, but with a type of porch called a veranda running the length of the third floor. "To use as a sitting room in the evenings, while the cool breeze from the ocean blew through the jalousies and cooled the upper stories of the house."

Francis obligingly listened to her memories of running through the dense forests that surrounded the plantation, playing beneath the aqueducts that ran water to the sugar mill, and sucking on fresh sugarcane given her by the slaves at their work.

She paused, the ever-present smile dimming as her countenance became reflective. "I thought they were workers, not slaves. I did not comprehend for many years what their situation was."

Francis regarded her. "Did you not know, then, that your mother had been a slave?"

A noise from Muncey's window seat alerted him that she took exception to this question, but Miss Willoughby hesitated only a moment before saying, "Not until I was older, for all my childhood she was the lady of the house." She turned resolutely to face him. "My father told me she had worked hard to purchase her freedom and then had sought work in his house. He caught her once looking at one of his books in the library, but rather than punish her, he had been intrigued, and taught her to read. It was not long after that he fell in love, and she too."

Her reminiscent smile was catching, and Francis found his lips responding in kind. "No doubt she was a handsome woman, as you never got your beauty from Willoughby's family."

Muncey's mutterings grew more insistent, and Miss Willoughby's eyes danced. "You are what I believe is termed 'a complete hand,' sir."

"Even if I was, you could not expect me to admit to it, seeing as how I am endeavoring to prove myself a gentleman."

She laughed, that lovely, delicious sound. "Then I shall not press you to do so. But if you truly are a gentleman, pray, will you extend your chivalry so far as to do something for me?"

Francis could think of several things he would gladly do on a gloomy day in front of the fire with a pretty girl, but as he was acting the gentleman, he merely said, "To be sure, it is in the nature of chivalrous knights to serve their ladies. What would you have me do?"

"You are very kind—and surprisingly trusting. I could ask for anything!"

His lips twitched. "I am not afraid of you."

"I am, in general, completely harmless," she said, her eyes averted. "But such is my present desperation that I will not scruple to impose on your trust."

"Come, tell me at once what you wish from me, or I shall lose my nerve completely and run away."

She pursed her lips against a grin. "Very well. Will you tell me about Nathan?"

He stared at her, nonplussed, and she hurried on. "You must imagine that my father did not think it important to inform me of my half-brother's disposition or habits. Indeed, I cannot imagine he even knew of them, for Nathan was only a young boy when our father left England, and had hardly formed his character. But if I am to live with him, I should like to know him better, so I may discover if there is anything I might do to reconcile him to the circumstance."

Francis rather thought Willoughby would never be reconciled to his sister's company, much less her existence, as it reminded him so plainly of his own insignificance in the eyes of their father. But being as he was in the guise of a gentleman, he could not say so. Nor could he refuse her very reasonable request, no matter how uninteresting it was. Gentlemen, it seemed, lived the blandest lives.

"Certainly." Francis confined his regret to a sigh as he sat back in his chair. "He is a fine fellow, I suppose. Always game for a lark. Good sportsman—though I'd not trust him with my horses, nor anyone's horses, really. But he's got bottom—that is, he's no coward. And he's right in matters of pay and play."

"You are very kind," she said, clasping her hands, her bright blue eyes gazing earnestly into his grey ones. "There is so much I should like to discover about him—how he likes his tea, how he orders his day—" She must have caught the slight lift to his brows, for she chuckled. "Never fear, sir, I will inquire of Mrs. Slade such mundanities."

Francis smiled at her perspicacity. "And now, I believe you must do something for me."

Muncey muttered something caustic, but Miss Willoughby merely gazed at him in surprise. "I should be glad to help anyone, sir, but I hardly know how I can be of assistance to you."

"I do not require your assistance, *per se*, but the laws of chivalry demand you give me something." He could feel Muncey's glare boring into the back of his head, but he continued matter-of-factly, "As it is the nature of a knight to serve his lady, it is the nature of the lady to grant her knight a boon when he has fulfilled her wishes."

Miss Willoughby blinked, but he detected the sparkle of mischief back in her eyes. "Of course. And I have just the thing: you may take me into dinner tonight."

"Ah, but you misunderstand. The boon is something the knight asks of his lady."

"I did not know the laws of chivalry were so exacting. Very well. You may ask, but as a lady, I reserve the right to refuse."

He smirked, impressed by her sharp wit, and determined to keep the upper hand. "A pity," he said, rising from his chair. "I had hoped you to be as unfamiliar with that rule as you were with the laws of chivalry. Now I must consider my request carefully, and ask it of you at a future date." Capturing her hand, he kissed it lightly. Before Muncey could exclaim, however, he released her and continued with a roguish twinkle, "But I have your word, now, so I will treasure it up against the day I find myself in need of a favor only you may bestow."

Miss Willoughby bit her lips in amusement, but this only made her dimples all the more evident. "I fear you have already disappointed yourself, sir. You just stole a kiss, so it seems we are even."

It took him only a moment to recover. "But the knight is required to kiss his lady."

"Only the hem of her garment, sir, or the ground whereon her feet have trod." She lifted her chin, the corners of her lips hovering in a smile. "You would be wise, perhaps, to reacquaint yourself with these chivalric laws about which you fancy you know so much."

"I am as conversant with them as is necessary, ma'am," he replied smoothly, adjusting his cuffs. "I merely could not reach the hem of your garment, and no one with any degree of sensibility—or mercy— would expect that I place my lips upon any of the floors in this house.

Mrs. Slade is an estimable female, but she is simply not equal to the sheer amount of dirt Will and all his guests track in."

"But as one of those guests, you could not imagine yourself above—"

"Therefore, Miss Willoughby," Francis interrupted her, holding a remonstrative finger up in front of him. "Therefore, it was entirely acceptable, not to say advisable, that I kiss what extremity I could."

She laughed heartily again, taking up her book. "We seem to be evenly matched, you and I. But as I am eager to begin reading, I concede the point. I will await your request with a good grace."

"Your mercy overwhelms me, my lady." He bowed in the manner of a medieval knight, with his fist pressed to his heart. "I shall go away to pray for your good favor."

He turned to nod to Muncey—who returned his civility with what he could only term the evil eye—and grinning, quitted the room.

Chapter 11

Returning to the billiard room, Francis found the others had abandoned the game and sat in the comfortable chairs scattered about the room, sipping at brandy.

Willoughby gave him a look over the top of his glass. "Thought you'd lost yourself in a maid's bosom."

"As none of your maids have seemed to have bosoms," retorted Francis, "I wonder that you could be so stupid."

"Been meaning to bring that up, Will," said Bellerton in a tone of disgust. "Seems there's never anything pretty to look at here anymore, much less get lost in."

"Could get lost in the formal gardens," put in George. "I did last spring."

Willoughby waved a hand. "Take it up with my housekeeper. She claims it's all she can do to get decent maids at all these days."

Charles grinned. "More likely, Mrs. Slade got so desperate to retain her staff with your lot running amok that she took to hiring only homely girls."

"An excellent solution," agreed Francis. "Mrs. Slade is more estimable than I imagined."

"Lucky your sister dropped into our laps," said Bellerton, smiling into his brandy.

George frowned. "She ain't the sort to drop into anyone's lap, much less yours, Bell."

"Wait until I've worked my magic on her," retorted Bellerton, waving his glass like a mystic.

Charles sat forward, his eyes narrowed. "And precisely how do you imagine your 'magic' could work upon Miss Willoughby? She is a lady, after all."

Bell glanced at him, hesitating at the intensity of the gaze directed at him. "I only mean to have a bit of fun—just a light flirtation. What else am I to do with her?"

Will grimaced. "Nothing. I won't have the Willoughby name tarnished any more than it is."

Francis turned a satirical gaze upon Willoughby. "It may be wiser simply to send her away. You could easily set her up with a companion in London or Bath."

"But my dear Mantell, that would be a waste of my dear father's money," Willoughby tossed off the remainder of his brandy. "I'll play the dutiful brother if I can get my share."

Francis shrugged off a feeling of mild unease at this summary dismissal of the witty and pretty Miss Willoughby's worth. "Perhaps you can marry her off. Then you can arrange for a generous settlement and be done with the business."

Will laughed bitterly. "So easy, eh, Mantell? And who, pray, would marry the chit? Would you?"

He looked challengingly at each of his friends, who seemed to find it suddenly difficult to meet his eyes. With a huff of disgust, he rose to pour himself more brandy.

Feeling somewhat guilty, Francis set his glass down. "Not everyone need know she is your natural sister, Will. You might introduce her as a wealthy relation from the West Indies. The girl is clever—she will recognize the need for discretion. With her fortune first and foremost in people's minds, you will have no trouble finding a gullible man to take her off your hands—for a price."

"I do not find myself as sanguine in the matter," was the sullen reply.

"Come, Will," pursued Francis, "You ought to know just how powerfully money works on people's minds. If you met a girl with half your sister's fortune, you'd leap into wedded shackles and thank her for it."

Willoughby grimaced. "That's how little you know me, Mantell. If all I wished for in a bride was riches, I'd marry Miss Draffin tomorrow. But I still have my pride, as I don't doubt the majority of gentlemen have—at least those I'd deign to call brother."

Muncey forbore to tease Eliza while she read her book, but when her mistress set it aside, she pounced. "Why do you encourage dat *ginnal*? He is de kind to take everyting, den cast you aside like a scrap."

Eliza sighed. "Even if he is a con-man, he has not deceived me. I know full well he is a flirt and, unless I am much mistaken, a rake. You must not fear for me, however. I will not allow him to touch my heart."

"Maybe," muttered Muncey. "Mr. Mantell does not seem de kind of man to be discouraged. What if he only tries all de harder, eh?"

Eliza chuckled, rising from her chair and taking her loyal hench-woman by the arm. "You are the best kind of friend, my dear Muncey, but you worry too much. Recollect, the gentlemen plan to go to Newmarket in the next week—which according to Mrs. Slade is quite a county away—and we shall be left in peace. I must only hold out against Mr. Mantell's wiles for a few days, a feat of which I believe I am capable."

Muncey only pursed her lips, emitting what seemed to be a low growl of vexation, but she allowed herself to be led out of the library. In the hall, however, they met Clayton, whose pleasant expression brightened to a grin upon seeing them.

"And 'ow are you this afternoon, ladies?" he inquired cheerfully, bouncing on the balls of his feet as though stillness were foreign to him.

"Very well, thank you, Clayton," replied Eliza, as Muncey's lips remained pressed tightly closed.

Clayton seemed unaffected by the maid's irritation. "You've been in the library, I see. And did you find anything to your liking there?"

Muncey flashed him an indignant look and Clayton, his eyes widening for a moment, chuckled. "Now, Miss Muncey, you know I meant books and nothing else, for what more could be found to your liking in a library? To be sure, there's gentlemen aplenty all about, but you fine ladies don't give owt for them, with your thoughts pure as angels, and likewise elevated above such unworthy beings."

Eliza watched as Muncey continued to spear him with her gaze, but she thought the tightness of her lips lessened, and did not think she imagined the ghost of a quiver at the corners.

"I found a lovely book on the flora and fauna of Lincolnshire," Eliza answered. "I read the day quite away, it was so absorbing to me.

Everything is different here, but I am glad to do what I can to acquaint myself with my new home."

"Ah," said Clayton, breaking eye contact with Muncey to nod to Eliza. "I'm pleased to 'ear it, ma'am, for the light of my days is to see my master's guests comfortable. But then, you are more than guests, being as you are the master's kin, Miss Willoughby, and Miss Muncey your dearest companion. Be assured, ma'am, all those serving at Penhurst Lodge are pleased beyond words to 'ave you with us, and are looking forward to becoming acquainted with you both."

"You are very kind," replied Eliza, wondering how it was that Muncey could keep back a smile after such earnest loquacity. But from the workings of the maid's jaw, Eliza judged it was only by mighty endeavor that she did so.

He seemed sensible of this fact, for as Eliza moved to excuse herself and Muncey, a smile tugged at the corners of his mouth, and he held up a hand. "I wonder if either of you might've noticed, during the long afternoon, if the small port decanter on the shelf behind Mr. Willoughby's desk requires a fill? Though I shouldn't expect you fine ladies to avail yourselves of spirituous liquor during daylight hours—and, indeed, I should never do so myself, believing it to be a deplorable 'abit and a waste of the God-given strength of man—the master or his male guests've been known to imbibe."

"I do not believe any of the gentlemen to have been near that port decanter today, Clayton," said Eliza, admirably preserving her countenance.

Clayton put a hand to his heart and bowed his head in gratitude. "Many thanks, ma'am, for saving a poor butler some difficulty. A penny saved is a penny earned, my dear mum used to say, and a minute saved is quite as valuable. Now I'll be on my way to prepare for the dinner hour, as I'm sure you ladies should like to do. Oh, and I've 'ad fresh flowers sent up to your rooms, to brighten them up in case you've been missing the warmer climes of Jamaica."

"Flowers?" said Muncey at last. "Where did you get flowers in de winter?"

"The 'othouses, ma'am," replied Clayton, looking vastly pleased with himself. "They're something like a bit of the West Indies in a glass 'ouse. If you find yourself curious, I'll be honored to take you for a tour. And you as well, of course, Miss Willoughby."

"How delightful!" exclaimed Eliza, seeing that Muncey was now tongue-tied from amazement—and perhaps gratitude. "You have been very kind. Perhaps when next it is sunny, we might trouble you for a tour. But now we must go up to see our flowers."

Beaming, Clayton bowed, stepping aside to allow them to pass, and watched them go with a deep sigh. But when he turned to enter the back hallway, he perceived Mr. Findlay, who was regarding him with undisguised interest.

'Allo sir," the butler said, bowing. "Is there owt I might do for you?"

"I believe there is, Clayton," said Mr. Findlay, beckoning him to follow him into the hallway. When they had penetrated nearly to the kitchens, he stopped and removed his glasses, polishing them with his handkerchief. "I wish to thank you for your goodness to Miss Willoughby. It seems that you have taken a liking to her," he replaced his glasses and gazed at the butler, "and to Miss Muncey."

Clayton looked him up and down, sizing him up as though for a fight. "And what if I 'ave, sir?"

Mr. Findlay smiled. "I am only glad to hear it. As Miss Willough-by's guardian, I have been anxious that she feel comfortable in her new home. It has been my disappointment to find, however, that she has not been made to feel so welcome by others in the household. Indeed, I have reason to suspect that my presence only is what keeps certain persons from becoming, shall we say, uncivil."

With dawning comprehension, Clayton drew himself up. "You wish me to watch over the ladies, do you?"

"I do," said Mr. Findlay simply, his sober gaze unwavering.

"Well, sir, I'll tell you a thing or two," said Clayton, grasping the lapels of his coat and rocking on the balls of his feet. "Mr. Willoughby's my master, sure as 'e pays good gold, and 'e's a right to order 'is own 'ouse, so far as I'm concerned. I'll knock the chatterers out of any catch poll that tries to mither 'im, and shut the door in the face of any ferret 'e wishes." He paused to flex his neck from side to side, and Mr. Findlay could hear the joints crack. "But if 'e thinks to mither our Miss Willoughby, or Miss Muncey, 'e'll have a brush with my fives sooner than 'e can blink."

Mr. Findlay's lips turned up in a full smile, perhaps for the first time in his life. "Well said, sir. Then I may count on you to see Miss Willoughby—and Miss Muncey—are properly treated after I am gone?"

"You've my 'and on it, sir."

They shook solemnly, though each held a glitter in his eye that bordered on the gleeful. Before turning to go, Mr. Findlay said reflectively, "I believe you may find an ally in Mr. Wraglain, and perhaps even in Mr. Hayes, should you require any assistance. But the gentlemen will be going on to Newmarket at the end of the week, and then we may all be easy for a while."

Clayton nodded briefly and Mr. Findlay went on his way, much relieved of a great weight. When he came down for dinner that evening, he picked up the newspaper as usual, propping it before him with a look of detached unconcern. But this attitude was merely a pretense, employed during the previous two evenings to facilitate his spying without compunction on his companions' conversations and actions. It was in this manner that he had quickly ascertained the characters of Mr. Willoughby's house guests, and determined from whom Miss Willoughby was more likely to receive insult or injury.

Mr. Wraglain he had quickly seen to be a good sort of fellow, who perhaps had poor taste in his friends, but who managed somehow to retain a moral compass. Mr. Hayes was very similar, but with a dull enough intellect that he might not be relied upon to act quickly in a crisis. Still, these two could be instrumental in keeping the others within the bounds of propriety, if not civility.

Mr. Bellerton and Mr. Mantell he was less comfortable with. The former was already in the habit of watching Miss Willoughby with an expression Mr. Findlay—or any honorable gentleman, for that matter—could not like. And Mr. Mantell, though not so outwardly disrespectful, had a careless way about him that, paired with his roving eye, boded ill for any young lady's peace. These gentlemen seemed more likely to turn a blind eye to any insult offered to a lady in their host's house, if not to be the one to offer it. And Willoughby, who ought to have taken his sister's safety as his personal charge, was least likely to guard it.

Findlay counted Mr. Willoughby's dislike of his sister as most unfortunate. He had not expected a warm welcome from his employer for the half-sister who had stripped him of his long-anticipated wealth, but he had hoped that family-feeling would engender in him at least a tolerance, if not a duty toward her. The sentiment Mr. Willoughby had shown toward his sister was so lacking even in tolerance that Findlay had felt it expedient to engage some sort of fail-safe plan for the protection of his ward. But until he had observed Clayton's rapt and respectful attentions to Miss Muncey, he had been at a loss as to how to achieve his ends.

Now, as he listened with distaste to the persiflage of the four other gentlemen in the room, his breast remained calm with the knowledge that he could without compunction return on the morrow to London, for Miss Willoughby—and Miss Muncey—ought now to be safe.

Miss Willoughby soon after entered the saloon in seeming contentment, bestowing her ready smile upon the gentlemen as though nothing caused her uncertainty. Her apricot-colored gown reflected the warmth of her disposition, and her blue eyes were bright with good-humor. But Mr. Findlay, through years of experience with persons of all types, could sense the anxiety latent beneath this mask, and it pained him. Indeed, during the weeks she had spent in London, his recognition of and respect for her cleverness, optimism, and generosity had grown until he had heartily wished his duty was not to deliver her into what surely amounted to a den of iniquity.

But what could he do? She wished to live at Penhurst as her father had decreed, and she was determined to win over her brother. At least now Mr. Findlay could be confident that she would not be left to bear her inevitable disappointment alone.

They went into dinner and he watched as she endeavored again to draw her brother out. His responses were curt and bordering on the uncivil—and this restraint was thanks only, Mr. Findlay believed, to his own presence at table. But Eliza, rather than taking umbrage at so obvious an affront, merely turned her civilities onto Mr. Hayes.

"And how did you spend the day, Mr. Hayes?" she inquired affably. "For I know you all were sadly confined to the house, which is of all things the most dreadful for gentlemen. For my part, I whiled away the day in the library with a good book."

Mr. Mantell interjected from across the table, "Your time was more enjoyably spent than any of theirs, I assure you."

Eliza darted her eyes to his, and Mr. Findlay was concerned to note a mild blush. But she answered archly, "In Jamaica, a heavy rain would drive all sorts of pests into the house, so it was not always enjoyable."

Mr. Wraglain, sitting on her other side, laughed. "I do believe she just designated us all pests, gentlemen."

"If she did," Willoughby retorted as he tucked away his lemon bream, "She would be obliged to include herself, for she also stayed inside today."

"Don't signify," said Mr. Hayes reasonably. "Rain didn't drive us in—already were in, so can't be called pests."

Nodding to him, Eliza said, "It is only unfortunate that all the neighborhood was similarly confined, for a caller or two would not have gone amiss."

"Not to Will," he replied, nibbling away at the roasted duck on his plate. "He don't like the neighbors."

"Unfortunate," she said, glancing at her brother. "But perhaps I should like them."

Bellerton, who had been listening in, said slyly, "You've much in common with Miss Draffin, I'll be bound."

Willoughby wiped his mouth with his napkin and glared at Bellerton. "There is no need to bring all sorts of Cits and petticoats into my house. I'll not allow the Lodge to become a gathering place for geese and hens."

Eliza blinked at him, but her lips twitched. "Certainly not, Nathan. I wouldn't dream of doing anything so improper. Should any of my guests wish to bring their fowl, I shall deny them instantly."

"You will not bring a parcel of females into this house," he declared in awful dignity. "I was forced to take in you and your maid, but that is where my hospitality to females ends."

Mr. Findlay, who seldom spoke at dinner, cleared his throat. "I believe it is your duty to introduce your sister to her neighbors, Mr. Willoughby."

Willoughby's gaze snapped to the solicitor's. "I am not obliged by the will to do anything of the sort."

"Perhaps not," said Mr. Findlay mildly, "but you are obliged as her guardian to see to her comfort and education. A lady who wishes but is unable to interact with her neighbors will be deprived of both."

Their gazes held, one fierce, the other bland, until Willoughby at last averted his eyes and took up his fork and knife again.

"Very well, but I'll not allow balls or parties," he said, addressing the food on his plate. "And I'll not do the pretty. She will receive them on her own."

Mr. Findlay was satisfied, returning to his own meal.

"Thank you," said Eliza, looking to Mr. Findlay first, and then to her brother, who did not look up. "It will be to your advantage for me to know my neighbors, you will see, for you will be vexed less often with my company."

Willoughby grunted, applying himself with more vigor to his plate and to his wineglass, but said no more against it.

Chapter 12

IN THE MORNING, Mr. Findlay took his leave of Eliza. She was saddened to lose her champion, but as he had largely refrained—wisely, she thought—from actively taking her part during the three days of his stay, she resolved that she could do well enough without him. Indeed, she must, for he could scarcely remain indefinitely at the Lodge.

As he drew on his gloves, she wished him a pleasant journey, and he turned his sober gaze on her. "Write to me whenever you desire, or if you are in any way in need of advice or assistance. You may trust Clayton to faithfully deliver your correspondence to the mails, so have no fear on that head." Taking her hand, he pressed it, adding, "I am assured that you are not friendless in this house. You will do very well, my dear."

Then he was out the door and stepping into his carriage, and Eliza, clutching her shawl about her in the cold of the morning, watched him out of sight on the drive. The coming days seemed to stretch interminably before her, and her mind plaintively inquired how she would survive her brother's ill humor, not to mention his guests' improprieties. But squaring her shoulders, she closed the door, reminding herself that she was no ninny, and that she had chosen this course with eyes open.

No sooner had she made this resolution than she turned to find Mr. Mantell, dressed for riding, propped against the stair rail and regarding her with his roguish smile.

"For a moment I thought you would disintegrate into a puddle on the floor," he said, moving toward her with lazy strides. "Are we that fearsome?"

"Nonsense," she said, forcing a smile. "It is merely that he has become like a father to me. I did not wish him to go."

Mr. Mantell tapped his gloves against his leg. "You will pardon my incredulity, ma'am. He did not seem to concern himself much with your welfare."

"You simply do not know him, sir." Eliza glanced about, wondering with a twinge of trepidation where her allies were to be found. "He has been of great help to me."

"Then you must wish for someone to take his place." Stepping close to her, he looked down with the same glint that had been in his eye when he had trapped her on the library ladder. "I am at your service."

As Eliza stood frozen, Mr. Wraglain appeared on the stairs, also dressed for riding. He paused a moment as he seemed to assimilate the scene before him before continuing on his carefree way down. When he reached the bottom of the steps, he strode toward them, tipping his hat to Eliza with a winning smile.

"Is he behaving himself, Miss Willoughby? If not, you may feel no scruple in telling him to go to the devil. I often do, and am none the worse for it, depend upon it."

Francis glanced at him askance. "Only because you are entirely insensible to even the broadest of insults, my dear Charles. Shall we go?"

"You see, ma'am?" said Mr. Wraglain, winking at Eliza. "Works like a charm."

They both tipped their hats to her, going to the back hallway to let themselves out the kitchen entrance, which was nearer the stables. Eliza watched them go with a relieved sigh. Mr. Findlay's assurances, it seemed, had not been misplaced.

After partaking of some breakfast, Eliza wandered into the library, thinking to find another informative book to read while Muncey mended some of her gowns. She was considering a book on the history of the Lincolnshire Fens when a knock sounded on the front door. Curious, she went to the door of the library, but it occurred to her that it was likely a male visitor for her brother, and she wondered if she ought to make her presence known.

But at that moment, Nathan, Mr. Hayes, and Mr. Bellerton erupted from the saloon, dashing across the hall and into the back corridor, and not half a minute later, the distant sound of an outer door closing met her ears. Eliza could only surmise that the saloon, which fronted on the drive, would have given an excellent view of the visitors, who must be some of the neighbors Nathan so disliked. Clayton, emerging just then from the back hallway, gave her a speaking look before striding to the door to answer the summons.

Eliza watched, wavering between intense curiosity and an irritation of nerves. There was nothing she should like better than to meet her new neighbors, and yet her imagination whispered that there may be some grounds for Nathan's dislike. What if they were horrid, these Cits he had spoken of? Clayton had likely been given orders not to admit them, but she wished to be allowed the opportunity to make her own assessment. Mr. Findlay had agreed that she should, but now that he had gone, Eliza was uncertain her desires would be attended to.

But then Clayton, as he reached to lift the latch, glanced back at her and winked. The door opened, and a female voice inquired in imperious tones after Mr. Willoughby.

"'E's just stepped out, ma'am," said Clayton, in as condescending a manner as his jaunty character could manage. The strident female tones began a demand, but he forestalled them by adding, "But perhaps you'd wish to make the acquaintance of 'is sister, Miss Willoughby."

There was a palpable silence before the female voice replied, "Indeed, we would, if there is such a person."

Clayton bowed, opening the door to admit two ladies, obviously related and even more obviously of wealthy, though likely plebeian, origins. The elder, a faded matron with hair an improbable red, wore purple taffeta with several flounces at the hem, gold braiding across the bosom, and an imposing turban sporting at least three ostrich plumes. The younger, a pretty girl with true auburn ringlets and a pert, heart-shaped face, wore pale blue silk adorned with innumerable white rosettes and ribbons, and a fantastic bonnet of blue net and lace. Both were bedecked with jewels, and wafted with them a strong odor of French perfume.

Upon perceiving Eliza in the hall, the ladies halted and subjected her to a thorough examination, the elder with the aid of a lorgnette attached to a ribbon at her gown's waist.

"Good lord!" the matron uttered, before recollecting herself and dropping the lorgnette. The younger one merely gaped.

Eliza, coming forward, put out her hand. "Good morning! I am terribly sorry that my brother is out, but so pleased to be here myself to meet you. Allow me to introduce myself: I am Eliza Willoughby."

The ladies exchanged a dubious look, but each dipped in the semblance of a curtsey before taking her hand in a limp handshake. The elder said, "I am Mrs. Draffin, and this is Sophronia, my daughter. It is a pleasure to meet you, Miss Willoughby."

"Please, come into the saloon," said Eliza, motioning them before her.

Clayton, stepping forward to hold the door, said in an undertone, "If they tend toward the catty, just pull the bell. I'll throw 'em out before the cat can lick 'er ear."

Eliza twinkled at him but shook her head. "That will be all, Clayton. Thank you."

Arranging their voluminous skirts on the sofa with a great many rustlings, Mrs. and Miss Draffin clasped their hands in their laps and regarded their hostess with critical eyes. Abruptly, Miss Draffin burst out, "We did not know Willoughby had a sister."

"It was not generally known," said Eliza imperturbably. "Have you come far? You will pardon my not knowing the neighborhood at all. I have only been here a few days, and have been unable to go about much."

Mrs. Draffin gave a thin smile. "Our estate is Draffinstoke Manor, about three miles to the east. It is easily seen from the post road, for it is situated perfectly on rising ground, and is surrounded by a lovely park—quite the largest house in the neighborhood, excepting perhaps Penhurst."

Eliza nodded civilly, attempting to recall another great house on her way to her new home. But everything had been so new and interesting that she had been unable to take note of any one sight in particular.

"Shall Mr. Willoughby return soon?" inquired the elder lady. "It seems he is too often out when we call."

"Forgive me, but I do not have any idea. Nathan is so accustomed to keeping his own schedule that he did not think to share with me his plans for the morning."

Miss Draffin glanced surreptitiously at her mother, then down at her hands.

"It seems strange that dear Willoughby never mentioned you, Miss Willoughby," said Mrs. Draffin with an assessing look.

Hesitating, Eliza considered how best to proceed. The Draffins had been specifically mentioned as undesirable neighbors, and she could perceive how this was so. But if she was to live at Penhurst for the foreseeable future, she had no wish to alienate any of her neighbors. "You may have learned that, many years ago, our father emigrated to the West Indies, where I was born and have lived the whole of my life. Nathan did not have a cordial relationship with my father, ma'am, which may have been the cause of his silence regarding me."

"To be sure," breathed Miss Draffin, still agog.

Mrs. Draffin sniffed. "You have come to visit, I assume? Did your father bring you to Penhurst Lodge?"

"My father is dead, ma'am. It was his parting wish that I come to live among my family here, in England. My stay is to be permanent."

The mother and daughter exchanged startled looks and when they turned again to Eliza, their expressions held far more warmth.

"Poor Miss Willoughby!" cried Miss Draffin. "Are you an orphan then? That makes dear Willoughby an orphan as well."

Mrs. Draffin, however, was unmoved by the romance of the situation, and bent a calculating gaze upon her hostess. "I believe your father owned a tidy property in Jamaica, Miss Willoughby?"

Smiling affably, Eliza decided Nathan had good reason to dislike the Draffins. "You are well informed, ma'am. But as the property in question is no longer in the possession of the family, I cannot say whether it is tidy or not. May I offer you any refreshment before you go?"

Perhaps sensing she had overstepped, the matron creased her face into a motherly smile. "My dear Miss Willoughby, you are too kind. How delightful to have another young lady to be a friend for my Sophronia."

"Oh, yes, Miss Willoughby," added the daughter, quite sincerely. "And we are so nearby, we might be meeting forever!"

Eliza smiled upon them, rising to ring the bell and musing to herself that it was a pity Mrs. Draffin was so vulgar, for Miss Draffin seemed truly to want a friend. They enjoyed some of Mrs. Slade's pastries while Eliza encouraged them to tell her of the other families in the neighborhood, and then they went away.

Eliza did not see her brother again until dinner, and she sensed immediately that he did not approve of her having entertained the very neighbors he most abominated. Sensible that her attention would only make his mood worse, she did her best to confine her comments to Mr. Hayes and Mr. Wraglain, who sat on either side of her. Conversation generally flagged under Nathan's darkling influence, however, and Eliza was grateful when she could leave the gentlemen to their port.

With Mr. Findlay gone, she was uncertain whether the gentlemen would follow her to the drawing room after dinner or disperse to their own amusements. Mrs. Slade had been fairly unhelpful on the subject, only supposing that Willoughby did what his guests liked. She had therefore determined to do what she had been trained to do of an evening, and allow them to choose what they did. Seating herself at the pianoforte, therefore, she let her presence in the drawing room be known, and awaited events.

The gentlemen wished for music, it seemed, for after only a quarter of an hour, they all arrived and disposed themselves in various states to listen to her playing. She was adept at the instrument, and Mr. Hayes and Mr. Wraglain evinced their appreciation, placing themselves so they could actively observe her. Mr. Mantell seemed tempted to join them, but Nathan invited him to a game of chess, pointedly ignoring her and her music.

Mr. Bellerton, however, leant his tall frame against the mantlepiece and watched her intently. After several minutes, the impression grew within her mind that his look was akin to that of a crocodile. Indeed, with his angular head and mud-colored hair, his wide mouth and intent stare, Eliza wondered that she had not seen the likeness before. It was disconcerting, and she could not feel comfortable in his company. But recollecting Mr. Wraglain's gallantry that morning, and determined to gain her brother's friends' respect, she was on her mettle.

This served her fairly well when Bellerton came up behind her at the pianoforte, bending rather close to inquire whether she knew any African songs.

"They use drums and voices rather than the pianoforte, Mr. Bellerton," she said, preparing to get up.

But he did not move away, saying with his disturbing gleam, "Then they're as wild as I've heard. I understand the women dance naked in Africa. Do they do so in Jamaica?"

Mr. Wraglain and Mr. Hayes both turned shocked gazes to him, and even Nathan and Mr. Mantell looked up from their game.

But Eliza, refusing to be baited into a blush, said pensively, "The women on Willow Plantation certainly never did, nor anywhere I visited in Jamaica. I'm sure I could not tell you how things are in Africa, however, having never been there."

"Stands to reason," said Mr. Hayes almost belligerently, directing a sober gaze at Bellerton.

With dignity, Eliza rose and moved to sit beside Mr. Hayes on the couch, but was consternated to sense Bellerton coming to stand behind them and bending over her as though to press her further.

But Mr. Wraglain said quickly, "Say, do you think we'll have some shooting tomorrow? Or will it still be too wet?"

"You may shoot at fish, perhaps," muttered Nathan, already returned to his game. "But watch for villagers—they seem to dispute the right of anyone they fancy is interfering with their livelihoods."

"I've no interest in shooting at fish," said Bellerton, still standing over Eliza. "I've a mind to stay in the house. Perhaps Miss Willoughby will teach me the Jamaican style of dancing."

"Do you know, I am put in mind of another West Indian spider," said Eliza in a bright tone to hide her unease. "Mr. Hayes mentioned the orb-weaver, which is a very large and colorful spider that builds webs all over Jamaica. But there is another type of giant spider, called the huntsman, that prefers, as its name suggests, to hunt its prey. It is quite terrifying—indeed, I saw a particularly large one, larger than a man's hand, catch a whole frog when I was young."

"Indeed, Miss Willoughby," uttered Mr. Wraglain, in awe. "And how did it eat the frog, I wonder?"

Eliza's eyes danced. "Well, I did not see it eat the frog, precisely, but that is what it meant to do, I assure you. It certainly incapacitated the poor creature, and then dragged it away. My mother told me that spiders suck the innards out of their prey, but I am not certain how that is achieved. Some spiders are certainly poisonous, and perhaps their venom has a dissolving effect. Whatever the case, I can only imagine my huntsman spider took the frog to its den and disposed of it there."

Mr. Wraglain looked on in rapt wonder, but Mr. Hayes appeared faintly ill, and Eliza was pleased to find that Bellerton, withdrawing a pace from her, grimaced in disgust.

Nathan, having lost the chess match to Mr. Mantell, stood and stalked over to her. "If you insist upon bringing spiders into polite conversation, you'll never find a husband."

"I don't know about that," said Mr. Wraglain, grinning at Eliza. "I'm half in love with her already."

Eliza returned his grin with a grateful look, before turning and saying somewhat stiffly to her brother, "Polite conversation, if my governess is to be believed, does not begin with references to nudity."

Nathan closed his eyes, clenching his jaw. "It will be hard enough to introduce you into polite society without your continually exhibiting these gruesome conversational habits."

"Be assured, my dear Nathan," said Eliza, edging on impatience, "when I find myself in polite society, I shall know what subjects are proper to introduce."

Mr. Mantell chuckled from his place at the chessboard, and Nathan turned on him. "You wouldn't allow your sister to make such a spectacle of herself, would you, Mantell?"

"It doesn't much signify, Will, as my sister does precisely what she wishes." He settled back in his chair, regarding his host in amusement. "Perhaps you ought to resign yourself to the fact that you can no more control Miss Willoughby than she can control you." Eliza flashed him a brilliant smile, and he added, "I ought to introduce Clara to you, Miss Willoughby. Then you will gain a proper appreciation of the freedoms obtaining in heiress's circles."

Nathan, muttering under his breath, returned to his seat, and Mr. Mantell, glancing sideways at him, said in a low tone Eliza could just make out, "Do not despair, Will. Perhaps Charles will take her off your hands."

After another quarter of an hour, during which Mr. Wraglain and Eliza conversed comfortably about the various species of spider to be found in Jamaica, Eliza rose to take her leave.

Mr. Hayes blinked at her. "Are you not to order the tea things?"

Eliza felt a trifle conscious. "Tea is a feminine custom. I did not wish to push such a thing on you gentlemen, simply for my sake."

"I like tea," said Mr. Hayes simply.

"As do I," added Mr. Wraglain, with a challenging look at Mr. Mantell.

His challenge failed there, but it succeeded in bringing a snort from Nathan. "You may as well do as you like, Eliza, for I seem to have no say in the matter. Let them maudle their insides if they wish, I don't care."

"I should like something stronger," muttered Bellerton, apparently laboring under a sense of ill-usage after Eliza's snub.

Nathan stood, moving to the door. "As do I. Care for a game of billiards?"

As the two quit the room, Eliza pulled the bell, smiling gratefully upon Mr. Wraglain and Mr. Hayes. Mr. Mantell looked on with a look of mild amusement as she regaled the others with a description of a species of small frog that made its home inland on water-gathering plants called bromeliads.

When Clayton brought the tea, she poured out then stood, taking a dish to Mr. Mantell. But when he reached to take it, she kept hold of it for a moment, saying, "Thank you, sir, for your support—such as it was."

He chuckled, giving her a roguish smile. "As I said, I am at your service."

Chapter 13

After breakfast the following morning, Francis went riding in the fields near Penhurst, keeping to the areas Willoughby had shown them to avoid stumbling into one of the blasted drains that crisscrossed the fens at odd and utterly unreasonable intervals. He could not fathom why it took so many ditches to empty the land of its abundant water, but he supposed it had something to do with its low elevation. Thank heaven he didn't have the sea to contend with in Warwickshire.

After a frustrating hour of picking his way over the fenland, he turned back, misliking the look of the clouds rolling in from the direction of the sea. He had come nearly to the line of trees at the border of Penhurst's park when he saw a lone, feminine figure wandering among them. It struck him that Miss Willoughby had avoided Bellerton's threatened company by the simple expedient of taking a walk, and he welcomed a flirtation to ease the frustration of his unfulfilling ride.

Cantering up to the trees, he hailed her and she turned, looking surprised and not a little consternated.

"Lovely day for a walk, alone and unattended," he said, glancing pointedly about. "You ought to be more careful, or you might be come upon by some rascally scoundrel."

The lovely blue eyes flashed, and she retorted, "As the country hereabouts seems to be overrun by rascally scoundrels, no amount of care could possibly help me to avoid it."

"Certainly the estimable Muncey would not agree."

"If you mean by that it is somehow unseemly to be walking about on my brother's estate at a respectable hour of the morning," she said archly, "then I can only claim some gross neglect in my upbringing. Muncey is helping in the kitchen and I wished for fresh air, trusting in my governess's teaching that damsels are perfectly safe walking on their own land in the country, even unattended."

He smiled wryly, perceiving that he had not succeeded in making her anxious in the least. He had caught her in a moment of weakness yesterday morning, just after Mr. Findlay had gone, but it seemed she had recovered, and was once more determined not to be intimidated. All the better—Francis did not favor shrinking violets.

"Do you return to the house," he inquired, "or do you intend to get caught in the impending rainstorm?"

She turned to follow his gaze, wrinkling her nose at the sight of the cloud bank rolling in. "Dear me. I had not been attending. In Jamaica, I could have been alerted by the rain trees, but they do not seem to be a species known to this island."

"Rain trees?" Francis looked curiously down at her. "How could they alert you, pray? Do trees speak in Jamaica?"

She laughed, that bright, cheery sound. "They tend to bloom yellow when it is going to rain."

"Excessively useful, I suppose, though in England they would be blooming so constantly that everyone should cease to heed them. Perhaps that is why we have no obliging rain trees here."

"It is very likely." She regarded him inscrutably for a moment then glanced back at the house. "Thank you for the warning. I shall turn back soon. Good morning."

Unwilling to allow her to go so easily, he dismounted and led his horse along beside her. "You really ought to turn back now, unless you feel the scoundrelly rascals in the house outnumber those outside it."

She cast him an impish look from under her bonnet. "As their numbers are about equal, I suppose I may as well cry craven and return."

"It pains me to find you remain unconvinced I am a gentleman," he said with a soulful sigh.

She huffed a laugh. "It may not be so difficult to convince me if you would cease to tease me at every opportunity."

"I've no notion what you are talking of."

She cast him a remonstrative glance. "You are also distressingly untruthful."

"And you are too observant for my taste, Miss Willoughby. But why, if you have seen me for what I am, do you walk with me now? You seem not the least anxious for your virtue."

"We have a chaperon," she said, indicating his horse, which walked placidly at his far side.

"But perhaps Sampson is my confederate."

"Even if he was, I know how you gentlemen prize your horses, and doubt very much you would engage in a seduction while he stood by, wanting his oats." He laughed, and she clasped her hands behind her back. "Did you enjoy your ride?"

"Not a bit. Have you any notion of the hazards awaiting a horseman in the Fens? They are almost as varied and tedious as those in a London ball-room. The approach also seems to be the same: one must only traverse the same roads in the same circuit to avoid being thrown in a ditch."

She looked up, her eyes comically wide. "Dear me. Perhaps I should not like a London Season, after all."

"Perhaps not, and it is a great pity, for I am persuaded you are better equipped to navigate London Society than most young ladies." At her inquiring look, he continued, "At the first sign of danger, you would simply launch into a description of the spiders of Jamaica, and the balance of power would shift instantly to you."

Her scandalized look didn't convince him for a moment as she cried, "But it would never do! Not after I have given my assurance to Nathan that I know how to comport myself in polite society."

"Knowing is one thing, but choosing what one does is an entirely different matter. It is not as though your brother—or anybody for that matter—could stop you."

"A philosophy you no doubt live by, Mr. Mantell."

"Oho! The lady has unbuttoned her foil," he cried, and his horse tossed its head. "Look, even Sampson finds your tactics unscrupulous."

She looked appraisingly at the horse and said, "And I fancied horses to be generally excellent judges of character—but I ought not to be surprised. You have obviously biased him."

"He is simply inured to my ways," Francis replied apologetically. "Do you ride, Miss Willoughby?"

"I do, sir, but it is unlikely that I should do so anytime in the near future."

"And why is that? Do you mistrust the fenland?"

"It is only that I doubt my brother has a suitable mount for me," she said, her tone less lively, "or that he would allow me to use it if he had."

Francis eyed her askance. "He will likely purchase you an animal at some point."

"Perhaps, but something tells me I dare not trust him to provide me with a decent one," she mused, not meeting his eye.

He felt a strange twinge of guilt and said, "Then you might commission Mr. Findlay to find you a suitable mount. Are not you in as good as full possession of your rather large fortune?"

She looked quickly at him, her brows drawing together. "Did Nathan tell you about my fortune? Does he mean to make my situation known generally?" When he merely shrugged, she shook her head. "I suppose it was inevitable. Things like this leak out, even if they are not broadcast. But as it may well increase my chances of making a good match, I must not repine."

"Indeed not, Miss Willoughby," he said. Then, he carelessly added, "You could cut rather a dash if you chose. You might even set up house with that maid of yours, and a paid companion of course. You could easily dictate to society how you will live your life."

"And become a social pariah—or worse, a prey to gentlemen such as you, looking for a lark? Are not unprotected women considered fair game even here in England?"

Her tone was still light, but she averted her eyes again as she spoke. Francis could almost believe she was possessed of some strange Jamaican magic—Obeah, Hayes called it—and could read his mind. He tugged surreptitiously at his cravat, feeling it was a trifle too tight of a sudden.

"Many spinsters live perfectly respectably in their own establishments," he managed.

"I am sure, but I should still far rather have a stable home life, with children and a proper place in society. I am even so romantic as to desire love."

Francis grimaced at the vision of her as the harried wife of a red-faced country squire, and surrounded by squalling brats, her spirit vanquished and her looks quite wasted. But a grumbling from on high suddenly reminded him that rain was imminent, and he cursed under his breath.

"I fear we are about to have a dunking, even without riding into a ditch." Stepping back beside his horse, he held out a hand to her. "Come, Miss Willoughby, you may sit up before me on Sampson."

She looked uncertain, glancing from the advancing storm to the house as though gauging if she could reach it in time.

"Come, Miss Willoughby, do not be missish," he said, gesturing impatiently. "Every young lady dreams of being thrown across a handsome scoundrel's saddle bow. But as that would be excessively uncomfortable, you must settle for riding sideways in the saddle."

She sighed. "Very well."

He helped her up and then swung himself up behind her, sitting pillion. When he placed his arm firmly about her waist, she stiffened.

With a low chuckle, he said in her ear, "I'm afraid I'm obliged to hold you, and you'd do better to hold onto me as well—you see, we must make haste."

Eliza swallowed but nodded, taking care not to look into his countenance as she put her arms tightly about his waist, for she did not doubt he was quite smug. To his credit, he did not openly gloat, but took the park at a gallop, reaching the house just as the heavens opened. He let her down by the kitchen door and she ran inside, hands shielding her head and face so that she did not see the figure coming down the hallway toward her.

Colliding with a solid chest, she uttered a startled apology and looked up into the face of Mr. Bellerton.

"There you are, Miss Willoughby," he said with his crocodile smile. "Out for a bit of fresh air?"

Eliza endeavored to hide her displeasure, as she had signally failed to avoid either one of her tormentors. Pursing her lips, she answered, "Yes, sir. I did not know it was to rain, or I might not have chosen such exercise."

"Didn't know you were one for a bit of exercise," he said, standing directly in her way. "Next time, I'll come with you. There are some very pretty little nooks about the estate I'd like to show you."

She readily believed this was so, but only smiled graciously, saying, "That's very kind. You will pardon me, sir. I must change my wet things."

"Pity it came on to rain." His eyes roamed freely up and down her person and Eliza was glad she had on a thick pelisse. "A dampened muslin can't be good for the constitution, though it can do wonders for a girl's figure."

Pink heated Eliza's cheeks, but her civility did not falter. "You may be assured, sir, that I shall never be so imprudent as to adopt such an extreme in dress, especially in this climate. My Jamaican blood is not suited to it."

"Not to worry, ma'am," he said, his gaze unwavering. "There are many other things your Jamaican blood ought to be suited to."

Eliza lifted her chin. "I believe Muncey is in the kitchen, concocting something to remind us both of Jamaica. Did I tell you she is an Obeah woman? That means, in simple English terms, something of a witch. She is quite skilled, and can do rather dreadful things. I can't wait to see what she has come up with."

She tried again to push past him, but he did not allow it.

"No cause to be frightened, Miss Willoughby," he said, and she could distinctly smell liquor on his breath. "I'll not harm you or Willoughby would have my head. I've simply a wish to get to know you better."

Eliza was about to tell him just what she thought of his daring to impede her, but a step was heard behind in the passage, and she felt the solid presence of another person behind her.

"Did it never occur to you she's no wish to get to know *you* better, Bell?" inquired Mr. Mantell's voice.

Eliza stilled, her composure slipping at being walled in by two large male bodies in the narrow hallway.

Bellerton glowered at him, releasing Eliza. "What's it to you, Mantell?"

As this was precisely what Eliza wished to know, she said nothing, only glancing quickly over her shoulder at Mr. Mantell. His languid smile gave her to wonder if her countenance betrayed the flutter of panic in her breast.

"Merely that I fear you must wait your turn," he said. "Having been so obliging as to ride with me, Miss Willoughby expressed a strong predilection for my company. As a gentleman, I could not refuse her, though scandalized by the notion."

Eliza gasped at this impertinence. "You know very well I did no such thing. If you will pardon me—"

"Now, Miss Willoughby," cut in Mr. Mantell, directing a look of injury to Eliza. "You simply cannot blow hot and cold on a gentleman like that. Perhaps it is acceptable in Jamaica, but here in England, such behavior is simply not the thing."

Eliza glanced quellingly back at him. "Perhaps this is a proper time to take Mr. Wraglain's advice and tell you to go to the devil.

You are quizzing me, and I cannot understand what I have done to deserve it!"

"Nothing, ma'am, absolutely nothing," said Mr. Mantell. "That is the problem. But you ought not to stand here chattering to us when you are soaked through. You'll catch your death, and then whom shall I tease? Come, allow me to escort you to your rooms." Placing a firm hand at the small of her back, he nodded in dismissal to Mr. Bellerton and shouldered past him. "Bell."

As his strides matched her own, Eliza could do no more than allow him to guide her along the passage and to the stairs. But there, she turned to face him.

"Thank you, sir, for your assistance, but I feel certain I am capable of reaching my room without an escort." So saying, she rushed up the stairs and to her rooms, only barely resisting the urge to turn the key in the lock behind her.

Her heart thumping in her chest, she threw herself on the bed, caring not that her pelisse was transferring its dampness to the coverlet. What had Mr. Mantell been about? He had surely saved her from an excessively disagreeable encounter, and for that she was truly grateful, but was that his only intent? After their rather enjoyable dialog during their walk, in the open air where he would not dare molest her, she had begun to feel easy with him. To be sure, in the few days of their acquaintance, he had never actually done more than flirt outrageously with her. But she knew she could not fully trust him. He was careless, selfish, and capricious, and only nominally a gentleman, and she could not depend on her being a lady weighing much at all with him.

Nor with Mr. Bellerton, she feared, though he did claim he wished her no harm. She could only surmise that Nathan had made his views on the sanctity of the Willoughby name—and its connection to her virtue—known to his friends. If this was so, she was infinitely grateful, for Bellerton seemed to be the sort of man her governess had warned her of, and would likely be running tame in the house for the foreseeable future. Even if he meant only to flirt with her, it still was rather worrisome, for she did not trust the power of his restraint, and she could not depend upon Mr. Mantell's—or anyone's—timely intervention.

Muncey entered the room, carrying a small bag that Eliza recognized as the spices they had brought from Jamaica. Attempting a light-hearted tone, she inquired how the experimentation had gone in the kitchens.

"Very well, Miss Eliza. I tink we shall have a tolerable chicken-foot soup tonight." Muncey placed the bag back among Eliza's treasures and turned to look at her, her eyes narrowing when she perceived the drawn and anxious look on her mistress's countenance. Crossing to her in purposeful strides, she held her hand to Eliza's forehead.

"I'm not ill, Muncey—"

"No tanks to dem wet tings! Why are you lying about in dem? Best get changed on the instant."

Eliza obliged, standing and allowing Muncey to help her remove the pelisse and her muslin, though only the skirts had got wet. She did not speak, unwilling to share her concerns with her overly pessimistic maid, but as she pulled on a new morning gown, Muncey eyed her sharply.

"Someting is wrong."

"It's nothing, Muncey. I am only tired from my walk."

Muncey clicked her tongue. "You never tire before noon! Someting has happened. Now, out wid it."

Eliza closed her eyes and sighed. "It was only another uncomfortable scene with Mr. Bellerton."

"He try to seduce you!" cried Muncey, fire in her eyes.

"No! No, nothing like that. He was simply rude, and would not allow me to pass him in the back passage. But Mr. Mantell came—"

Muncey gasped. "Dey catch yuh in de passage? Oh, mi break dem deh necks—mi set Obeah on dem deh—wheh de parrot beak—mi get a spell, fix dem deh good good."

"Muncey!" cried Eliza, recognizing in the maid's slip into Patois the extremity of her agitation. "There will be no need for Obeah. Mr. Mantell defended me—that is, he put Mr. Bellerton in his place."

The maid grunted, looking unconvinced. "Mi tell yuh nah come."

Eliza gave a forlorn smile. "But I had to come, and now I must make do. And I have you to help me. Really, it was not so bad. I will simply take care never to be alone in the passage again."

The maid regarded her mistress in sympathetic frustration. Then she stood briskly, brushing off her skirts. "Stay in bed, Miss Eliza. I will bring you a tray for dinner, and say you are sick from de cold and rain." As she opened the door, she said with a grim smile, "I tink I will add someting special to de chicken-foot soup, just for de gentlemen tonight."

Chapter 14

MUNCEY BROUGHT ELIZA a tray in the morning as well, reporting that the gentlemen had been so amazed by the chicken-foot soup that none could speak for several minutes. They had also drunk copious amounts of water and wine in a vain attempt to douse the fire of the bonney peppers Muncey had used liberally to flavor the soup. In a rather self-satisfied tone, the maid suggested her mistress wait upstairs, as the gentlemen had announced their intention of going out shooting right after breakfast.

When the men had gone away, Eliza dressed and went down to the library, assured to have it to herself. She had been reading an exceedingly interesting book on local fishing for some time when the bell rang at the front door to the house. She heard Clayton's jaunty step across the hall and the door opening, then a murmur of voices. Clayton soon opened the library door and announced, "Miss Draffin to see you, ma'am."

Eliza's visitor—resplendent in a primrose muslin gown sprigged with pink roses and with several flounces, two strings of beads about her neck, and a straw and ribbon confection on her head—glided into the room, glancing about as though certain someone else were to be found lurking there. Eliza went to her, hand outstretched.

"Miss Draffin! What a lovely surprise. How do you do?"

Miss Draffin took her hand, more firmly today than the day before yesterday. "I am very well, thank you. How delightful that you are receiving. I declare, I was so worried when I set out from Draffinstoke that you would not see me—that is, that you would not be home to visitors."

"Dear me, Miss Draffin, what could give you such a notion of me?" inquired Eliza, somewhat chastened. "I hope I was not uncivil at our last visit."

Her visitor lifted a shoulder. "Oh, no. Only, that is how Mr. Willoughby is. Upon our first visit, he was all affability, even offering to show me some paintings in the gallery, and stealing a ki—" She glanced quickly at Eliza, coloring. "That is, he was all that was friendly and obliging. But when next we came, he was out, and ever after that, it seemed. The only way to see him was to lie in wait for him in the lane—" Again she glanced at Eliza, then turned her face away.

Eliza, smiling to herself, said, "It is very bad of him, and I must apologize in his stead. Personally, I am of the opinion that one must always start out as one intends to carry on."

"Certainly, Miss Willoughby," said Miss Draffin, gazing at her in relief. "That is precisely my feeling. Indeed, once I had seen Mr. Willoughby, I determined to have him, and that is how I have gone on!"

Eliza hid her amusement at this artlessness in a cough. "I wonder, had you not heard of my brother before meeting him?"

"Oh, yes!" cried Miss Draffin. "When Papa bought his land—and very inexpensively, too, you must know, being in the Fens—Mama made it her business to investigate all the landed families in the area. She thought it prudent to discover the eligibility of the bachelors hereabouts, since I'd be out by the time Draffinstoke was built. Almost as soon as we had taken possession, she began her visits. I thought the other gentlemen very amiable, but when we visited Penhurst, I saw that Mr. Willoughby was beyond compare my favorite!"

"How fascinating," replied Eliza, truly amazed and not a little curious how her brother behaved himself in company. "May I inquire what it is you like best about him?"

"Oh, he is ever so handsome. And he can be very pleasing, when he is alone with one."

"Very true," said Eliza, though she had never seen it. Nathan had worn a scowl nearly all the time she had known him. On the rare occasions his friends had made him smile or laugh, it had still been jeering in nature. Still, she was certain he would be rendered more handsome with a pleasing manner, and wondered if it was only the guarantee of Miss Draffin's kisses that made him capable of assuming such.

Miss Draffin seemed to be meditating on the same lines. "Willoughby has been cross with me, of course, but only when I speak of marriage. And he is cross with Mama at all times."

"I am quite ashamed of him," said Eliza, no longer quite so amused. "I believe I comprehend the matter perfectly. Gentlemen can be excessively fickle, and require a vast amount of cosseting to put them in better frame. I do wonder, however, if you have hardly been able to find him at home when you call, how have you discovered so much about his character?"

"Oh, it is simple," answered Miss Draffin readily. "After I had met him in the lane a few times, he took to sending me little notes by the groom, asking to meet at the copse near the dike. I've met him there ever so many times."

And doubtless allowed him ever so many kisses, thought Eliza. Out loud, she inquired, "Does your mama sanction these meetings?"

Miss Draffin reached a hand to her cheek, which had become quite pink again. "No, she had no notion of them. Oh, do not think me undutiful, for it was only for her own good! She made such a poor impression on him at our first meeting that, he told me since, he would rather be in Bedlam than be in the same room with her again. She would be so mortified to know it. The only course was to meet with him alone, for I could not face the prospect of never seeing him again! But it was to no avail."

"What do you mean?"

Her visitor sighed. "It was the most unfortunate thing, Miss Willoughby. After nearly six months of our meeting in secret, Mama stumbled upon us, and though I assured her we had only just kissed, she went on a rampage, calling him a rake and a scoundrel and claiming that he had forced himself upon me. I instantly told her it was nothing like that, and I had gone willingly to meet him, but she flew even higher into the boughs, saying I was a jade and a wanton to meet him clandestinely. He rode away directly, but she stormed here to demand that he marry me! I was so terribly mortified, for I knew he would only give her one of his set-downs—if he saw her at all. And he did not, but set that impertinent butler of his to bar her entry, until at last he went away and Mama could not discover where."

She reached into her reticule and pulled out a handkerchief, blowing her pert little nose into it and sighing. "I have not seen him in over a month, and I do miss him so."

Eliza was no experienced Society lady, being out only two years herself, but she knew enough to feel certain that Miss Draffin was flirting with danger. The poor naive girl did not mean to, of course, being one whose grasp of the moral expectations of a lady was apparently wanting. Eliza expected it was bewildering to be caught in the current of upward mobility.

She also knew too well that, regrettably, many gentlemen believed that only young ladies of their own station merited respect. Indeed, if it had not been Nathan arranging these clandestine meetings, she would believe Miss Draffin headed for certain ruin. But though he had not treated Eliza very kindly, and his friends' characters tended toward the ungentlemanly, he did seem to value virtue in a female.

Still, she felt responsible to warn Miss Draffin, and said kindly, "Perhaps it is for the better that you have been separated, Miss Draffin. I cannot help but feel it was improper of him to meet you so many times unchaperoned."

"But it was the only way!"

"Perhaps, but do not you think it unwise to encourage the advances of a gentleman who is at violent odds with your mama? He could not seriously consider marriage with one whose parent so terribly irritates him. Even were you to be married, he would likely forbid her the house, and she would be lost to you. There simply does not seem to be a happy issue in store for you with my brother."

Miss Draffin sat wide-eyed for some moments, digesting this. Then she sniffed and, blinking back tears, wailed, "But I love him so, Miss Willoughby! There is not another man in the world with whom I wish to be. Oh, what am I to do?"

Eliza, stunned by this excess of emotion, instantly changed her seat for one beside her visitor, putting an arm about the girl's shaking shoulders and patting her hand. "My dear, I had no notion your sentiments were so strong. Indeed, I did not believe you could love him when he is so odiously uncivil to your mama, and even to you!"

"But he is n-not uncivil to m-me, Miss Willoughb-by," she hiccupped, dabbing at her eyes with the now sodden handkerchief. She took a deep breath and continued, "At least, he was not. He confided all s-sorts of things to me, about dikes and flooding and windm-mills, and hunting and larks and—it is all so excessively interesting. I could listen to him talk all day, and never find it tiresome. And when he took me in his arms—Oh! It was entirely delicious. I cannot imagine feeling so with anyone else."

Murmuring something soothing, Eliza gazed into space, pondering the inexplicability of human attraction. She was as ready as the next fond sibling to consider her brother capable of exciting a maiden's admiration, but Nathan had not yet merited such fondness. She could not, in sincerity, recommend him to Miss Draffin as a desirable husband, at least as yet. But Miss Draffin seemed truly to have formed an attachment which, after six months' duration, could not be easily disregarded, and ought to be given due consideration.

Coming to a resolution, Eliza said bracingly, "Then you must no longer be parted. Should you like to spend the day with me, Miss Draffin? Nathan cannot possibly avoid you if you are hours together in the same house."

"You are so very wise, Miss Willoughby!" said her visitor, her gaze filled with admiration. "And so agreeable. Mama said I should have to work on you to become my friend, but I see she was mistaken. I feel that we are friends already!"

Eliza bit her lip against a smile at this artless confession. "Then I insist that you call me Eliza."

Miss Draffin went pink, but this time with pleasure. "Certainly, Eliza! But only if you will call me Sophy. Oh, I am certain I shall like being your sister!"

Smiling despite her doubts, Eliza gave her newfound friend one last squeeze. She did not tell Sophy that she had a deeper motive for making her a friend. It had occurred to Eliza that, just as keeping Miss Draffin by her side would prevent Nathan from making improper advances upon the naïve young girl, so would having another lady in the house keep Mr. Bellerton and Mr. Mantell from imposing upon Eliza. As they had only a few more days before they intended to remove to Newmarket, it seemed a perfect arrangement, and if it succeeded in strengthening Nathan's attachment to her friend, all the better.

She took Sophy up to her room so that she could put off her pelisse and hat, introducing her to Muncey and expressing her intention of having her new friend to stay the afternoon. Muncey acknowledged this with her customary pessimism and followed her mistress and her visitor to the drawing room. Ringing the bell, Eliza then offered Sophy her choice of embroidery basket or book to occupy her while Eliza joined Muncey in mending.

After a very short time Clayton entered in all his buoyancy, inquiring what he could do for the ladies.

"Miss Draffin is staying the day, Clayton," said Eliza brightly. "Would you please send a note to Draffinstoke Manor informing her mother, and instruct the messenger to bring back her workbasket?"

Clayton stilled his rocking on the balls of his feet, gazing with uncertainty upon his mistress. "Staying the day, ma'am? 'Ave you spoken to Mr. Willoughby, perchance? May very well be 'e has something to say on it, that's best said in private."

Eliza bit her lip, but only against her ready humor. "Nathan will find out in good time, Clayton. But thank you for the warning. You may send the message—I will bear any blame."

"Not if I've anything to do with it, Miss Willoughby," the butler said, with a defiant set to his chin. "But I thought as to warn you, on the chance 'e takes it into 'is 'ead to be disagreeable when I'm out of earshot. I own I find it mighty pleasant to see you with another lady, and so contented, and Mr. Willoughby can try to sack me for saying so."

As Eliza fancied he knew very well his position was secure, Miss Draffin ensconced in the drawing room or no, she thanked him with real sincerity. He bowed as only he could and with a charming smile to Muncey, who merely glanced up momentarily in acknowledgment, he went away.

Not an hour later Sophy's workbasket arrived, and with it Mr. Bellerton. He strode into the room with his crocodile smile and rubbed his hands together.

"Now here's a lovely sight," he said, eying the ladies at their work. "Not one, but two fine ladies to feast my eyes on."

"Then it's true," came a grumble from the door, and Nathan precipitated himself into the room.

He stopped short, glancing from Eliza to Sophy, who started up in hopeful delight. His irritation seemed to waver at this, and after a moment, he came forward, taking her hand and bowing in stiff formality. Her delight dimmed somewhat, but revived when he took a seat beside her in a chair.

"Pardon my surprise, Miss Draffin," he said, his countenance unyielding. "I had not thought to see you here."

"No," she said apologetically. "I fancy Clayton forgot your instructions when he let me in. But you mustn't be angry, for I did ask to see Miss Willoughby."

Nathan cast Eliza a glare, but she merely smiled and said, "It has been so lovely to entertain callers! It is not entirely comfortable to come to a new place, knowing one will be a stranger and without friends. But now, after only two visits, I am beginning to feel quite at home."

"As you ought, Miss Willoughby," said Bellerton, seating himself on her opposite side. "A lady is never so charming as when she is with her friends, especially when they are such pretty things, eh, Willoughby?"

Sophy colored, and Nathan's grimace looked to Eliza to hold something of a warning for Bellerton. But Bellerton merely grinned, sitting back in his chair with his long legs stretched out before him.

"You have been gone such a long time, Willoughby," said Sophy. "May I inquire as to your whereabouts?"

"Went to Mantell's hunting lodge. Leicestershire. Fine country."

"Oh, yes, I recollect," she said, sitting almost at attention, her wide blue gaze locked on his face. "Tell me, how was the hunt?"

He managed a smile, though it seemed more of a sneer to Eliza. "Bellerton got himself stuck in a hedge. Jobbed at his horse's mouth and got thrown clear over its head. You should have seen it, Miss Draffin. Flew right through the air like a shuttlecock."

She clapped her hands. "I should have liked to have been there. I enjoy Shuttlecock."

Bellerton's enjoyment had vanished, replaced with a grimace as surly as Nathan's had been. But after a moment, he turned to Eliza with a look of piteous courage, saying, "Injured my arm, Miss Willoughby. Had to be carried home, and every jolt of the carriage hurt like h—that is, hurt amazingly. But not a word did I say, not a moan nor groan passed my lips. You should have been there, ma'am. You'd have admired my fortitude."

"I'm sure you were very brave, sir," said Eliza kindly.

He bent toward her, over the arm of his chair. "If I had been here, you could have nursed me, rather than that crone Mantell has for housekeeper."

Eliza smiled weakly, but merely turned to Sophy. "Do you ride, Miss Draffin? I have decided to buy myself a mount. I had a pony at Willow Great House, but he was too old to bring on the ship."

"How very sad," said Sophy, truly moved. "I remember my pony, who had to go with the knacker man when I was fifteen. I thought I'd cry my eyes out. He had been with me twelve years in Southampton, and another three after we removed to London. I have a lovely, sweet mare now, however, who carries me nearly as quietly."

"I believe I should like something a bit more dashing," said Eliza, directing her impish look at Nathan. "Mr. Mantell suggested I commission Mr. Findlay to find a suitable mount for me in London. With your leave, of course."

Nathan nodded curtly. "Of course. You may have whatever you wish. It's your money."

"Do you have money, Eliza?" inquired Sophy. "That is ever so nice. I do not know how it is to be forever at low-tide, but Willoughby assures me it is dreadfully uncomfortable."

"Should you like to go to the gallery, Miss Draffin?" inquired Nathan, jumping to his feet.

She smiled brilliantly, putting her hand in his with alacrity. "Oh, I should like it above all things, Willoughby!"

Before Eliza could blink, they had quitted the room, and Bellerton sat staring at her.

"They make a fine couple," he said, tapping his fingers on the arm of his chair. "Makes one wish one had a sweetheart."

"I own, I cannot find I am envious of Miss Draffin," replied Eliza matter-of-factly. "Nathan is an eligible match, but not the kindest or most generous of persons."

Bellerton leant forward, elbows on knees. "Miss Draffin don't seem to mind. She's the sort who likes a kiss and a cuddle, and don't press for more."

"Mrs. Draffin, however, does mind," said Eliza firmly, "as would any sensible female. Indeed, I am disappointed that Nathan should take such advantage of Miss Draffin's naivete."

He was gazing intently at her—or, more precisely, at her lips. Muncey, making her presence known with a loud clearing of her throat, drew Bellerton's annoyed gaze. But though she gave him an excessively evil eye, he merely resumed his intent scrutiny of Eliza.

"It don't signify if her mama don't hear of it. What's a little kiss amongst friends?"

Abruptly gathering her sewing things into the basket, Eliza said crisply, "It is a significant thing, I assure you, sir, and not to be taken lightly."

But Bellerton only murmured, "Come now, you must be curious."

"Pardon me, sir, but I believe I will go to the gallery with Sophy and Nathan." Eliza stood, making for the door.

Before she had taken three steps, however, and before Muncey could even stand, he had jumped up after her, and had taken her roughly into his arms.

Chapter 15

MUNCEY THEN EXHIBITED the agility and strength for which she had been known at Willow Great House, leaping the sofa in a single bound and swinging her workbag at Bellerton's head in one swift and powerful motion. Eliza, who had been straining her head away from his as she kicked at his shins, avoided the blow, but Bellerton's grasp was only partially released in his surprise as he lost his footing and fell to the floor. Eliza, still tangled somewhat in his arms, fell with him, only barely missing the side table that broke his fall—or rather, was broken by his fall.

He lay amongst the wreckage, stunned long enough for Eliza to disentangle herself and to stand, with Muncey hovering about her and cursing in strong Patois. When Bellerton sat up, the ladies had turned to make a hasty exit, but at that moment the door flew open and Clayton strode in. His keen blue eyes took in the scene before him and he was on Bellerton in a flash, taking him by the collar and hoisting him up.

"Now, then, Mr. Bellerton," he said in a dangerously conversational tone, "I believe you've been misbehaving, and that I can't allow. You know full well Mr. Willoughby's got no patience with the furniture getting broke, seeing as it'll cost 'im more of the ready 'e don't have. And you've gone and put our fine ladies in a mither, when they only wished to see to their stitchery in peace. But I suppose Mr. Willoughby took that Miss Draffin off to the gallery again, more's the pity. 'E won't be 'ere to chide you, but perhaps I'll see my way to brushing this all under the rug, so to speak. The ladies will excuse you now to clean yourself up, for they oughtn't to be made to see a man with 'is face broken."

Bellerton, a trifle wild-eyed at this rough-and-ready treatment—which until then had been reserved only for uninvited tradesmen and other debt-collectors on the doorstep—gasped out, "My face ain't broken!"

"Not yet," murmured Clayton as softly as a man in a barely controlled rage could do. "Only give me cause to lose my temper, sir, and it'll be as broken as an old cook pot, quicker than you can wink."

Hauling his captive to the door, Clayton paused to incline his head to Eliza and Muncey. "Pardon me, ladies, as I assist Mr. Bellerton to 'is room. 'E's suddenly indisposed, and shall not be seeing you till dinnertime at least."

They watched them go, and only when Muncey had hurried to close the door behind them did Eliza collapse onto the nearest chair. Muncey hastened back to her side, clicking her tongue and speaking in agitated accents.

"Dis all Willoughby's doing, Miss Eliza. Him nah should 'a keep dat Bellerton deh heah, to make free wid yuh. Mi set Obeah on him now."

"I own to being quite tempted to allow you to, my dear," said Eliza, somewhat hazily. She put a hand to her forehead. "It was rather stupid of me to trust to his sense of honor, I now perceive. But I must be excused, for I could not believe that he would actually attempt to accost me, and in full view of my chaperon!"

Muncey answered only with more muttered curses, gently inspecting her mistress's head and arms for any signs of injury.

"I am unhurt, dear," said Eliza, smiling weakly. "Only shaken. Thank you for your prompt response to my distress. If not for you—"

"Bah!" replied Muncey, standing and beginning to pace. "Lucky Mr. Clayton take care of him. Dat Bellerton tink hard before he touch you again."

Eliza sat up, frowning. "Perhaps we should go to London."

"If only we could!" Muncey gestured emphatically with her hand. "We have no way to get dere ourselves. You must write Mr. Findlay. He will come take us away."

"I will, certainly," said Eliza. "But then again, the gentlemen will be gone to Newmarket the day after tomorrow. Perhaps then we will be safe."

"Dey will not stay away." Muncey shook her head, pressing her lips into a tight line. "Dey are too great friends to Willoughby and will come back again and again."

"Very well, I shall write to Mr. Findlay." Eliza stood, fatigued by the events of the morning. "But later. I do believe I shall lie down upon the bed, though how I shall close my eyes, I do not know. I'll not soon forget the way Clayton hoisted Bellerton up like a pile of old blankets. Bellerton is the taller of the two, and yet he seemed to shrink. A satisfying memory to treasure against the times he is impertinent."

"He is no match for Mr. Clayton, sure enough," said Muncey with a chuckle. "Dat butler has a way about him."

"He certainly is charming," said Eliza, taking her arm with a know-ing grin.

Muncey cast her a quelling look. "I never said so."

But the corners of her mouth tugged upward as she walked to the door and up to their rooms. Tucking her mistress up in bed, she went to make some chamomile tea in the kitchens, taking care to lock the door behind her and pocket the key.

Eliza did sleep, and woke some hours later to the sound of a key grating in the lock. The door opened, revealing Clayton carrying a tray with tea and a hot scone. Bowing his head to her, he carried the tray into the room and set it on the dressing table. Muncey was right behind him, wearing a look somewhere between consternation and pleasure.

"It's good to see you slept, ma'am," said the butler, "as I feared you'd be suffering from nerves the remainder of the day. But I know that was quite foolish, for you've never been the sort of lady to swoon or 'ave the vapors. Indeed, I congratulate you on your cool 'ead this afternoon, when you'd ample cause to faint dead away, or drum your 'eels on the carpet. I only wish I knew what 'appened to make the fellow fall down, for it does make a body curious."

Eliza could not but smile, flicking a glance at her maid. Putting a hand to the side of her mouth, she whispered loudly, "Muncey knocked him down." In a more normal tone, she added, "She has always been quite protective. She once took a stick to a giant iguana—that is a lizard the size of a large child—when it was frightening some children on the beach. This time, however, she used her workbag as a weapon, and to good effect."

"Is that a fact?" The blue eyes that turned to Muncey were bright with more than admiration. "I'd give a year's wages to 'ave seen it, ma'am. A flush 'it, to be sure, and knocked 'im clean off 'is feet. I've seen plenty of wisty castors in my day, but that I'd like to 'ave seen."

Muncey blushed, struggling to remain on her dignity. "Dat shows you I could have carried de tray myself. It's not'ing to me."

"Ah, but the wages go to the victor," replied Clayton, grinning. "You've earned a bit of rest after so brave a display of loyalty to your mistress. I'm right proud to bear your burden, ma'am, and thank you for allowing it."

"Nonsense," muttered Muncey, blushing more deeply in her delight.

Clayton, gazing some moments more upon the object of his admiration, turned at last to Eliza. "But I've another motive for insisting I accompany Miss Muncey up to see you, Miss Willoughby, and that's to beg you not to 'ide away in your rooms today, nor any other day. Now, I've told Miss Muncey I know you've plenty of spirit, for only a looby could take you for a die-away miss. But I'd not 'ave you fear you'll be troubled more by a certain gentleman, for I've put a flea in 'is ear, and I've a strong notion 'e'd rather poke out 'is own eye than give me another cause to dislike 'im."

"You're very kind," said Eliza, biting her lip. "I had wondered whether it might be best if I kept to my rooms, at least until the gentlemen remove to Newmarket in a day or two. However, I cannot like to be so easily intimidated."

"Aye, and that you're not, Miss Willoughby," said Clayton. "I've no doubt your presence in the dining room tonight would be the best reminder of that. And as I've reason to believe at least 'alf of the gentlemen live up to the name—and I'll be 'overing about all dinner time—you can 'ave no fear of a distressing recurrence."

"Very well," said Eliza. "With such able support, I believe I have no cause to shrink."

Evidently pleased, Clayton nodded, dusting his hands together. "Then I'll be seeing you at dinner, Miss Willoughby."

Eliza started in sudden recollection. "Dear me, Clayton, what has become of Miss Draffin? I fear I forgot all about her in the hubbub earlier. She must think me a very strange sort of hostess."

"I'll wager she's not given you another thought, ma'am," said Clayton, a wry light in his eyes. "Mr. Willoughby handed her into her carriage not an hour since, and very merrily did she go. Seeing as how she had lost herself in the gallery with him for quite an hour before that, it's safe to imagine she's more than satisfied with her visit today."

"Oh dear." Eliza sighed, feeling that her resolution to keep Miss Draffin and herself safe this afternoon had gone terribly poorly. "Well, if she was happy when she went away, that, at least, was well-done." Oh, if only Nathan would be kind to poor Sophy!

Clayton went away and Muncey helped Eliza dress for dinner, telling her she would be near at hand if any of the gentlemen stepped out of line again, and muttering dire imprecations if they did. Fortified by this show of support, and by the clear memory of Mr. Bellerton's wild eyes as Clayton told him his face could easily be broken, Eliza went down to the saloon in good spirits.

Meanwhile, Francis, George, and Charles, who had stayed out shooting into the afternoon, had come back in time to witness Willoughby handing a pretty young lady into a carriage. Will having vanished by the time they had come in from the stables, their curiosity must wait until they met for dinner. But it was only the more piqued upon arriving in the saloon, for they perceived Bellerton standing in stony silence at the window, while Willoughby leaned against the mantlepiece, gazing gloomily into the fire. The restrained tone instantly alerted the others that something of significance had occurred during their absence, and they inquired of Willoughby what was toward.

He pursed his lips. "Bell thought to steal himself a kiss of my dear sister, despite my precise instructions not to touch her, but that virago of a lady's maid attacked him and knocked him down. Broke one of the tables to bits, too."

There was a moment of silence as the gentlemen digested this. Then Francis, unable to restrain his delight, said, "Is it too much to hope it was by breaking the table over his head she knocked him down?"

Charles, apparently recovered from his shock, whistled. "Bell, knocked down by a lady's maid? Oh why, by all that's holy, did we stay out today of all days?"

"Fiery tempers, these West Indians," remarked George. "Best not test them."

"That's something they've in common with Mancunians, by all appearances," said Willoughby in a tone of disgust.

Francis quirked an expectant eyebrow. "I sense that Clayton had something to say in the matter."

"Bell would have it I've nurtured a snake in my bosom," replied Willoughby. "Clayton stormed in, summed up what had happened in an instant, and hauled Bell away, with a marked threat to break his face if anything else untoward happens. Useful scoundrel."

Bellerton grunted from the window. "Ought to sack him."

"No one to keep the duns away, if he did," said George.

Willoughby snorted. "I might just, however. He allowed Miss Draffin in to visit again with Eliza, and what does she do? She invites the chit for the day! I never was so incensed in my life."

Francis, eying him askance, said, "One would not have guessed it as you handed the chit, smiling, into the carriage."

"Because I am not a man to spurn an opportunity," said Willoughby, the hint of a smile at the corners of his mouth. "I had occasion to take her to view the paintings in the gallery, and we were detained there alone some time."

Charles huffed in disbelief, but Francis merely shook his head. "Dangerous doings, old boy. For one anxious to avoid parson's mouse-trap, you're distressingly careless."

"They're Cits," replied Willoughby disdainfully. "Mushrooms. I'll never join my name with theirs."

Eliza entered then, and the group at the fire watched intently to see how she would act. To Francis's eyes, she seemed unchanged, though a trifle paler than usual. The gold of her dress accented her coloring beautifully, and her blue eyes sparkled with determination. She greeted them pleasantly, but before Francis could so much as attempt to elicit a blush to brighten her cheeks, Clayton announced dinner.

The meal passed pleasantly enough, with Willoughby in better spirits than he had been all week and Charles and Francis scarcely containing their glee. Eliza behaved with her usual cheerful humor, but Bellerton was sulky as a bear. He ate his food in simmering silence, casting pointed glares at Clayton whenever he came near the table to serve them, and consuming several glasses of wine. At last, Eliza rose to retire to the drawing room, and when the door closed behind her, all the gentlemen turned their gazes to Bellerton.

Charles began chuckling first, followed by Francis, and then Willoughby, with George joining in at the last. Their chuckles gave way to laughter, then to guffaws that rang in the dining room for some minutes. When they had laughed their fill at their unfortunate friend, they wiped streaming eyes with handkerchiefs and passed the port around.

"A toast to the most ham-handed lover in Lincolnshire," said Charles, raising his glass.

Francis joined him. "I am in your debt, Bell. Doubtless Miss Willoughby will now turn to me for comfort."

Bellerton, who had suffered their laughter with only the grinding of his teeth, slammed his glass to the table. "She'll have me sooner than you, Mantell—my life on it!"

"Not if Muncey and Clayton have aught to do with it," supplied George.

Bellerton jumped to his feet. "They're nothing but meddling idiots!"

Charles, grinning, remarked, "I believe Clayton's fives are more than nothing."

"Not enough," retorted Bellerton, but he slumped into his chair. "It was just to be a kiss. Pretty girl like that ought to be pleased a gentleman admires her."

Highly amused, Francis set his glass down. "If you truly believe Miss Willoughby will simply fall into your arms because you admire her, you're a greater cod's head than I took you for. Did you learn nothing today? Even without Muncey and Clayton to protect her, she's a million miles from the sort of woman who would take *you* up." He tutted, picking up his glass again. "Your delusions will be your downfall, Bell, mark me."

Bellerton grabbed up his glass, ready to throw it, but Willoughby forestalled him, saying, "Stow it, Bell. I'll not have my crystal wasted on Mantell's sorry head. If your admiration of my sister is in earnest, you'll have your chance with her, never fear."

All eyes turned to him as Bellerton set the glass back on the table, looking pugnacious. "I'm dead earnest."

Willoughby smiled smugly. "Let's go play billiards, Bell. A good game will clear your head."

With that, he stood, pulling Bellerton up by the arm and leading him from the room. The others exchanged looks, and Charles silently placed his glass on the table.

"I don't like the sound of that," he said, his gaiety vanished.

George nodded, pouring another glass for himself. "Sounds ominous, to be sure. Bell's drunk as a lord."

"Really, Francis," pursued Charles, "you know Willoughby. He don't like his sister above half. What would he let Bell do to her?"

Francis shrugged, tossing off his drink. "Nothing he hasn't already attempted, and you heard how that ended. Miss Willoughby is safe enough."

"Not if Bell fixes Muncey and Clayton," said George.

Charles cast Francis a meaningful look.

"It doesn't signify," replied Francis, standing. "He could not do it. You have taken this far too seriously, Charles. Now, stop being a bore and come along to the drawing room. I wish to press my advantage with the fair Miss Willoughby."

They all rose to go, George ambling ahead, but Charles grasped Francis's arm, detaining him in the dining room.

"I believe this is more serious than you think," he said in an urgent undertone. "What if Will were to allow Bell to force himself upon Miss Willoughby?"

Francis paused, but said only, "Are you forgetting the Willoughby pride? Her virtue is worth too much for Will to sacrifice it to a gudgeon like Bell."

"He has something in his mind, Francis, and it cannot bode well for Miss Willoughby, I am persuaded!"

"If you are so concerned, my dear Charles, by all means, place yourself at her service. You might become her watch dog."

"I must leave tomorrow!" Charles scowled, shaking his head. "My mother has written twice now, urging my return to Somersetshire. I've promised myself to them in two days and must not fail. But I fear that Miss Willoughby is in some danger. I may yet be wrong, but—Give me your word, Francis—with what little honor is in you, promise me you will watch over her."

Francis looked away, unable to meet so earnest a gaze. "What is she to you, Charles? I vow you seem as though you have fallen in love with the girl."

"It's not that," said Charles, dropping his hand. "It's common decency! I have sisters, dash it, and I wouldn't wish for them to be in Miss Willoughby's situation. Come, Francis, even you would look after Clara were she so circumstanced."

Francis laughed, a somewhat forced sound. "Clara would either eat Bell alive or shoot him. She requires no protection."

"But if she found herself in a situation where she could not protect herself, would you not feel it your duty to do so?"

"Miss Willoughby is not my sister."

"No, but her brother has failed her, and she has no father to protect her." Charles gazed at Francis, his brow furrowing. "I never imagined you would act the hero, to be sure, but neither did I believe you a coward."

At that, Francis's gaze flicked to his and held for some moments. Then he looked away, running a hand through his dark locks. "It often amazes me we are friends. Very well, Galahad. I shall do my possible to thwart Bell in his little campaign. I have already done so, twice—it should not be difficult to do it again. It may even be amusing."

Charles's shoulders relaxed, and he nodded. "You go to Newmarket soon enough. She will be safe then."

"Unless she is as troublesome on her own as she is with four gentlemen in the house," replied Francis, his lips quirking in a wry smile.

Chapter 16

CHARLES WAS GONE with the first light of day, and Francis, wondering bemusedly that he had actually agreed to be some sort of guardian to Miss Willoughby, thought he might as well seek her out. He found her in the library, but rather than Muncey as her companion, she was attended only by Bellerton. This discovery gave him nearly as much annoyance as it seemed to give her, for though he delighted in vexing Bellerton, he was now obliged to do so.

"See here, Miss Willoughby," he remarked, making his presence known, "I take exception to your varying principles. When last I came upon you in the library, your dear Muncey was here to deter me in my nefarious purposes. But here you are alone with Bellerton! I cannot accept this as fair."

Her usual confidence was strained at best, and he felt a strange twinge in his chest as she turned to him in obvious relief. "Mr.

Mantell! I do not know how to account for it. My dear Muncey went for my shawl some ten minutes ago, and has not returned."

His gaze flicked to Bellerton. "Did you suggest she go? Such a simple expedient—I commend you, Bell. I wouldn't have conceived of our clever Miss Willoughby falling for it."

"I did not!" cried Eliza. "That is, he was not here. But the window had been left open during the night, and the room was very cold. I rang for a fire but as you can see, it is not much help, so Muncey went for my shawl."

Glancing at the pathetic little flame on the hearth, Francis thought he would sack the maid who built so puny a thing—unless she had been ordered to do so. The thought gave him pause, and he glanced again at Bellerton, who stood glaring at him in much the same manner as he had the night before. He had the uncomfortable feeling that Charles had been right, and that Miss Willoughby was in some danger, for it seemed that Willoughby was, indeed, in collusion with Bellerton. Just what good that would do Willoughby, he could not tell—nor could he tell what good it would do himself to intervene. But as he looked into Miss Willoughby's pleading blue eyes, he felt something, deep within him, stirring.

Bowing gracefully to her, he said, "Will you sit with me, ma'am? I came searching for you, after all. I had hoped, of course, to find you with Miss Muncey, for I have never been so entertained in my life than when I scandalized her by flirting outrageously with you. Bell is far less easily scandalized—a shocking truth, I know—but I suppose he will have to do."

Bellerton, at last moved to action, stepped forward. "Take yourself off, Mantell. Miss Willoughby is sitting with me."

Francis languidly looked him up and down, then Miss Willoughby.

"You neither of you seem to be sitting. Is this a new fashion? Are we now to stand up to dinner and sit down to dance?"

Bellerton became almost irate. "Miss Willoughby don't wish to hear any more of your rattling on!" he growled, stepping between them.

Miss Willoughby straightened. "Indeed, I do not. I beg your pardon, gentlemen, but I must go see what is keeping Muncey." She darted around them and was gone.

Francis, satisfied she had got away, gazed imperturbably at Bellerton, a maddening smile upon his lips. He considered there *was* a calculable benefit to himself in rescuing Miss Willoughby from Bellerton's advances in the pleasure of thwarting him so neatly.

With something like a roar, Bellerton suddenly pulled back his fist and plunged it toward Francis's face. Fully anticipating the blow, Francis slipped to the side, coming in with a hook to Bellerton's ribs. The man grunted, returning a hook that Francis blocked with his bent arm, then followed up with a jab to Bellerton's face. Bellerton fell back, tripping over a short table and landing halfway on the sofa to the side.

Shaking out his smarting fist, Francis grinned down at his adversary. "I believe that's my point—again." And he strode from the room, believing that if watching over Miss Willoughby was this entertaining, he would not regret his promise.

But some time later, Willoughby came upon him in his room as he read a letter from his land agent. He looked up, finding his friend scowling as usual.

"I'll thank you to leave Bell to his business, Mantell," said Willoughby.

Francis regarded him. "I'm happy to do so, Will. Has he given a complaint?"

"You darkened his daylights this morning. That's complaint enough."

Francis huffed, returning to his letter. "He never was much for a mill."

Willoughby came forward, twitching the letter from Francis's hands and tossing it on the desk. "I gave him my leave to court Eliza. Stay out of his way."

Gazing intently at Willoughby, Francis wondered vaguely why he felt disgust. "It's not very sporting of you, Will. She does not seem to like him in the least."

"It doesn't matter what Eliza likes," snapped Willoughby. "Bell will give me half the money when he marries her. I'll get my due, and she'll be off my hands. The deal is made, now keep out of it."

Francis stood slowly, rising to his full height, which was only slightly taller than Willoughby. He gazed directly into his eyes and said, "I'm afraid I can't do that, Will. You see, I've made a deal as well. I've challenged Bell to a friendly competition for your amiable sister's attentions."

"That deal is off," declared Willoughby with a swipe of his hand. "Bell wants her for his wife, not just for a flirt. You'd best leave off."

Francis crossed his arms, looking away. "I really cannot. You see, I've been terribly busy the past few hours, doing all sorts of honorable things. Just last night I promised Wraglain I'd look after Miss Willoughby."

"Wraglain?" cried Will. "What does Wraglain have to say to anything, pray?"

"He seemed to believe Miss Willoughby had no one else to protect her. He did not think you had her best interests in mind." Francis regarded him coolly. "I must own, I'm beginning to believe him."

Willoughby gazed at him in open incredulity. "You, Mr. Francis Mantell, rakehell and Man of the Town, stand there and lecture me about protecting a female? You, who have never raised a finger in the protection of a woman in your life? You, who couldn't care less if your sister lives or dies? How dare you spout such nonsense to me when you'd do precisely the same as I have done, were you in my shoes?"

"I beg to differ, Will," said Francis, inspecting his nails. "I would not have sold my sister to a man she despised. Granted, if I had made the attempt, she would have laughed in my face and likely challenged the poor sot to a duel. And she'd have killed her man, too, which would have been horridly inconvenient."

Willoughby rolled his eyes, turning to pace angrily away and back. "You may make light of my predicament, but you've no notion how it weighs on me. I require that money—I rely upon getting that money! Eliza has no right to my father's fortune—he owed it to me, after abandoning me to this god-forsaken estate—and I am determined to have it."

"You need not force Bell on her, however."

"Who else will take her? Will you?"

Francis averted his eyes, effectively silenced.

Willoughby barked a brittle laugh. "You see how quickly your true character asserts itself? What were you thinking, to take on so gallant a charge, when you topple at the merest hint of opposition?"

He turned and stalked out, leaving Francis a prey to unpleasant thoughts. It was true that he was playing the hypocrite—he had known that from the moment he had made his promise to Charles. What did he know of protecting women? The entirety of his life had been spent in disdain of the female sex, and in avoiding anything resembling attachment. His chief focus in his interactions with Miss Willoughby had been flirtation, without any thought to her sentiments or comfort. He had even determined to keep his promise to

Charles out of spite for Bellerton, rather than any thought for the lady—except perhaps in the delight of her impish company.

Pushing that thought aside, he pondered Willoughby's claims, and could only agree that he, Francis, was in no position to champion the lady's cause. Indeed, upon reflection, he could find in Will's deal with Bellerton no distinct detriment to Miss Willoughby. It would give her what she wished: a place in society and a family and home of her own as a married lady.

The recollection that she had also expressed a desire for love gave him pause, but as he held love so cheaply himself, he could not believe the lack of it to be so very disappointing. In fact, by marrying Bellerton rather than some imaginary gentleman who professed love to her, she may be spared the pain of discovering just how flimsy love's promises were.

Besides, while Francis disliked the idea of her being forced to marry against her wishes, he could not say he was convinced that Willoughby would succeed. Miss Willoughby was possessed of cleverness and spirit, and she had Muncey and Clayton on her side. And the gentlemen were all to hie to Newmarket on the morrow, at any event. If she found Bellerton's suit disagreeable, he would soon be gone—as would Francis.

It seemed reasonable to assume that, despite Charles's insistence, Miss Willoughby was better off without any of Francis's help. There was really nothing more for a rakehell and Man of the Town to do but go find something more in his line to occupy him while Bellerton went about his business. Taking up his coat and hat, therefore, he left the house, calling for his horse to be saddled and making for the Pig and Whistle.

Eliza's instinct was to avoid Bellerton, but as she had told Clayton, she did not wish to give him reason to believe she was a weakling to be preyed upon. She had determined to abide by the advice she had given Miss Draffin: to begin as one intends to go on. Even if she was not, after all, to live in Nathan's household, his friends must learn that she was to be treated with respect. When Bellerton had come upon her in the library that morning, therefore, she had been prepared to explain her sentiments precisely, so that no misunderstandings could occur.

Mr. Mantell's subsequent appearance had caused her mixed emotions. She was sorry that he had interrupted her efforts, but she was forced to admit that her defense was not proceeding as planned. While Mr. Bellerton had not attempted to accost her person again, he had redoubled his efforts to monopolize her and seemed incapable of comprehending her dislike of his advances. It had occurred to her that he had somehow arranged Muncey's disappearance, for he seemed unconcerned at coming upon her alone in the library and had detained her most improperly for some minutes when Mr. Mantell had entered.

She wished she knew what that gentleman's intentions were. He was as persistent as Bellerton and nearly as improper, but he had never forced himself upon her. He had teased her that he would do so, on the library ladder and again on their walk, but so far it had all been flirtation. And when he had taken her up before him in the saddle, and she had been forced to cling to him in a thoroughly discomfiting and distracting manner, he had not imposed upon her.

Was his timely intervention in the passage and again this morning proof of his desire to help her or only a product of his enjoyment in vexing Bellerton? She could not help but feel she had become a pawn in a game between them, and she could not like it.

But when she would have had a tray brought to her room for dinner, Willoughby came to request her presence in the dining room, and she thought perhaps he meant to protect her. The meal was, indeed, as uneventful as she could have wished, for Mr. Mantell did not put in an appearance, and Bellerton—his right cheek bruised and puffy—merely regarded her sullenly as she enjoyed a discussion on Jamaican tree frogs with Mr. Hayes.

When she rose to retire to the drawing room—where Muncey awaited her—however, Bellerton followed her, taking her arm and drawing her toward the saloon, saying, "I've got something to say that you'll be pleased to hear."

Pulling away from him, she replied, "You will excuse me, Mr. Bellerton. You are very kind, but I had rather not be private with you."

"Go with him, Eliza." Willoughby's stern voice forestalled her, and she turned to find that he had come out of the dining room and was gazing sharply at her.

"Gladly, Nathan," she replied pleasantly, "if you will go with me."

"You do not need me, but I insist you go and hear what he has to say."

With an exasperated sigh, Eliza stepped close to him, lowering her tone. "I do not wish to be uncivil, but I do not feel he can be trusted."

Willoughby gave a curt shake of his head. "He won't harm you, Eliza. He has asked to address you, and you will hear him, or I will be seriously displeased."

So this was the sum of Bellerton's attentions, thought Eliza with some surprise, and Nathan had approved it! Surely he could sense her dislike of his friend, and yet he insisted she hear him. She was not a little disappointed. She had not expected sympathy, but nor had she anticipated so thorough a disregard for her wishes. But his very look spoke his inflexibility, and she knew that she must do as he wished.

"Very well, Nathan," she said and turned, allowing Bellerton to usher her into the saloon. She would hear him, but she would not accept him.

Seating herself primly in a wing chair, Eliza arranged the skirts of her pale green silk gown and awaited the proposal with dignified resignation. With his customary confidence, Bellerton pulled a chair close to hers, lowering himself into it and leaning forward to rest his hands on his knees.

"No need for this display of maidenly modesty, Miss Willoughby," he said with his crocodile smile. "I believe I've made my intentions plain."

Elizabeth huffed. "Your frequent insinuations and unsanctioned handling of my person have rather obscured your purpose, sir. I could have no notion you meant marriage."

"There's nothing in that, my dear," said Bellerton, sitting back. "Perhaps I didn't always mean to marry you, but I do now. It's more than anyone else would do."

She stiffened, striving against a sudden urge to hit him. As if in response to her mood, rain began pelting against the window glass.

"I believe, sir," she said in a carefully controlled tone, "it is customary for a lady to thank a gentleman in these situations, but I fear I cannot find it in me to do so. I have endeavored to disabuse you of the notion that I should receive your attentions gladly, but still you persist. Forgive me, sir, but I cannot accept your very obliging offer, nor do I wish to be importuned by you—in any way—again."

She stood to go, but he leaped up, grasping her wrist. "Don't be like that, my dear. Consider a moment! Will has given his permission, and you'll not receive a better offer."

At that moment, the door opened and Patty, Nathan's ill-favored maid, entered, gingerly carrying a large tray with the tea things. Bellerton let Eliza's hand drop, but he did not move away, watching the maid with narrowed eyes.

Patty set the rattling tray on the table before Eliza, sighing and rubbing her nose with her hand. Then, recalling her duty, she bobbed a curtsey, saying, "Miss Muncey said as how you'd be wanting tea, and she said she'd made it the way you like, specially, and that she's sorry she can't come herself but she's been obliged to speak with the master." The girl stood for a moment, eyes darting up and around as though looking for any instructions she had forgotten.

"Thank you, Patty," said Eliza, assimilating that Nathan had intentionally detained Muncey—and likely Clayton as well—to ensure the success of the interview. Seating herself gracefully and smiling at the girl, she said, "Muncey is perfectly right—I was just wishing for tea. Will you have some, Mr. Bellerton? I believe tea is just the thing for our raddled nerves. Patty, would you pour?"

Patty put her hands behind her back, saying, "Mrs. Slade said as how I'm not to touch the Wedgwood, seeing as how I broke two plates already, and I'm to come back quick-like, since Miss Muncey don't have call to take me from my duties."

So saying, the maid bobbed a curtsey and left the room, and Eliza, pressing her eyes closed, inhaled deeply.

"I'll take tea, my dear," said Bellerton, resuming his seat with a smug look. "Won't do to let it go cold. Will might take a pet at the waste."

Her chin up, Eliza sat and poured out the tea, all cool civility. She handed him his dish, studiously avoiding his gaze, then poured herself a cup. Raising it to her lips, she instantly sensed a strange smell.

It was not unpleasant to her—indeed, it was very familiar, but not from England. With a thrill of comprehension at Muncey's message, she sipped, and savored the burn of bonney peppers on her tongue.

Across from her, Bellerton spluttered, then coughed. "What the devil—" he wheezed, but could say no more.

Eliza regarded him placidly from her seat, tolerably masking her triumph. "Is something the matter, Mr. Bellerton? Do you dislike the taste? I own it is one of my favorite ways to take tea—a trifle hot to the tongue, I suppose, but so comforting. Muncey knew just what I wanted."

She sipped again, smiling as Bellerton jumped up, coughing and choking. He rushed to the fire, tossing the remainder of his tea into the grate. Then he staggered to the decanters on the sideboard and poured wine into his cup, gulping it down.

Setting down her teacup, Eliza rose, moving toward the door. "You will excuse me, as I believe we have nothing more to say on the subject we were discussing," she said.

She went out of the saloon, closing the door behind her, and raising her eyes to the stairs, perceived Willoughby midway down. He eyed her imperatively, and she smiled sweetly back, but as she took a step toward the stairs, a bellow issued from the saloon.

"What have you done?" exclaimed Willoughby, rushing down the stairs.

Eliza, emboldened by her small victory, refused to allow him to take it away. He and Bellerton would be gone in the morning, and if she had anything to do with the matter, she would be gone when they returned, and they could no longer press her.

With a rush of rebellious energy, she darted across to the back passage and out of the house before he could detain her.

Chapter 17

FRANCIS RODE SLOWLY back from Swineshead, hat tugged down and the collar of his coat turned up against the sudden downpour. He swore softly, cursing himself for a fool. He had given up a night at the inn with the promise of a soft companion in his bed—precisely the distraction he had gone to the Pig and Whistle to seek—and for what? A moonless ride on a lonely road, and now a soaking that would likely lead to an inflammation of the lung.

A vague voice in his mind whispered that he deserved it. Charles had accused him of being a coward, and much of his time in the Pig and Whistle, nursing a mug of ale as the noise and colors and smells of humanity shifted about him, had been spent arguing against the idea. Francis owed Miss Willoughby nothing. She had no ties to him, either of friendship or of blood—not that either of these had ever held much sway with him—and if she had, his friendship with Willoughby should have come before any obligation to her. Besides,

Charles had pressed him to involve himself, and a promise made under duress was unenforceable.

But as the light had faded and Molly, the pretty serving maid, had attempted to lure him out of a brown study with her charms, all these arguments had failed. Miss Willoughby's situation was precarious, and even Molly's coy inquiries as to his plans for the night could not dispel his growing conviction that Will's agreement with Bellerton would not only destroy all Miss Willoughby's hopes for happiness, but strangle her vibrant spirits in one stroke.

In obstinate rebellion, he had ordered a fish pie, rehearsing to himself as he ate it Willoughby's justifications of the afternoon. Willoughby had as much right to his father's fortune as did his sister, and what if Bellerton wished to assist in obtaining his share? Francis, as selfish in practice as he was in precept, was in no position to cavil. But the more he indulged this line of thinking, the more his stomach revolted, and the desperate order of a second fish pie had utterly failed its purpose. Unable to face either the hearty pastry or Molly's swaying hips for the agitation of his mind, Francis had admitted defeat, tossing a few shillings on the table as he made for the door.

Now, plodding back to Penhurst Lodge in the dark and wet, he was cold and miserable and wondering what the devil ailed him. How could he, an admitted despiser of all duty and gallantry, have anything to do with the protection of a lady for whom he did not even cherish any designs? She was a mere acquaintance, not even the full sister of his friend, and he could do very well without the insistent memory of her pleading blue eyes, thank you very much.

He turned in at the gate, picking his way up the drive in the gloom. Lights shone in the saloon, casting rectangles of light onto the drive as he made his way around the back of the house and into the stables.

As he dismounted, handing his reins to Hatten, his groom, he thought he heard a shout of outrage. He removed his hat and shook off the accumulated water, walking to the open stable door and squinting through the rain at the house.

Suddenly, a slight figure in pale green erupted from the back passage door, flitting erratically down the path, as though it had no clear notion of where it was going. Francis watched, brow furrowing, from the doorway, until the figure—Miss Willoughby, unless he was much mistaken—hurtled toward the stables. The rain must have hampered her sight for, rather than slowing or going around him, she barreled directly into him, uttering a surprised "Oof!"

He grasped her arms as they both regained their balance, and looked into her face. "What the devil is toward?"

She blinked up at him, winded and utterly shocked. "Pardon me, Mr. Mantell. I did not perceive you there—your coat—the darkness—the rain—"

"Good heaven, Miss Willoughby," he said, amused. "Can it be that you are running away? I cannot advise it. The hour of the night, the state of the weather—and your gown! Even you can have read enough novels to understand that one must wear a hooded cloak, or at the very least a veiled hat. And where is your bandbox, filled with your most cherished treasures?"

She recovered her breath enough to retort, "I am not running away! Only from Nathan—Oh, gracious, I must hide!"

Glancing back at the house, Francis pulled her around him into the stable, so that his back, made broader by his great coat, shielded her from view. His eyes searched her face in the dim light thrown from the house, aided slightly by the groom's lantern, which hung far at the back of the building. It was difficult to tell from the brightness of her eyes and the set of her jaw if she was merely frightened or—was that exultation?

"Something has happened," he said, still regarding her keenly. "What is it? Tell me."

"I cannot—there is no time!"

He gave her a gentle shake, a ghost of a smile hovering on his lips—she always had this delightful effect on him. "I'll have it out of you one way or another. Now, what devilry are you up to?"

She huffed. "It is no devilry. Nathan wishes me to marry Bellerton, but I refused him, and now—"

A shout came from the direction of the house, and Francis hastily walked them both out of sight into the corner by the door. Craning his neck back, he peeked around the door frame to see if he could make out what was happening at the house. Through the drizzle, he thought he perceived Willoughby, having exited the back passage, hunching against the rain and peering this way and that in the darkness.

"Eliza!" Willoughby shouted, then uttered something that could have been a curse.

Another man—Bellerton—joined him, rubbing his face and speaking rapidly. After a brief conference, Willoughby returned into the house, but Bellerton, holding up an arm to shield his face, made for the stables.

"Blast," muttered Francis, mashing his hat back onto his head and working at the buttons on his great coat. "I don't know what sort of refusal you made, ma'am, but there seems to be the devil to pay!"

"What are you doing?" whispered Eliza, staring in anxious suspicion at his hands as they threw open his coat.

He grinned roguishly but only had time to sweep her and her pale green dress into his coat, pressing her deep into the corner to hide both himself and her entirely in the shadows, before Bellerton came puffing through the door.

"Miss Willoughby!" Muttering imprecations on the rain, Bellerton swiped at his coat sleeves, shaking his arms and head. Droplets sprayed out, hitting the floor and the stall doors with a patter. "Come out, Miss Willoughby. I'm not too angry. If you come back now, I'll speak to Will for you, tell him it was a good joke."

Miss Willoughby pressed her forearms against Francis's chest, holding a small distance between them, but remained silent and still. He kept his head down, hunching his shoulders to push the collar of his great coat up over his neck and breathing as quietly as possible.

He heard the light shuffling of Bellerton's steps as he walked through the stables, stopping at each stall to peer in as he went, and finally the murmurs of his questions to Hatten at the back.

"They was someone here, sir," Hatten drawled, pausing long enough to look about, "but they must have gone."

"Devil take her," muttered Bellerton as he strode back. His steps halted at the outer door as he muttered more curses on women and the weather, then he took off running through the rain toward the house.

After a moment, Francis lifted his head, turning it toward the door and straining for sounds indicative of Bellerton returning. There were none, and he looked down to where Miss Willoughby yet held him off, eyes wide and lips parted as she, too, listened. She was trembling, and Francis instinctively tightened his arms about her.

But she pushed away from him, meeting his gaze and, with an imp of mischief dancing in her eyes, she began to giggle. Regarding her sternly, he said, "You abominable girl! What did you do to poor Bell?"

She began to laugh then, stepping away and wrapping her arms about herself. Her shoulders shook, and her rich, melodic laughter filled the stables. He watched her, a wry smile on his lips, admiring the curve of her neck as she threw her head back and brought it forward again in her increasingly futile attempts to reign in her mirth. Tears streamed from her eyes, flowing down her cheeks and mingling with the wet curls that clung there.

"It is my belief you are hysterical," said Francis, remarking a strange desire to capture all that delicious frivolity.

She peeped up at him, but was laughing too hard to properly speak.

He heaved a sigh, his eyes rolling heavenward. "I know not who to pity more, Bell or myself."

"Crocodile," wheezed Eliza, in a vain attempt to steady herself. She wiped her streaming eyes, gasping for breath.

"I beg your pardon?"

"He smiles—" she managed, still giggling uncontrollably, "like a crocodile!"

Fighting to maintain a show of displeasure, Francis clenched his jaw, his lips twitching. What was it about this woman that brought him such delight? Other women could draw him in with their wiles and coquetry, but they were easily charmed and just as easily forgotten. His usual style of female could not even compare to Miss Willoughby— she was so pure and unaffected.

How he yearned for her to respond in kind to his flirtatious sallies—yearned for it and dreaded it. The moment she did, he imagined she would lose all fascination for him. But she could not disappoint him so now—not while she laughed to tears without a care for what he thought of her.

She gasped, "Oh, if you had seen his face!" Inhaling desperately, she went off into another peal.

Her dimples came and went in the pale lamp light as she endeavored to calm herself, those lovely lips parted and her cheeks pink. Gazing down on her, he became suddenly aware of the memory of her body pressed against his, of how well she fit into his arms. He was seized by a desire to take her in his arms again, but—uncharacteristically—knew he could not give into it, for it would mean the end of her delight. And he had no wish to end the pleasure of this moment.

His heartbeat quickened, and with a slight gruffness in his tone, he said, "I perceive I will simply have to hold you hostage here until you recover your wits enough to tell me what I wish to know."

That sobered her a great deal, her gaze flicking to his and her smile fading. Then she glanced back toward where Hatten had popped his head above the stall to look inquiringly at them. Francis caught the groom's eye, shaking his head and smiling as a signal that the lady was safe with him. Hatten nodded, finishing his work and going out the back door to the stairs that led to the rooms over the stable.

Miss Willoughby rubbed her arms in some agitation. "I must go back inside, sir, and find Muncey," she whispered, moving to go around him.

But caught in her strange enchantment, he shifted so she could not pass. "You must pay a forfeit," he said, his eyes locked on her face.

She did not meet his gaze. "Pray, do not—I thank you for assisting me, but—"

"That is three times I've got you out of trouble," he persisted. "It is long past time I exacted a forfeit. Indeed, I seem to recall you owe me a boon. By Jupiter, a boon must be worth three forfeits at least."

"Pray let me go!" She began to tremble, but he merely swept off his coat and put it about her shoulders, enveloping her in its damp warmth.

"Now, Miss Willoughby," he said, narrowing his eyes in thought. "What might I ask you to do? A boon and a forfeit—together they add up to something grand, I should think. Now, if only I could recollect whether I had succeeded in proving myself a gentleman, it might assist me in determining the scope of my choice."

She pulled the heavy coat tighter about her, peeking intently up at him from the corner of her eye. He thought he saw the moment she recognized he meant her no harm, for her shoulders relaxed and she huffed.

"Shame on you, sir!" she said in a somewhat shaky voice. "You are roasting me—taking advantage when I was afraid for my life! Gentleman indeed—"

Her tone was disdainful as she lifted her chin in challenge, but Francis detected the relief in it also. It gave him a peculiar, but oddly pleasant, feeling in his chest.

"You were no more afraid for your life than I was gentlemanly. Indeed, I am of the opinion that you were not a little thrilled." The cold air from outside the stables was beginning to seep into his clothing, but he merely tipped his head, regarding her with dark eyes. "I own to a great curiosity as to what has inspired such triumph."

She looked up at him with a disapproving moue. "There is not much to tell. Nathan forced me to listen to Mr. Bellerton's addresses. I very graciously declined his offer of marriage—"

"I somehow highly doubt that, Miss Willoughby."

"Do not interrupt," she said, casting him a disparaging glance. "You are only attempting to prolong this excessively impertinent—and improper—interview. Where was I? Yes, then I poured out the tea—"

"You had tea? Do you tell me it was Clayton who brought it? Dare I hope he had cause to floor Bellerton?"

She glared at him. "Clayton was *detained* by Nathan, as was Muncey, I can only assume as a security against their interference. But they managed to send the tea by Patty, who was unable to remain to pour out, as Mrs. Slade would not allow her to handle the Wedgwood—"

"Now you are prolonging the interview with needless detail," he said, his lips turning up in a smile.

"Incorrigible, detestable man." Rolling her eyes away from him, she continued, "I poured out the tea and Bellerton began choking—"

"You poisoned him!" Francis gazed at her in awe. "I had not imagined you capable of such infamy, Miss Willoughby. But then, he did not seem much affected just now. How has he survived, I wonder?"

Not deigning to dignify this with an answer, she went on, "And he was so very busy drowning his burning throat in Madeira and water, I excused myself—"

"Minx!" Francis barked a laugh. "You used that odious West Indian spice again!"

She primmed up her mouth in an unconvincing show of propriety. "I did not. Muncey put it in the tea, and all I did was pour it out. And that is all! Now, pray, step aside, so that I may go back into the house and get out of these wet things."

"You seem fond of chatting away in wet things, Miss Willoughby," he said dryly, forestalling her attempt to remove his coat by grasping the collar gently together. "You have not fulfilled your part of the bargain, however. Your exceedingly interesting story did not explain Willoughby's ire."

She looked away, her humor evaporating. "Willoughby is angry that I refused Bellerton."

Francis gazed into her pretty face, now shadowed by something other than darkness. He knew an urge to cradle her cheek in his hand and kiss the frown away from that forehead. But he believed that she had chosen to trust him in some measure—an odd sensation that made him loathe to make any sort of move that would harm their fragile accord.

"You do not like Bellerton," he said.

Her eyes flashed up. "Does it surprise you? He is like a crocodile, always lying in wait to pounce. And he is even more odious and insinuating than you."

He smiled ruefully. "How horrid for you to land amongst such uncivilized heathens."

"You state the matter quite perfectly," she said with an arch look. "However, you know it is not true. Mr. Wraglain and Mr. Hayes are quite civilized. I wonder that they suffer the rest of you."

"They are not often called upon to suffer us all at once," he said. "Charles has known me from childhood, and has learned to bear my odd starts, but he does not much like Bellerton, nor Willoughby."

She huffed. "I cannot much blame him. Nathan is—well, he has his disappointments to excuse him. But Bellerton is simply intoler-able! No matter how firmly I push him away, he comes back again, convinced I am not in earnest."

"He is much like Charles—impervious to hints."

"He is nothing like Mr. Wraglain," she said, spearing him with a deprecating look. "Mr. Wraglain is a *gentleman*."

Francis chuckled. "Are you on about that again? Forgive me, Miss Willoughby, but I find you unreasonable. What must a man do to prove he is a gentleman?"

She was quiet, regarding his waistcoat buttons. "A gentleman would not have kept me here in this intimate attitude, teasing me to earn my freedom." She raised her frank eyes to his for a pregnant moment, then went back to inspecting his buttons.

Something in Francis's chest twisted, and he stepped back. She glanced quickly up at him, then removed his coat, handing it to him. He took it automatically, but she immediately crossed her arms over her chest, grasping her damp sleeves in an attempt to ward off the chill that now swept around her. He made to give it back to her, but she stopped him.

"It is only a step to the house," she said with a quick glance, "and then I may go up the back stairs to my room. I am obliged to you, Mr. Mantell, for your assistance. Good night."

She ducked around him and ran up the path. Francis watched her go, glad the rain had stopped, but feeling he had lost something, and wishing he knew whether he wanted it back, or whether it was better to let it go.

She reached the door, but just when she should have disappeared into the house, she jerked to the side, leaping into the shrubbery. Francis swore, swinging on his coat and striding up the path, just as Bellerton appeared in the back passage doorway.

Chapter 18

ELIZA CROUCHED IN the shrubbery, shivering and trying with all her might to stop her teeth from chattering. Bellerton stood only two paces from her, muttering to himself. She could hear snatches of what he said—outside the noise of her teeth—including her name, and "where in thunder has she got to," and sundry epithets.

She squeezed her eyes shut, cursing her bad luck—she ought to have taken Mr. Mantell's coat. Perhaps she was being silly, hiding like a recalcitrant child, but she was not about to allow Bellerton to find her, when it had been his ridiculous insistence on pressing his suit that had driven her to flee. And with Willoughby firmly in support of Bellerton's right to address her, she did not intend to offer him any chance to renew his suit, especially when he would be going away in the morning to Newmarket.

She was just formulating a desperate plan to risk a dart around the back of the house in search of an open window, when she heard a firm step on the path, and Mr. Mantell's voice.

"Why, Bellerton, how solicitous of you to come and meet me. Did you see me ride up? But how touching—I didn't imagine you would have missed me so."

Bellerton snorted. "Thought you'd gone back to Warwickshire, and good riddance."

"Then what the deuce are you doing out here, muttering to yourself? Best hold it in, dear boy, or the servants will think you mad."

"Miss Willoughby's gone, you cod's head. Vanished over half an hour ago."

"And you imagine she'll come running back if you wait here to meet her, scowling like Beelzebub?"

Bellerton made a low noise. "Stubble it, Mantell. She's got to come back sometime."

"Has it occurred to you that she's probably safely in her room?"

"Dash it, we've looked in her room! She ain't there!"

Francis chuckled. "She's more clever than you take her for, Bell, poor man. Carlton House to a Charlie's shelter, she's fooled you—with the help of that maid of hers, no doubt—and is at this moment snug in her bed, laughing at you."

Bellerton cursed, shuffling as though uncertain what to do.

"You may stay out here, making a fool of yourself," continued Francis, moving toward the door, "but I am going inside. Good luck!"

His steps continued into the house and Eliza held her breath, shivering so hard she could hardly keep quiet. After an interminable few moments, she heard Bellerton turn and follow Mr. Mantell into the passage.

Holding still for as long as she could stand, to give Bellerton time to go through the passage, she at last jumped up and ducked into the house. Numb and stiff, she tiptoed clumsily down the passage to the servants' stairs and hurried as swiftly as her shivering legs could carry her up to the first floor. As she rounded the corner, however, she heard voices in her room, and had just enough time to stumble back out of sight before Bellerton and Willoughby stomped into the corridor, slamming the door after them.

"That means she's still on the grounds," growled Bellerton.

But Willoughby snapped, "I'm even more convinced Mantell's right and she and that virago of a maid are playing you for a fool. Her woman isn't the least bit worried—did you see her? Sewing as though nothing were amiss. Leave off, Bell. Eliza's won this round. She'll show herself eventually, and then you'll have another go."

"We'll be gone to Newmarket tomorrow," was the sulky reply.

"All the better. She'll have ample time to consider her situation. But don't fret, Bell. She's nowhere else to go. If she knows what's good for her, she'll have you."

Eliza waited until she could not hear their voices anymore, then limped to her door and stumbled through it. Muncey startled so badly she dropped her mending, a scold bubbling instantly from her lips.

"Whah in God's eart' yuh been, Miss Eliza? All de gentlemen deh lookin' for yuh, and tink mi hidin' yuh! And mi worryin', tinkin' yuh fall down a hole, and dead!"

She stopped abruptly, assimilating Eliza's wet hair and dress, and her uncontrollable shivering. Pressing her lips into a tight line, she flew into action, unfastening Eliza's gown and stripping it from her quicker than a wink. Pulling off her damp shift, Muncey bundled her into her dressing gown, pressing her into the bed and pulling the blanket up around her chin. The pins in her hair were plucked out and the hair loosened, then dried and wrapped in a warm towel. At last, going to the fire, Muncey took down the warming pan, dropped in a few hot coals, and wrapped it in another towel, thrusting it under the bedclothes at Eliza's feet.

"Th-thank you, M-muncey," stammered Eliza, her eyes fluttering closed as the cold and her exertions overcame her.

"Hush, now, Miss Eliza." Muncey stroked Eliza's brow as she crooned to her, "Sleep now. I'll not go away."

A few minutes later, as Eliza slept peacefully in her bed, a knock came at the door. Muncey opened it to find Clayton there, his arms crossed and the fingers of one hand worrying his lip.

"Has she come back?" he inquired urgently.

"Yes, Mr. Clayton. She is safe enough." Muncey glanced back at the sleeping form in the bed. "Dough I would like to tear de gizzard out'a dat Bellerton deh!"

Clayton's eyes glowed at her display of temper, but he merely peeped over her shoulder, humming in agreement. "Not to worry, Miss Muncey. All the gentlemen are leaving tomorrow morning, and you'll be free of them and their tomfoolery for a fortnight at least."

"Den dey come back, Mr. Clayton! What den, eh? Miss Eliza nah wish to marry Mr. Bellerton, but Mr. Willoughby gwan make her!"

In a swift movement, Clayton took her hand, pressing it between his own. Looking down at her, a mischievous but earnest glint in his eye, he said, "It won't come to that, my dear. Don't forget Mr. Findlay! He'll put everything to rights, just as soon as Miss Willoughby acquaints him with our fine gentlemen's plans."

Muncey looked down but did not attempt to withdraw her hand. "I hope you're right, Mr. Clayton. Miss Eliza deserves to be happy."

Pressing her hand once more, Mr. Clayton bowed and withdrew to report to Mr. Mantell, who had alerted him of Miss Willoughby's whereabouts. Assured of her safe return to her room, Francis strolled into the billiard room to find George, Willoughby, and Bellerton all at play. George greeted him, inquiring how his jaunt to Swineshead was.

"Entertaining. Took my dinner at the Pig and Whistle," said Francis, disposing himself in a comfortable chair. "That Molly is an obliging little thing. Sends you her love."

Will glanced sharply at him. Then, clenching his jaw, he bent again over the table.

Francis chuckled. "I hear there was some excitement this evening. Any sign of Miss Willoughby yet?"

Bellerton only favored him with a glare, then turned it to the table as Willoughby lined up his shot.

"She's hiding somewhere about," said Willoughby, with a dismissive air. "Would have the house in an uproar, I suppose, but I've not the patience to play her games."

"No, it seems you don't," mused Francis. He sat back in his chair, clasping his hands at his waist. "You're not anxious, then, lest she be really lost or, heaven forbid, injured?"

Bellerton glared at him again. "Make up your mind, Mantell! A moment ago you were sure she was safe in her bed! Now you're insinuating we've been neglectful in discontinuing the search. Well, you can't have it both ways, and I'll not be made a fool of by you nor her. If she ain't got the sense to do what's good for her, she can bear the fault. She's a grown woman, and I'm sick to death of her. Sick to death of all of it."

Bending over the table, he took his shot and missed.

"Come, Bell," said Francis, tutting. "Mustn't say such things in front of Will. He's counting on you to repair his fortune, after all. Can't be sick of it all yet. Not the thing to be so cavalier with Will's future."

"Going to help him out of his embarrassments, Bell?" inquired George with interest. "Mighty good of you."

"Not if that jade's this troublesome all the time," muttered Bellerton. "Wouldn't shackle myself to her for half a kingdom, much less half her fortune."

"Stow it, Bell!" commanded Willoughby with a darkling look. Putting down his stick, he went to pour himself a drink. "She's likely just tetchy. Off her balance, moving halfway across the world, and not knowing how to go on. She'll come around—best think before you toss away such a plum. Not everyone can find a wife that is pretty and rich."

George blinked from Willoughby to Bellerton, brow furrowed. "Going to marry Miss Willoughby, Bell?"

Willoughby ignored him. "Perhaps we rushed things a trifle, but we'll come about. She'll calm down and get settled while we're off to Newmarket. When we come back, you'll take your time. Woo her properly."

"Woo her, wed her, bed her," said Bellerton, coming to take the glass Willoughby held out to him. He took a deep swallow, grunting in satisfaction.

Francis tapped his fingers on the arm of the chair to mask his irritation. "An admirable plan, gentlemen, but with an unfortunate flaw. What if the lady does not wish to be wooed?"

"Stands to reason," said George. "Ran from you tonight, Bell."

Bellerton clenched his jaw, glaring at George. "She's only playing the coquette. Likely a teasing sort of woman."

"Or she despises you." Francis stood, going to pour his own drink. "Seems to me you ought to be wary of a lady who would poison you rather than consent to become leg-shackled, Bell."

George chuckled, and even Willoughby's lips twitched.

"You can all go to the devil," said Bellerton, grabbing the decanter and sloshing more wine into his glass.

"Just offering a bit of advice, dear boy. Always best to thoroughly understand the character of the lady for whom you mean to be a tenant for life." With a smirk, Francis tossed off his drink, leaning back against the billiard table and crossing one foot over the other.

"As though you were any sort of authority, Mantell," Willoughby scoffed. "You'll never marry—or if you do, you'll make certain to snatch a lady that won't interfere with your wishes."

Francis smiled thinly, looking down into his empty glass. "To be sure. A pity Miss Willoughby is not that sort. I'd not begrudge her fine portion."

"Are you changing your tune, then, Mantell?" asked Willoughby, flicking a glance at Bellerton, who was regarding the fire with sullen intensity.

"Not at all." Francis shrugged. "As you said, I require a lady who is willing to wink at my habits, and not make a fuss. Miss Willoughby shows an alarming tendency to not only accurately judge one's character, but to point it out to one with distressing precision. She is remarkably adept at the shot across the bow. Too fatiguing by half. But *you* won't mind that, Bell."

"So she has spirit!" said Willoughby, his mouth tightening. "It'll add spice to the marriage. She'll never bore you."

"If I can manage to get my hands on her," grumbled Bellerton.

"Aye, there's the rub," said Francis, nodding in sympathy. "It's the very devil to get an unwilling lady to sign away her life to one. I wish you luck, Bell."

Bellerton's scowl deepened and he pushed himself up from his chair. "I'm going to bed."

They watched him stalk out and George said philosophically, "Too much to think over in one evening. Don't blame him." He put down his glass. "Early start tomorrow. Think I'll go to bed, too."

He went out and Francis moved to follow, but Willoughby stopped him.

"I don't know what you're playing at, but it won't succeed."

"Playing, my friend? Oh, no. I know very well you only play your own games."

Willoughby's lip curled. "Eliza will take Bell, sooner or later. She'll not receive another offer of marriage, and marriage is what she wishes."

"I'm aware of what she wishes, Will," said Francis, his eyes hooded as he regarded his friend, "and you are mistaken. Miss Willoughby does not simply wish for marriage—she wishes to be *happy* in marriage. She wants a home and children—a family, not just the name of the man who has taken her for her fortune."

Willoughby huffed. "That sounds as though you had it out of a cheap novel, or an improving tale."

"No, only from the lips of your sister." Francis moved to the sideboard, gazing unseeing at the decanters as he held his empty glass in his hand. "Nauseating drivel, isn't it? One cannot conceive what ails females that they look for warmth and companionship in marriage, and not simply a business arrangement. Everyone knows marriage is a farce, where the two individuals unite in the hopes of bettering their circumstances, and more than likely end by loathing one another, and plaguing each other's lives out."

"Precisely," said Willoughby, pointing around his glass at Francis for emphasis. "The chances of happiness in marriage are as good with one person as with another. So Eliza would do better to accept the offer that is forthcoming, than to hold out hope for a better."

Francis turned to regard him. "A compelling argument. However, you forget one thing: there is generally benefit to each of the parties. What does Eliza receive in return for her marriage to Bell, that she doesn't already have?"

"She'll get children," huffed Willoughby. "Bell's more than eager to get on with that part of the bargain."

With a grimace, Francis placed his glass on the tray. "When you put it that way, I must own to a rather old-fashioned notion. It seems only sporting that Miss Willoughby ought to be the one to choose the man who will 'get on with that part of the bargain.' And the law, I believe, agrees with me."

"Why the deuce don't you mind your own business, Mantell?" growled Willoughby, slamming his glass down on the tray as well. "The chit don't know what's good for her—just look at the *fracas* she caused tonight, all because she took a pet and ran off into the night. Bell likes her well enough, and he's willing to overlook her anteced-ents and illegitimacy. He'll treat her decently—it's not as though I'm asking her to wed a beast, or even a skinflint."

"Like you? No, I suppose you're right." Francis put up a hand to toy with his neckcloth. "It's entirely unreasonable for one to expect that you look about a bit, perhaps even take her into society, so that one might test that theory you seem so fond of, that no one else will have her. One is completely unjustified in believing that you're afraid she might actually find someone she prefers, and that they won't be quite as accommodating with her fortune as Bell will be."

Willoughby ground his teeth. "That money ought to be mine, Mantell! She has no right to it! She's nothing but the natural-born daughter of a slave, and isn't worth the snap of my fingers!"

Something snapped in Francis's mind, and he took a menacing

step toward Willoughby, only barely keeping his hands from his throat. "According to your father's will, she is worth far more than that, Will. Perhaps he guessed how you would look down on her. It would not surprise me if that is precisely why he left his fortune to her, so that you would be obliged to grovel for it. You may congratulate yourself that you have at last lived up to his expectations."

With a last look of disgust, he turned away and strode from the room. Obtaining his own room, he shut the door and went to the dressing table, leaning with both hands on its surface and gazing with amazement at the furious countenance in the glass.

Francis was uncertain what had engendered such anger in him, for he was not an impetuous individual, liable to fly into a passion, especially in defense of a female. But he felt somehow responsible for Miss Willoughby's safety, thanks to his promise to Charles, though he did not believe she was any more to him than that. An agreeable companion, perhaps, and a delightful sparring partner—a spirited adversary capable of inspiring him to press more and more for the appearance of those adorable dimples. Pretty and lively, patient and kind—

He straightened, wincing at the insipidity of his thoughts. When had he ever held patience and kindness as virtues, either in women or men? His exertions today must have fatigued him beyond rational thought, so he readied himself for bed and climbed into the four-poster. But instead of falling asleep, he stared into the darkness of the canopy, reliving the delight of holding Miss Willoughby in his arms as they hid from Bellerton. Did he feel something for her? Of course he did not. Rolling over, he closed his eyes and attempted to sleep.

But sleep did not come. He tossed and turned, thinking of Willoughby's hateful self-interest and Bellerton's lust—and of how often he had acted and thought in precisely the same way. It had never troubled him before, yet now he could not cease to find it disgusting and wrong—was he becoming a prude? Or was he at last experiencing remorse?

How did Miss Willoughby affect him so? He had a vision of her impish blue eyes, laughing up into his, and he marveled that she could laugh so, when she had so much with which to contend. She had held her own against all of them—including Francis—and she had done it ably, but even with Muncey and Clayton on her side, she had been vulnerable to Willoughby's willful manipulation. And Bellerton was not the most patient of men—he had attempted force once, and there was no guarantee Will could keep him from using it again.

Anger surged up in him again, and he fought it down, blinking in the darkness of his bed. What the devil was the matter with him? He may not approve of force in relations with women, but he had never before been provoked into such a primitive response. Yet he was consumed by a desire to break Will's face and to tear Bellerton limb from limb if they did not desist in their persecutions of Miss Willoughby. Surely, it could only be that he was becoming annoyed at their society, for truly, they were such boors. He wondered that he had not seen it before.

He slept poorly, and seriously debated whether to accompany the others to Newmarket, since he had lost all desire for their society. But he had a horse running, and it was unreasonable to expect that he should cast everything to the wind simply because he suddenly did not like his friends. Besides, once they all left Miss Willoughby to her peace, he could hold his promise fulfilled, and then perhaps his reason would be restored.

But at breakfast, as George buttered toast and Bellerton shoveled ham into his mouth, Clayton appeared at the door.

"Miss Muncey is inquiring whether you are taking all the grooms, sir."

Willoughby hesitated, his mouth full of kidneys. "What the devil does she care if we take them all?"

Clayton's jaw clenched, and he seemed unwilling to look at any of them. "She wishes to summon the apothecary. Miss Willoughby, it seems, is seriously ill."

Chapter 19

Tʜᴀᴛ sᴛʀᴀɴɢᴇ sᴇɴsᴀᴛɪᴏɴ, that had been cropping up in relation to Miss Willoughby, twisted in Francis's chest. He put down the plate he was holding to serve himself from the buffet, then took it up again, wondering why he suddenly felt uneasy.

Willoughby was in no such quandary. "Serves the chit right, gallivanting about in the rain. Perhaps now she'll learn to do as she's told."

He continued to eat his breakfast, and Bellerton, after pausing a few moments to look dismayed, did as well.

George wiped his mouth, his brow furrowed. "Might be serious. Terribly common for persons from the West Indies to take a chill here in England. Not accustomed to our air. Miasma and all that."

Willoughby stared at him. "My what?"

"Miasma," repeated George. "Bad air. Responsible for the spread of disease, or so they say."

Francis, who had been slowly and mechanically filling his plate, inquired, "Is this miasma only in England?"

"Wouldn't think it is," said George, sober. "Disease everywhere. Several epidemics in Jamaica while I was there. Must be different sorts of miasma."

Willoughby huffed, taking a bite of egg. "Eliza's a healthy young woman. She'll recover."

"Can't die—has to marry me," added Bellerton.

Clayton had remained expressionless, though his nostrils flared. "Then you won't spare a groom for 'er, sir?"

"No," said Willoughby, scraping up the last of his kidneys and standing. "You can send the footman—on the old nag! I'll not risk him ruining one of my horses."

"John doesn't ride, sir."

"Then he can take the dogcart. Dash it, man, we're in a hurry. Got to leave within the hour if we're to reach Newmarket before dark."

Francis set down his plate. "I'll go."

The others looked at him and Willoughby laughed. "Of course you'll go. You've a horse running."

"Not to Newmarket." Francis swallowed, his throat dry. "I'll take my curricle and bring back the apothecary. I can follow you all tomorrow."

"Nonsense!" exclaimed Willoughby in disdain. "The servants will look after all that. Not your responsibility, Mantell. What's come over you?"

"She's ill, Willoughby," said Francis, though his habitual thoughts had been running in much the same vein. "It could be serious, and it's common decency to see she's properly cared for. Order the curricle, Clayton."

Pausing only to look Francis up and down, something akin to respect in his eye, Clayton went away.

Willoughby shook his head. "All this fuss over nothing. The chit's got a cold! And all because she took a pet and flung out into the rain. I say it's a salutary lesson for her."

"Perhaps I'll stay behind as well," said Bellerton, gazing with suspicion at Francis.

Will took his arm, giving it a shake. "Don't be a gaby. Let him play Galahad, while we fill our pockets at Newmarket. Come along Hayes. Enjoy minding the nursery, Mantell."

With much stomping and muttering, he and Bellerton disappeared into the hall, but George stood uncertainly by the door.

"Nasty things, colds," he said, swinging his hands as though unsure what to do with them. "Never know when one will carry a person off."

Francis exhaled, stifling the sharp pang in his gut at the possibility of Miss Willoughby's death. "She won't die. She's too headstrong."

George hesitated, brow furrowed. "Don't have a horse running, myself," he remarked.

"Go along, George," said Francis, patting his shoulder. "If I'm unable to join you at Newmarket, you might bet on my horse for me, and bring me the winnings."

Seemingly satisfied, George shook his hand, then turned to go.

"And George?" He looked back at Francis. "I'll be obliged if you'll keep Will and Bell at Newmarket. It oughtn't to be very difficult. Convince them to stay for the Houghton meeting in three weeks, if you can. Just keep them away from Miss Willoughby as long as possible."

The furrow on George's brow cleared, and he nodded. With a determined stride, he followed after the others.

Francis slumped into a chair, rubbing his eyes with a thumb and forefinger. What the devil had he been thinking last night, to keep Miss Willoughby so long in the stables, and after she'd run through the rain? The fact was, he hadn't been thinking—she was too fascinating a creature. But even he knew this was a paltry excuse. It had been fairly warm within the confines of his coat, but the cold air had necessarily crept in about her feet and head. It was certainly that had done the business, and he couldn't deny it.

He found this realization of responsibility incredibly discomfiting—all the more so for being one to which he was wholly unaccustomed. Until now, he had happily lived his life caring not a jot for the well-being of others. Indeed, he was persuaded, if it hadn't been for that promise Charles had exacted from him, he would not be experiencing his present discomfort.

However, that was obviously untrue. He had to own that Miss Willoughby had intrigued him from the beginning, with her impish humor and talk of spiders at table. He had unconsciously grown to admire her over the past week. He may have begun by viewing her as a diversion, or at best a challenge to unravel, but had quickly been charmed by her imperturbability and spirit and, with the advent of those strange sensations in his chest, to dislike her circumstances. If he were entirely honest, Francis suspected that, even without Charles's blasted interference, he should still be disturbed by the events of the past several hours.

As it stood, she was ill and he was at fault. The bit of honor he possessed—and that Charles, drat him, had known he possessed—demanded he do what he could to rectify the situation. In this conviction, he rose and went out into the hall, taking the stairs two at a time to the first floor. At the landing, he hesitated, then turned into the family wing, going to Miss Willoughby's door.

Muncey answered his knock, greeting him with her customary dignity, but with something of a softness to her glare.

"I've come to inquire if you require anything for Miss Willoughby's care. I'll be leaving momentarily in search of the apothecary, and might obtain what you want in Swineshead."

She nodded. "No, tank you, sir. I tink we best bring de apotecary witout delay."

"Is Miss Willoughby worse?" Francis felt his chest tighten as he attempted to peep into the room.

"No, sir. But she is feverish. I have brewed a tisane, but de apotecary will know more about English sickness."

Remarking her tightly clenched hands, Francis nodded and instantly took leave, striding quickly down the corridor to his own room. Within a very few minutes, he had donned his driving coat, hat, and gloves, and was climbing into his curricle.

Driving along the road to Swineshead, he cursed himself again for his part in Miss Willoughby's illness. At least Willoughby shared the fault with him, for his selfishness had driven her from the house, and with Bellerton, who had affronted her so greatly that she had rather freeze to death than return into the house under his eye. But the thought gave him little comfort, and he took the turning into town without slowing, nearly colliding with a dray-cart and earning himself a colorful epithet.

The apothecary, an able gentleman of middle age, was available, and listened with some concern to Francis's explanation of the situation.

"It sounds as though her constitution is strong, but we must take great care," he said, in response to Francis's query about her chances of recovery. "Being West Indian, she certainly would be more susceptible to our climate, but I will not hazard an opinion until I have seen the patient."

"Are you concerned for the effects of ... miasma?" pressed Francis, feeling sheepish he didn't know enough about the term to use it correctly.

The apothecary looked somewhat startled. "Dear me, no. Miasma is concerned only in the transmission of disease, sir. If there had been an outbreak of influenza hereabouts, I should respond affirmatively. However, as such is not the case, Miss Willoughby's danger is in the lungs. In foreign persons, especially those from warmer climes, a moderate to severe chill may be productive of pneumonia, and must be tended carefully."

Sobered by this view, Francis was grateful he had not tarried in fetching the apothecary. Upon arriving at the Lodge, he handed the apothecary into Clayton's hands, who ushered him upstairs and into Miss Willoughby's room. Francis then stood dumbly in the hall, wondering what he ought to do. After his guilt-induced burst of activity, his usefulness seemed to be at an end, and habit would have him be glad. He had done as he had promised, and could go about his business with a clear conscience.

But that little-used mental appendage seemed unwilling to be done with the matter, and Francis, strangely, agreed. When the butler came back, Francis was standing in the hall, still in his greatcoat and hat. He looked up as Clayton came down the stairs.

"How does she do, Clayton?"

The butler looked grave. "Feverish and fretful, sir." Francis flinched and Clayton added, "But the apothecary's a good man. 'E's been called 'ere before, to look after one or the other of us, and 'e always sees us 'ale and 'earty in the end. Your fetching 'im was kindly felt, and 'as put us all more at ease."

Reflecting that it had not put himself at ease, Francis inquired, "You've seen the ladies have all they require?"

"Oh, they've what they'll be needing for now. Miss Muncey seems to know 'er way about a sickroom. She's quite a collection of medicines from Jamaica, and 'as already used some to good effect."

Francis nodded, looking about as though he had lost something. Clayton reached out a hand and patted his shoulder in a brotherly way.

"She'll do, Mr. Mantell. No need to worry yourself to a flinder."

Huffing a laugh that was more incredulous than helpless, Francis said, "I fear I don't know quite what to do, Clayton. This is not my usual territory."

"It's not a man's province, sir, or so my mum used to say," replied Clayton with a tilt to his lips that could have been understanding or amusement. "The womenfolk tend to bear the lion's share when there's illness in the 'ouse, but they'll be sure to tell us when they need our 'elp."

This prognostication proved correct, for as soon as the apothecary had finished his examination, he began to issue orders for mustard foot baths and chest poultices. Mrs. Slade and Patty were sent scurrying, and made a list of necessary items that must be purchased in the town. Francis ordered his groom to ready his curricle once more, meaning to procure the items after returning the apothecary to his dwelling, but just as he was about to climb in, Patty came rushing out. She handed him a note from Miss Muncey, which at once rescinded half the apothecary's orders and added several of her own, and commanded that he not allow the apothecary to know that she had done so.

Unsurprised at this high-handed dealing from the virago Obeah woman, Francis mounted into his curricle beside the apothecary and went on his way. The apothecary was forthcoming with his diagnosis of Miss Willoughby's illness, which was almost exactly what he had feared. "A severe chest cold, brought on by exposure to night vapors and exacerbated by chill. If we had not caught it so quickly, she could be in great danger, but I am quite sanguine that my remedies will arrest the progression of the illness, and with proper treatment and attention, she will make a full recovery.

Rather than soothe Francis's guilty conscience, this information only served to confirm that he was almost solely to blame for Miss Willoughby's illness, and any consequential suffering. Whatever defense his subconscious had mounted against the necessity of putting himself out further on Miss Willoughby's behalf crumbled to pieces, and as soon as he had returned to Penhurst, bearing his load of medicinal odds and ends, he placed himself entirely at Miss Muncey's service.

Thus commenced four days of unprecedented selflessness for Francis, as he neglected his own wishes for the needs of a sick female. His fast pair and curricle were always ready at a moment's notice, as was their driver, to be put to use in procuring needed supplies from Swineshead and beyond, and fetching the apothecary to and from the Lodge. As the staff at Penhurst was meagre at best, Francis's groom, Hatten, was also put to work, cutting wood for fires and anything else that John and Clayton needed help to do.

The apothecary seemed generally pleased with the efficacy of his remedies, as evidenced by Miss Willoughby's rapid improvements. Muncey did not deign to tell him she had substituted several of her own remedies for his, and was equally proud of their effects.

"She always was strong, Mr. Clayton," she said on the fifth day, after the apothecary had pronounced himself satisfied he was no longer needed. "I have never worried too much for her—only dis English climate is not so wholesome, wit it's cold and wet."

"Do you miss the warm climes of Jamaica, Miss Muncey?" Clayton inquired. "For I know just where to take you to make you feel at 'ome. I wonder, now Miss Willoughby's out of danger, and resting just as peaceful as a babe, will you accompany me to the 'othouse?"

Miss Muncey blinked, a bit of color coming into her cheeks. "Miss Eliza—she may wake—"

"Ah, but we'll ask Patty to sit in with 'er," said Clayton reasonably, his charming smile in full force, "and she'll come right out to find you if our patient does wake."

Muncey uttered a few more protests, but Clayton had already taken her shawl from its peg on the wall and placed it about her shoulders. Recognizing the futility of refusal, she bit her lips on a smile and allowed him to lead her out and into the gardens.

It was for this cause that Francis, who had taken up his post in the library—ready lest Miss Muncey discover something else her mistress required for a full recovery—was obliged to answer the front door, being summoned with repeated attacks at the knocker. He had been feeling a trifle fatigued—with the beginnings of a headache, of all things—and had just reclined comfortably on the sofa when the pounding began. This would normally have brought on a blast of temper but, having become inured to his new role as general factotum, he merely muttered under his breath about the quality of servants prevailing in Lincolnshire and opened the door.

The very pretty, very vulgarly attired young lady whom Francis had witnessed Willoughby handing into her carriage a few days earlier stood in some agitation on the doorstep.

"Oh! I beg your pardon," she said, blushing a deep rose. "Can it be that you are a new footman?"

Francis, looking down at his raiment, which had been chosen

for its ease and comfort in field sports and was in nowise his usual style for social calls, said, "Why, no, ma'am. I fear I should not pass muster—Clayton is excessively snobbish regarding his subordinates."

The lady's mouth formed an O, and she glanced from side to side as if in search of another entrance. "I wonder if I might see Miss Willoughby. I am her friend, and neighbor, and—Oh! I am in such terrible need of her advice!"

"Miss Draffin, I presume?" said Francis, summoning up his Society manners despite his headache. "I beg your pardon, but being neither footman nor butler, I'm not entirely certain how I should handle this situation. Clayton is heaven knows where, and so is John the footman—probably cutting wood for Miss Willoughby's fire, as it must be stoked day and night. She is ill, you see."

"Oh no!" cried Miss Draffin, her large blue eyes wide. "Oh, that is horrible. Oh, what am I to do?"

Perhaps due to the subjection of his pride and the rebirth of his conscience during the past week, Francis held the door wide, inviting Miss Draffin into the saloon. He seated himself across from her on the settee and, rubbing his temples, heaved a sigh.

"Now, Miss Draffin, I am at somewhat of a disadvantage, for I am a stranger to you and a man, so I cannot tell how I might be of assistance. But I have become rather used to putting myself out for females of late, and might as well add you to their number, for ten to one I shall somehow convince myself I am responsible. Are you in some sort of trouble?"

She blinked at him, then clasped her hands at her bosom, shifting to the edge of her seat. "Oh, yes, sir! But, dear me, you must be a friend of Willoughby's! I don't know if I ought to confide in you."

Francis waved a dismissive hand. "Have no fear of that, ma'am.

Willoughby and I are at outs at the moment. Besides, he is at Newmarket, and will know nothing of it. Does your trouble have to do with Will?"

"I suppose it does—that is, my mama insists I must find a way to make him marry me. But I do not think I can, sir! He has told me a hundred times he is not the marrying sort, and that if I wish to see him again, I must not think of marriage."

Resting his chin in his hand, Francis gazed blankly at her. "You are precisely correct, ma'am. Willoughby will not marry you. He thinks you are a cozy—that is he admires you, but, not to put too fine a point on it, he wishes, when he looks for a bride, to find her among the gentry."

"I know." Miss Draffin sniffed and a large tear rolled down her cheek. "But Mama insists that he has ruined me, and must marry me, though I vow and declare we have only ever kissed—and—and embraced."

"Truly?" inquired Francis, brows rising. "I must own to some surprise. But though your mama does have a point, Willoughby will be difficult to pin down. Slippery as an eel is Willoughby. But I should like him to be made to feel responsible—it's rather a unique experience—so I will attempt to advise you."

Miss Draffin clasped her hands. "You are very kind. But what can I do? It seems hopeless."

"You might bring a breach of promise against him, if you could prove he has given you expectations."

"But you know he has not! I have told you so, and Mama!" She let out a little huff, her brow contracting. "He tells me all sorts of sweet things, and that he loves me, even, but he will not say he will marry me."

Francis smiled at a most pleasant idea. "Then you must write to him. I daresay it will be nothing to you after all those stolen kisses. He is at the Red Lion in Newmarket, and will be for a fortnight at least. If you write him a letter, he may answer you using those endearments with which he is so free. Then you will have proof that he is abusing your trust, and you may have him."

"You think so?" She blinked, looking about as she considered, much like a bird looking for a worm. At last, she beamed upon Francis. "I believe you are right, sir! Thank you! Oh, thank you from the bottom of my heart."

Francis stood, holding his hand out to her, but before he could bow and invite her to go away, the room spun, his hearing became muffled, and everything went dark.

Chapter 20

Francis was riding in the rain, soaking wet and unable to see clearly, but possessed of an urgency to arrive at his destination. The harder he pressed his horse, however, the more sluggish it became, until it disappeared from under him entirely. He was anxious, fearful—of what he could not fully comprehend. Snatches of memory teased him—Miss Willoughby trembling in his arms, then Bellerton leering down at her in the passage. He had a hazy conviction that he must save Miss Willoughby, but he did not know how—he only must keep moving.

Francis pushed on, striving for speed, but his limbs were impossibly heavy, and when he looked down, he found to his befuddlement that he was waist-deep in mud. He had hardly assimilated this strangeness when the mud turned to water and he was slipping under, swirling darkness closing over him. In rising panic, he struggled to lift his arms, but they were unresponsive.

He cried out, expecting a rush of water to choke him, but it did not. Taking courage, he cried out again, and a soft rushing noise filled his ears, then a cool pressure relieved his aching forehead. Only then did he realize he was very hot, and the fear assailed him that he must have drowned—died, and was surrounded by the fires of hell. But a breeze wafted over his burning limbs, and something cool and soft touched his cheek with the scent of oranges and lemons. Hell, surely, could not be so gentle and calming.

Something was pressed to his lips and he drank, choking a bit on the bland mixture, but a soft voice encouraged him and he drank more before slipping again into restless sleep. His dreams continued distressful and foreboding, however, always haunted by an urgent deed undone. Miss Willoughby's voice and visage was now interspersed with those of his mother and sister, and visions of Bellerton in anger transformed into images of his dead father berating him.

At last he woke, bleary and fretful, and heard a soft feminine voice entreating him to be still. Then a masculine voice rumbled nearby, and he felt a sudden rush of panic.

"No!" he cried, eyes shut tight against what he feared. "You're dead! Leave me in peace!"

The feminine voice hushed him gently, saying, "You're dreaming, sir. No one here has died, least of all Hatten."

His agitation paused as a face rose lethargically to the surface of his mind—a kind and wise face, to which he could turn in times of trouble. In desperation, he groped weakly toward the voice he remembered. "Hatten?"

His hand was taken in a reassuring clasp. "Aye, sir. I'm here."

A wave of relief washed over Francis. "Hatten, you'll keep them away? My father and my mother—they are holding me back. I've too much to do—something—I cannot recollect—"

"That'll do, sir," said Hatten, his voice soothing. "You're beset by nightmares, is all. But Miss Muncey and Miss Willoughby have taken care of you, and you'll pull through."

Francis shook his head on the pillow. "Miss Willoughby is in trouble. I must—but I cannot, Hatten! I have failed them all! I cannot—but she will be lost if I do not."

A shadow hung over him, and the feminine voice murmured, "I am well, Mr. Mantell. I am Miss Willoughby, and I am out of trouble, you see?"

Francis gazed up through misted eyes but could not discern any features in the shadow above him. His hand clutching Hatten's convulsed, gripping him tighter.

Turning in the direction of the groom, he whispered hoarsely, "Hatten, I must not fail. You'll help me? Do not let my father hinder me—he does not understand—he never understood."

"He'll not put a spoke in your wheel, sir, if you don't let him," said Hatten calmly. "Now drink this, sir. It's a mite tastier than that orange whey the apothecary made you take. Miss Muncey made it special."

"But you'll help me?" insisted Francis, turning from the cup pressing to his lips.

"Aye, I'll do that, sir. Now drink up and sleep."

Francis did, and when he slept, he found that some of his nightmares had been done away, though Bellerton still leered at him from the dark. He woke on and off through the day and night, unable to fully recognize those who nursed him, and requiring constant soothing and attention until he took whatever draft they gave him and drifted off again.

At last, after what seemed an eternity of fruitless wandering down dark paths, he woke to sunlight streaming in the window, and curtains fluttering in a light draft. He shivered, pulling the bedclothes tighter around himself, and a weight lifted from the bedside.

He turned to see Miss Willoughby seated beside him, regarding him in sleepy astonishment. She must have fallen asleep with her head on the bed. He gazed at her, the mists of his dreams receding at the reality of finding her in his bedroom, and seemingly unconcerned at it.

"What are you doing here?" he inquired, his voice rusty.

She smiled, rubbing her eyes. "I am merely spelling Hatten, who was so hagged from keeping vigil that he seemed likely to take ill himself. Your sleep has been terribly fitful, you know."

Francis frowned. "I had the strangest dreams."

"You certainly did." She chuckled at his look of surprised inquiry. "You were quite vocal in your delirium."

Realization dawned that he had been ill, and moreover was in his nightclothes, and he let out an exasperated breath, saying gruffly, "You ought not to see me like this. It is too mortifying."

"Not to fret, sir. My memory is amazingly poor when it suits me." Her blue eyes twinkled as she reached a hand to his forehead. "Your fever seems finally to have broken. I congratulate you, sir! You'll do, as Hatten said."

"Where the devil is he?" Francis strained to sit up and failed, falling back to the pillows. "I'm weak as a kitten."

"Which is how I convinced the others to allow me a turn at watching by your bedside. You could hardly seduce me. Indeed, if you are able even to flirt, I shall be utterly astonished."

Francis sighed, closing his eyes and shivering as another draft wafted about him. "How long have I been delirious?"

"A trifle more than four days." She stood to retrieve a coverlet, which she draped over him and tucked up around his shoulders.

"Thank you." He opened an eye to watch as she went to the window and closed it. "What the devil happened to me?"

"You were taken exceedingly ill—far worse than I. The apothecary diagnosed you with a putrid fever, brought on by a chill exacerbated by your general decadence and overindulgence in spirits."

He closed his eyes again. "That gleeful tone is wholly unsuitable to one who has assumed the role of nurse."

Her eyes widened, as did her smile. "There! You are already being superior and disapproving. It is my belief you are firmly on the road to recovery."

She pulled the bell rope and bent to bundle up a sheet that had been discarded sometime during the night. Francis regarded her from under drooping eyelids.

"You really ought not to be here, in your situation."

She glanced at him, a slight arch to one brow. "If you mean by that, my reputation cannot stand the scandal of my being alone with a sick man in his room when all his friends have forsaken him, then I thank you for your solicitude, but I believe I am safe."

"It would only take one idle tongue, you know."

As he uttered the words, the door opened and Patty entered. She bobbed a curtsey and almost without a pause took the bundle of sheets from Miss Willoughby's arms.

"Thank you, Patty," said Miss Willoughby. "As you see, our patient is finally sensible and is very likely hungry. Will you bring back some gruel, with the thyme tea Muncey had prepared?"

"Gruel?" croaked Francis with a grimace. "What have I done to deserve that pap?"

Miss Willoughby turned to regard him with sympathy. "Nothing but be deathly ill for several days, sir. The apothecary assures me that a bland and light diet will restore you faster than a rich one."

"But gruel? I won't have it."

"I doubt you could resist, sir," she said, a martial light in her blue eyes.

Francis groaned, turning his head away. "Very well. But if I waste away on this flummery, my death is on your hands."

She laughed and ushered Patty out, returning to sit in the chair beside his bed. "What would you like me to do now? Muncey and Hatten are likely still asleep, or they'd have come at the bell, and Clayton is likely gone in the dogcart to town for supplies, so you must abide my company a little longer."

He huffed. "I cannot even lift my arms to play at cards."

"I could read to you."

"What is there to read?"

She picked up two books that had been placed on the nightstand. "*A General View of the Agriculture of Lincolnshire* and *The Modern Angler*. The former is deceptively entertaining, I assure you." Rolling his eyes, he turned his head away, making her say impishly. "I suppose I might discourse more to you on Jamaican spiders."

He turned his head back to eye her incredulously. "Good gad, are there more? It seems to me Jamaica is an excessively unpleasant place."

"How like a little boy you are," she said, laughing merrily at his frown. "You are so cross and disagreeable when you cannot get your way. Well, I shall do my best to entertain you—and to disabuse you of the notion that Jamaica is unpleasant. To be sure, there are nasty things, like hurricanes that can lift the roof off a Great House as though it were *papier mâché*, and scorpions whose sting can be excessively painful. But there are things that are beautiful and mysterious too—"

The door opened, and Patty came in bearing a tray with Francis's meager meal. He groaned, but Miss Willoughby simply helped him to sit up, saying soothingly, "You will feel much better once you have taken some food. You have had only broth and medicines for days."

"I had rather have some cold beef and ale," he said with a grimace at the bowl she held before her.

She looked stern. "That would only unbalance your humors—at least according to the apothecary. Muncey scorns the idea of humors, but she agrees a return to your normal diet now would likely give you indigestion. So you see, it is all for the best."

"You may all go to the devil."

"I am not nearly so susceptible to that phrase as you, sir. And I'll warn you that my memory gets stronger the more contrary you are," she said tartly. "Now stop being difficult and eat your gruel."

His gaze flicked between her face and the spoon of gruel she now presented to him. "You are not very accommodating. I have always believed that patients are to be indulged and coddled, or they might suffer a relapse. You must be a very bad nurse."

"Then I will prove my worth," she said archly, "by allowing you that opinion simply because you are an invalid. Now, if you will eat up your gruel like a good boy, I have hit upon just the thing to entertain you."

Interest gleamed in his eye and he opened his mouth to take a spoonful of gruel.

"Very good," she said, giving him another spoonful as she went on. "You may recall one evening I told Mr. Wraglain about the tiny frogs we have in Jamaica, who make their home in the water reservoirs of bromeliads. Well, there is also a species of crab that lives in the bromeliads, quite inland and away from any other water."

He interrupted her to inquire what precisely bromeliads were, and she explained that they had curved leaves that collected rainwater at the base, and thus created reservoirs for the plant to use against dry seasons. Thus it was that creatures, who normally required immersion in water to survive, could live quite independently of other bodies of water on or surrounding the island.

She was so animated in her discourse, and the subject so intriguing, that Francis had eaten up his gruel before he knew it, and she set down the spoon with a satisfied smile.

"There. Now, do not you feel more the thing?"

"I suppose I do." He allowed her to pat his lips with a napkin. "And I suppose I must thank you, as well, for dealing so generously with me. Have I been a cantankerous patient throughout?"

"Yes," she said without hesitation. But with a softened look, she added, "Though it was not without cause. You have suffered a great deal these past days, and before that, it was you who dealt generously with me. Mr. Mantell—" She clasped her hands in her lap and looked earnestly at him— "I cannot begin to thank you for your kindness to me while I was ill. There was nothing to compel you to stay behind—"

"No, that responsibility belonged to your brother," he interjected somewhat gruffly.

She bowed her head for a moment, then looked gratefully at him. "And when he rejected his duty, you took it up. We might have got along, but without you and Hatten—"

"And my horses and curricle," he said, rather embarrassed by her praise and wishing to deflect what he could.

She smiled. "Yes, those too. With all of what you so generously provided, my recovery was swift and complete."

"And timely, too," he said, glancing at her from the corner of his eye. "If you had not recovered so quickly, I might have stuck my spoon in the wall."

"Well, I fancy that between the two of us, we should certainly have run all our servants into the ground with our arduous and unremitting demands."

He rested his head back against the pillow. "I must be grateful, though I yet feel that you have placed yourself in an awkward position. If Will were to find out what you have done, he should believe your reputation compromised beyond repair. Indeed, it is, and only an idle word will broadcast it to the world."

She lifted a shoulder in unconcern. "I seem to have single-handedly charmed the staff—that is, if I am being perfectly honest, Muncey has charmed them, and they have accepted me as their mistress in turn. Therefore, unless Hatten is not, after all, to be trusted, there is none to tell the tale."

"What of the apothecary?"

"We took care that I should not be present in your room when he called."

Francis exhaled deeply, his eyes drifting closed. "It still is unseemly that the task of nursing should fall to you."

"Well, sir, I will choose not to take umbrage at that remark, for I have come over the past few days to fancy I am a capital nurse, and you did only just own you are not dissatisfied with your care at my hands." He peeked through one eye at her and she gave him her mischievous smile. "However, again I must be honest, and admit to you that Muncey has been your principal nurse, with Hatten second, and Clayton and I merely poor bystanders. Clayton has become what you were to me—though he did not trust himself with your horses, so you need not fire up. My part you have chiefly seen, as a waiter and a watcher when all others were too exhausted even to argue propriety. You are more able this morning in that area than they were last night, and so you have found me here."

"I suppose I must be satisfied that you are right." He sighed, his eyes closing again. "Though it is a rather odd circumstance, for the sight of a pretty woman in my bedchamber is usually productive of a deal more activity on my part."

She gasped, but as it quickly became evident he had fallen asleep on the words, she merely closed her lips in a smile and, tucking the coverlet more securely about his shoulders, went away.

Chapter 21

After another few days of what Francis affectionately termed "Muncey's infernal quacking," with thyme tea and gruel giving way to chicken-foot soup and carrot-orange juice, he declared himself liable to throw himself out his window rather than endure another day in his bed. Thus warned, the staff judged it prudent to allow him to join Miss Willoughby in the drawing room, where her bright but calming influence might keep him from unwise exertion.

She greeted his advent with a broad smile, refraining from leaping up to assist him as Clayton was now doing. Francis swatted the butler's hands away and sank into the wing chair, too exhausted to refuse the placement of a blanket over his knees.

As Clayton took himself off, Francis sighed. "It seems I am to continue infirm, like an aged man ready to pop off."

"Take heart, sir—you are a very well-looking aged man," said Eliza, her dimples peeping.

He eyed her askance. "You are far too chipper for my company. Do not you comprehend I am laboring under extreme distress?"

Miss Willoughby instantly sat forward. "Has leaving your room caused you pain?"

"No, no," he said, waving a weak hand. "I simply am unused to the discomfort of gratitude. Not only do I find myself obliged to all the servants, but to you as well, a lady whom I have teased and tormented for my own amusement. It is not at all comfortable. I might have known Mr. Noyce would be right—he is my stepfather, and warned me once regarding such emotion."

"Well, sir," was the gentle reply, "As there is something of an apology in your discomfort, I believe I can see my way clear to forgive you."

He bit his lips. "Thank you, Miss Willoughby." Looking away again, he said in a rueful tone, "And you are far too gracious, I am persuaded. I fear I shall continue to be made uncomfortable for some time, especially in your presence. Perhaps that is the true meaning of 'imbalance of humors.'"

"It certainly would be apt," she said with a twinkle returning to her eye. "And if my presence cannot ease your distress, I will take myself off instantly."

He gave her a darkling look. "Stay where you are, if you please. I would rather endure discomfort than solitude. I'm sick to death of quiet. Would that I were strong enough to go driving."

"I might drive you about in the dog cart," she offered helpfully.

"No. I never allow females to drive me, no matter the state of my health."

She chuckled, then said, "I will take you at your word, sir."

He glanced quickly at her, but as she was studiously regarding her mending, he turned away again. "Have you heard from Willoughby?"

"No, I have not. It's been blessedly silent in that quarter, and I can only be grateful they have stayed away so long. However, Mr. Hayes wrote today to you, sir. Should you like to read his letter now?"

He did, and she went to the tray on the side table, bringing back a letter. He perused it briefly. "He says only that they have all decided to stay for the Houghton Meeting, which ought to be starting next week. That means we might expect them home in another fortnight."

"You do not think they might go on to London, or somewhere else entertaining?" She kept her head bowed over her mending as she spoke.

Francis refolded the letter, tossing it onto the end table beside his chair. "As much as we might wish it, it is unlikely."

She glanced up. "I know I do not wish for their return, but do not you?"

He cast her a wry glance. "Will and Bell have proven by their actions they are not my friends. They left me behind as easily as they did you, you know, with no thought for the consequences."

"Nathan can have no notion you have been ill."

"No, but he did not shrink from abandoning his family duty to my care."

She was silent, stitching away until she at last raised her eyes to look him full in the face. "It is no wonder you regret staying behind. It is entirely possible I am to blame for your illness, after all. I do not blame you, and only wish you to know that my gratitude is unchanged."

"Miss Willoughby," he said in an earnest tone that made her look up once more. "It is not regret I feel, but anger on your behalf. Willoughby ought to have taken more care of you." She blinked, looking taken aback, and he huffed a caustic laugh. "I do not fault your surprise. It is perhaps the first time in my life I have been possessed of unselfish feelings, having been far too often in Willoughby's shoes and of his mind. Indeed, I cannot be certain it will not be my last. I am no saint, nor am I even good. I am scarcely a gentleman, as you well know. But the fact remains that I chose to stay behind the others because I felt responsible while no one else did."

Her brow furrowed. "But you had no cause—"

"I kept you in the stables in your wet things. I held you back when you would have returned to the house. When at last I let you go, Bellerton had returned to block your entrance into the house, causing you to become even more wet and chilled." He gave a shrug. "If anyone is to blame for your illness, or for mine, it is I."

She blinked at him for a moment, then exhaled. "Well, I suppose we could argue for the greater share of the blame that night, but as it seems impossible that I should win, I feel it unnecessary."

He glanced up quickly, meeting her laughing eyes and mischievous smile. He huffed. "Minx."

She returned more happily to her mending and Francis watched as she set neat stitches in the garment draped over her lap. No matter Willoughby's or Bellerton's notions, she was every inch a lady.

"Did your mother teach you to sew?" he inquired.

"No, it was Miss Tibble. Apparently, my mother was a terrible needlewoman." She looked up, her courageous optimism shining in her face. "My father told me she was far too interested in herbs and plants to waste precious time with mending." She paused, her reminiscent smile transforming to a reflective look. "I believe it was because she had worked the plantations all her childhood. She had an affinity for the land, despite being forced to labor. But she was never strong, and field work was exceedingly taxing for her. I do not know what might have been her fate if she had not been able to purchase her freedom."

She said it simply, but Francis perceived a change in her demeanor. He was amazed at his own discomfort at the knowledge that, were circumstances only slightly altered, Miss Willoughby could very possibly be laboring at present in a sugarcane field halfway across the world.

"Does it distress you," he inquired gruffly, "knowing your mother was once a slave?"

She set a few more stitches before answering. "The horrors of slavery were kept from me for the early part of my life, you see, so for my formative years, I simply did not understand what it meant to be a slave. My mother had been freed before I was born, and was treated with dignity and respect in our home. I was loved and indulged, and the slaves I saw—I thought they were merely workers on our land, and they seemed to my innocent eyes no different from the servants in the house. However, my father was a better master than most." Her eyes grew haunted, and she looked down again. "I did not know how much better until he began to take me around to other plantations. I was about sixteen, and I will never forget what I saw during those visits. It certainly caused me to struggle with the fact that I, who bore the same looks and ancestry as the slaves, was treated so differently."

Francis considered this in silence for a few moments, wondering that a girl who felt so keenly could witness the horrors she had clearly seen and retain such ebullient optimism. That strange emotion he had experienced so often lately in connection with Miss Willoughby reared up again in his chest, and he knew a desire to shield her from the injustices and dangers of their world.

Eliza raised her eyes, her smile slightly forced. "Even my birth did not cause me so much distress. I did not learn until just before my father's death that he and my mother had not married until I was five years old. And my father did what many other Englishmen would not—he acknowledged me and provided my fortune. I have more and more cause to be grateful to him for that."

"He must truly have loved your mother," remarked Francis, his voice gruff with unaccustomed emotion. "Was it her influence that led him to free his other slaves?"

She nodded. "My mother was understandably distressed by the plight of her people, and that distress spoke more powerfully to my father's heart than any discourse on anti-slavery. I believe as soon as he fell in love with her, he began to view his slaves in a different light—not as chattels, but as fellow human beings. By the time I was eight or so, he would speak of making recompense, but he could not bring himself to free them yet."

She looked up again, her eyes intent. "He was used to the way things were, I think. My father and mother spoke often of it. He did not trust he could still make a profit on the plantation if he freed his slaves and paid them a working wage. He did not even know if they would stay to work for him, for all he was a good master. Many freed slaves join the Maroons up in the mountains, and participate in raids on the towns and plantations. Others would understandably rather make a living any other way than on the plantation. Knowing this, he feared freeing them would prove the destruction of his living, and he would be unable to provide for my mother and me."

"Yet he did it."

"He did," she said, and a sort of mournful pride glowed in her eyes. "It took losing my mother to yellow fever, but he did what he knew to be right at last. After her death, the Willow Plantation slaves were all given certificates of freedom, and many of them stayed on. Paying their wages did change our pecuniary situation greatly, but he was at peace. He saved every penny he could to amass my fortune, then, at his death, willed that the plantation be parceled up between his former slaves."

"Did he know he was dying?"

She sighed, looking down at her stitchery. "I can only guess he did. His urgency was very great."

Francis regarded her with unexpected tenderness. "You miss him."

She looked up, her eyes glassy with unshed tears, though she smiled her almost ever-present smile. "I do. And my mother. I miss Willow Great House and the sugarcane fields and all the workers who are now free to rule their own lives. I miss the cicadas that sing in the evening stillness, and the whistling frogs that chirp with them. I miss the sun that is so bright and hot it warms one quite through, and the turquoise waters of the bay that are so clear and warm and beautiful one can see straight to the conches and sea stars at the bottom." She paused for a moment, her voice suspended by emotion. Brushing tears from her eyes, she said raggedly, "It quite desolates me that I have lost all I know and love for naught, for the family I hoped to find here in England does not exist."

The yearning in her voice pierced his soul and, driven by that deep desire to shelter her, he impulsively extended his hand. Eliza blinked back her tears, gazing uncomprehendingly at his hand for a moment before tentatively placing hers within it. His fingers closed around hers in a warm clasp, and held. She did not at first look up into his eyes, but when he did not release her hand, she at last met his gaze.

Francis could not define what he felt as she had confided her inmost sorrow, having never experienced so strong an emotion before. In the past weeks, he had learned to care for her safety, to rely on her optimism, and to respect her person, but until this moment he had not considered that he could be falling in love. The idea jarred in his mind even now—love was the folly of the weak-minded, the trap set by the rapacious, the fantasy of the fledgling. It was no part of his character, nor his plan, to fall in love.

Nevertheless, he could not bear the ache that her words had brought to his heart, as it broke in sympathy with hers. He gripped her hand, unwilling to allow her to bear her sorrow alone, wishing he could somehow restore her peace and protect her from future injury. He would have been satisfied to be whole enough and man enough to take her in his arms and reassure her that all would be well. But he was not.

Pressing her hand once more, he released it, saying with difficulty, "I would that you had not been obliged to come here, Miss Willoughby."

"Oh?" She looked on him in surprise, and some hurt.

He glanced away. "You have already borne so much, and must yet bear more. You were made for joy, not sorrow."

She was silent for some moments, then said, "Sorrow is the lot of every human on earth, sir. It is not a matter of if, but when it will strike. When one comes to accept that fact, one must only choose how one will face one's particular sorrows."

"It is hardly fair," he said, looking at her again. "I cannot comprehend how you remain optimistic, in the light of all your hardships."

"I choose joy," she said simply. "But I hardly fancy myself put upon. Many persons are far worse off than I—it would be unpardonable in me to complain of my situation. No, I have much to be grateful for, and much to which I look forward—even considering the obstacles in my way. I had rather laugh than cry, at all events."

She had recovered both her composure and her cheer, and he marveled at the ease with which she set aside her cares and looked with hope on her future. But the strength of feeling that possessed him now could not allow her to face that future blindly.

"Miss Willoughby, I must warn you." She looked quickly at him, and he went on, "Your brother is dangerously jealous of your fortune."

"I am aware," she said, exhaling. "I should be glad to give him the half of my fortune, for I believe as he does that it is as much his as it is mine. However, it is tied up in the trust, and Mr. Findlay insists it must be used as my marriage portion."

"As it should!" said Francis forcefully. Her gaze was both startled and inquiring and he continued, "Forgive me, but your brother does not deserve a penny of your fortune. He has the income from Penhurst estate, and the use of Willoughby House in Town, and should require nothing more if he would only live more responsibly. But more to the purpose, he has treated you with nothing but carelessness and disdain since first he knew of your existence, and can have no claim on your good will."

"Perhaps not, but I had hoped—" She hesitated at his stern expression, looking away. "I had hoped his brotherly feelings might be warmed toward me if he did not feel so slighted by our father."

"I doubt Will's heart is so easily worked upon," said Francis bluntly. "Besides, were you to give him the money, I fear he would quickly waste it. I know well enough the sort of habits he keeps, having kept much the same myself—only he plunges far more deeply when gaming than I ever did. Mr. Findlay is certainly intimately acquainted with your brother's expenses, and is best heeded."

"But Nathan is so concerned for the land!"

"He blames the land, perhaps, but he is less concerned with righting past wrongs as he is catching up foregone pleasures. If he were to get hold of your fortune, or even a part of it, he may pay his most pressing debts, and perhaps even make some essential repairs about the estate, but be assured he should use the remainder to improve his situation in Society sooner than invest it in Penhurst's future."

Eliza was quiet, regarding the mending in her lap with unseeing eyes. "But what can be done? Will he lose Penhurst?"

"Your love for your brother is commendable, to be sure," observed Francis, regarding her with a furrowed brow. "However, I am astonished you can feel so about a man who has only been a distress to you."

"Nathan is my only kin, Mr. Mantell," she replied with emotion. "He is all I have left."

"But he does not care for *you*, ma'am," he pressed. "Nor do I believe that time will change Willoughby's outlook. It pains me to disabuse your mind in this matter, but it is imperative that you understand your brother sees you only as a means to his father's fortune."

"I cannot believe that, sir," she said quietly.

With a deep sigh, Francis said, "Miss Willoughby, your brother has contracted with Bellerton to split your fortune on your marriage. That is why he will not allow you to refuse Bell's suit. That is why Bellerton pursues you with such vigor. They have agreed to strip you of both your freedom and your fortune in one blow, with no thought to either your happiness or your comfort. And they certainly are not above using force to obtain their ends."

The sharp pain he saw in her eyes nearly unmanned him, but he did not look away. She must not doubt his sincerity, for her safety and peace were in the balance.

"You must not accept Bell's suit, Miss Willoughby," he said. "No matter how you are pressed to do so."

"No," she replied, then moved the repaired garment from her lap and stood, beginning to walk somewhat aimlessly about the room. "I had not intended to. Indeed, I would sooner set up my own establishment than be pressed into marriage with Bellerton."

"Willoughby would attempt to thwart you in that."

"Perhaps," she said, still wandering the room. "But Mr. Findlay would support me. Indeed, I had meant to write to him before the others removed to Newmarket, but I became ill, and then you—"

"You ought to write to him now. At least to let him know what is in the wind."

She glanced at him. "But what if I speak to Willoughby—tell him I will share my fortune with him if I may choose my husband—make it a condition of the marriage?"

Francis could not meet her eyes. "He is certain there will not be another offer of marriage."

She sighed, sinking back down onto the sofa. He felt her eyes upon him as she hesitated then said, "Do you believe so too?"

Chapter 22

Eliza watched mr. Mantell with some anxiety lest her question had been too forward. His face took on an arrested look, and his gaze became quite intense. But then he blinked, looking away as though distressed, and said in a gruff tone, "I believe you could easily receive many offers, if given the chance. Did you not meet any gentlemen during your sojourn in London?"

She averted her eyes, disappointment at this vague answer bringing a slight color to her cheeks. But what had she wished him to say? That *he* would marry her? That he had fallen in love with her? She scarcely knew him, and though the shared experiences of this past week had forged a bond between them, she could not rely on it to last. He was a rake and a flirt, whose charm extended only so far as he wished.

When he had taken her hand and pressed it just now, she had felt a well of emotion within her, strong enough to convince her that something significant had occurred—that he was becoming a very different man than he had hitherto been. But that did not necessarily signify a romantic attachment.

She therefore replied with tolerable composure, "I met only a very few gentlemen. Mrs. Riddle's purpose was more to accustom me to England than to introduce me into society. Indeed, I believe she was somewhat discomfited by her role as my chaperon. We did not attend any routs or balls, and though we made several calls and entertained some visitors ourselves, we went to only two dinner parties."

"I see," said Mr. Mantell, his expression dark. "It is the way of the world, I suppose. The circumstances of your birth are not such as are forgivable in their minds, though you are entirely innocent. But though they preclude you from a proper Season in Town, you may still find a footing somewhere."

"I believe I am beginning to comprehend my father's great anxiety regarding my future. His great generosity to me, even in light of Nathan's pecuniary troubles, is not so very unjust after all."

"No," Mr. Mantell said emphatically. "Willoughby has created his own trouble—you had no part in yours. It was only right that your father try to make amends to you."

She averted her gaze to the fringe of her shawl, which she twisted in her fingers. With a sigh, she said, "I cannot help but pity Nathan. Our father was nothing but loving to me. I never knew a day's heartache at his hands. If only you could have seen how he doted on me and my mama, you would understand how unimaginable it is to me that he was the same man who abandoned Nathan and his mother all those years ago. It was shameful, and I can comprehend why Nathan cannot forgive him—or me—for it."

His look was grave as he said, "Do not allow yourself to soften too much toward him. He must not prevail in his plan with Bellerton. You ought to be allowed at least to mingle in genteel society, and the use of your reason to choose a husband. I will even engage to convince Willoughby of it, with all my energies. These are not quite as robust at the moment as I could hope, but such as I can offer is at your service."

She was moved by his friendship, and said with a resolute smile, "I thank you, Mr. Mantell. Forgive me for wearying you with my troubles. What a maudlin mood I have fallen into—it was not my intention to be so tiresome a companion! On the contrary, I had resolved to cheer you with inconsequential chatter—at which I have signally failed, and I beg your pardon. But we will ring for nuncheon, which I do not doubt will serve to cheer us both. Muncey has been at work with Mrs. Slade in the kitchen, and promises a most delicious repast."

The meal that afternoon proved both fortifying and tasty, and Francis was liberal with his praise of Miss Muncey's efforts. Miss Willoughby fell as easily as ever into banter with him, and he would have found this as delicious as the meal, but for the resolution with which it was presented. He was certain their talk before had broken something within her—some hope he could only guess was connected to her desire to be loved. When she had asked if he thought she would receive no other offers than Bellerton's, a sharp yearning had struck him, and he had wanted to leap up and take her into his arms and assure her there would be at least one more. But as that would have been productive of a fall flat on his face—literally at least, if not figuratively as well—he had kept his peace.

His momentary excitement at the prospect of having Eliza for his own had thrilled him, but he had also shrunk from it. Just how did he expect to make her his? He had never before considered matrimony—indeed, he was sure he was not any woman's idea of a husband.

Could he imagine she should agree to become his mistress? That was preposterous—she was a lady, no matter her illegitimacy, and the thought of offering so base a position to Miss Willoughby disgusted him as it had never done so with any other woman.

She, more than anyone he had known, deserved to be happy—she deserved to have everything she wished for: a comfortable home, children of her own, a loving husband who would cherish and respect her—if indeed such a relationship could exist. But what a monumental task it must seem to her, to pursue the dream of a future as a wife and mother, after the rejection of both society and her only kin. It was a crushing blow, yet she bore it with such dignity.

The better he knew her, the more Francis was determined she should realize her dream. Her illegitimacy may be too great an obstacle to eligibility in the eyes of the *ton*, but lower circles may overlook it, either from laxer scruples or in deference to her vast fortune. She simply must escape the confines of Penhurst Lodge, and Francis was determined to assist her. It caused him a pang to imagine her sharing her dimpled smiles and clever repartee with other men, but there was nothing for it. He had promised to press her case with Willoughby, and as his conscience had shown no evidence of returning into dormancy, he would do so.

First he must recover, and he intended to accomplish this as quickly as possible, so as to enjoy her company to the fullest before Willoughby and the others returned. He therefore allowed Clayton to support him on walks through the halls and eventually up and down the stairs, until Miss Willoughby's arm was found to be sufficient, and he gladly basked in her smiles as they shuffled about.

Though her spirits seemed dimmed, they conversed now as naturally as old friends. She no longer seemed to fear his intentions, and he no longer endeavored to make her blush. He still flirted quite shamelessly, but only to break the gravity which too often hampered her mood.

"I ought to have invalided myself long ago," he remarked one chill day as they meandered about the hothouse.

"That is a nonsensical thing to say, sir," replied Miss Willoughby.

"Indeed, it is not! It cannot have escaped your notice that I have received abundant attention from pretty women with little to no effort on my part, but only since I became an invalid."

She chuckled. "From the profusion of your complaints since becoming an invalid, sir, I had taken quite a different view of the matter."

"As had I, and I cannot imagine why. I must have been a simpleton not to have taken advantage of illness before."

"I am persuaded you mean 'a gaby.'"

He cast her a deprecatory glance but said, "Perhaps I do, for I even had the benefit of example: my stepfather, Mr. Noyce, has been afflicted with weak legs all his life, and has been the recipient of all sorts of female attentions. He could not walk the length of the high street without being accosted by every female about, stopping to inquire how he did and if he had received her pot of jam or knitted scarf. My mother was forever sending him baskets of our choicest hothouse fruits and finest viands, even before my father's death."

"If you had rather I should shower you with fruit than accompany you about, I would gladly do so," she replied, gesturing to the pineapple bushes nearby with a twinkle in her eye.

He raised an imperious brow. "But you are missing the point, ma'am. It is the sum of these attentions that makes being an invalid so felicitous. I perceive you have been slacking in your duty, however—when, pray, do you intend to knit me a scarf to put about my knees against the draft?"

"Goodness me," she said, in mock solemnity. "I do not know how I shall ever accomplish such a task when my arm is continually claimed for your support."

"Then I am in a quandary," he mused, squinting in consideration. "The notion of clothing even my knees in a garment made by such lovely hands is infinitely delightful. However, if I redouble my efforts to get well, you will no doubt claim I no longer require a scarf." He sighed. "I suppose it is not so very enviable to be an invalid after all."

She laughed. "Perhaps if you ask it as your boon, I may still knit you a scarf, even when you are well."

"Now you are talking nonsense," he exclaimed, looking quickly at her. "To waste my boon for something that ought to be mine by rights?"

"But if you are no longer an invalid, it is no longer your right."

He humphed and looked away.

"Goodness, you are become a greybeard in spirit as well as constitution," she said with a teasing smile.

"A pity it does not earn me your respect," he retorted.

"Yes, it is a great pity, and I am persuaded that, as you are deriving no benefit from being either an invalid or a greybeard, you may as well cease such speculation and put all your energies into getting well."

He did, and when he managed to walk all round the perimeter of Penhurst Lodge without support or even a sign of fatigue, Eliza's congratulations were immediate and sincere. Muncey declared herself satisfied at his complete recovery, and he declared himself amazed to have survived her excessive solicitude.

"You really are too hard on Muncey, sir," said Eliza as she meandered with Francis along the path in the formal gardens. "If it were not for her vigilance, you could very well have 'stuck your spoon in the wall."

"If she is affronted by my cajolery, I shall instantly beg pardon," he replied, "but I believe she could not be so poor-spirited. I, however, am considerably affronted to find you imagine me insensible of my great debt to her. As a gentleman, I must always be sensible of my debts, whether they be to the tailor or to the banker at White's."

"As I never was able to convince myself you are a gentleman, sir, you must pardon me."

She made fun, but Francis was not deceived; even after a week, her natural optimism had not yet fully reasserted itself. She did not mention her situation, nor did she allude to his promise to convince Willoughby to allow her to choose her own husband. He could only conclude that she did not believe him capable of fulfilling his promises, nor could he blame her.

"Where is the estimable Muncey, by the by?" he inquired lightly. "Is she not tasked with playing propriety? I am no longer too weak to accost you, you know."

She chuckled. "She has developed a marked preference for the hothouse, sir."

"But not when I walk there with you, which you must own is curious."

"Indeed," she said wryly. "She tells me that not only does the hothouse remind her of Jamaica, but she finds we are wanting fruits and flowers at all times of the day. The oddity is she seems continually to be getting lost, for these forays take longer and longer each time."

"That is odd. And the affliction seems to be catching, for it seems Clayton is also forever getting lost somewhere. One can never find him when one needs him."

Miss Willoughby nodded gravely. "We must not think they are neglecting us. I can only imagine they are both caught up in seeking for ways to increase our comfort."

"Admirable servants, are they not?" Offering his arm, Francis said, "We must make what shifts we can to occupy ourselves while they are so hard at work."

As these shifts took the guise of long walks in the gardens, long talks in the library and drawing room, cozy suppers in the breakfast parlor with no thought for the niceties of port or tea, and at last comfortable drives about the neighborhood, neither party found much to repine.

At the end of another week, Francis drove with Eliza to the dike, about whose failings they had heard so much. Eliza, who had seen it only from the coach on her first arrival at Penhurst, expressed surprise on closer inspection at its ordinary appearance, and Francis agreed that it looked far too innocent for so treacherous an object.

"To be sure," Eliza said, "it ought at least to bear some resemblance to a brooding beast, ready to strike when least expected."

Francis nodded. "It is perhaps best that it does not, however, for then I should be expected to play Galahad and slay the dragon."

"I fear the metaphor is unsuitable, for in slaying the dike, you should almost certainly bring watery disaster upon our heads."

"You are perspicacious as usual, Miss Willoughby. Perhaps we ought not to survey it so closely. If it does take into its mind to burst and your brother discovers we were nearby, he will certainly hold us to blame for it."

"To be sure, you are right," said Eliza, somewhat subdued.

Francis, chiding himself for thoughtlessness, led her back to the curricle and handed her in while searching for a way to soften his appraisal of her brother. When he had settled next to her and given his team the office to go on, he mused, "I must own I do not envy Willoughby this estate. To be forever holding back the sea must be a gargantuan undertaking, and far too fatiguing for my comfort. It is no wonder he is tetchy on the subject. I may dislike Gracely Hall, my estate in Warwickshire, but at least it is not always threatening to flood."

She glanced quickly at him. "You do not like your home?"

He hesitated, then shrugged. "It is well enough, I suppose, as estates go. But I do not care to reside there more than is necessary."

"I find that sad," she said, her brow furrowing. "I have always associated home with family, so I loved Willow Great House almost as much as I loved my father and mother."

"It is precisely my family associations that sour Gracely's attractions for me," he said dryly. "Not everyone loves their family—I barely tolerate mine."

She considered this. "But you speak kindly of your sister, and of Mr. Noyce, your stepfather."

"I do not know that either of them would agree with you that my quizzing references are the product of kindness."

"Surely you care for them," she said, regarding him intently.

He hesitated again, unwilling to disabuse her of a notion so natural to one of her goodness. At last, he said, "My father was not so loving as was yours, and nor was my mother. My brother and sister and I were not reared on principles of virtue and goodness, but rather of selfishness and spite. I have very few fond memories of my childhood, unlike you, Miss Willoughby."

Her gaze grew pensive, and not a little sorrowful. "I believe I begin to understand you, sir." She turned forward again, watching the horses' heads as they trotted briskly down the road, passing fields and crossing over ditches. "I expect the idea of a family of your own is almost abhorrent to you. There can be nothing in the notion to attract you after your own experience."

"There is not," he said, but then wished he had not spoken so quickly, for her sigh was eloquent with dismay.

In the silence that followed, he wondered at the vast dissimilarity between their upbringings. She had rejoiced in love and light and laughter while he had known only irritation, malice, and disillusionment. He suddenly knew a pang of envy for her experience—and a desire to know the joy and contentment that a loving family could bring.

A sudden vision leapt into his mind of Miss Willoughby at Gracely, her dimpled smile and bright enthusiasm casting a cleansing light over the distressing memories of his youth. He saw her keeping the house, ordering the servants, and moving in Southam society with her generous and indomitable spirit. He even imagined her holding a child—his child—and that strange twinge in his chest became a rich ache that took his breath away.

He did not dare to look at her again, for fear what he had seen would show in his face. Was such a future even possible? For a rakehell and Man of the Town to find peace and contentment and even joy in the companionship of one woman, and the family that would follow?

His heart beat rapidly at the thought, even while his mind endeavored to beat it into submission. He would never be so foolhardy as to bow to the conventions—they were lies, anyway. Happiness in marriage was a facade covering trouble and strife—hadn't he witnessed this in his parent's marriage? Even Miss Willoughby's father had been unfaithful to his first wife, and had abandoned her with their child.

As they tooled up the drive, he tried to shake off the intensity of his feelings, uncertain and even fearful of probing into them further. Even was marriage not a burden of lies, he was who he was and a life with the likes of Miss Willoughby—no matter how intriguing—would not be likely to change him. Indeed, it could only lead to disappointment and misery on her part.

They both continued silent and grave as the greys came round the house, but all thoughts were arrested at the sight of the stables milling with grooms leading Bellerton's ill-favored team to their stalls.

Chapter 23

Francis tensed, but his first thought was for Miss Willough-by. A glance told him she was as displeased with and unprepared for the return of her brother and her would-be swain as was he.

Pulling up near the kitchen door, he jumped out to help her descend, saying, "I'll take you in the back door and watch you safely up the servants' stairs. Stay as long as you like in your rooms—I'll see they are settled."

She only nodded, going before him up the path to the kitchen door. After she disappeared up the back staircase, Francis made his way to the saloon, where he found Bellerton and Willoughby, still in their dirt, enjoying glasses of Madeira.

"I see you have returned," he said with an amiability he did not feel. "But where is Hayes?"

Willoughby turned as he entered. "Hayeswas summoned to the ancestral home, and good riddance. I've had about as much of his witless witticisms as I can take." He measured Francis with a knowing glint. "You don't look too much the worse for wear, Mantell. Enjoy your stay?"

"Not terribly, no," Francis replied, casually placing his hands in his pockets. "You do recall I stayed behind to care for your sister during her illness."

Willoughby grimaced over a slow sip of his wine. "She must be recovered now. Can't make me believe she was ill the whole four weeks."

Bellerton, glancing quickly between the two, suddenly started to his feet. "You ain't stolen a march on me, Mantell? I tell you, she's mine! Will promised her to me!"

"Take a damper, Bell," said Willoughby, coolly regarding Francis. "She's still yours, even if Mantell here thinks he's played us for fools. Trying your hand at an heiress, eh?"

A muscle twitched in Francis's suddenly tight jaw. His inexplicable rage of a few weeks ago seemed to have returned, for he knew another powerful urge to send both Willoughby and Bellerton to grass. It occurred to him that his languid boredom had been noticeably absent these four weeks, replaced by these strange, intense emotions over which he had no control.

With infinite care, he poured himself a drink. "What kind of sapskull do you take me for, Will, to try for an heiress when I've made it my life's work to avoid parson's mousetrap? Of course, I ought not to be surprised at your reasoning, when you are so careless about it yourself."

Willoughby scowled, taking the decanter and pouring another measure of wine. "It's why we were in Newmarket so long."

"How odd. I thought it was for the Houghton Meeting."

"George wished it, though none of our horses were running."

Bellerton goadingly added, "Got a note from Miss Draffin, as well."

"Did you?" Francis regarded Will with no little curiosity.

He scowled at Bell. "Yes, the little jade. Reminded me of her persistence in visiting my dear sister, so I stayed away."

Fervently and not a little spitefully hoping Miss Draffin had got the evidence of false promises she required to trap Will at last, Francis inquired in a carefully languid tone, "Was it worth the sacrifice?"

Bellerton smirked. "Dipped pretty badly, our Will. Hedged on two losing prads, then played a Martingale on the last, but it didn't fadge. No luck."

"My condolences, Will," said Francis, still firmly detached. "But I always did hold such desperate practices as useless. And you, Bell? Did you fare any better?"

"Went down heavy on the last winner," Bellerton announced proudly. "Might get Miss Willoughby a handsome engagement present."

Balling his fist in his pocket, Francis somehow managed not to shatter the glass in his other hand. Instead, he inquired calmly how his own horse had done at the October Meeting, and Willoughby sighed, pulling out a roll of bills.

"I had hoped you wouldn't recollect your request of Hayes to bet for you, but I suppose I am honor-bound to give you this." He handed over the bills, which amounted to just under a hundred pounds. "As ever, Hayes's cards were all trumps. One would never guess such a nitwit could be so knowing."

Bellerton snorted. "Only reason we tolerate the fellow."

"Indeed," said Francis, pocketing the bills. "Well, you'll like to get cleaned up. I'll see you at dinner."

He left them to their Madeira, making his way up to his own room. It rankled that Bellerton was so proprietary of Miss Willoughby, who would never accept his suit in her life—but neither did she have an understanding with Francis. He knew he had no right to be offended on her behalf, but he was, and he no longer cared to wonder at it. She had somehow touched his stony heart, and he would dashed well do what he could to protect her.

A wild notion of eloping with her overcame him. He could snatch her out from under Bellerton's nose, take her away under cover of darkness and hie to the border—but he dismissed the idea out of hand. Miss Willoughby wished for propriety, decency, and love—how could he imagine she should agree to elope with him? He must simply fulfill his promise to her and convince Willoughby—somehow—to relinquish his claim to her fortune.

When she came into the saloon before dinner, as bright and cheerful as ever, he therefore made sure to subvert Bellerton's confidence by monopolizing her attention, making many references to private jokes and generally giving Bellerton to understand he stood on no common ground with her. At dinner, he sat beside her, making himself so agreeable with his wit and vivacity that Bellerton could only subside into grim mutterings.

At last, Miss Willoughby stood. "You'll pardon me, gentlemen, if I do not join you in the drawing room. I am a bit fatigued, and believe I'll retire to my room. Good night."

They bid her good night and Francis relaxed back in his chair, ready to take the tongue-lashings he knew Bellerton was more than eager to deliver. But Willoughby spoke first.

"You're mighty intimate with dear Eliza, Mantell." He poured the port into his glass, passing the decanter to Bellerton. "Seems you've put a fine one over on her. Fairly glows in his company, eh, Bell?"

Bellerton was scowling. "What you mean to do about it is what I'd like to know."

"Not to worry, my friend. Our agreement still stands."

"The agreement wasn't for damaged goods!" snapped Bellerton, sloshing the port into his glass.

Willoughby grimaced. "You know Mantell never seduces innocent maidens. Besides, Eliza was damaged the moment she was born out of wedlock. But I'll agree that Mantell here has certainly overstepped his privileges. Without his raising her expectations while we were at Newmarket, Eliza would have been easy to bring round your thumb. Now we shall have to take more drastic measures."

"That's right!" exclaimed Bell. "I believe compensation is in order."

"For both the wronged prospective groom and the outraged brother," agreed Willoughby.

They both turned to regard Francis, who had only just maintained his composure through this exceedingly infuriating dialog. Lifting a hand, he made sure it wasn't trembling with rage as he made a show of inspecting his fingernails. "Though I maintain my opinion that Miss Willoughby will never entertain Bell's suit, no matter what measures you choose to employ, I will agree to talk compensation. As you have outlined my offenses, you will now allow me to outline yours."

Willoughby snorted. "What the devil are you going on about, Mantell? We weren't even here!"

"That is precisely the issue," said Francis, smiling unpleasantly and clenching his fists safely in his lap. "You did, after all, leave your household in my care, a member of which was seriously ill, and for whose well-being I was obliged to put myself out. I was called upon at all times of day and night to take out my curricle and my thoroughbreds for purposes of summoning the apothecary, retrieving medicines, or otherwise running mundane errands. This continued for several days without stop. I further believe—but you shall have to inquire of the apothecary to be sure—that I was instrumental in saving Miss Willoughby's life, for he intimated that without my services she should have been lucky to have recovered at all."

Bellerton looked uncertainly at Willoughby, but before either could retort, Francis held up a hand.

"Now," he narrowed his eyes in thought, "even without weighing the cost to my energies, the money I was obliged to put out, and the wear on my horses and vehicle, I should think that in saving your sister's life, I have more than compensated for the—imagined—affront you each have received to your very fine sensibilities."

Willoughby huffed. "Better to have let her snuff it, Mantell. Then I should have got her entire fortune at a stroke."

Glaring at Will as though betrayed, Bellerton cried, "But then I'd have got nothing!"

"Precisely," said Francis dryly.

Will grimaced, and it was some moments before he muttered, "You were little better than a nursemaid, Mantell. Worth no more than a few shillings."

"Ah, but I have yet to explain that as soon as your sister began to recover, I, myself, fell ill as well, and just as dangerously. If I had not been forced by your dishonorable conduct to stay, I would not have subjected my person to a contagious miasma, and would not have suffered the agonies of fever and delirium." He put up a finger. "First, I saved your sister's life. Then," putting up another, "I risked my own. Two lives' worth of compensation, gentlemen. Even if I had ruined your plan to dispose so satisfactorily of your sister, as you infer, Willoughby, I argue that you could only reasonably ask one life's compensation."

"Probably would have been ill anyway," muttered Willoughby, grasping the port decanter and refilling his glass. "Even without staying behind."

"In that case, you certainly would be obliged to me," retorted Francis, the rein on his temper slipping, "for I have no doubt you'd have left me to suffer unattended while you caroused at your leisure at the races, just as you did your own flesh and blood."

Willoughby did not answer, merely swallowing down his port and planting his glass back down on the table. After an uncomfortable silence, he raised dark eyes to Francis. "You've become insufferably high in the instep, Mantell. Dashed if I've ever heard such a chaff-cutter in my life. But I'm willing to let that go. There'll be no lady awaiting us in the drawing room and I've no wish to do the pretty at all events. What say we stay here and toss the bones?"

He pulled out a pair of dice and Bellerton gave what sounded like a bark of a laugh quickly smothered in a cough. Francis, putting himself on guard, agreed to play.

They decided on Hazard, Francis casting first, with Willoughby as banker. The game was friendly enough, progressing from quiet play to more jovial quizzing of the losers and booing the winners, their moods assisted by the frequent refilling of each other's glasses with the free-flowing port which Clayton replenished at intervals. Francis, who had been watching closely their increasing luck, soon suspected they were playing with loaded dice.

When Willoughby and Bellerton exchanged a gleeful look after Francis's third straight loss, he was convinced of it, but rather than allow a rather reasonable anger to overtake him, he smiled, a warm sense of well-being filling his mind.

"See here, Bell," Willoughby said, waving his refilled glass in front of his friend's face, "Mantell's got himself a bit of a losing streak. Looks like we'll have our compensation after all!"

"Serves him right," said Bell, nodding sagely. "Was prob'ly lying, at all events. Couldn't have been so ill, him or Miss Will'by."

Francis allowed the dice to make the rounds until Clayton came in with more port, then said amiably, "I'm out of cash, gentlemen, but I've a feeling my losing streak is about to end. Are you willing to take a different sort of wager?"

Bellerton snorted. "Going to bet your greys, Mantell? I'll take them!"

"Not quite, Bell. What would you say to a wager on Miss Willoughby?"

Bellerton growled, moving to rise, but Willoughby, eying Francis with narrow interest, held him back. "What do you mean?"

Francis smiled, beckoning to Clayton. "I bet that Bellerton will leave tomorrow, and you will vow not to interfere in Miss Willoughby's choice of her husband, or how she chooses to dispose of her money after her marriage."

Both Willoughby and Bellerton gaped at him. After some minutes of absolute silence, Willoughby huffed, "You're mighty bold, Mantell. You must be drunk as a lord."

"I assure you, I am perfectly sober. To prove it, I will promise to leave Penhurst tomorrow if my conjecture is wrong."

Bellerton exchanged a significant glance with Willoughby, who nodded, an unpleasant smile growing on his features. "Very well, it's a bet. We'll see tomorrow who is the winner, and who is out on his ear. What say we go to the saloon to celebrate our winnings, Bell?"

"Not so fast, if you please." With a languid movement, Francis took up the dice, weighing them in his hand. "The deciding factor is not so arbitrary as chance."

Willoughby's smile faded. "What the devil are you going on about, Mantell?"

Francis held the dice on his open palm, glancing at Clayton. "I've a fancy to smash these dice, Clayton. Would you bring a hammer?"

"What the deuce?" cried Willoughby, leaping up. "Do you call me a cheat? Don't you dare fetch a hammer, Clayton!"

But Francis nodded at Clayton, who went away. "Why, yes, Will, I do call you a cheat. It is only one more in a rapidly lengthening list of epithets I've called you recently."

"That's a dashed miserable thing to do, you scroof! Come into my house and eat my food, drink my wine, and ogle my sister— why, I ought to have Clayton throw you out!"

Francis's eyes glinted, but he merely shrugged. "I fancy Clayton won't see it your way, Will, especially as he agrees that you are deeply in my debt. But there is only one way to settle this. The hammer will tell."

Bellerton let out a string of oaths directed at Francis, his ancestry, and his ability to choose cattle, while Willoughby shouted his innocence, but when Clayton returned with the hammer, they fell silent, staring red-faced at the implement.

"Shall I smash them, sir?" Clayton inquired, his expression smug.

Willoughby hit a fist on the table. "I won't have it, Mantell! Not in my own house! I'll have you both out before I'll submit to this indecency!"

Francis turned his steely grey eyes upon him. "You will have to pardon me, Will, but this is the deciding factor. Per the terms of our wager, I'll go if I am wrong."

"It wasn't fair play, dash it!" Willoughby clenched his fists, look-ing from Francis, sitting at his infuriating ease, to Clayton standing almost protectively beside him. "The wager was a trick—the bet is off."

"Whether or not you honor the bet, Will, is your prerogative." Fran-cis laid the dice on the table. "But if these turn out to be Fulhams—as I've suspected for more than an hour they are—you are a cheat, and I've a fast pair and curricle to take me to London to publish the whole of the business at the clubs."

"No one will believe you," blustered Bellerton, but Willoughby only looked green.

"If you please, Clayton," said Francis, waving a hand toward the dice.

Clayton raised his hammer and Willoughby choked out, "I'll do as you wish. Bell will go, and—and Eliza may choose her husband, with no more interference from me."

The butler glanced sideways at Francis, who nodded. The hammer fell, and the dice shattered. Gathering the pieces, Clayton showed them to Francis. There was a hollow with a lead weight embedded on one side near the four and five of each die.

"Thank you, Clayton." Francis stood, loosening his cravat. "A game well-played, gentlemen. I condole you on your losses. But I own to disappointment in you, Will. Though I have known you capable of almost every other perfidy, I had long fostered every confidence in your sense of honorable play." He put a hand up to stifle a yawn. "Good night, and goodbye, Bell. Clayton, might I depend upon you to call this gentleman's carriage, and his odiously ugly team, at, say, half-past eight? An early start to speed him on his way."

Willoughby looked murderous at this usurpation of his authority, but Clayton only nodded, almost gleeful, and went out.

Bellerton glared in red-faced outrage at Willoughby. "You're going to toss me out? Without so much as a by-your-leave?"

"Stubble it, Bell," ground out Willoughby, pouring himself more port. "Go to the saloon and await me there. We'll drink to your newfound freedom."

Bellerton began to protest, but a look from Will silenced him. Snatching his winnings from the table, he strode out the door, slamming it behind him. Francis coolly ignored this, gathering up the bills he had lost to Willoughby and stacking them neatly in his hand.

Willoughby turned on him. "Not enough to steal away my inheritance—you must clean me out, too! Fine, take back the money! It wasn't fair play to use Fulhams, I'll admit to it openly—but nor was your wager. You hunted me admirably, and led me right into a dead set!"

Francis regarded him blandly before holding out the bills. "You may have these with my good wishes. Only leave Miss Willoughby—and her fortune—alone."

"You are the worst sort of hypocrite," snarled Willoughby, ignoring the money. "Oh, yes, you stare, but I know what you've been about! Once I let fall the grossly disproportionate size of my sister's fortune, you could scarcely keep the drool from your lips! What a honeyfall to grace the Mantell estate! You've meant to have her ever since, and I never suspected until we went to Newmarket."

He laughed bitterly. "What gulls we were! Thinking you were touched in the upper works, yet leaving you behind to fix her interest. I came back to find you practically lord of the manor, with my sister dear hanging on your every word, and the two of you smelling of April and May! Even then, you had me fooled, for I thought you couldn't abide the thought of her illegitimacy. For all you hated your father, I swore you wouldn't besmirch his name with marriage to a base-born female. But you said it yourself, didn't you? When one has no pride, money speaks louder than birth.

"Well, I'll have the last laugh, Mantell. Don't think my sister will leap into your arms without full knowledge of what you are. I'll tell her all about your mistresses, your hatred of women, your pathetic parentage and your hoyden of a sister. I'll make dead certain she knows your justifications for marrying her are even worse than Bellerton's, for you don't even wish to help a friend find his feet again with your ill-gotten gains! Then we shall see who has won. Oh, I'll do as I promised and not interfere in her ultimate choice, but I sure as hell won't just stand back and watch you take everything away from the Willoughby name."

He stormed out, slamming the door behind him, and Francis stood silently for a while, his elation at having fulfilled his promise to Miss Willoughby evaporating.

Chapter 24

A SURPRISING SENSATION OF dread filled Francis's chest. He sank into his chair, reaching for the port and wondering if Willoughby knew just how well-aimed was his threat. A month ago, Francis would merely have shrugged and looked about himself for another flirt, but in that time Eliza had become far more to him than a passing fancy. The thought of Willoughby flinging all Francis's faults up for her inspection struck something very like horror into his heart, and he cast about for a reason he should not care so very much.

But as he considered how he had conducted himself, he could find no such reprieve. The carelessness with which he had treated all women in his sphere now struck him as odious and unforgivable, as well as utterly immoral. Even his self-imposed restrictions against seducing innocents or taking unwilling lovers seemed but flimsy excuses to behave himself licentiously in all other cases.

It was a shock to find that his conscience had so quickly outgrown itself as to begin to change the very fiber of his moral being. He had been so taken up with the enjoyment of Eliza's company that he had been oblivious to anything else. But this was cold comfort, for his acknowledgment of his sins could do nothing to make them less abhorrent, especially to one as virtuous as Eliza.

He tossed off the port, striving to convince himself that all would not be lost if Willoughby carried through his threat. It was not as though Eliza thought him perfect, after all. She was well aware he was a flirt and a scoundrel—how often had she questioned his being a gentleman? It was all in light-hearted banter, to be sure, but he knew she was too clever to believe him anything but what he was. Even after three glorious weeks in her company, she did not seem a whit less wise as to his true character. She had perhaps gained confidence that she was safe in his company, even while he flirted outrageously, but she had never responded in kind.

Would it be so very terrible for her to know the odious details of his life? If anything, the knowledge would simply cement her estimation of him, and they would continue as they had done. It was not as though she had ever thought of him as more than a friend.

Though, a soft look stole into her eyes from time to time when she regarded him, and he did not think she pretended the delight that always lit up her features when he came into the room. Since his illness, she had never hung back from conversing with him, or demurred from taking his arm when offered. Was this the response of a mere friend?

Could it be she was in love with him? He took another ruminative sip of the port. Willoughby had said she glowed around Francis, that she hung on his every word—but it was not out of love, surely. She merely delighted in sparring with him, and quizzing him into better humor. Francis had often imagined she gloried in her own wit, but a brief reflection convinced him that could not be so. She was too generous to glory in herself, and more likely gloried in making others forget themselves or their cares. That was why she glowed—not for love of him.

He could not allow himself to believe it, for all he longed for it to be so. His previous visions of her lighting the stark portals of Gracely Hall returned in full force, and an aching longing filled his chest as he considered the hopelessness of it all. He was certain she could fill his days with interest and delight—teasing him with those deliciously impish looks and peeping dimples in her cheek. She could be the only female ever to cross the threshold of his hunting lodge, and George could have his pick of the rooms with Francis's good will.

He mused miserably on the inevitable issue of this dreaming. She might be capable of giving him all he could wish for, but what could he offer her in return? He had never been faithful to one woman in his life—even during his two years with Jane, he had entertained a mistress in London and dallied with barmaids from Southam to Swineshead. Could his newly emboldened conscience allow him to give her a proper church wedding, only for him to chafe against the vows he would make?

Francis retreated again into the port. He would change—he had changed. Did he not refuse Molly at the pub in Swineshead, all for anxiety over Eliza's well-being? There had been no understanding between him and Eliza then, nor was there now, but the thought of paying attentions to any other female repulsed him.

Indeed, recollections of the sort of attentions he had been used to pay to females made him almost ill. How he had not felt the shamelessness of his actions all these years he could not tell—certainly, he had never given them a thought. But now, knowing that Eliza might hourly be in possession of all the horrid facts of his life, he wished to bury himself rather than face her.

He groaned aloud, refilling his glass. He could never make her happy. Even if she did consent to marry him, it could not be a happy issue. Within a very short period his low character would be sure to reassert itself, undermining her optimism and killing her joy. All her friendly feeling for him would vanish and he would be responsible not only for her grave disappointment, but for the destruction of all her dreams.

The now familiar clenching in his chest penetrated the fumes of the port, telling Francis he cared more for her happiness than he did his own. He could not offer for her, no matter how much he wished it. He would not risk her future happiness only to fulfill his own desires, just as he would not leave her at Willoughby's mercy.

Staring into his empty glass, he contemplated drearily the futility of all his good intentions. What good was a conscience, after all, when it only militated against what one wanted? For it was no longer any use to dispute that he wanted Miss Willoughby—but he knew, without a doubt, he could not have her. Pushing the glass away, he stood and wove his unsteady way out the door and up the stairs.

Eliza had gone to her room, but though she had claimed fatigue, she could not think of sleep—not with such disturbing thoughts cluttering her mind. From the few comments Bellerton had made during dinner, she feared he yet considered her his property and intended, as Mr. Mantell had warned her, to press his suit despite her rejection a month ago. Willoughby's manner had not changed toward her, and she imagined he would uphold Bellerton's claim to her hand as before.

She had written a long-overdue letter to Mr. Findlay that evening after dinner, outlining her fears, and given it to Clayton to post the following morning. She ought to have written earlier, when Mr. Mantell had urged her to do so, but without the constant shadow of her brother and Bellerton in the house, she had been able to convince herself that the danger was far off. Mr. Mantell, in his humbled and dependent state, had been so enjoyable a companion that she had fallen into something of a beguiling dream, and had quite lost track of all else.

But she had at last recognized that he was not the man for her—not truly. She sighed heavily. He was lately everything a lover should be—charming, attentive, even gentlemanly—and yet he did not wish for a family, or marriage. His views on the matter seemed unalterable, which was not only a terrible pity, but a heartbreaking disappointment, for she had fallen hopelessly in love with the man she had imagined he had become.

She had not long believed him so. Before her illness, he had been merely an interesting sparring companion—a charming thorn in her side. But when she had discovered how he had served her during her illness, she began to suspect that she had misjudged him. And then, when he had needed her assistance so much himself, and had expressed his gratitude for it, she felt certain of it. Through the ordeal they had developed a bond, and she could discern a goodness in him that had been latent but was beginning to stir.

Since he had begun to recover, she had delighted in his company and their friendship had quickly developed. Indeed, they had been much to each other during the two-and-a-half weeks of his convalescence, having no other companions but Muncey and Clayton—who were more often than not off somewhere by themselves. While Mr. Mantell's teasing flirtation had returned as he had gained strength, she did not believe she had imagined his softened attitude toward her, nor his heightened concern for her welfare. She no longer felt she was a pawn in his game, but someone dear to him.

She was not dear enough, however, for him to offer himself as a suitor in Bellerton's place. Though he cared enough for her to promise to further her cause with Nathan, he had not changed so much as to wish to offer his heart. It was a severe disappointment, but she supposed her romantic ideals were to blame, for he was who he was. Still, she cherished these past weeks together even though she had not found what she had set out for after all: someone who could love her as she loved him.

It pained her to think of all she had hoped for that had not materialized. She had promised her father she would endeavor to heal the family breach, and though startled by Nathan's animosity at her arrival, she had been certain she could overcome it with her optimism and love. Then he would assist her in finding a proper husband who would cherish and protect her, despite her illegitimate birth. She would be a Cinderella winning her way from isolation and obscurity to family and fulfillment.

She had been wrong. Nathan's disdain was, as yet, unshakable. And the man with whom she had fallen in love did not exist. It was a discouragement almost rivaling that of leaving Jamaica and all she knew and loved. But Jamaica could not be her home, just as her love for Mr. Mantell was barren. He was a scoundrel and a rake, after all. She did not know precisely to what extent of immorality he had descended during his life, but she had gleaned enough from his manner and the odd comment here and there from the other gentlemen that he was wont to be quite shameless.

Though lately he had materially changed, her common sense told her a gentleman who had been inconstant and self-absorbed the whole of his life did not transform completely in a matter of weeks. She felt the Francis Mantell she had known the past fortnight was a man she could happily marry, but what if he was a figment that disappeared as quickly as it had emerged? Her heart whispered that she would be willing to take the risk, if only he would endeavor to love her, but there was little likelihood that he would.

So she had sent off her letter to Mr. Findlay, who would come to take her away, and she fully expected that she would never see Mr. Mantell again. She could not move in his circles, situated as she was, so no matter where she set up house for herself, there was little chance their paths would ever cross. But it was all for the better, for she still was wont to slip into a dream world where Mr. Mantell truly had changed, and that simply would not do.

She must steel herself for the time left in his company. It would be at least three days before Mr. Findlay could return to Penhurst from London—and that was only if he was able to leave instantly he received the letter. So she must endure however long of wishing and wanting what he could not give before she would be given space and time to forget him.

A sudden knock startled her from her musings. At Muncey's entrance, Eliza rose from the chair by her fire to meet her, and was surprised to find Clayton entering the room behind the maid.

"We must get you away from here, Miss Eliza," Muncey cried. "It's not safe for you."

"Our Miss Willoughby *is* safe!" exclaimed Clayton, visibly agitated. "It'll come to nowt!"

"Of what are you speaking?" inquired Eliza, surprised.

Clayton said quickly, "Mr. Bellerton will be on 'is way tomorrow, so there's nowt to mither you."

"Dere is plenty to mider her!" retorted Muncey.

Eliza frowned at them both. "What do you mean? Bellerton is leaving tomorrow?"

"Mr. Mantell forced 'im to it, 'e did," Clayton said, a gleam in his eye. "Caught Mr. Willoughby cheating at dice and threatened to make it known in the clubs unless 'e gave Bellerton the boot and let you and your fortune be."

Eliza blinked. "Good heaven. He has done it. Then I am safe, for Bellerton will no longer importune me—"

"He does not mean to ask you," retorted Muncey, mouth grim. "He means to carry you off wid him tomorrow!"

Shocked, Eliza said, "I don't understand. How can you have discovered this? Are you certain that is his plan?"

"Mr. Willoughby and Bellerton were speaking of it in the saloon," said Clayton. "I listened at the keyhole, for I did not trust them after Mr. Mantell served them that trick. And it's well I did not, for Mr. Willoughby said 'e'd not repine if you were to go missing in the morning at the same time Bellerton were off 'ome, and Mr. Mantell could do nowt about it."

"That is despicable," murmured Eliza, putting hands to her heated cheeks.

"But I won't let 'im take you," insisted Clayton. "*We* won't!"

Muncey shook her head, her gaze fiery. "Too many times we could not protect her. I will not risk it."

Clayton clenched his jaw. "The letter to Mr. Findlay—'e will come up from London to talk sense into Mr. Willoughby."

Muncey reached a hand out, placing it on his arm. In a low tone, she said, "No more delay, Matt'ew. Miss Eliza and I must go away tonight."

Her touch had done something to soften his irritation, and he took up her hand, holding it gently between both of his. "Oh, no, my Phoebe. You munna leave me like that."

Eliza stared at the two of them standing so intimately together, gazing intently into each other's eyes. She had suspected a romance, but this was something altogether more serious.

Clayton kissed Muncey's fingers, releasing them to pace about the room. His blue eyes flicked back and forth, unseeing, as his brain worked. "There's no moon for traveling, and no use in running off 'alf-cocked. I'm to wake Mr. Bellerton in the morning—I simply won't."

"But he will waken sometime," said Eliza.

"When he does, we will be long gone," said Muncey firmly.

Clayton halted his pacing, gazing intently at her again. "Yes, you'll be gone, my love, but I'll be gone with you."

Muncey's eyes widened, but at his unflinching gaze, her countenance softened. Her eyes glowed and her lip trembled, but she merely nodded, averting her eyes.

"How will we go?" inquired Eliza, bewildered. "And to where?"

Clayton tore his gaze from his beloved long enough to say, "To London on the stage. And never you worry, Miss Willoughby, nor you, my Phoebe. I've a notion who'll 'elp us."

He left them then, and went purposefully down the corridor to the servants' stair, but stopped at the sound of an awkward step on the main staircase. Turning, he went to the landing and found Mr. Mantell teetering on the top stair.

He grabbed at his arm, hauling him onto the landing. "What, are you foxed, sir? It's a fine thing to celebrate a victory, but not by breaking your neck. I can think of more than one of us as would find that not to our taste."

Mr. Mantell turned blearily to him. "You're too kind, Clayton—and I mean that. One less scoundrel in the house will rather relieve several persons, I fancy."

"Ah, but we'll be one less scoundrel tomorrow, sir, so no sense in trying to steal a march on 'im." He supported Mr. Mantell across the landing and into the guest wing. "Miss Willoughby were proper grateful to hear you got Bellerton to go away."

Mantell blinked at him. "Did Will tell her?"

"No, sir, I did. And it's none too soon, I'd say. Lucky you spotted the Uphills, or there'd have been nowt to hold over Mr. Willoughby."

"Indeed," said Mantell blankly. "If it had not worked, I should have counted myself obligated to offer for her myself—"

"No need to feel obligated, sir," said Clayton in annoyance as he opened the door to Mr. Mantell's room.

Mantell glanced up in muzzy surprise and said, "Do not eat me. You know as well as I that it would be nothing short of a disaster for me to offer for anybody, much less a divine creature such as Miss Willoughby."

Clayton's gaze softened, and he helped Mantell off with his coat. "She deserves a sound man, sir. A man who'd love her as she'll love him."

"Yes, certainly." Mr. Mantell looked drearily away. "One may only wish her luck."

Clayton was quiet a moment as he helped Mantell to his bed. "It's a difficult task set her—unless you've someone in mind?"

Mr. Mantell sat staring unseeing past Clayton. "That is precisely what I have endeavored these past few days not to think of, Clayton." His bleak gaze met the butler's. "I can't bring myself to do it—she deserves infinitely better."

Clayton pursed his lips, pulling off Mantell's boots. "Well, sir, either you do or you don't, but you ought to consider what she'd like." He bowed, moving toward the door. Before he exited the room, however, he said abruptly, "If you'll pardon the liberty, sir, I believe you're a better man with a better chance than you like to think. It'll only take some conviction."

He pulled the door closed behind him, striding to the landing and down the stairs, and wondered if he ought to apprise Mantell of their plans, or simply put a flea in Hatten's ear to be used at the most opportune time.

Chapter 25

THE FOLLOWING MORNING, Francis woke with an exceedingly bad head. It had been months since he had succumbed to strong drink, as it had been months since he had allowed any cares to cause him enough worry to do so. He swung his feet out of bed, leaning on his knees. It was then he realized he had his breeches on and soon discovered that he was almost fully clothed. He must have been so far gone as to fall asleep without disrobing. Hadn't Clayton brought him to bed?

He pressed his palms to his eyes, willing away the burning. He was beginning to recollect snatches of conversation, in which Clayton had encouraged him in some way. He opened his eyes, squinting against the morning light and wishing his head would not pound so. Was it a dream? He rubbed his eyes again, willing his brain to slough off its heaviness and show him the truth.

Clayton had told him Miss Willoughby was grateful that he had won her freedom. But then he had said something about Francis being a decent man. Had he as much as said Eliza would welcome his addresses? Clayton could only be deluded. How could anyone believe that sweet, virtuous, lovely woman would ever entertain the suit of a rake?

Francis groaned, passing a hand over his face before reaching for the bellpull. When the footman came, he asked for strong coffee, then sat in a brown study until it came. After sending the footman away again, Francis leaned back against the headboard and sipped at his coffee.

Perhaps Clayton, being himself in love, saw more than what was real between Francis and Eliza. They could not be together. She wanted love in a marriage, and he had never believed in love, nor had he ever planned to marry. Marriage had never been in his mind through all his careless flirtations with Eliza. Even after Charles had exacted his promise, Francis had used it as an opportunity to vex Bellerton rather than endear himself to Miss Willoughby. And when she had fallen ill, he had only put himself at her service out of an indignant sense of duty.

But when he had woken from his delirium to find her by his side, joking him from his megrims, he had felt gratitude for the first time in his life. And when he had sat broken and weak in her presence and witnessed her strength, he had yearned to support and protect her. But even then, when marriage had at last suggested itself, he had dismissed it, for who was he to consider marriage?

He was a fool, to be sure, for now, in the cold light of morning and without the fumes of port to muddle his thoughts, he still could think of nothing he would like more than to marry Eliza. But there was no way he could convince her to accept him. He could promise not to touch her until she was certain of her choice, and he could arrange for her fortune to be placed in a trust for her use alone—he could even take up residence in Swineshead and court her properly, allowing her whatever time she required to come to a decision. But it would never be enough—not after Willoughby revealed to her the extent of Francis's depravity.

The mortification of this conviction gave him an ill feeling in the pit of his stomach, and he put down his coffee. He ought not to think more of it. Even were a miracle to occur and she to overlook his faults, she deserved far better than he could ever be.

He came to a decision. He could not bear to remain at Penhurst to see her gentle smiles and hear her vibrant wit and know she was forever beyond his reach. He had done what he could to protect her—Bellerton would be gone within the hour and would antagonize her no more. Willoughby's hands were tied as to her marriage—she was free to choose her own future. She had no more need of Francis, and he must away to Southam, and try to forget her. He would steel himself to face her at breakfast, and then bid her goodbye forever.

Ringing for the footman, therefore, he desired him to pack his things, and he took himself down to the breakfast parlor, finding it empty. This was advantageous, for his thoughts continued to circle on the impossibility of his situation, made the more maddening by the encouragement of well-meaning persons like Clayton and Mr. Noyce.

What was it that made them think more highly of him than was reasonable? Mr. Noyce was probably simply naïve, but Clayton was much more a man of the world. Where Francis had summarily dismissed Mr. Noyce's opinion, he was actually inclined to at least consider Clayton's—though it went against the grain. It was more in Francis's nature to run away from problems, or to foist them onto someone else's capable shoulders.

Absently placing a few kidneys and ham onto his plate, he glanced out the windows, noticing the activity in the yard. Bellerton was, indeed, removing from Penhurst today, which was well and good. He had at least given Eliza that.

It was about all he had given her, however, except vexation. He had quizzed her that day in the library, then again when he had come upon her in the park. Their dialog had been lively, though, and he thought that perhaps she had derived some enjoyment from it. She had allowed him to hold her before him in the saddle, which he had been sorely tempted to use to his advantage, but somehow could not bring himself to do. He had enjoyed it far too much to spoil it—his desire had been to capture the whole of the experience and put it in his pocket for a dark day. So he had teased Bellerton instead, using Miss Willoughby as a pawn. True, he had essentially protected her from Bellerton, but he still had used her to his own ends.

And she had not grudged him for it, in the end. She had twitted him for not being a gentleman, to be sure, but when he had required her help, she had given it freely. And when he had recovered, she had not retreated back into her teasing distance, but had opened her heart to him. If Clayton were to be believed, it was not in friendship, but in love. Had he broken her heart by claiming he did not wish for a family?

The immensity of that possibility pained him deeply, and he was forced to pause in his mechanical consumption of breakfast. Had she truly loved him, and he had denied her? If so, he had lost even her friendship, and was an even bigger fool than he had known. The future stretched out gloomily before him, without the sunshine that was Eliza Willoughby to warm and enliven it.

He was obliged to sternly remind himself he was no sort of husband for so bright and trusting a creature. She loved with her whole heart, while he hardly knew how to love, much less if he were capable of it. How could he ask her to throw in her lot with his, with no better guarantee of happiness or stability than with Bellerton?

He grimaced. He might have a chance if he were able to reform his ways—it could be possible. He, who had never thought for another soul, had experienced a multitude of refining emotion in the past month. Perhaps if he continued to allow his conscience liberty, it might eventually cure him of base desires. He already had lost his taste for the company of loose women—but was it enough?

Having never considered his own redemption, Francis was at a loss as to how to effect it. He supposed he ought to have paid more notice in church, but it had been years since he had even bothered to attend. Now it was probably too late—he was so set in his ways that he expected he would simply return to his old habits once Eliza was out of his reach.

But how could he not even make the attempt to change when his happiness might depend upon it? And yet, how could he ask Eliza to accept his transformation as real and lasting, when he could not trust it being so?

After traversing this ground in his mind over and over, he knew there was nothing more he could do. He wanted to be with Eliza more than anything in the world, but he could not bring himself to offer for her and risk her future happiness. In any event, it was not likely she returned his affections—despite Clayton's opinion—or that she would accept him once Will had had his say. The only thing for it was to retire to Southam and leave Eliza to find her own path and her own happiness.

He did not know how long he had been gazing blindly at the wall, his breakfast going cold on his plate—perhaps a little less than an hour, judging by the clock. The activity in the yard had subsided, and he was pleased to see that Bellerton's chaise was gone. He noted, however, that his own team and curricle were also gone, and upon inquiry of a groom, he was told that Hatten had taken them out early for an airing.

Francis did not think much of this—knowing full well he had neglected his pair during his convalescence—and only felt vexation at the delay. He turned his steps instead to the guest wing, to inspect Bellerton's room to satisfy himself that his departure was no trick. The room was empty—all sign of him was gone.

Grateful that he had, in fact, done the thing for Miss Willoughby, Francis steeled himself to face her once more and took himself to the drawing room to take his leave. It was her habit to spend time either there or in the library, and when he found the drawing room empty, he went downstairs. The library, too, was empty, and Francis began to feel ill-at-ease. He went to the saloon, but found only Willoughby there, pacing back and forth with a thunderous expression.

"Dear me, Will," he said in a sardonic tone, "do you miss Bell so much? One would think he was a lover, but that he is too much of a boor."

Willoughby whirled, a look of intense hatred in his features. But then the fury left his eyes, and his snarl was replaced with a sneer as he said, "Always the cynic, eh, Mantell? Well, you are wrong this time, for I am certain to see Bell soon. He is to be my brother-in-law, after all."

Francis stopped mid-stride, his heart freezing in his chest. Then he almost leapt at Willoughby, taking his coat lapels in his fists. "What have you done, Willoughby? I swear to you, I will strike you down where you stand if you dare to tell me you have sold your sister to that scoundrel!"

"I did nothing," said Willoughby, tolerably keeping his countenance. "I have kept my promise to you, my dear Mantell—no interference."

"Amazingly, I am not satisfied," growled Francis.

Willoughby broke Francis's hold and stepped away. As he readjusted his coat, he said calmly, "It is unnecessary that you be satisfied, Mantell. That was never my purpose, after all—indeed, it was quite the contrary. I wish only to satisfy myself, and in doing that, I must teach you never to meddle in my affairs again."

"Where is Eliza?" Francis demanded.

"Surely, you have guessed," said Willoughby with a patronizing smile. "I warned you I would tell her about your exploits—the many women you have known, offered protection, and discarded. You could not imagine that she should desire to remain here any longer, with only your company and mine. She took the best chance that offered."

"What are you saying, Willoughby?"

Willoughby smiled grimly. "She is gone, along with Bellerton. Before you again put hands on my person, Mantell, recollect that I did not interfere. She went willingly, and took that virago of a maid with her. I could not be more pleased, for I have my house, my fortune, and my revenge, all in one fell swoop."

Francis's vision threatened to go red, and he commanded himself with a supreme effort. "Have they gone to London or to his estate at Swaffham?"

Willoughby snorted. "I wouldn't know, having no say in the matter. He will proceed as he sees fit."

"You cannot convince me she went willingly, you snake," said Francis in a dangerously controlled tone. "She never would do so."

"Are you so sure?" inquired Willoughby. "Consider, Mantell, the disappointment she has sustained. Her savior, the man who so tenderly cared for her during her illness, has been revealed as an unrepentant rake and a charlatan. The shock of this betrayal was enough to rob her of all desire to pursue the course you so cleverly won for her. I suppose she could no longer trust that her freedom would be hers after all, if you were to have a hand in it, and took Bellerton's more honest offer."

Francis felt the color drain from his face, leaving him feeling ill and weak. Nevertheless, he stepped close to Willoughby and said in a menacing tone, "I will find them and see for myself—and heaven help you if you are deceiving me."

Will let out a mirthless chuckle. "Were you truly fool enough to hope she had fallen in love with you?"

"It's none of your business, Willoughby," said Francis curtly. "Whatever Eliza feels for me, I will ensure that she is not being forced into this marriage."

"Suit yourself, Mantell. She's no longer my concern. I never wanted her and I say good riddance to that greedy, encroaching daughter of a slave whore—"

Francis laid him flat with what Clayton would have called "a Floorer." As he moaned on the rug, Francis rubbed his knuckles and said, "If I find you have done anything to harm Eliza, I'll make certain your gaming days are over."

"Rot in hell," uttered Willoughby through the blood in his mouth.

Francis strode away—but before he reached the door, the sight of a carriage coming up the drive caught his eye. Willoughby, now sitting on the floor with his back to the window, did not see it. But

Francis, recognizing the carriage, hastened out of the saloon and to the front door, before Clayton could come to turn away the visitor.

Opening the door wide without waiting for the knock, he said in a low but amiable tone, "Welcome, ma'am! Come in, come in. You will pardon my asking you not to speak, or Willoughby may just escape you again. Do I hope too much that the letter I see clasped in your hand is from him to your daughter? No, no, do not waste your breath with me. Willoughby is just here, in the saloon."

And ushering Mrs. Draffin into the room before Willoughby knew what he was about, Francis closed the doors, calling for Clayton. John, the footman, came out of the back corridor, straightening his neck cloth.

"He's not here, sir. May I help you?"

"Where has he gone, John?"

The footman looked embarrassed. "We don't know where he's gone. Up and left this morning—all his things is gone, Mrs. Slade says."

Francis exhaled, puzzled, but nodded. "It seems there is to be a mass exodus this morning. Would you bring my trunk to the yard?" Then he went upstairs and collected his driving coat, hat, and gloves, and hastened downstairs and out the back passage door to the stables. He called for Hatten, then inquired of one of Willoughby's grooms, "How long ago did Bellerton drive off?"

The groom considered. "About twenty, thirty minutes, I reckon, sir."

That did not give him much of a head start, but Francis nodded, desiring the groom to ready his curricle.

"But the greys was just out, sir."

Francis went to his horses' stalls and, running an expert eye over the pair, was pleased to see them looking none the worse for their early exercise. "They'll do. Hitch them up."

Hatten appeared, raising a brow at the greys being led from their stalls.

"Get your things, Hatten," said Francis. "We're leaving on the instant."

Hatten nodded but said, "They're a touch winded, sir."

"No matter. We won't be going far, then they can have a rest."

"Very well, sir." Hatten went back up to the loft to retrieve his own bag while John strapped Francis's trunk to the back of the curricle, and in a few minutes they were off. "Are we headed home, sir?"

"Yes," answered Francis through gritted teeth, "but we've a short stop along the way."

Other than that, he was in no case for conversation, and it suited him very well that Hatten was his usual taciturn self as they flew down the drive. They took the post road south, for if Bell wished to marry Eliza quickly, he could do no better than obtain a special license in London. But Bellerton's family estate was in Norfolk, and it was possible he had taken her there. Bell's father was a blustering man who chided his heir at every folly but never failed to pay his debts, and his mother was a querulous woman who doted on him. Neither was likely to prohibit the marriage if Bellerton insisted upon it, especially after discovering the size of Eliza's fortune.

Either destination took the same road for about fifteen miles, however, and unless Francis missed his mark, Bellerton's showy nags were incapable of making that distance in less than an hour and a half. His own pair, driving the light and well-sprung curricle, could catch them well before they would have turned one way or the other.

He did not much care what Bellerton would think upon seeing him, but he could not be certain what would be Eliza's response. If she had, as Willoughby claimed, gone with Bellerton willingly, she may well be irritated by his interference. But he could not believe it—unless Bellerton had succeeded in forcing himself upon her, and she had determined that her best hope of saving her reputation was simply to appease him by marrying him. But this notion brought a white-hot flame of jealousy into Francis's chest, for if she simply wished to save her reputation, she dashed well could marry *him*!

But he highly doubted the clever and resourceful Eliza had fallen to such foolish thinking—even considering Willoughby's revelations regarding Francis's past—which meant she had been abducted. And if she had been taken against her will, he hoped she would view his intervention as providential—and perhaps even some small atonement for his larger sins.

After half an hour, he saw a swaying vehicle ahead, and he whipped up his horses. Taking advantage of a bend in the road, he passed the carriage, satisfying himself that it was indeed Bellerton, with his ugly team at the fore. He urged his pair ahead, then pulled his curricle across the road to block it, and got down, handing the reins to Hatten.

"Hold them, please. I'll not be long."

Bellerton's carriage slowed to a stop and its owner thrust his head out the window. "What the devil are you about, Mantell? You wanted me gone, and now you're stopping me in my tracks. Are you mad?"

Francis strode up to the door, pulling it open. Bellerton exclaimed as Francis gazed all about the interior of the chaise. There was no one else inside.

Chapter 26

FRANCIS TOOK HOLD of Bellerton's coat. "Where is she?"

"Who in blue blazes are you blustering about?" cried Bellerton, his muddy brown eyes flashing.

Francis let him go. "Miss Willoughby. Will told me she left with you."

Bellerton exclaimed, then huffed a laugh. Then he began to guffaw.

"What the deuce is the matter?" Francis demanded, extremely annoyed.

"Did Will tell you that?" inquired a breathless Bellerton. "Oh, would that I were there to see it. What a joke! He gulled you properly. Oh, but you deserve it—sweet, sweet revenge."

Francis took hold of his coat again and pulled him from the vehicle. "You'll tell me what you've done with her, or I'll murder you right here on the road."

Bellerton stopped laughing, his features contorting into a look of disdain. "She ain't with me, Mantell, nor was she ever. Not for lack of trying, mind you. I worked it out last night that you never made me promise to keep my hands off Miss Willoughby, so I decided to nab the girl as I was going off this morning. A forced elopement, you might say." He shoved Francis's hands away. "But sweet Eliza wasn't there. Nor was her maid—couldn't find hide nor hair of them. Put Will in a fury, I tell you, because it would have been the perfect revenge. Well, it looks as though he got his revenge after all, and so have I."

Francis, assimilating all this, released his coat. With a heavy exhale, he closed his eyes. Will really had gulled him, but it was of no consequence if Eliza was safe from Bellerton at last.

"So neither of us gets her, Mantell," said Bellerton with a smug expression. "But don't think I won't do my possible to keep her from marrying anyone else. I'll see to it everyone who is anyone knows just what she is."

In a rush of fury, Francis hit him square in the jaw, sending him careening backward. Bellerton shouted with outrage and came back at him, swinging wildly and clipping Francis on the shoulder. But Francis caught his jaw again with an uppercut, then followed with a wicked hook to his face. Bellerton slumped against the carriage, groaning.

Taking Bellerton by the lapels once more, Francis growled into his face, "If you dare to say one word against Miss Willoughby, I swear to you, Bellerton, I'll knock those crocodile teeth of yours right up into your brain."

Bellerton spat out blood, but Francis shoved him into the chaise and back against the squabs. Slamming the door on him, Francis stalked to his curricle, signaling for Hatten to lead the pair off the road and motioning Bell's coachman to move along. As the chaise rumbled by, Francis rubbed his knuckles.

"Do we go on, sir?" inquired Hatten diffidently.

Francis grimaced, fixing his hat upon his head and feeling his shoulder where Bellerton had hit him. "I don't know yet, Hatten. I must think."

Where in thunder was Eliza? Pacing up and down the road, Francis tried to order his thoughts. Both Will and Bell said she had gone from Penhurst—there was no trace of her or Muncey. Could they be hiding somewhere on the estate, awaiting Bellerton's removal? Or had they found a way to transport themselves to London? He had advised Eliza to write to Mr. Findlay—perhaps he had somehow arranged for their removal without anyone else knowing. But without returning to Penhurst and ransacking the house and the grounds, there was no way for Francis to discover which was the case.

He kicked a carriage wheel, his heart tight in his chest. He could not go on to Southam now. It was one thing to leave Eliza, as he had planned this morning, safe and secure at Penhurst Lodge, and another entirely to leave her to an uncertain and possibly dangerous fate.

"I feel as though I'm going mad not knowing what has become of her," he said aloud.

Hatten scratched his nose. "If I may, sir, I know where she's gone."

Francis's gaze snapped to his face. "You know where Eliza's gone? Why the devil didn't you say so before?"

"Beggin' your pardon, sir, I'd no notion you cared, haring off home as I thought you was."

Cursing himself for an impetuous fool, Francis scrubbed a hand over his face. "Forgive me, Hatten. I ought to have told you. Just where the deuce *is* Miss Willoughby, pray?"

"She's gone on the stage to London, sir. Took her at daylight this morning."

Fury rose in Francis's chest. "Do you mean to tell me that is where you took the curricle this morning? I could boil you in oil, man! Why did you do such a thing? She doesn't know her way to Swineshead, much less across half the kingdom! Anything could happen to her! We must—"

"Clayton's with them, sir," put in Hatten calmly. "He'll see them right."

Taking a breath, Francis begged pardon again. John had said Clayton was gone, and Will had said Muncey was with her too—that certainly mended matters. But even knowing she was well looked-after, he still thrilled with the urgency to find her.

"Where in London do they mean to stay, Hatten?" he pressed. "With Findlay?"

Hatten regarded him, his grizzled features intent. "Just what is it makes you wish to chase after her, sir? She ain't in your usual style, if you'll pardon the liberty."

Running a hand through his disordered locks, Francis looked away, considerably discomfited. "I know it. I don't know why I must find her—I don't even know if she wishes to be found, or if I am part of the cause of her running away. But I must find her, Hatten. On my honor, I wish her no harm. I simply cannot go on without knowing she is safe and well—indeed, I begin to wonder how I shall go on without her at all."

After a long moment, Hatten remarked, "Seems you've discovered that love is worth any trouble or expense."

Francis blinked at him, vaguely recalling their conversation before he had provided for Jane to marry her long-time admirer. Was this how Jacob Hatchett had felt? This yearning for his beloved's society, this desire for her best welfare, this agony over her safety—even when his love may not be reciprocated? Was this what it was like to love? It seemed preposterous, and yet it was how he felt.

He had scorned love so long, there was a surreal quality to the thought. He was in love. He tested the notion in his mind, almost sounding it out on his tongue, but refraining in the presence of Hatten, who already was regarding him dubiously. It seemed impossible that he could be in love, but the heart-rendings that had engrossed him the past few days confirmed it. For all his languid worldliness, he had fallen in love with the most unlikely lady—an impish, delightful, pure-sunshine girl.

It was a disaster. He knew it, and Hatten probably knew it, from the way he regarded his master in silent appraisal.

"Am I mad, Hatten?"

Rubbing his nose, the groom said, "Only if you don't mean to tell her how you feel when you find her."

Francis groaned, slumping against the curricle. "You know I've no business telling her, Hatten. I have no business loving her, so what's the use in making it known?"

"It's my belief she ought to have a say in the matter, sir." He crossed his arms, his gaze steady and not unsympathetic. "If she's no notion how strongly you feel, she'll never know what it is she's lost."

Snorting, Francis straightened and began pacing again. "She's lost nothing but a selfish, odious, rakish flirt who made her stay at Penhurst a torment."

"That'd be Bellerton you're describing, sir, not you."

Francis gave him a disparaging look. "Perhaps I was not so much a torment as I was a trial."

Hatten's lips tilted in a half smile. "You didn't see her while she nursed you through your fever, sir. She couldn't be kept away, no matter how Muncey railed about the impropriety. She was always inquiring what else she could do to ease your distress. She it was who sat with you hour after hour while me and Muncey caught some sleep. Your fretting now reminds me of her."

Francis stilled, staring at his groom. "Surely not. It was only that she is so generous and kind—"

"I never saw a lady so joyful as the day you finally woke sensible. She fairly danced downstairs to spread the news, then redoubled her energies to make you well."

"Why have you never spoken of this before, Hatten?"

The groom shrugged. "Wasn't certain of your sentiments, sir, knowing you almost as well as I know myself. Thought much the same as you seem to do—only now I'm fair convinced you're not yourself, nor will you ever be again. You've the capacity to change, sir, and become what Miss Willoughby deserves. Ought to try."

Francis stood gazing at him in wonder, the angry, mocking voices in his head quieted for once. The possibility that he *could* be worthy of Eliza, that she would accept him—it was too wonderful, too terrible to contemplate. Hatten could be utterly wrong in his conclusions, but he could also, possibly, be right. The hope this thought inspired was almost unbearable.

"I scarcely know what to think."

Hatten replaced his cap on his head. "On the drive to the Pig and Whistle, Miss Muncey carried on about returning to Jamaica, but Miss Willoughby spoke of a governess in Bristol—believe the name was Tinley or Tindle—Tibble?"

Even as he straightened with hope, dread pierced Francis's heart. London, it seemed, was not to be her final destination. What if she heeded Muncey's wish to return to Jamaica, and this governess in

Bristol was only another stop on her journey? How would he ever find her then?

But if he had learned one lesson today, it was not to go haring off without vital information. Their primary destination had been London—he would go there. Mr. Findlay was there, and Francis could speak to him and discover if he knew anything about Eliza's flight, and where she had gone. He said as much to Hatten, climbing into the curricle.

"As you wish, sir," said Hatten.

The horses had rested long enough during this period to carry them without complaint to Spalding, where the two men baited at the inn. Then Hatten stayed behind to bring the horses by easy stages to London while Francis continued on with a fresh pair.

He had hours to contemplate the futility of his actions. She may not wish to see him, and if she did, she may well change her mind once Francis declared himself. Even if Will had not, after all, revealed Francis's exploits to Eliza, he knew he must confess them to her before asking for her hand. It made him feel sick to think of doing so, but Hatten was right—she deserved to have her say, and Francis wished her to have full knowledge to make her decision. But he believed the possibility of her deciding to accept him on the promise of his full transformation—which he himself did not yet trust—was almost nil.

And yet, he remembered her generosity and goodness, and the warmth of her gaze when it had rested upon him in their closest times. Perhaps Clayton had been right that Francis had more of a chance with her than he thought. But how could she put faith in his love when it was so new and untested, and how could he live with himself if she did so and he failed to change?

His mind went round and round with longing, hope, crashing reality, and doubt. He loved her—he did not deserve her—she might wish to be with him—she could not yet trust him—she would never have him—he could not live without her. It seemed a hopeless situation, and he continued on only because he could not rest without at least knowing she was safe and well.

He arrived in London late on the second day and went straight to the Saracen's Head—the posting inn where the Lincolnshire stage stopped. Here he discovered that two West Indian women had disembarked from the afternoon stage and had hailed a hackney. Without the number of the hackney, he was unable to pursue this lead further, so he went on to his club for dinner before retiring to his lodgings in Ryder Street. He spent the remainder of the evening gazing tensely into the fire, a glass of brandy near to hand but hardly touched, contemplating the hollowness of his life and despairing at his sudden overwhelming conviction that the only thing to fill it was Eliza Willoughby.

Just before ten o'clock, a messenger arrived with a scented note on hot-pressed pink paper. The landlady presented it to him with her customary moue of distaste, but Francis recoiled. How Eglantine had discovered he was in Town, he did not know, nor did he wish to find out. They had parted amicably months ago, but now he did not feel the slightest interest in renewing their relationship, or even in seeing her again.

"Tell the messenger there is no reply," he requested his landlady, adding, "And if you would, toss that note on the fire—in another room."

Francis slept fitfully that night, plagued by dreams of former mistresses revealing all to Miss Willoughby—who turned from him in horror, just as Willoughby had insisted she would. But he doggedly presented himself at the offices of Windle, Windle, and Findlay in the City at half-past nine o'clock the following morning. He was made to wait nearly a half hour to see Mr. Findlay, and when he was at last ushered in, the solicitor did not greet him with warmth.

"Mr. Mantell," he said gravely, shaking his hand. "What brings you to London?"

"I hope you know, sir," replied Francis, feeling unaccountably mawkish under the venerable man's gaze. "I am anxious to have information of Miss Willoughby—she vanished from Penhurst day before yesterday and was last known to have embarked on the London stage from Swineshead."

Mr. Findlay removed his glasses, polishing them on his handkerchief. "It is still unclear to me why you have come, Mr. Mantell. Do you act as someone's emissary?"

Francis frowned. "If Willoughby had any sense of duty, I should be his emissary, sir. However, he does not. I come of my own volition."

"You will pardon my curiosity, sir. Just what do you hope to accomplish in discovering Miss Willoughby's whereabouts? You see, as one of her guardians, I am responsible to safeguard her."

"Then you know where she has gone?" Francis's heart leapt, and he sternly tamped it down.

Mr. Findlay made a minute adjustment to the arrangement of papers on his desk. "If I did, I would make a poor guardian to simply relay that information to just anyone who inquired."

Francis wilted a trifle. Mr. Findlay did not know him well, but he knew Willoughby's friends by reputation, and had seen Francis interact during his brief stay at Penhurst last month. He likely had not missed the air of careless flirtation Francis had employed with

Miss Willoughby, and judged, very reasonably, that he could have no honorable cause to wish to find her.

"Does Mr. Bellerton, perhaps, have aught to do with your search?" inquired Mr. Findlay flatly.

Glancing quickly up, Francis replied, "Yes. He has much to do with it."

Findlay's gaze grew hard. "Then we have nothing more to discuss, Mr. Mantell. Good day." He rose to his feet.

"No, sir—you mistake." Francis stood as well, putting out a hand. Eliza must have come to Findlay and told him all about Willoughby's plan to wed her to Bellerton. "I wish to find Miss Willoughby to preserve her from Bellerton's attentions."

"By exposing her to your own?"

He opened his mouth and shut it again, giving a quiet growl of frustration. "That is not my wish at all, sir."

Mr. Findlay resumed his seat, gazing reflectively at his visitor. "If you have no personal interest in my ward, Mr. Mantell, I cannot conjecture why you should wish to find her. You are not a relation, nor do you seem to be on good terms—at present—with her brother. You will pardon my belief that you have no business knowing the whereabouts of Miss Willoughby."

Rubbing a hand over his face, Francis slumped back into his chair. "You're perfectly right, sir. I have no business seeking after her. But it is not that I have no personal interest. I care deeply for Miss Willoughby—for her safety. She has been singularly unlucky in her family situation—she has very few friends, and I fear she may come to more trouble. I should like to be assured of her welfare."

"Hmm." Mr. Findlay fiddled with his pen, laying it at right angles to the papers on his desk. "Then I may satisfy you, sir. You may be assured she is very safe, and shall be well guarded from the importunities and machinations of all kinds of fortune hunters."

As this statement was accompanied by a pointed look, Francis stared at him, aghast. "I don't want Eliza's money."

Mr. Findlay's brows rose. "Would you acknowledge it if you did?"

"Fiend seize it." Francis put his head in his hands. This was proving much harder than he had supposed—he had given no thought to what obstacles might arise at the solicitor's office. He had assumed he would be able, in a few short sentences, to convey to Mr. Findlay his very disinterested desire to find Eliza, and the solicitor would assist him. Now he was under suspicion of being a fortune hunter, or at the very least, in league with Bellerton and Willoughby.

With a heavy exhale, Francis said wearily, "Mr. Findlay, I cannot explain to you why I am compelled to be of service to Miss Willoughby, for I do not understand it myself. I have been a self-absorbed, careless, rackety creature all my life, and have never put myself out for anyone. But Miss Willoughby—" He shook his head helplessly. "She has sparked a change in me, such that when I discovered she had run away, I could not rest until I had seen with my own eyes that she was safe. I should easily have been able to go home to Warwickshire and never have given her another thought. Instead, I drove a hundred miles only on the hope that I might find her here with you, or that you might know where she means to go. If you will not help me, I will be forced to hire a Bow Street Runner to find her, for I cannot rest until I may satisfy myself that she is safe and well."

Mr. Findlay listened without expression, then dropped his eyes to his desk, moving his pen from one side to the other. "No need to hire a Runner, sir. I believe you are sincere. But I have promised Miss Willoughby to conceal her whereabouts. However," he said, raising a hand against the protest he could sense poised on Francis's tongue, "I will write to her and inquire if she will allow you to know where she is. If you have come to care so much for her, she must have felt it, and will respond accordingly."

Francis's heart sank to the bottom of his boots. Eliza could know nothing of his true feelings, for he had only just begun to understand them himself. He sighed, standing and handing his card to Mr. Findlay. "Thank you sir. I will await your answer. But if I am not satisfied, I cannot promise not to involve Bow Street."

Chapter 27

THE FOLLOWING DAY brought Hatten with his horses, and the groom found his employer taut as a bowstring.

"What news of Miss Willoughby?" he inquired with his customary placidity.

Francis threw up his hand as he paced the rug. "None that satisfies me. Findlay very kindly informed me she is safe and well, but refused to supply me with her direction until he has received her permission to do so."

"Seems reasonable."

Throwing him a disgusted glance, Francis continued to pace. "I know it. Eminently reasonable! After all, I am merely another scoundrelly rogue who must be after her fortune. She essentially ran from me as well as Bellerton, so why cannot I leave her alone? Findlay assured me she is safe and well-protected. Why do I not simply go back to Southam and forget her?"

"Love is a powerful motivator, I reckon."

"It is agony." Francis put fingers to his forehead, pressing his eyes tight shut. "When Mr. Noyce said love is excessively uncomfortable, he vastly understated the matter."

Hatten regarded him with a ghost of a smile. "Perhaps Mr. Noyce is the man you want. He's as wise as he is good, and at Bath he's on the road to Bristol, too."

Francis gaped at the groom, then strode over and pumped his hand. "You're a great gun, Hatten! Let's be off!"

They were on the road to Bristol at first light, and during that day's travel, Francis maintained his hope at a manageable level with the conviction that Mr. Findlay would not have suggested he wait for a letter if Miss Willoughby had boarded a ship to Jamaica—or if she intended to do so in the near future. Thus, she must be within a reasonable distance from London, and if she was not at Bristol, this governess would likely know her intended destination.

Still, despite the fact that both Hatten and Clayton had offered him encouragement, the realities of his situation continued to mock him, and he was chafing with uncertainty and self-recrimination by the time he sighted the Bath road and veered southwest.

Francis tooled the curricle straight to Laura Place, drawing up before Number 8. "See to the horses, will you, Hatten?" he requested as he jumped from the vehicle.

Taking the steps two at a time, he plied the knocker, being admitted by the staid butler. His inquiry as to the family's being home was answered in the affirmative, and he was ushered upstairs into the drawing room. His mother and sister, only, were there, however, and he was made to endure an uncomfortable interview with them before Mr. Noyce at last came to deliver him.

They retired to his study on the first floor, where he invited Francis to sit in one of the overstuffed chairs by the fire, saying as he lowered himself into the other, "Forgive me, my boy, for being unavailable when you came in. I was going over some letters from my steward at Wesley Abbey, but I am now at your service. Your mother mentioned a pressing problem—how might I be of assistance?"

The kindness of his tone and the earnestness with which he delivered this speech worked like a tonic on Francis's frayed nerves. Exhaling as though a great weight had been lifted, he began to talk. He told Mr. Noyce of his meeting with Miss Willoughby, of his early shameful abuse of her friendship, and of the gradual growth of his respect for her. He told of Bellerton's advances and of Willoughby's agreement with him to divide Eliza's fortune between them, and of his part in Eliza's sudden illness.

Mr. Noyce, brows raised in surprise, interjected, "You stayed behind from Newmarket? Did not you have a horse running?"

"Yes, yes," said Francis, waving this irrelevancy away. "I could do nothing other than stay. Don't you see it was the least I could do after causing her illness?"

Mr. Noyce, blinking, instantly agreed, and bade him continue. Francis told of his succumbing to his own illness and of waking to find Miss Willoughby as his caretaker. The enjoyment of her company over the proceeding days came through more in his tone and look than in specific details, and Mr. Noyce found himself smiling at his own conclusions.

"Then Will and Bell returned from Newmarket, and were as keen as ever to go forward with Bell's engagement to Miss Willoughby. I knew she didn't like him—she had told me as much—so I forced Willoughby to relinquish his plan."

"And just how did you do that, my boy?" inquired Mr. Noyce, bending forward in his deep interest.

Francis shook his head. "I caught him out in cheating at dice, and threatened to noise it about the clubs if he didn't leave her alone."

Mr. Noyce leaned back, nodding. "I suppose that is the only sort of honor he respects."

"Precisely."

"It seems that you have done Miss Willoughby a very good turn."

Francis stood, pacing quickly about the room. "I do not know that I have, sir. During all this time, I was developing feelings—I did not realize just how strongly—" He hesitated, rubbing a hand over his face—a gesture he had not been wont to use in Mr. Noyce's memory. "Sir, you will think me mad, or joking, but—I believe I have fallen in love with Miss Willoughby."

"That is wonderful, my boy!" cried Mr. Noyce.

But Francis only said wretchedly, "It is not, sir! It is not! Have you not heard me describe her? She is all goodness and light, vitality and generosity! I am a selfish, odious, careless rake, not worthy even to think of her."

Mr. Noyce, undeterred, said, "You might once have been, Francis, but I am persuaded you are no longer. No, do not protest. You have changed—I could see it even before you began to speak to me."

"But it is not enough!" cried Francis, throwing up a hand. "I must make a complete reformation, and what if I cannot do so? What if the devil in my nature cannot be contained, and I succumb to what I have always been?"

Gazing ruminatively at him, Mr. Noyce said, "It is entirely possible, I suppose. And yet, you may recall that I always thought you better than you think you are, Francis."

Francis sank back into his chair. "She deserves far better—more than what I can give, sir. She deserves warmth and fidelity and love—things I have never felt or shown to anyone. Would that I could! I want her so badly I can scarce think of anything else."

"Then I am even more strongly persuaded you have the will and the strength to continue to reform," said Mr. Noyce. "I fancy there is an angel in your nature that has finally got free of the devil. Why else would you suddenly yearn after a life and a lady whom you would hitherto have scorned?"

Francis huffed. "It may be the devil has simply turned all its energies to tormenting me. She is precisely the sort of creature with whom I have no business falling in love."

Mr. Noyce regarded him keenly. "But you could make it your business, and I believe you have already begun. Do you not see, Francis? You say you want her, but as I hear you speak of her virtues and excellence, I know you do not want her as Bellerton did—as a trophy for a collection. You do not simply want another willing woman for your bed. What you want, Francis, is Miss Willoughby as a companion and confidante, as a mother to your children, as a keeper of your home and happiness. In short, you have become the sort of man to want a loving marriage and a family. And you want it so badly you can scarce think of anything else."

The strange tightness in Francis's chest shuddered and his throat caught on the truth of Mr. Noyce's words. The explanation was so simple it was astounding, and yet it unwound all the complexities of Francis's emotion. He did want a loving marriage and a family, if it could be with Eliza. The vision of her holding his child rose up again in his mind and that undeniable yearning returned. But he was even more convinced that this yearning, this desire to continue to become the man she wanted, was not enough.

"I dare not approach her," said Francis, almost in a whisper. "I cannot offer myself to her when I have no assurance that I will not disappoint her in the end."

Mr. Noyce considered his stepson with compassion. "None of us can ever become a perfect being, Francis. It is the nature of humanity to fall short. But it is what keeps us humble and ever reaching, I believe, and is essential to our eternal welfare. Everyone must try to do better, I am persuaded—to reach higher, for that is what we are made for. When we do not attempt to better ourselves, there is a littleness to our lives that leaves us empty and unfulfilled."

Francis glanced up at this, recalling his dissatisfaction with his life when considering replacing Jane with another mistress. Perhaps the changes that had occurred over the past weeks had actually begun then, and were merely accelerated by Eliza's influence. If that was so, Francis's inner angel may truly have freed itself, and may be strong enough to perpetuate his change. But it would take time.

As though reading his mind, Mr. Noyce said, "Redemption is not done overnight, you know—not even in a month. I suspect you feel the truth of that, for you would never have faltered if you did not. You have done much of which you must be ashamed, to be sure, but that is the beauty of repentance, Francis. You may be forgiven of all your sins, and leave them behind. It takes work and conviction, but it is a gift of God to all mankind. It may, perhaps, be advisable to attend to that before declaring yourself to Miss Willoughby."

"I have never been a patient man, sir."

"Perhaps not. But oftimes love wants time to clear the mind and comprehend what it really wants. You must know that your mother and I loved each other when we were young, but she accepted your father instead. It was many years before she was ready to understand her own heart, and many more before she was again free to choose me." He chuckled at Francis's bleak look. "Now, do not think that I remind you of this because I believe you will be made to tread the same weary path. But I do think you have an opportunity to give both yourself and Miss Willoughby some needed time. If you are not sure of your ability to be constant, and if you truly love her, you ought to take the time to repent and reform, so that you may approach her with confidence. And she may look about her to make sure you are the man she wishes to be with the rest of her life."

Francis looked down, his heart sinking. "She may well find another, better, man."

"If she does, you must accept it as the hand of Providence. But you need not wait to approach her until you have entirely transformed, for that will never happen. You may simply wait until you are certain of yourself." Mr. Noyce bent forward to pat Francis on the knee. "Do not despair! It is exceedingly likely she is as unhappy as you, for not knowing your sentiments. It may well be you will not be hard-pressed to win her."

Francis was silent for some moments, digesting this advice. At last, he looked up to meet Mr. Noyce's sympathetic gaze. "Then you think I ought not, at present, to attempt to find her?"

Mr. Noyce chuckled. "On the contrary, I believe you are likely to die of suspense if you do not find her and assure yourself of her well-being. Whether or not you show yourself in the process is your decision, and may depend on circumstances. But I do believe you both will be happier if you are given the opportunity to make an informed decision."

Francis closed his eyes tightly and inhaled. Then, exhaling heavily, he said, "Thank you, sir. It is a hard course you have set me, but I must own, it does seem the wisest."

Mr. Noyce smiled broadly, struggling up with his canes to stand. "You are closer than you think you are, my boy. I venture to predict a happy outcome between you and Miss Willoughby." Then he clapped Francis on the shoulder as they went together to join the ladies for dinner.

Francis slept well for the first time in a week, having a peace at heart he had never before experienced. He awoke betimes, and having ordered his curricle at seven, set off punctually, but not in the direction of Bristol. He had realized that it behooved him to avail himself of some assistance in searching for Miss Willoughby's governess, as he did not know Bristol well. Thus, he turned his team in the direction of the village of Cleeve, and the abode of Charles Wraglain's parents, the Finchleys.

Having no wish to present himself at Captain Finchley's home, and thus waste precious time being regaled with dubious tales of wartime bravery, Francis hoped he might find one of the many Finchley children about, who could fetch Charles to him. He was in luck for, coming near to the cottage, he observed a young red-haired lady walking along, a basket held in the crook of her arm. He drew up and called to her. Her freckled cheeks blushed a bright pink when she saw Francis in his curricle, and she tightened the shawl about her shoulders in a shyly conscious gesture.

"Hello, Mr. Mantell," she said, her blue eyes bright but flicking about timidly.

Francis tipped his hat. "Hello, Lyddie. Pleasure to see you. I declare you've grown into a lady since last I saw you!" She blushed even rosier, looking down at her feet, and Francis continued a trifle urgently, "I had hoped to meet with Charles. Is he about?"

She shook her head and his heart fell, but then she peeped up and offered helpfully, "He's gone off again to the Lord Nelson. You might find him there, if you hurry."

Francis thanked her, bidding her good day and setting his curricle in motion. The Lord Nelson Inn was in the High Street, and only ten minutes from the Finchley's door. Hatten drove the curricle around to the stable yard while Francis went in, inquiring for Charles at the bar. The tapster grinned and motioned Francis down the hall to the kitchens.

Surprised and intrigued, he went along the passageway, entering the kitchens and nodding insouciantly to the various menials who were visibly startled by his entrance. Sweeping the kitchen with his gaze, he found Charles propped up against the edge of the washbasin, looking infinitely pleased with himself as he chatted away to the scullery maid who scrubbed at the dishes with an almost angry vigor. If he were to judge, Francis would say she was incensed by Charles's attentions.

Francis gazed narrowly at his friend—this was not his usual style of flirtation. Charles charmed the serving wenches in the taproom and was known to flirt with the maids who did out his room at the inns where he stayed. But unlike Francis, he was not known to single out any young lady, much less one from the serving classes, and goad her with an unwanted flirtation.

After a very few moments, Charles felt his friend's gaze upon him—or became aware of the general unease in the kitchen occasioned by the sudden addition of a second member of the Quality—and looked up. He grimaced, striding across to Francis.

"Blast you, Mantell," he muttered, hustling him out the back door. As it closed behind them, Francis peeked back at the scullery maid and glimpsed a rather ordinary, if very pink, face. Charles admonished him directly they had obtained the yard.

"What the devil are you doing here?" He paused, a light of memory in his eyes. "Miss Willoughby—Did Bell and Will—"

"They have not succeeded, Charles," said Francis, brought back to his cares with a jolt. "I've come because Miss Willoughby has fled Penhurst, and I must find her."

Eying Francis narrowly, Charles made particular inquiries and within ten minutes, Francis had acquainted him with the whole of the business.

Charles grinned. "Thought you had a softness for her. It's just a pity we never shook on our wager, or I'd be the proud owner of your bay gelding."

"Can you help me to find her, Charles?"

Relenting, Charles said, "I'm only somewhat conversant with Bristol myself, more's the pity. But I can't gad about just now." He looked away. "Business, of a sort. I wish I could help—Stay! I know a man who might be of use. He's a friend of my brother William—Peter Guthrie, tapster at the Plume of Feathers in Wine Street. A mite shady, but a good man to have in a corner. If you give him my name, I'll wager he'll know how to find her."

Francis added this hope to the growing number. "I'm in your debt, Charles. Thank you."

Charles nodded, holding out his hand. "I'll see you back in Southam after Christmas, Mantell. And I expect to hear all about the end of your adventure—may it turn out as you hope."

"Not so fast, my friend," said Francis, taking Charles by the shoulder. "What do you have to do with that little scullery maid?"

Charles scowled, but his eyes danced. "You needn't have become curious as well as humble—curiosity used to fatigue you."

Francis snorted. "Suspicion, conversely, is quite enervating. What are you up to, Charles?"

"It's none of your business, Mantell." Charles put his chin up, crossing his arms over his chest.

"Come now, you're the last man to take up with a village maiden. There must be something in the wind."

Charles looked mulish, and seeing Hatten walking across to them from the stables, nodded curtly to his friend. "Good luck with Miss Willoughby."

His brow raised, Francis watched him stride to the kitchen door. "Very well, keep your secrets! But you owe me an explanation when next we meet, if you wish to learn mine!"

Opening the kitchen door, Charles flashed him an impudent grin and was gone.

Chapter 28

Francis assisted Hatten in hitching up the horses, and they were on their way again within a quarter hour. As they neared Bristol, he found himself bristling with nervous energy in the expectation of the end of his chase. He pulled up in front of the Plume of Feathers in Wine Street and directed Hatten to walk the horses.

Entering the tavern, he was obliged to duck his head under the low-beamed ceiling. It was dim despite the afternoon light filtering in the windows, but he made his way to the bar and addressed himself to the tapster.

"Peter Guthrie?" he inquired.

The tapster's eyes narrowed. "Who's asking?"

"Charles Wraglain sent me to you." Francis introduced himself and described his problem.

Guthrie nodded, chewing at something in his cheek. "It'll cost you a crown, but I can find this Miss Tinley, or Tindle, or Tibble."

Francis handed over the coin, then grimaced as Guthrie instructed him to take a room at the White Hart on Broad Street and await his information.

"How shall I know you're not simply taking my coin and laughing up your sleeve as I await your information?" he inquired irritably.

Guthrie regarded him blandly. "Beggin' yer honor's pardon, but it takes time to ferret out the whereabouts of a lady with three names. Big city, Bristol—lots of people milling about, working, hiding. Never you fear, however. Peter Guthrie's got a knack for these jobs, and give it two, three days, I'll find your Miss What's Her Name."

Francis could do no other than obey, and he went out to the curricle, allowing Hatten to drive them to the inn. He could not simply sit in his room all day, however, so after a nuncheon at the inn, he sent Hatten off to enjoy himself however he liked, but himself whiled away the afternoon with a walk toward the docks.

There was much bustle and activity on the streets for, as Guthrie had stated, Bristol was a busy city. The custom brought by hundreds of ships each year, full of trade goods and passengers, had encouraged a thriving populace. Francis witnessed the scores of new buildings for commerce and comfort that had appeared in response, as well as dwellings to house the varying sorts of humanity drawn to the city. It could have been inspiring to one who did not face the impossibility of discovering one woman among such hordes. His vexation had reached a peak when he came upon the noisesome River Frome, and he instantly turned back, holding a handkerchief to his nose and questioning aloud the sanity of so many persons who chose to flock to so wretchedly stinking a locality.

Guthrie having been entirely honest that his request may take some days, Francis was forced early to practice his resolve to reform.

It was his greatest temptation to tear Bristol to pieces in an effort to locate Miss Willoughby, but he manfully restrained himself, and thus was not taken up by the Watch for hounding strangers on the street, nor for wandering up and down the rows of neat houses vociferously calling Miss Willoughby's name.

His success was due, in part, to the continuation of his lately-born habit of introspection—which he supposed was a thing he must get used to if he was finally to live up to his name of gentleman. It did, after all, bring notice to even the smallest devilish inclinations, causing him to consider how he had ever justified them before. Whenever he began to slip into his habitual ways, his conscience—or what Mr. Noyce would likely call his "angel"—would instantly bring to mind Eliza regarding him askance, as though ready to tease him into better behavior. This almost constant remembrance of Eliza served to galvanize his restraint, and he quickly found he had lost the desire to even look twice at a comely barmaid.

Indeed, he found himself regarding with distaste the efforts of a particularly vulgar individual whose advances toward a barmaid were actively—but unfortunately ineffectually—rebuffed. Another man came to the young woman's aid, and as he watched appreciatively the tormentor's flying exit from the inn, Francis wondered if he had ever been so close as that scoundrel to having been served up the home brewed. If he had not, it was likely only his station that had pre-empted it, and it was with some dismay he recognized such allowances were a sad abuse of his duty.

It might have been this realization that prompted him to give an extra shilling to the maid who came to turn out his room, for though she was as plain as Patty, she had a kind face—something he'd never given notice to before—and did her duty well. She thanked him, blurting that she could buy a present with it for her brother, and it struck him that she was a person, with a background and a history—just like Miss Willoughby. He recalled how Eliza had told him of her father's change of heart toward his slaves—that once he had fallen in love with her mother, he had ceased to view her people as chattels and come to regard them as fellow human beings. It seemed that love did have power to soften and change many things.

After two days of such fruitful moral activity, Francis went down to order breakfast, his formerly roving eye exceptionally diffident, and received a twisted note from the tapster. Untwisting the screw, he quickly took in the contents, then grabbed up his coat and hat and made for the street.

He met Guthrie in front of the Plume of Feathers and was led immediately down the street, across two roads, and into a small, neat neighborhood. Halting in Water Street, Guthrie motioned to the tiny row houses on the far side.

"They's two Miss Tibbles what lives there, in the third house. Both spinsters, one a governess returned from service in Jamaica two years or so ago."

Francis's heart sped. This was surely Eliza's former governess. He thanked Guthrie, slipping him another coin as the tapster turned and went away.

Turning back to observe the house, Francis was torn between charging into it in search of Miss Willoughby and standing frozen in place on the pavement. If Miss Tibble was there, would she give him the intelligence he sought? And if Eliza was there, what should he say? In all his frantic rush to find her, he had not taken a moment to consider how to explain himself to her. Mr. Noyce's observation, that circumstances would decide whether Francis ought to show himself to Eliza or not, had been exceedingly wise. He thought it would be simpler, and kinder to his heart, if he did not meet her just yet.

But he must discover where she was, and how she did, and to do that, he must approach Miss Tibble's door, no matter the risk of seeing Eliza prematurely. So, at last, he made his feet carry him up the steps and plied his hand at the knocker. After a few excruciating minutes, the door opened to reveal a faded woman of medium height and birdlike eyes that surveyed him with no small curiosity.

"Miss Tibble?" inquired Francis, his throat dry.

"Yes. May I help you?"

"I hope you may—that is—I am Francis Mantell. I am lately come from Lincolnshire—"

"Dear me! Mr. Mantell!" The lady drew the door wide and stepped aside. "Do come in, sir. It is not terribly cold today, but the wind can bite at this time of year, and I would not leave one of my dear Eliza's friends on the doorstep."

The lady continued to chatter about the weather as Francis stepped into the house, a weight lifting from his shoulders. Eliza had at least communicated with her governess recently, and with enough commendation of himself that she had not slammed the door in his face. She led him through the narrow entry and into a tiny parlor, barely large enough to seat three or four persons in the shabby but clean sofa and chairs arranged there.

"Do sit, sir," said Miss Tibble, indicating a chair as she took another for herself. "I fear there is no refreshment to be had, for I never expected a visitor today—we do not receive many visitors, you know, our situation being so humble. But you must not think me ungrateful, for my dear sister Beatrice has been ever so good to me. I should have been obliged to take rented rooms if she had not agreed to take this house with me, and though it is cramped in many ways, it has been more than adequate for our needs."

"You are very fortunate in your—your family, ma'am," said Francis, somewhat overwhelmed by her volubility. Hastening on, he said, "Miss Willoughby was obliged to leave Penhurst quite suddenly, and did not leave a forwarding address. As I had heard you were her governess, I determined to come and see if you might direct me to her new location."

"You came all the way here from Lincolnshire, sir? Oh, you are a most ardent friend, I must say. To have such a friend must be a delight to Eliza—and I will instantly own *she* is just such a friend! She came all the way from Jamaica to see me—though in all honesty, she only did so on her way to live with her brother. Such a disappointment that she was made unhappy at Penhurst. But she will be so pleased to find you have made the journey hither!"

"I have not come to see her, ma'am," said Francis, his heart stuttering with the fear that Eliza would appear at any moment. The governess regarded him, tipping her head in inquiry, and he thought furiously, saying, "I was on business in this area with a friend—indeed, he is also acquainted with Miss Willoughby—and thought to try if I might locate her as well."

Miss Tibble's birdlike eyes blinked, bright with interest. "Another acquaintance? I wonder who it may be. Eliza would be delighted to find there is someone nearby with whom she is already familiar. Might I know him? He is in Bristol, I suppose."

Unable to withstand the expectant look in the governess's countenance, Francis said, "I do not know, ma'am, if he is known to you— Mr. Charles Wraglain. He is presently at Cleeve, but only until after Christmas."

"Mr. Wraglain? Could he be Lord Wraglain's eldest son? To be sure, he must, for Mrs. Franklinson mentioned Mr. Willoughby was his friend. And he is at present at Cleeve? So near, and Eliza never mentioned it—but I believe she must not have known, for gentlemen are always going here and there at the slightest inclination. What liberty you men have! She certainly could never have guessed Mr. Wraglain might be in the neighborhood, for Lord Wraglain's seat is in Warwickshire, which is quite a hundred miles off! I suppose Mr. Wraglain must be visiting someone at Cleeve?"

Francis merely nodded, glad that Southam *was* a hundred miles off, for if he were ever to win Eliza, he conjectured even his inner angel would be hard-pressed for patience if he were obliged to entertain this voluble lady more than once or twice a year.

Miss Tibble had paused a moment, as though hopeful of more precise information regarding Lord Wraglain's son's friends, but when this was not forthcoming, she continued, "Well, he must have a wide acquaintance, being the son of nobility. At any event, it is delightful that his staying so close brought you here! Eliza will be sorry she missed you."

"Missed me?" Francis's strained civility grasped this pertinent detail. "She is not here?"

"No, for she and dear Muncey, and that lovely butler Clayton, are gone to secure lodgings for the winter. Miss Muncey has never stopped grumbling over the cramped rooms and the lack of privacy— she is ever so dour, but the dearest friend! And Eliza agrees that we are almost on top of one another in this tiny house. As you are well acquainted with her, you will not be astonished in the least to find she has very generously offered to purchase a house large enough for all of us! Imagine, Mr. Mantell, how delightful that my dearest

Beatrice will not be obliged to find some other companion who may not be quite so familiar, nor so comfortable, as myself. But dear Eliza is such an angel that she assures us she has more than enough funds to put us all up in very good style! Mr. Findlay, her man of business, has looked out some prospects that were advertised, and they hope to choose one today. I must own I longed to accompany them, but dear Beatrice reminded me that, as it will be Eliza's house, she must be allowed to make the choice. We will simply be her companions, and can have no opinion on the matter."

When she paused for breath, Francis interjected, "Then Miss Willoughby intends to stay for the winter, here in Bristol?"

"In Clifton, to be precise, sir. Mr. Findlay, who is so very knowledgeable, advised her to look in that locality, as it is farther from the docks and the rougher areas of Bristol. There are several new and larger houses there, as well, that could accommodate all of us quite comfortably. Beatrice is rather pleased, for it has been her dearest wish to remove from this neighborhood so near the Frome, but more salubrious areas have been quite out of our reach—that is, before Eliza's obliging offer. Clifton is a lovely village, right off the Downs and with such a country-like air. And though the hot spring is no longer quite so popular, Clifton society remains a notch or two above that of Bristol, attracting as it does those of finer sensibilities and breeding. There is a new Hotel and Assembly Room, and I have it on exceedingly good authority that the assemblies are quite respectable, unlike those in Bristol, which tend to draw some quite shockingly improper persons. One must only pay the subscription fee, you know, to attend. One does often wish there were another means of restricting admission."

"You may be certain I am glad to find Miss Willoughby will be settled so comfortably, ma'am," he said when given the chance. "I suppose Clayton means to serve as her butler?"

"To be sure! And what a lovely man he is—so devoted to our dear Miss Muncey! I do believe they shall make a match of it—but not until Eliza marries, for Muncey refuses to leave her, and if Eliza's husband will not take Clayton on, Muncey vows she will not take him either. Poor man! But he is optimistic, and one cannot blame him, for who cannot be charmed by the fellow? Surely Eliza's husband will find a position for Clayton, if he has no need for a butler, for Clayton is as useful in the yard as he is in the house! And he watches so carefully over us all—it is a comfort to know we will never want for safety."

Miss Tibble ran on in this fashion, and Francis allowed it, having heard enough to satisfy him as to Eliza's well-being. She would be comfortable and secure in Clifton, and surrounded by persons of refinement and propriety. And if any improper persons were to approach her, surely Clayton's fives would have something to say to it.

But now that he was assured of not meeting Eliza, he was loathe to take his leave. He could not but think that had he come on a different day, or only earlier that morning, she would have been there, and he could have seen her smile, heard her voice, and felt her nearness. But it would only have been exquisite torture, for he still could not bear to offer himself to her without knowing he was capable of being the man she deserved.

Mr. Noyce was wise—time was what they both wanted. After all, Eliza was doing as Francis had suggested during his convalescence, and setting herself up in a circle of society that was far more likely to accept her than that in London. She would find her feet and learn more of what she looked for in a husband. He feared to leave her to her own devices, for he could not imagine anyone withstanding her charms long enough for him to make the necessary adjustments to his character. It was a very real possibility that she would receive an offer of marriage before he was ready to offer for her himself.

But then an idea started into his head, that would allow him the strength to leave her—for he knew in his heart—that organ that had so recently been as cold as stone and now was as tender and untested as a newborn babe—he must leave her to have any chance at winning her. Thus, as soon as he was able to guide Miss Tibble's monologues to a proper closure, Francis excused himself and, leaving his very sincere compliments for Miss Willoughby, went away.

When he reached the White Hart, he asked for paper and pen and wrote a letter.

> *Dear Clayton,*
>
> *You told me that I'm a better man with a better chance than I thought. I've decided to trust your instinct, but there is more I must do before I can bring myself to offer for an angel. If you truly believe me capable of securing Miss Willoughby's affections, I must beg a favor—write me at the enclosed address if she seems on the point of receiving or accepting another offer. Then I might let go my fear of losing her to chance and keep all my strength for the work I must do.*
>
> *Your servant,*
> *Francis Mantell*

Slipping his card into the folded page, he sealed it with a wafer and addressed it, giving it to the tapster to post. The following morning saw him driving with Hatten on the Gloucester Road, toward Southam. He had much to do.

Chapter 29

Three months later

THE MUSICIANS IN the alcove of the Assembly Room played a lively reel, but Eliza had elected to sit out the dance, having exerted herself rather excessively during the evening. Mr. Slimstock, her previous partner, was as energetic as he was tall, and she had been grateful to her current partner, Mr. Danson, when he solicited her hand, for his sensibility in suggesting they rest themselves rather than dance. He was gone to procure her a glass of lemonade, and Eliza was at liberty to consider, as she often did, the variety of gentlemen who were her admirers.

Nathan had been utterly wrong in his conviction that Eliza should receive no interest in her hand. While some people in Clifton and Bristol openly stared at her West Indian looks, many admired, and people did not, in general, look askance. There was so much trade coming through Bristol to and from the West Indies, that persons hailing therefrom were frequently to be seen, even in the more refined circles of society. She had heard herself described as a lovely girl, possessed of charm and a lively wit, and had quickly gathered about her a group of admirers who were quite assiduous in their attentions.

Certainly, no question had arisen as yet surrounding her birth, an advantage owing to the less exalted society which obtained at Clifton as opposed to London or Bath—there was not so much urgency among the persons who congregated there to make a match as spotless as it was splendid. She knew the time would come when she must admit to her illegitimacy, but felt sure it would be private with the man with whom she wished to spend her life, and she was sanguine that the revelation need not be made more than once, unless her choice was a poor one.

She was, therefore, taking her time—which, if the mutterings which occasionally came to her ear from some of her admirers were to be understood, did not suit them in the least. Mr. Rutger was the most impatient, judging from the frequency with which he found occasion to expound on the evils of her situation as a spinster set up in her own household. But Clayton had overheard him speaking to a crony of an estate for sale near Bath, at the same time lamenting his lack of funds, so she did not take him quite so seriously as he should probably like.

Sir Godfrey Villiers, who even now watched her with his smoldering gaze from his post across the room, most flatteringly ignored all other women when Eliza was in the room, and took every opportunity to murmur phrases into her ear calculated to bring a blush to her cheek. But he was usually disappointed, for his brand of flirtation fell so far short of another, particular gentleman's that she could only smile and shake her head.

Eliza had endeavored to forget Mr. Mantell, but found it exceedingly difficult. It seemed that every gentlemen with whom she interacted meant to bring him to her remembrance in one way or another. If a gentleman asked about Jamaica, she saw in her mind's eye Mr. Mantell's sincere and emotional response to her recollections. If a gentleman flirted, she could only compare his wit—or lack thereof—to Mr. Mantell's. If a gentleman was gallant, she could only recall Mr. Mantell's protecting her from Bellerton in the stables, and then his profoundly generous assistance during her illness.

Even now, as Mr. Danson returned with her lemonade, handing it to her with a slight bow and a smile, she could only think of Mr. Mantell placing a shawl tenderly about her shoulders in the chill of the library. Mr. Danson was a kind man, and good, but his valiant attempts to attach her were, she feared, in vain. He simply did not have that spark of something that she had yearned for ever since her removal from Penhurst.

He was also blond, and she simply could not bring herself to like blond men. There was something alluring about dark hair, and grey eyes. Yes, she thought she liked stormy grey eyes—Sir Godfrey's were green, which were all very well, but they seemed to her like a cat's. Her ideal man was also tall—though not so tall as Mr. Slimstock, nor so thin, for he must also be possessed of broad shoulders that could shield one from view if the occasion demanded. Indeed, her ideal was very like the gentleman who had just entered the hall, and was removing his chapeau bras to run a hand through his dark locks.

The gentleman raised his head, and she gasped as his eyes found hers. There was a moment during which she could not breathe while his gaze searched her face, and she had the distinct impression that he was drinking her in, like a starving man. Then he was coming toward her, so intent that he nearly shouldered through the lines of the dance in his haste and was obliged to divert around the edge of the floor. He disappeared from view behind a group of ladies with plumes in their hair and Eliza inhaled, pressing a hand to her heart and attempting to order her thoughts. But then he was at her side, and her thoughts fluttered away like so many butterflies in her head.

"Miss Willoughby," he said, bowing.

Still unable to form speech, she simply extended her hand to him, her gaze locked on his beautiful storm-grey eyes. He hesitated only a moment, then took her hand and pressed it.

The contact seemed to jolt her mind into action. "Mr. Mantell," she said at last, color tinging her cheeks. "What a surprise—I had not expected to see you here."

She saw his throat bob as he swallowed. "I hope my coming is not unwelcome."

"No! No," she said, still holding to his hand. Abruptly, she smiled, her shock giving way to delight. "You cannot imagine how good it is to see a friend."

"Ah." He gave a rueful smile and let go her hand. "I have wondered how you have been these months."

She looked keenly at him. "I was sorry to have missed your visit after I—well, after I removed from Penhurst." She suddenly became aware of their surroundings, and of Mr. Danson watching them with stiff curiosity. "I beg your pardon, but I am being remiss. Mr. Mantell, may I introduce Mr. Danson? He has been so kind as to sit out the dance with me."

The two gentlemen exchanged bows, and Mr. Mantell turned again to Eliza. "Do you not dance tonight?"

"Oh, I have danced nearly the whole evening, and have enjoyed myself hugely—so much so that I am quite exhausted at present."

He bit his lips, casting a somewhat challenging glance at Mr. Danson. "Then, as the dance is just ending, I wonder if you would care to walk with me in the corridor. I should like to catch up on your movements since last I saw you."

"I should like that immensely," she said, smiling again and taking his arm.

With a nod and thanks to Mr. Danson, she allowed Mr. Mantell to lead her from the hall into the corridor that connected the Assembly Room to the Hotel, where only a few persons walked in search of a respite, either from the heated ballroom or the exertions of dancing.

"Who is Mr. Danson?" Mr. Mantell abruptly asked.

Eliza was somewhat startled at his tone. "He is another resident of Clifton. Why do you ask?"

"He admires you."

She lifted a shoulder. "I suppose he does, as do several other gentlemen. Nathan would be disappointed, to be sure."

"Nathan was a fool," said Mr. Mantell, somewhat somberly. "I anticipated you should have many admirers. You are looking very well, Miss Willoughby."

"As are you, sir," replied Eliza. There was an odd silence, so she inquired, "What brings you to Clifton? Are you visiting Mr. Wraglain again?"

He glanced at her, then said, "No. Charles is home in Southam— that is, he has returned to Lord Wraglain's estate."

"I see." She did not really see, for she wished to know if he had come for her, as his intent look had intimated, but she dared not inquire so specifically.

"I have only just come into town," he supplied. "I stopped in the Crescent and Clayton informed me you were here."

"He is an excellent butler, as ever," she said with a chuckle. There was another silence between them and she plucked up the courage to say, "I had an interesting letter from Mr. Findlay only a day or two before you came to Miss Tibble's house. I own, its contents surprised me, and I was never more disappointed in my life than when I missed your visit."

He looked quickly at her. "Truly?"

"Yes, for I was terribly curious as to how you could precede a response to him."

She thought his face paled. "Did you not reply?"

"Certainly I did," she said with an outraged look. "I am not so lost to all decorum as to ignore a letter from my solicitor—as my brother is wont to be. However, as my letter had gone out only the day before your visit, I could not conjecture how you could have received his information and arrived in Bristol all in one day."

He huffed, the taut lines of his face relaxing into what seemed to be relief. "You awakened something in me, Miss Willoughby, that drove me to superhuman exertions."

Her heartbeat sped up a trifle. "I? Now you must certainly elucidate, sir, or I vow I shall die of suspense."

He chuckled then, and she thrilled at the sound. "We seem to have much the same impatience, for it was not long ago I thought I should die of suspense. Your precipitate exit from the Lodge, without word to anyone, was so disconcerting as to bring me hotfoot to London in search of you."

Her cheeks heated at this information, so pleasing to her bruised heart. "I own, I was consternated to be obliged to leave Penhurst so suddenly."

"I'm glad you did—" She blinked at him, taken aback, but he hurriedly added, "That is, it was lucky you went away when you did, for Bellerton had planned to take you with him by force."

"That was why I left so suddenly, Mr. Mantell. Clayton overheard his plans and Muncey and he insisted we leave as soon as could be contrived."

"Yes." He looked away. "I nearly bit Hatten's head off when he admitted to taking you to the stage without my knowledge. But he redeemed himself, for when Findlay refused to tell me where you were, Hatten supplied Miss Tibble's name and the fact that she resided in Bristol."

She gazed at him in wonder. "You searched Bristol for me, rather than wait." Pressing her hands to her heated cheeks, she averted her eyes, saying, "You must forgive me, sir. I had no notion you would be so affected by my leaving. I see now it was a horrid trick to play on so dear a friend as you had been to me."

"Yes," he said, his eyes fixed on her face with a somewhat desperate look. "But there is another reason I had to find you."

She could only stare at him and he set his jaw, glancing quickly around before taking her hand and pulling her into an anteroom. Closing the door behind her, he inhaled deeply.

"Miss Willoughby, I believe I am in love with you."

Her lashes fluttered as her breath caught. Surely he did not mean it. He despised love—he had always disdained love and marriage, and abhorred the idea of family. He could only mean he desired her in a way she could not abide. Her heart seized at the thought, but her native optimism bid her not to be a goose, for men did not chase women across the country simply because they desired a mistress.

But where had he gone after he had spoken to Miss Tibble, her reason demanded? If he truly loved her, why did he not return to speak with her until now?

She looked away, speaking hesitantly. "Mr. Mantell, you must pardon me for asking, but just what do you mean by that?"

He took a step toward her. "I mean I am nothing without you. I wish always to be with you. I—" He paused, and she peeked up to see him visibly struggling with his words. "Miss Willoughby, I can only admit to having been a careless, selfish man. I have been guilty of loose and disrespectful conduct, and am ashamed of how shabbily I have treated nearly every woman of my acquaintance. It was not until I met you that I ever began to care for someone, and even then my thoughts did not have a proper turn. I did not think of marriage, and when you inquired about my family, I told you truthfully I never wished for my own."

She nodded, heaving a sigh of dismay, but he went on. "I quickly realized my mistake, Miss Willoughby. I soon comprehended the feelings that had formed within my breast were irrevocable, and that I was at last experiencing what it means to love. I wrestled within myself, for I could believe it only with difficulty. But in those days without you, I was forced to admit that I had fallen utterly and hopelessly in love with you."

"Then why did you not come back to tell me, once you had found me?" she whispered.

He reached a hand out to her. "Because I could not offer myself to you knowing what sort of dastard I have been. After I assured myself that you were safe and well-looked-after, I went home to see if I could become a man who could someday deserve you. I have worked hard for redemption, and may honestly say I am on the road to reformation—though I yet have far to go. I would not even now have allowed myself to offer for you, but that Clayton wrote to warn me that you might be on the verge of accepting Mr. Danson."

Her hand found his and held tight. "Clayton was mistaken, but I am glad it brought you back. I have wished many a time that I could have known what is in your heart." She looked into his eyes, her brow furrowing intently. "I had persuaded myself you were not the man for me, but there is something different about you, Mr. Mantell."

He stepped closer and said, "I hope there is, and I pray it is enough to convince you of my sincerity. I want to make a family with you, Miss Willoughby. I want to have a home with you, and children, and I want fidelity and joy. I want you to become my wife, Miss Willoughby, so I can give all these things to you. Do you think that you could ever come to overlook my past failings, and accept me?"

At these words, confirmed by the sincerity in his lovely grey eyes, a smile spread over her face. Here was the man with whom she had fallen in love—indeed, here was a better.

With a happy little sigh, she said, "Mr. Mantell—Francis, I believe I have loved you since I discovered how you served me through my illness. I could not discern the depth of your feelings for me, however, and when you said you never wished for a family—it seemed I had been foolish to care for you. But I could not help it. It is true you have not always been what you ought, but I witnessed a change in you over those last weeks at Penhurst, and I perceive that you have continued to change. I believe you are in earnest."

With a look of wild hope, he clasped both her hands. "I have never been in such earnest in my life, Eliza. It is shameful, I know, but at least I am honest. I *have* changed, and I can promise you that I will do my utmost to allow the transformation to continue, so that I might become even one tiny bit worthy to have you as my own."

She closed the distance between them, putting one hand up to his cheek. "Then I am ready to grant your boon. I am willing to take the chance that you will continue to change, Francis. It might even be worth all I owe—a boon and a forfeit."

"Oh, my dear Eliza, your trust would be worth infinitely more than that to me."

Smiling tenderly, she said, "My own father held quite unsatisfactory views for a very long time, but he was a good man at heart. He did not always do what he ought, but he tried, and in the end, he did what was right. You are quite as redeemable as he."

"Darling Eliza," he whispered, taking her into his arms and holding her pressed to his heart. "Will you marry me?"

"I will, Francis."

He tightened his hold on her, and her joy was so great she laughed. Her hand came up to cradle his head against her cheek, and she felt the warmth of tears between them.

Pulling away just enough to cup her cheek in his hand, he looked an inquiry, and she closed her eyes, tipping her head up to meet his lips. The kiss was sweet and tender and more beautiful than she had thought possible.

When they pulled back from the embrace some time later, Francis gazed in joyous relief down at her. "What a fool I have been these many years, to militate against love."

"Don't you mean a gaby?" she said, the impish twinkle appearing in her eyes.

He grinned. "Or a cod's head, or a simpleton, or any manner of fool you wish to call me, my love."

She put up a finger to trace his lips. "I do not believe any manner of fool could kiss me like that."

"No, that is a privilege I claim for myself alone." His eyes seemed to darken, and his smile took on a rakish tilt. "As is the privilege to kiss you like this."

And he bent again to kiss her with a passion that drove every other thought from both their heads for quite some time.

Clayton chuckled to himself in satisfaction as he turned away from the parlor, wherein Miss Willoughby and Mr. Mantell were taking quite some time to say their goodbyes. His letter, it seemed, had been timely, and had had the desired effect: Mr. Mantell had brought himself to the point at last.

As he stepped into the corridor, however, Muncey appeared from the kitchen, storming toward him.

"How dare you leave dem alone?" she demanded, pushing past him. "Even if he is reformed, he is still a man!"

He grasped her waist, swinging her about to face him. "Which is not a bad thing, in this case. They're an engaged couple now. We can give 'em a moment longer."

Muncey protested, struggling against him, but Clayton, with a wicked gleam, said, "Besides, we 'ave cause to celebrate. Mr. Mantell wants a new butler and housekeeper, so we'd best leave 'em be and look to our own future, my Phoebe."

She stilled, her wide gaze snapping to his, and Clayton pulled her to him, pressing his lips to hers in so fervent a manner as to quite remove all thoughts of interruption from her mind.

Epilogue

Five months later

MRS. ANAMARIA NOYCE stood at the window of Gracely Hall's well-appointed sitting room, gazing out at the sloping lawn behind the house. The wood bounded the lawn on two sides, and the rooftop of another manor could be seen some way off.

"I must admit to being pleasantly surprised at the new occupants of Chandry Manor," she remarked to the other two ladies in the room.

"The Pitfords?" inquired her daughter, Clara Simpford, who sat with her new sister-in-law, Eliza Mantell, on the settee. "What could be surprising? They are a most respectable family—indeed, more so than we ever were."

Her mother lifted a petulant shoulder. "One assumed the Manor was so tainted by odious Sir Anthony's influence that no family residing there could ever be pleasing."

"*One* may have assumed it," replied Clara, casting a humorous glance at her sister, "but *I* never did. Such superstition would render this house as tainted as Chandry Manor, for my dear departed father was quite as odious as Sir Anthony. And yet, Gracely is delightful, is it not, my dear Eliza?"

Eliza, her eyes dancing, said, "To be sure! I believe I loved it from the moment I first stepped over the threshold."

"But you did not step over the threshold," chided Clara. "Francis carried you over."

"Which is why, I believe, I loved it so much."

Clara chuckled, placing a hand over her sister's. "Well, I must say you have brought a light into it that never was here before."

Mrs. Noyce sniffed, but then sighed, turning to bestow a genuine smile upon her daughter-in-law. "I've not enjoyed any visit to this house until you came, my dear. Indeed, I should be well-satisfied in everything should my children only begin to fill their nurseries."

"As only Geoffrey has been wedded long enough to do so, Mother," replied Clara, "you ought to be thankful neither Francis nor myself have yet to present you with offspring."

"I should expect Geoffrey to oblige me sooner than either of you, to be sure," said her mother, pursing her lips. "He has ever been my most obedient and thoughtful child, never causing me a moment's vexation."

"Except when he was nearly hanged for murder."

Eliza and Mrs. Noyce both gaped at Clara, who blinked innocently. "But he was! Did not Francis tell you the story, Eliza? Dear me, what an unforgivable lapse. I shall certainly have to tell you. It is the only interesting thing that has ever happened in our family."

"But I should have considered your having eloped, not once but thrice in as many days, as another," said Eliza, her look impish. "I certainly found it interesting."

Clara laughed, taking Eliza's hand and pulling her to her feet. "But I did not run afoul of the law, which renders my adventure a mere indiscretion. Come, let us walk in the gallery and I shall relate Geoffrey's tale in all its glory—it is, in fact, a love story, you know."

They went out and Mrs. Noyce resumed her vigil at the window. Soon, three horsemen appeared out of the wood, and she hastened to open the French door, stepping out onto the terrace. Shielding her eyes against the sun, she watched their approach, an appreciative smile on her lips, for her husband was a fine specimen, especially on the back of one of his thoroughbreds. They cantered by on their way to the stables, and Mr. Noyce blew her a kiss, causing a delighted blush to warm her cheeks.

She was seated primly on a settee when the three gentlemen at last entered, heated and dusty. But when Mr. Noyce bent to place a salute upon her cheek, she did not shrink back, only inquiring after their ride.

"Dashed hot," said her son, Francis, as he poured himself some sherry from the decanters at the sideboard. He offered Mr. Noyce and Lawrence Simpford, Clara's husband, a drink, which they accepted. Sipping his sherry, Francis glanced about the room. "Where have Eliza and Clara got to?"

"They are walking in the gallery."

"Whatever for?" inquired Francis, tossing off his drink and moving toward the door.

Mr. Noyce stopped him with a hand on his shoulder. "Best not disturb them, my boy. Young ladies enjoy their little private talks."

"More likely, Clara's filling Eliza's head with all sorts of information about my misspent youth."

Lawrie snorted. "Or she's teaching Eliza to fence."

The two young men glanced quickly at each other, set their glasses down, and dashed from the room.

Not two minutes later, Clayton entered the drawing room with a letter on a salver. "But where might Mr. Mantell be? I thought 'im returned from riding."

Mr. Noyce looked up. "Ah, Clayton! Francis and Lawrie went to find their errant wives. And how do you and Mrs. Clayton go on?"

"Very well, sir," Clayton said, bowing. "She's taken right to 'ouse-keeping like it was 'er first calling, she 'as. And Cook don't mind her 'elping out in the kitchen, as long as she keeps the bonney peppers to a minimum."

"Ah! Yes, Francis told us of her facility with West Indian spices. A highly useful gift, I understand."

"That it is, sir," said Clayton with a grin. "I know just when I'm in 'er bad books, for the burn of my tongue at dinner. But our Miss Eliza—or rather, Mrs. Mantell likes a bit of spice in her dish, so the Missus'll likely be in the kitchens more often than not."

"She seems to enjoy being busy," remarked Mr. Noyce.

"Aye, sir. It's not certain she'll soon give up waiting on our Mrs. Mantell."

Mr. Noyce chuckled. "That is understandable, as they have been through much together, have they not? At least they are to be in the same household, no matter what they decide regarding Mrs. Clayton's responsibilities. I hear the Grimsleys are very pleased with their little cottage and pension."

"That they are, sir, and quite 'appy to advise us in anything about the running of the 'ouse. It was a sound arrangement, all around, I'd say."

"Most providential," agreed Mr. Noyce.

Clayton gave a jaunty bow, placing the letter on the table before he went away.

Mrs. Noyce sniffed. "He's an odd sort of person to hire as butler. So familiar and coarse. One would think that Francis could have done better—but I suppose it was out of compassion they hired him."

"I should rather think it was out of gratitude, my dear," said Mr. Noyce, smiling. "Recollect, Clayton and his wife were instrumental in preserving our dear Eliza from her brother's machinations. You might say they made Francis's present happiness possible."

"I suppose they did," said Mrs. Noyce, never proof against her husband's generosity of spirit. "And Clayton will doubtless learn how to go on, now that he is in a true gentleman's house."

"And even if he does not, he could not be more loyal to both Francis and Eliza, which, I am persuaded, is an infinitely desirable trait in a retainer."

Francis and Lawrie had discovered their wives arm in arm in the gallery, heads together, giggling like schoolgirls. The ladies glanced up when their husbands' footsteps came to their ears.

"Good heaven, Francis," exclaimed Clara, turning toward her brother. "Cannot you be parted from your wife for even a few minutes?"

Taking his wife's other arm, Francis kissed her cheek and said, "Certainly I can, Clara. I have been parted from her for over an hour, which is more than long enough."

"There ought to be a limit to reformation," returned Clara, relinquishing Eliza to him. "I declare, you have swung too far the opposite of what you were before."

"Come now, my love," said Lawrie, taking his own wife onto his arm. "Were not you pining to see me?"

She allowed him to kiss her, but wrinkled her nose. "You smell of horse."

Eliza laughed, covering her nose and glancing mischievously up at Francis. "It is true, you know. But I suppose you simply could not wait to be with us again."

"On the contrary," said Lawrie, "we thought it best to find you before Clara took it into her head to teach you any of her unladylike habits."

"But she has already promised to teach me to fence," said Eliza, "and I should dearly love to do so."

"Yes," said Clara, "and when I have done that, I shall teach her to drive."

"I forbid it," said Francis, raising an imperious eyebrow. "I intend to teach her to drive."

"Goodness! What is the world coming to?" cried Clara, exchanging an astonished look with Lawrie before gazing dumbfounded at her sister. "Francis is never driven by females, Eliza. He has only ever allowed his own sister to take the ribbons a short while, and that under duress. He truly has gone mad for love of you."

"Or perhaps," said Eliza, gazing laughingly up at her husband, "he has simply swung far to the opposite of what he was."

"Not completely, my dear," said Francis. "You are the only female I shall teach to drive."

"Not our daughters?"

He grimaced. "Perhaps our daughters, but no others."

Clara laughed. "Then *I* shall teach Eliza to shoot, for you cannot very well forbid that, Francis. I am indisputably the better shot, not only than you, but Lawrie as well."

"You never bested me, Clara, and Lawrie did so only the once!" protested Francis.

Clara held up a hand, counting off her fingers, "He bested you that summer, then again at Michaelmas. And as I had bested him twice before and once again after, it's as though I bested you five times."

"There is much in what she says, my love," said Eliza gravely. "I do believe I ought to be taught by the very best."

Francis opened his mouth to argue, but Clara said quickly, "But you may procure her a pistol, for she will require one of her own, and you did very well in choosing mine."

Eliza turned expectant and shining eyes to her husband, who swallowed the cutting remark he was about to make and merely said stiffly, "It is excessively kind in you to say so, Clara."

Lawrie, pulling Clara away toward the stairs, said in a low tone meant for all to hear, "Best leave it at that, my love, or he will challenge you to pistols at dawn. I fear neither I nor Eliza could wish to be widowed so soon. Only think of the scandal."

They all returned to the drawing room, each couple arm in arm. Francis, passing the table, saw the letter and reached for it.

"It's addressed to you, my love," he said, giving it to Eliza. "But I'd swear that's my sister-in-law Emily's hand."

"How lovely," said Eliza, sitting down and regarding the address on the letter. "It is posted from Bombay. Ought I to read it now?"

As everyone agreed she ought, for they were all eager for news of the traveling couple, she broke the seal and spread open the pages.

> *Dearest Eliza (and of course Francis),*
>
> *Both Geoffrey and I are delighted with the news of your marriage, and sincerely wish you all the happiness we, ourselves, have found together. How interested I am in Jamaica, even without having lived in India these several*

*months. I hope you will not dislike discussing the similar-
ities of the two regions—or telling all about yourself, for
that matter—for I should dearly love to know you better.*

*We shall have the opportunity to meet soon, as Geof-
frey and I have determined upon making our way back
to England in anticipation of a happy event in the spring.
We intend to take in Greece, or at least Paris, on the way,
if all goes well with my condition, and ought to be back
in Warwickshire by Christmas.*

*If they will have us, we intend to stay at Wesley Abbey
with Mr. and Mrs. Noyce until we might find a suitable estate
to purchase, close by our dearest relations in Southam.*

The remainder of the letter outlined their recent travels in India, which were heard with great interest by all, with many exclamations on the pleasant turn of events that would bring Geoffrey and Emily back to England so soon.

"You see!" said Mrs. Noyce. "Geoffrey has been the first to oblige me in the way of grandchildren. It is just as I expected."

"Then you must be satisfied, Mother," said Clara, "for you are never more happy than when you are right."

Mrs. Noyce clenched her jaw. "I should be happier to be wrong in this situation, Clara; however, as I know you are being impertinent to be interesting, I shall not heed you. You may do as you wish."

"Thank you, Mother. I am excessively relieved of care, for it happens that I have undertaken to teach Eliza to fence, and I could not possibly do that if I were in a delicate condition."

Mrs. Noyce's eyes fluttered closed, and she uttered in accents of mortification, "Good heaven, Clara."

Patting his wife's hand, Mr. Noyce smilingly said, "You must pardon her, my dear, for you have always known Clara has no delicacy."

Clara merely looked arch and said, "It is not for lack of trying, sir. Indeed, if what I am to believe is true, I shall sooner or later fall excessively delicate."

As Lawrie blushed scarlet, Francis said dryly, "I fear the term 'delicate' could never be applied to you, Clara, no matter the issue of your endeavors."

Mrs. Noyce stood abruptly. "It is time we were leaving, William. You must perceive that my children mean to vex me, but I will not allow it. I will take myself out of their reach, and will think on pleasanter times, when they did not cause me to wish to strangle them. Perhaps when they were too young to speak."

"You are very wise, my dear," said Mr. Noyce, standing with the help of his canes and flashing a knowing grin at his step-children. Going with his wife to the door, he called back, "Goodbye, Francis, Eliza. We will see you for our dinner party Tuesday next. And you also, Clara, Lawrie."

They exited the room, and Clara and Lawrie soon took themselves off as well, leaving Eliza and Francis to meander up the stairs to dress for dinner.

"Speaking of delicate conditions, my love—" began Eliza.

Francis stopped short, turning her to him, his face covered in shock and his eyes searching hers.

But she only giggled, putting a hand up to his cheek. "No, my dearest heart, I am not making an announcement. There is no cause for anxiety just yet!" She kissed him, then went on, "I had a letter from Sophy, who is overjoyed at her situation, for Nathan has been strutting about like a peacock and ordering the nursery set up, with no expense spared. That is telling, do not you think? I only hope that he has been taking more care of her as well."

Drawing her into his arms, Francis brushed her cheek with the backs of his fingers. "You will never cease to hope for your brother, will you? No, I suppose it is in your nature—and I must be grateful for it, for without that generous optimism, you might never have believed I could change, nor accepted me only on the promise of it. And I should be the most miserable man on earth."

"And I should not be much happier, sir," said Eliza, putting her arms about his neck. "But you have fulfilled your promise, and made so material a change as to stun even your nearest relations. I believe your mother almost enjoyed herself today."

He kissed her forehead, then her lips, and said, "I would endeavor to oblige even my mother to please you, Eliza."

"Goodness, Francis," she replied with an impish grin. "You know not whereof you speak. You must not have comprehended that her dearest wish is for her children to fill their nurseries."

With a rakish tilt to his smile, Francis kissed her again, long and deep, then whispered into her ear, "I know precisely whereof I speak, my love."

If you enjoyed this book, please consider leaving a review at the library or store site where you found it, or on your favorite review site.

Reviews help others find their next favorite read and are extremely helpful to authors. You can find store links, where you can leave reviews for *The Branwell Chronicles* series, by scanning the QR code below.

Thank you!

Author's Note

THIS BOOK TURNED out to be far more challenging to write even than I imagined. I knew attempting to create a believable redemption arc for a true rake would be very difficult, but with the addition of two female Jamaican characters, I found myself in fraught territory. I could only do my best to faithfully portray very difficult subjects while allowing for the sensibilities and sensitivities of my readers. I hope that you can appreciate my good-faith endeavors, and that the story ended up being an uplifting and enjoyable one. I learned a lot while I wrote, and though some topics I researched were pretty horrible, most were just plain fascinating, and I was glad to have been introduced to all of them.

A note about the accents: Jamaican Patois, though somewhat similar to English, is its own language, with its own structure, grammar, and vocabulary. Because I have no personal expertise in

Jamaican Patois, I made the choice to have my Jamaican characters speak English, with Muncey only having a mild accent. Since she was a lady's maid, and would have been trained to speak the King's English, this worked well, and only in a few circumstances she slips into Patois. I did the translations for those moments myself, and did find a Jamaican reader to proofread, but my arrangements fell through at the last moment. I hope that my readers familiar with Jamaica and Jamaican Patois will forgive any mistakes I made, and know that I did my best!

The British occupation of Jamaica began in 1655, when it was captured from Spain. The island already had a very mixed population, with native Tainos, Spanish colonists, free Africans called Maroons, and also enslaved Africans. England at first used Jamaica as a penal colony for indentured servants and Scots and Irish prisoners, but when sugar became a lucrative crop, thousands of English settlers flocked to Jamaica to make their fortunes. By the late 1700's, there were 80,000 English colonists in Jamaica, and three times as many slaves. Jamaica had a terrible reputation for brutality in its treatment of enslaved Africans, and there were several slave rebellions and Maroon uprisings. There is no doubt that slavery was a horrific practice, but I did find an incidence of one "good" master, whose slaves protected him and his property during an uprising because they cared for him enough not to wish harm to come to him. I used this master as my pattern for Eliza's father in this book. England abolished the slave trade in 1807 but slavery itself was not abolished in England and its colonies until 1834.

Bristol is an inland port, serviced by the tidal River Avon, which at high tide could accommodate very large ships. But when the tide went out, ships would become stranded, necessitating the building in

1809 of the Floating Basin, or a man-made port controlled by locks on the Avon and Frome rivers. This solved the problem of the tide, but the locks kept the water mostly stagnant, increasing the problem of pollution from the disposal of human and other waste in the river. In 1817, Queen Charlotte's carriage was held up at the drawbridge over the River Frome, and she complained of the revolting smell, but this only resulted in largely unsuccessful efforts to alleviate the problem. Devastating cholera epidemics followed by public outcries in the 1840s at last prompted the council to act, and a Sanitary Committee was established in 1850 that at last made major improvements to health and sanitation.

The draining of the Fens was attempted as early as Roman times, but it was the concerted efforts of various corporations in the 1630's that resulted in wide-scale drainage. These efforts were violently opposed by locals, whose livelihoods in fishing and wildfowling were threatened. It also caused the uncovered peat to shrink, lowering the land elevation even more, and constant flooding from both rivers and sea plagued the area. Windmills were introduced to pump water into drainage ditches cut across the land, including the South Forty Foot Drain, which curves from Boston around Swineshead and down to near Pinchbeck. These windmills were not powerful enough to pump the necessary amount of water, however, and were in constant danger of sabotage by local fishermen, with riots often resulting in the destruction of dikes. Landowners prevailed only when the windmills were replaced by steam pumps in 1820, which successfully drained the land faster than it could be flooded.

One of the most fascinating subjects I researched for this story was the flora and fauna of Jamaica. Being an island, Jamaica is home to many unique endemic species, including the bromeliad frogs and crabs Eliza describes. These creatures have evolved to live in the vase-like bases of the leaves of epiphytic bromeliads, which grow on other plants, especially trees, in the forests of Jamaica. The crabs and frogs live their entire life cycle in the bromeliads, requiring no other water source. The other creatures that made their way into the story are the Jamaican Iguana, which Muncey beat off in protection of some children on the beach, and various spiders. Though many spiders inhabit the island, there are only a few poisonous species, including what was known as the Black Spider (aka the North American Black Widow Spider). The Golden Orb Weaver and the Huntsman Spider are not poisonous, and being fairly common in the Caribbean, are useful as predators of pest insects.

Illegitimate births were a circumstance dealt with differently in England, depending largely on class. Upper classes had successions of titles and estates to ensure, and thus legitimacy was crucial for the heir. Lower classes had no such pressures, so legitimacy was less of a concern, at least socially. When an illegitimate child cropped up—as the widely flexible moral framework for men almost guaranteed—and its parentage could be traced to one of noble or gentle birth, the issue was often decided based on the child's gender. Males were more often acknowledged by their fathers, especially if there were no other male offspring, or if the child proved handsome or clever. But such was the stigma surrounding loss of virtue in women that female children were generally bundled off to a remote cottage to be raised in ignorance of their parentage, and their memories consigned to oblivion. Some illegitimate female children were lucky enough to be acknowledged, however, as was Dido Elizabeth Belle by her father Sir John Lindsay, and even given legacies by their fathers. I decided this would be the case with Eliza in this story.

There was an unfortunate tendency during the Regency for immorally-minded men to assume that all lower-class women were open to improper advances, as my rakish gentlemen do. But though some lower-class females in this story have rather free morals, they are not meant to represent the generality of their class. Virtue was highly prized in females of every class during the Regency, and it only depended upon the strictness of the girl's upbringing or her choices upon sexual maturity whether she welcomed or shunned male advances (and I am only speaking of women who were given the choice, not forced—that's a topic for an entirely different story). For a young lady attempting to move upward between classes, like Sophronia Draffin, the shoals were many and difficult to navigate, for though the degree of one's moral rectitude did not depend upon class, the degree of one's openness about it did. Those young ladies in the lower classes who held morality cheaply, like the maid Jane, could commit indiscretions without lasting repercussions far more easily than could those in the upper classes. Gently bred women, restricted as they were by concerns of succession and reputation, would do everything they could to hide indiscretion. An upper-class female found in a compromising situation must be married quickly, if possible, like Lydia in Jane Austen's *Pride and Prejudice*, and if not, as with Maria Bertram in *Mansfield Park*, sent away from public eyes. Even a kiss or a private interview, as Sophy had with Nathan Willoughby, were far more damning to her aspiring reputation than she imagined.

Many readers of Regency fiction are aware of the pervading fear during the era of night air. But this fear stemmed from the belief in what was scientifically known as miasma, which was held to be responsible for the spread of disease such as cholera, chlamydia, and even the plague. It was basically a theory that pockets of noxious air trapped and transported contagious diseases, and one only needed to be exposed to this miasma to become infected. As the night air was already suspected of causing everything from colds to diseases of the lungs, it seemed logical that the miasma was most active at night. Thus the belief that being out at night, or even having a window open at night, was dangerous.

Sources:

https://en.wikipedia.org/wiki/The_Fens#Draining_the_Fens

https://en.wikipedia.org/wiki/Miasma_theory

https://lntreasures.com/jamaica.html

https://victorianweb.org/history/empire/westindies/jamaica.html (particularly photo of William Carr Walker headstone)

https://www.bristolmuseums.org.uk/blog/how-improved-sanitation-in-bristol-transformed-lives/

Ash, Eric H. *The Draining of the Fens: Projectors, Popular Politics, and State Building in Early Modern England.* Johns Hopkins University Press. 2017.

Hakewill, James. *A Picturesque Tour of the Island of Jamaica.* Hurt and Robinson. 1825.

Livesay, Daniel. *Children of Uncertain Fortune: Mixed-Race Jamaicans in Britain and the Atlantic Family, 1733-1833.* Omohundro Institute and UNC Press. 2018.

Mason, Fergus. *Dido Elizabeth Belle: a Biography.* BookCaps. 2014.

Morrison, Robert. The Regency Years. W.W. Norton and Company. 2019.

Reece, Richard. *The Medical Guide, for the Use of Families and Young Practitioners in Medicine and Surgery. Being a Practical Treatise* on the Causes, Prevention, Cure, Etc. of the Diseases Incident to the Human Frame, Exhibiting the Latest and Most Important Discoveries in Medicine, Pharmacy, Etc. In Two Parts .. 5th Ed., Considerably Enlarged and Improved, pgs. 113-114. Longman, Hurst, Rees, and Orme. 1808.

Wells, Charles. *A Short History of the Port of Bristol.* J.W. Arrowsmith. 1909.

Acknowledgments

I HAVE WANTED TO tell Francis's story for a long time, ever since he first appeared in all his insouciant rakishness in Forlorn Hope. Because of the challenges involved as his story unfolded, I sometimes wondered if I would ever finish! But after much input from excellent people, and several long days and late (late!) nights, I think it turned out pretty well.

I hope it brings enjoyment to you, my wonderful readers! Without your encouragement, reviews, and support, my writing would be pretty unfulfilling.

The subject matter in this book required a lot of consideration, reworking, and revising, and I could not have done it without my fantastic beta readers. Diane Paredes, Liz Prettyman, Emily Menendez, Alondra Uhi, Karen Pierotti, Laurie Zobell, Marianne Harris, and Chelsea Mortensen, your comments, corrections, and feedback improved the original story immensely. Thank you so much!

Special thanks to Anna Cherry, whose insights into the Black experience opened my eyes and helped me more sensitively and dynamically portray my Black characters and their history.

Thanks as always to Clare Wille, my narrator, and Paul Midcalf at Audio Sorcery for your wonderful work bringing my books to sparkling life on audio.

Thanks again to Rachel Allen Everett for the beautiful, unique, and eye-catching cover!

Thanks to my kids for getting me out of the house for walks, and doing your chores so the house doesn't completely fall apart while I'm madly revising.

And no book would be complete without a dedication to my husband, Joe, who is right by my side in all of this, reading, encouraging, assisting, and generally being my rock and my stay. I am so grateful you took a chance on an imperfect girl who had a lot to learn about life, love, and relationships. Your unconditional love is my inspiration.

Judith Hale Everett is one of seven sisters and grew up surrounded by romance novels. Georgette Heyer and Jane Austen were staples and formed the groundwork for her lifelong love affair with the Regency. Add to that her obsession with the English language and you've got one hopelessly literate romantic.

You can find JudithHaleEverett on Facebook, Twitter, and Instagram, or join her newsletter at judithhaleeverett.com.